GOD: *Stories*

GOD

STORIES

EDITED BY

C. Michael Curtis

A MARINER ORIGINAL

HOUGHTON MIFFLIN COMPANY

BOSTON · NEW YORK

1998

For information about permission to reproduce
selections from this book, write to
Permissions, Houghton Mifflin Company,
215 Park Avenue South, New York,
New York 10003.

Library of Congress Cataloging-in-Publication Data
God : stories / edited by C. Michael Curtis.
p.   cm.
"A Mariner original."
Includes bibliographical references.
ISBN 0-395-92677-7 (cloth). — ISBN 0-395-92971-7 (paper)
1. Religious fiction, American. 2. English fiction — Irish
authors. 3. Religious fiction, English. 4. Belief and doubt
— Fiction. 5. Spiritual life — Fiction. 6. Faith — Fiction.
7. God — Fiction. I. Curtis, C. Michael.
PS648.R44G64   1998
813'.0108382 — dc21   98-42585 CIP

Printed in the United States of America

Book design by Robert Overholtzer

QUM 10 9 8 7 6 5 4 3 2 1

Permissions for the stories are on page 400.

For Dock

....

I know that there is nothing good
for anyone except to be happy and live the
best life he can while he is alive.

— ECCLESIASTES 3:12

ACKNOWLEDGMENTS

I owe a debt of thanks to several people whose efforts contributed, in important ways, to the making of this book. First is Kate Fraunfelder, whose tact, patience, and attention to detail prevented the project from foundering in a sea of bureaucratic minutiae. For her early assistance I'm grateful to Kitty Guckenberger. For inspiration and guidance, I thank the Reverends James W. Crawford and James Keck, and their congregations at Old South Church and West Concord Union Church. To Elizabeth Cox, who makes all things possible, I owe far more than these words can convey.

CONTENTS

INTRODUCTION

THIS IS A COLLECTION of stories about spiritual experiences of several sorts. Some are comic, some vaguely anticlerical, some only grudgingly engaged with any sort of denominational mainstream, at least a few outwardly skeptical of a divine presence or intention at any level. Others, however, make their way shrewdly into the perplexities and challenges of belief, explore the hazy perimeter of unconditional love and forgiveness, examine sympathetically the paradoxes of discipleship. Above all, these stories encounter spirituality in its human dimensions. They are about men and women, children and venerables, proselytizers and skeptics, the obsessed and the weak at heart. They tell us something important about our literary culture, point to the impact of religious sensibility in the way we lead or question our lives. Holding them together is a recognition that God, however conceived, challenges our deepest yearnings, provides our greatest comfort, assures us of our fundamental worth, grants us the only absolution we fully trust, makes possible, in ways both mysterious and immense, a loving regard for other characters in the larger narrative of life.

Until the spring of 1977 I had never opened a Bible, never been baptized, never been a church member, never appeared in or observed a church Christmas pageant. I had not set foot in a church building since 1961. I had not asked for, nor been granted, forgiveness for my sins, had not enjoyed measuring the level of piety against the standard advanced sternly, even pridefully, by others. If I thought about religion at all, it was with a sort of good-natured tolerance, with wonder at the strength of its hold on believers, and a feeling of mild self-congratulation at my good judgment in avoiding what I thought of as its anti-intellectualism and cant. Then a family member with a long-dormant experience of the church had a conversion experience that might have stepped full-blown from the pages of William James's *The Varieties of Religious Experience.* This "reawakening" was powerful, all-consuming, and an unavoidable challenge to the patterns and expectations of a sixteen-year marriage that had produced three young children.

After my initial astonishment had subsided, I decided to take a closer look at the phenomenon that seemed about to radically transform my life. Like the graduate student I had once been (I spent four years at Cornell working toward a Ph.D. in political science before joining the editorial staff at *The Atlantic Monthly,* where I remain), I went to a good-sized Boston book store and asked to be pointed to the "religion" section. There, to my great good fortune, I discovered a set of books that permanently changed my way of thinking about religious matters. Among them were the William James tome mentioned above, Hans Kung's *On Being a Christian,* Deitrich Bonhoeffer's *Ethics,* Edmund Wilson's *The Dead Sea Scrolls,* a collection of essays by Reinhold Niebuhr, sermons by Paul Tillich, Bertrand Russell's cranky *Why I Am Not a Christian and Other Essays,* and a few others. I read these books as if I were learning a new language, and in a sense I was. I opened a Bible for the first time and found there, to my amazement, cultural artifacts — metaphors, similes, other figures of speech — that I realized had been a part of my literary and cultural armament for years. If religion was superstition, I realized, its intellectual trappings were formidable. It seemed no more puzzling, and surely as resistant to proof texts, as the social science and literary/critical propositions I'd been wrestling with for years. And in Tillich, Niebuhr, Kung, James, and Bonhoeffer, I found thinkers one could prop up next to Freud, Marx, or James Joyce without fear of descending into simplicities or reductionism.

I joined a group of ministers and theologians at Andover-Newton Theological School who met early each Monday morning to read and discuss new and challenging books about theological and church life matters in a number of denominational traditions. I became a member of Boston's Old South Church, where I discovered the inner workings of a church community, the tensions between congregation and minister, the richness and almost comic variety of models of church membership, and the potency of that deepest mystery — the will to believe.

Originally this collection of stories was the outgrowth of an effort I made several years ago to find a text suitable for an adult education class at a church in West Concord, Massachusetts. Seeking a way to combine my professional concern for "story" with an ongoing interest in religion, I decided to bring to the class a set of stories recently published in *The Atlantic,* stories that had either directly or implicitly to do with the chemistry between pastor and congregation, or with one or another strain of Christian belief.

My class responded enthusiastically. Buffered by literary forms from the intimidation of theological hair-splitting or the weight of highly specialized scholarship, they seemed more willing than usual to discuss articles of faith, the efficacy of prayer, ecstatic experience, the range of human frailty, and other such matters. Once I'd worked through the *Atlantic* stories, I began to cast a wider net, bringing in the work of other writers or work by *Atlantic* contributors that had appeared in other magazines or collections. The tradition I know best, and with which I most often resonate, is Protestant. So the bulk of the stories here collected are recognizably Protestant in their concerns. Others, however, are explicitly Catholic or Jewish in outlook or orientation.

As I sorted through these stories, I was struck by the way religious matters and clergymen (and, in recent years, clergywomen as well) are portrayed in mainstream fiction. Many clergy/characters pridefully accept the exalted status thrust upon them by needy parishioners; others are plainly made uncomfortable by worshipful admiration, are keenly aware of their "humanness," and are occasionally maddened by what they think of as the unrealistic expectations of their church members. Some writers, like Cynthia Ozick or Bernard Malamud, contemplate God as mischief-maker; others, like Flannery O'Connor, Eileen Pollack, and John Updike, have written stories that are less about God, per se, than about the perplexity — often the confusion — of individual believers who yearn for the strenuousness of absolute faith but lose sight of, or never encounter, the bounteousness of absolute love and forgiveness.

Some of these stories are about parish life. As portrayed by Alice Munro, Bobbie Ann Mason, or Eudora Welty, church membership can be an ordering mechanism, a source of regulating norms in a world of erratic impulses and desires. In other stories, by Tobias Wolff, Peggy Payne, Mary Ward Brown, or Elizabeth Spencer, for example, belief is questioned, even repudiated, and the strength of ancient convictions is challenged by narrow secularism or misguided evangelism.

Some of these stories celebrate the variety and intensity of religious belief; others call into question its efficacy or legitimacy. But all are about people caught up in a life informed by visions of the sacred, and by the institutions we have constructed to give those visions full play. They are about triumphs of the spirit, and about the desolate failure of empty spirituality. Some are amusing and some are tragic, but each of them asks, in a voice however idiosyncratic, where, if anywhere, is the place for God in the life we live, and how is one to tell.

In the hands of William Hoffman and Richard Bausch, among others, clergymen are treated kindly. The characters in their stories are aware of their limitations and realize that too much is expected of them by parishioners who need reassurance in the face of disappointment. John Hersey's minister is a tyrant prototype, a man who willingly identifies himself with the God of righteous anger in order to reinforce his own faltering sense of personal competence — but also to make sense of that other indelible mystery, human suffering.

Louise Erdrich's itinerant evangelist uses the currency of spiritual enthusiasm to exploit a young woman's vulnerability. Other clerics, as in stories by J. F. Powers, Joe Ashby Porter, and William Trevor, have moved beyond the stirring battles for inspiration or orthodoxy but find themselves helpless to resist old and honorable habits of mind. In several stories, by Brendan Gill, Andre Dubus, James Baldwin, James Joyce, and John Gardner, the church is largely off-stage, though its teachings reverberate in unexpected and unsettling ways.

This collection is about lives intertwined with religion, with the church, with clergy gone awry, and with clergy speaking to the heart. What it lacks in precision it provides in range. At the very least, it speaks to the variety and richness of lives touched by the spirit.

C. Michael Curtis

GOD: *Stories*

James Baldwin

....

Exodus

I

S HE HAD ALWAYS SEEMED to Florence the oldest woman
in the world — for she often spoke of Florence and Gabriel as the
children of her old age; and she had been born, innumerable
years ago, during slavery, on a plantation in another state. On this
plantation she had grown up, one of the field workers, for she was very
tall and strong; and by-and-by she had married, and raised children, all
of whom had been taken from her, one by sickness, and two by
auction, and one whom she had not been allowed to call her own, who
had been raised in the master's house. When she was a woman grown,
well past thirty as she reckoned it, with one husband buried — but the
master had given her another — armies, plundering and burning, had
come from the North to set them free. This was in answer to the
prayers of the faithful, who had never ceased, both day and night, to
cry out for deliverance.

For it had been the will of God that they should hear, and pass it,
thereafter, one to another, the story of the Hebrew children, who had
been held in bondage in the land of Egypt; and how the Lord had
heard their groaning, and how His heart was moved; and how He bid
them wait but a little season till He should send deliverance. She had
known this story, so it seemed, from the day that she was born. And
while life ran, rising in the morning before the sun came up, standing
and bending in the fields when the sun was high, crossing the fields
homeward while the sun went down at the gates of heaven far away —
hearing the whistle of the foreman, and his eerie cry across the fields;

in the whiteness of winter when hogs and turkeys and geese were slaughtered, and lights burned bright in the big house, and Bathsheba, the cook, sent over in a napkin bits of ham and chicken and cakes left over by the white folks; in all that befell, in her joys — her pipe in the evening, her man at night, the children she suckled, and guided on their first short steps — and in her tribulations, death, and parting, and the lash; she did not forget that deliverance was promised, and would surely come. She had only to endure and trust in God. She knew that the big house, the house of pride where the white folks lived, would come down: it was written in the Word of God. And they, who walked so proudly now, yet had not fashioned, for themselves, or their children, so sure a foundation as was hers. They walked on the edge of a steep place and their eyes were sightless — God would cause them to rush down, as the herd of swine had once rushed down, into the sea. For all that they were so beautiful, and took their ease, she knew them, and she pitied them, who would have no covering in the great day of His wrath.

Yet, she told her children, God was just, and He struck no people without first giving many warnings. God gave men time, but all the times were in His hand, and, one day, the time to forsake evil and do good would all be finished: then only the whirlwind, death riding on the whirlwind, awaited those people who had forgotten God. In all the days that she was growing up, signs failed not, but none heeded. *Slaves done riz,* was whispered in the cabin, and at the master's gate: slaves in another county had fired the master's house and fields, and dashed their children to death against the stones. *Another slave in hell,* Bathsheba might say one morning, shooing the pickaninnies away from the great porch: a slave had killed his master, or his overseer, and had gone down to hell to pay for it. *I ain't got long to stay here,* someone crooned beside her in the fields: who would be gone by morning on his journey North. All these signs, like the plagues with which the Lord had afflicted Egypt, only hardened the hearts of these people against the Lord. They thought the lash would save them, and they used the lash; or the knife, or the gallows, or the auction block; they thought that kindness would save them, and the master and mistress came down, smiling, to the cabins, making much of the pickaninnies, and bearing gifts. These were great days, and they all, black and white, seemed happy together. But when the Word has gone forth from the mouth of God nothing can turn it back.

*   *   *

The word was fulfilled one morning before she was awake. Many of the stories her mother told meant nothing to Florence, she knew them for what they were, tales told by an old black woman in a cabin in the evening to distract her children from their cold and hunger. But the story of this day she was never to forget, it was a day like the day for which she lived. There was a great running and shouting, said her mother, everywhere outside, and, as she opened her eyes to the light of that day, so bright, she said, and cold, she was certain that the judgment trump had sounded. While she still sat, amazed, and wondering what, on the judgment day, would be the best behavior, in rushed Bathsheba, and behind her many tumbling children, and field hands, and house niggers, all together, and Bathsheba shouted, "Rise up, rise up, Sister Rachel, and see the Lord's deliverance! He done brought us out of Egypt, just like He promised, and we's free at last!"

Bathsheba grabbed her, tears running down her face; she, dressed in the clothes in which she had slept, walked to the door to look out on the new day God had given them.

On that day she saw the proud house humbled, green silk and velvet blowing out of windows, and the garden trampled by many horsemen, and the big gates open. The master and mistress, and their kin, and one child she had borne were in that house — which she did not enter. Soon it occurred to her that there was no reason any more to tarry here. She tied her things in a cloth, which she put on her head, and walked out through the big gate, never to see that country any more.

And this, as Florence grew, became her deep ambition: to walk out one morning through the cabin door, never to return. . . .

II

In 1900, when she was twenty-six, Florence walked out through the cabin door. She had thought to wait until her mother, who was so ill now that she no longer stirred out of bed, should be buried — but suddenly she knew that she would wait no longer, the time had come. She had been working as cook and serving girl for a large white family in town, and it was on the day that her master proposed that she become his concubine that she knew that her life among these wretched had come to its destined end. She left her employment that same day (leaving behind her a most vehement conjugal bitterness) and with part of the money which, with cunning, cruelty, and sacrifice, she had saved over a period of years, bought a railroad ticket to New

York. When she bought it, in a kind of scarlet rage, she held, like a talisman at the back of her mind, the thought: "I can give it back, I can sell it. This doesn't mean I got to go." But she knew that nothing could stop her.

And it was this leave-taking which came to stand, in Florence's latter days, and with many another witness, at her bedside. Gray clouds obscured the sun that day, and outside the cabin window she saw that mist still covered the ground. Her mother lay in bed, awake; she was pleading with Gabriel, who had been out drinking the night before, and who was not really sober now, to mend his ways and come to the Lord. And Gabriel, full of the confusion, and pain, and guilt which were his whenever he thought of how he made his mother suffer, but which became nearly insupportable when she taxed him with it, stood before the mirror, head bowed, buttoning his shirt. Florence knew that he could not unlock his lips to speak; he could not say Yes to his mother, and to the Lord; and he could not say No.

"Honey," their mother was saying, "don't you *let* your old mother die without you look her in the eye and tell her she going to see you in glory. You hear me, boy?"

In a moment, Florence thought with scorn, tears would fill his eyes, and he would promise to "do better." He had been promising to "do better" since the day he had been baptized.

She put down her bag in the center of the hateful room.

"Ma," she said, "I'm going. I'm a-going this morning."

Now that she had said it, she was angry with herself for not having said it the night before, so that they would have had time to be finished with their weeping and their arguments. She had not trusted herself to withstand, the night before; but now there was almost no time left. The center of her mind was filled with the image of the great, white clock at the railway station, on which the hands did not cease to move.

"You going where?" her mother asked, sharply. But she knew that her mother had understood, had, indeed, long before this moment, known that this moment would come. The astonishment with which she stared at Florence's bag was not altogether astonishment, but a startled, wary attention. A danger imagined had become present and real, and her mother was already searching for a way to break Florence's will. All this Florence, in a moment, knew, and it made her stronger. She watched her mother, waiting.

But at the tone of his mother's voice, Gabriel, who had scarcely heard Florence's announcement, so grateful had he been that something had occurred to distract from him his mother's attention, dropped his eyes, and saw Florence's traveling bag. And he repeated his mother's question in a stunned, angry voice, understanding it only as the words hit the air:

"Yes, girl. Where you think you going?"

"I'm going," she said, "to New York. I got my ticket."

And her mother watched her. For a moment no one said a word. Then, Gabriel, in a changed and frightened voice, asked:

"And when you done decide that?"

She did not look at him, nor answer his question. She continued to watch her mother. "I got my ticket," she repeated. "I'm going on the morning train."

"Girl," asked her mother, quietly, "is you sure you know what you's doing?"

She stiffened, seeing in her mother's eyes a mocking pity. "I'm a woman grown," she said. "I know what I'm doing."

"And you going," cried Gabriel, "this morning — just like that? And you going to walk off and leave your mother — just like that?"

"You hush," she said, turning to him for the first time; "she got you, ain't she?"

This was indeed, she realized, as he dropped his eyes, the bitter, troubling point. He could not endure the thought of being left alone with his mother, with nothing whatever to put between himself and his guilty love. With Florence gone, time would have swallowed up all his mother's children, except himself; and *he,* then, must make amends for all the pain that she had borne, and sweeten her last moments with all his proofs of love. And his mother required of him one proof only, that he tarry no longer in sin. With Florence gone, his stammering time, his playing time, contracted with a bound to the sparest interrogative second; when he must stiffen himself, and answer to his mother, and all the host of heaven, Yes, or No.

Florence smiled inwardly a small, malicious smile, watching his slow bafflement, and panic, and rage; and she looked at her mother again. "She got you," she repeated. "She don't need me."

"You going North," her mother said, then. "And when you reckon on coming back?"

"I don't reckon on coming back," she said.

"You come crying back soon enough," said Gabriel, with malevo-
lence, "soon as they whip your butt up there four or five times."

She looked at him again. "Just don't you try to hold your breath till
then, you hear?"

"Girl," said her mother, "you mean to tell me the devil's done made
your heart so hard you can just leave your mother on her dying bed,
and you don't care if you don't never see her in this world no more?
Honey, you can't tell me you done got so evil as all that?"

She felt Gabriel watching her to see how she would take this question — the question, which, for all her determination, she had dreaded
most to hear. She looked away from her mother, and straightened,
catching her breath, looking outward through the small, cracked window. There, outside, beyond the slowly rising mist, and farther off than
her eyes could see, her life awaited her. The woman on the bed was
old, her life was fading as the mist rose. She thought of her mother as
already in the grave; and she would not let herself be strangled by the
hands of the dead.

"I'm going, Ma," she said. "I got to go."

Her mother leaned back, face upward to the light, and began to cry.
Gabriel moved to Florence's side and grabbed her arm. She looked up
into his face and saw that his eyes were full of tears.

"You can't go," he said. "You can't go. You can't go and leave your
mother thisaway. She need a woman, Florence, to help look after her.
What she going to do here, all alone with me?"

She pushed him from her and moved to stand over her mother's
bed.

"Ma," she said, "don't be like that. Ain't a blessed thing for you to
cry about so. Ain't a thing can happen to me up North can't happen to
me here. God's everywhere, Ma. Ain't no need to worry."

She knew that she was mouthing words; and she realized suddenly
that her mother scorned to dignify these words with her attention. She
had granted Florence the victory — with a promptness which had the
effect of making Florence, however dimly and unwillingly, wonder if
her victory was real; and she was not weeping for her daughter's
future; she was weeping for the past, and weeping in an anguish in
which Florence had no part. And all of this filled Florence with a
terrible fear, which was immediately transformed into anger.

"Gabriel can take care of you," she said, her voice shaking with
malice; "Gabriel ain't never going to leave you. Is you, boy?" and she

looked at him. He stood, stupid with bewilderment and grief, a few inches from the bed. "But me," she said, "I got to go." She walked to the center of the room again, and picked up her bag.

"Girl," Gabriel whispered, "ain't you got no feelings at *all*?"

"*Lord!*" her mother cried; and at the sound her heart turned over; she and Gabriel, arrested, stared at the bed. "Lord, Lord, Lord! Lord, have mercy on my sinful daughter! Stretch out your hand and hold her back from the lake that burns forever! Oh, my Lord, my Lord!" and her voice dropped, and broke, and tears ran down her face. "Lord, I done my best with all the children what you give me. Lord, have mercy on my children, and my children's children."

"Florence," said Gabriel, "please don't go. Please don't go. You ain't really fixing to go and leave her like this?"

Tears stood suddenly in her own eyes, though she could not have said what she was crying for. "Leave me be," she said to Gabriel, and picked up her bag again. She opened the door; the cold morning air came in. "Good-by," she said. And then to Gabriel: "Tell her I said good-by." She walked through the cabin door and down the short steps into the frosty yard. Gabriel watched her, standing magnetized between the door and the weeping bed. Then, as her hand was on the gate, he ran before her, and slammed the gate shut.

"Girl, where you going? What you doing? You reckon on finding some men up North to dress you in pearls and diamonds?"

Violently, she opened the gate and moved out into the road. He watched her with his jaw hanging, until the dust and the distance swallowed her up.

Richard Bausch

....

Design

THE REVEREND TARMIGIAN was not well. You could see it in his face — a certain hollowness, a certain blueness in the skin. His eyes lacked luster or brightness. He had a persistent, dry, deep cough; he had lost a lot of weight. And yet on this fine, breezy October day he was out on the big lawn in front of his church, raking leaves. Father Russell watched him from the window of his study, and knew that if he didn't walk over there and say something, this morning — like so many recent mornings — would be spent fretting and worrying about Tarmigian, seventy-two years old and out raking leaves in the windy sun. He had been planning to speak about it for weeks, but what could you say to a man like that? An institution in Point Royal County, old Tarmigian had been pastor of the neighboring church — Faith Baptist, only a hundred yards away on the other side of Tallawaw Creek — for more than three decades. He referred to himself in conversation as Reverend Fixture. He was a tall, frail man with wrinkled blue eyes and a wisp of fleecy blond hair above each ear, and there were dimples in his cheeks. One of his favorite jokes — one of the many jokes he was fond of repeating — was that he had the eyes of a clown built above the natural curve of a baby's bottom. He'd touch the dimples and smile, saying a thing like that. And the truth was he tended to joke too much — even about the fact that he was apparently taxing himself beyond the dictates of good health for a man his age.

It seemed clear to Father Russell — who was all too often worried about his own health, though he was thirty years younger than Tarmigian — that something was driving the older man to these stunts of killing work: raking leaves all morning in the fall breezes, or climbing a ladder to clear drainspouts, or, as he did one day last week, lugging a bag of mulch across the road and up the hill to the little cemetery where his wife lay buried, as if there weren't fifteen people within arm's reach on any Sunday who wouldn't have done it gladly for him (and would have just as gladly stood by while he said his few quiet prayers over the grave). His wife had been dead twenty years, he had the reverential love and respect of the whole countryside, but something was driving the man, and, withal, there was often a species of amused cheerfulness about him almost like elation, as though he were keeping some wonderful secret.

It was infuriating: it violated all the rules of respect for one's own best interest. And today, watching him rake leaves, Father Russell decided that he would speak to him about it. He would find some way to broach the subject of the old man's health, and finally he would express an opinion about it.

He put a jacket on and went out and walked up the road to Tarmigian's church. The road went across a stone bridge over Tallawaw Creek and up a long incline. The air was blue and cool in the mottled shade, and there were little patches of steam on the creek when the breezes were still. The Reverend Tarmigian stopped raking, leaned on the handle of the rake, and watched Father Russell cross the bridge.

"Well, just in time for coffee."

"I'll have tea," Father Russell said, a little out of breath from the walk.

"You're winded," said Tarmigian.

"And you're white as a sheet."

It was true. Poor Tarmigian's cheeks were pale as death. There were two blotches on them, like bruises — caused, Father Russell was sure, by the blood vessels that were straining to break in the old man's head. He indicated the trees all around, burnished looking, still loaded with leaves, and even now dropping some of them, like part of an argument for the hopelessness of this task the old man had set for himself.

"Why don't you at least wait until they're finished?" Father Russell demanded.

"I admit, it's like emptying the ocean with a spoon." Tarmigian put his rake down and invited the other man into his kitchen for some hot tea. Father Russell followed him in, and watched him fuss and seem to worry, preparing it, and then he followed him into the study to sit among the books and talk. It was the old man's custom to take an hour every day in this book-lined room, though with this bad cold he'd contracted, he had lately done little of anything with regularity. He was too tired, or too sick. It was just an end-of-summer cold that he couldn't get rid of, he said, but Father Russell had observed the weight loss, the coughing; and the old man was willing to admit that lately his appetite had suffered.

"I can't keep anything down," he said. "Sort of keeps me discouraged from trying, you know? I'm sure when I get over this cold . . ."

"Medical science is advancing," said the priest, trying for sarcasm. "They have doctors now with their own offices, and instruments. It's all advanced to a sophisticated stage. You can get medicine for a cold."

"I'm fine. There's no need for anyone to worry."

Father Russell had seen denial before: indeed, he saw some version of it almost every day, and he had a rich understanding of the psychology of it. Yet Tarmigian's statement caused a surprising little clot of anger to form under the flow of his mind and left him feeling vaguely disoriented, as if the older man's blithe neglect of himself were a kind of personal affront.

Yet he found, too, that he couldn't come right out and say what he had come to believe: that the old man was jeopardizing his own health. The words wouldn't form on his lips. So he drank his tea and searched for an opening — a way of getting something across about learning to relax a little, learning to take it easy. There wasn't a lot to talk about beyond Tarmigian's anecdotes and chatter. The two men were not particularly close: Father Russell had come to his own parish from New York only a year ago, believing this little Virginia township to be the accidental equivalent of a demotion (the assignment, coming really like the draw of a ticket out of a hat, was less than satisfactory). He had felt almost immediately that the overfriendly elderly clergyman next door was a bit too southern for his taste — though Tarmigian was obviously a man of broad experience, having served in missions overseas as a young man, and it was true that he possessed a kind of simple grace. So, while the priest had in fact spent a lot of time in the first days trying to avoid him for fear of hurting the poor man's feelings, he had learned finally that Tarmigian was unavoidable, and had come to accept him as one of the mild irritations of the place in which he now found himself. He had even considered that the man had charm, was amusing and generous. He would admit that there had been times when he found himself surprised by a small stir of gladness when the old man could be seen on the little crossing bridge, heading down to pay another of his casual visits, as if there were nothing better to do than sit in Father Russell's parlor and make jokes about himself.

The trouble now, of course, was that everything about the old man, including his jokes, seemed tinged with the something awful that was clearly happening to him. And here Father Russell was, watching him cough, watching him hold up one hand as if to ward off anything in the way of advice or concern about it. The cough took him deep, so that he had to gasp to get his breath back; but then he cleared his throat and sipped more of the tea and, looking almost frightfully white around the eyes, smiled and said, "I have a good one for you, Reverend Russell. I had a couple — I won't name them — in my congregation, come to me yesterday afternoon, claiming that they were going to seek a divorce. You know how long they've been married? They've been married fifty-two years. Fifty-two years and they can't stand each other. I mean, can't stand to be in the same room with each other."

Father Russell was interested in spite of himself — and in spite of the fact that the old man had again called him Reverend. This would be another of Tarmigian's stories, or another of his jokes. He felt the need to head him off. "That cough," he said.

The other man looked at him as if he'd merely said a number, or recited the day's date.

"I think you should see a doctor about it."

"It's just a cold, Reverend."

"I don't mean to meddle — " said the priest.

"Yes, well. I was asking what you thought about a married couple, can't stand to be in the same room together after fifty-two years."

Father Russell said, "I guess I have to say I'd have trouble believing that."

"Well, believe it. And you know what I said to them? I said we'd talk about it for a while. Counseling, you know."

Father Russell said nothing.

"Of course," said Tarmigian, "as you well know, we permit divorce — when it seems called for."

"Yes," Father Russell said, feeling beaten.

"You know, I don't think it's a question of either one of them being interested in anybody else. Nobody's swept anybody off anybody's feet."

Father Russell waited for him to go on.

"I can't help thinking it's a little silly." Tarmigian smiled, sipped the tea, then put the cup down and leaned back, clasping his hands behind his head. "Fifty-two years of marriage and they want to untie the knot. What do you say, shall I send them over to you?"

The priest couldn't keep the sullen tone out of his voice. "I wouldn't know what to say to them."

"Well — you'd tell them to love one another. You'd tell them love is the very breath of living or some such thing. Just as I did."

Father Russell muttered, "That's what I'd have to tell them, of course."

"We concur." Tarmigian smiled again.

"What was their answer?"

"They were going to think about it. Give themselves some time to think, really. That's no joke." The Reverend Tarmigian laughed, coughing. Then it was just coughing.

"That's a terrible cough," said Father Russell, feeling futile and afraid and deeply irritable. His own words sounded to him like something learned by rote.

"Do you know what I think I'll tell them if they come back?"

Father Russell waited.

"I think I'll tell them to stick it out anyway, with each other." Tarmigian looked at him and smiled. "Have you ever heard anything more absurd?"

Father Russell made a gesture he hoped the other took for agreement.

Tarmigian went on: "It's probably exactly right — probably exactly what they should do, and yet such odd advice to think of giving two people who've been together fifty-two years. I mean, when do you think the phrase 'sticking it out' would stop being applicable?"

Father Russell indicated that he didn't know.

Tarmigian merely smiled.

"Very amusing," Father Russell said.

But the older man was coughing again.

From the beginning, there had been things Tarmigian said and did which unnerved the priest. Father Russell was a man who could be undone by certain kinds of boisterousness, and there were matters of casual discourse he simply would never understand. Yet, often enough over the seven months of their association, he had entertained the suspicion that Tarmigian was harboring a bitterness, and that his occasional mockery of himself was some sort of reaction to it, if it wasn't in fact a way of releasing it.

Now Father Russell sipped his tea and looked out the window. Leaves were flying in the wind. The road was in blue shade, and the shade moved. There were houses beyond the hill, but from here everything looked like a wilderness.

"Well," Tarmigian said, gaining control of himself. "Do you know what my poor old couple say is their major complaint?"

Father Russell waited for him to go on.

"Their major complaint is they don't like the same TV programs. Now, can you imagine a thing like that?"

"Look," the priest blurted out, "I see you from my study window — You're — you don't get enough rest. I think you should see a doctor about that cough."

Tarmigian waved this away. "I'm fit as a fiddle, as they say. Really."

"If it's just a cold," said Father Russell, giving up. "Of course — " He could think of nothing else to say.

"You worry too much," Tarmigian said. "You know, you've got bags under your eyes."

True.

In the long nights, Father Russell lay with a rosary tangled in his fingers and tried to pray, tried to stop his mind from playing tricks on him: the matter of greatest faith was, and had been for a very long time now, that every twist or turn of his body held a symptom; every change signified the onset of disease. It was all waiting to happen to him, and the anticipation of it sapped him, made him weak and sick at heart. He had begun to see that his own propensity for morbid anxiety about his health was worsening, and the daylight hours required all his courage. Frequently, he thought of Tarmigian as though the old man were in some strange way a reflection of his secretly held, worst fear. He recalled the lovely, sunny mornings of his first summer as a curate, when he was twenty-seven and fresh, and the future was made of slow time. This was not a healthy kind of thinking. It was middle age, he knew. It was a kind of spiritual dryness he had been taught to recognize and contend with. Yet each morning his dazed waking — from whatever fitful sleep the night had yielded him — was greeted with the pall of knowing that the aging pastor of the next-door church would be out in the open, performing some strenuous task. When the younger man looked out the window, the mere sight of the other building was enough to make him sick with anxiety.

On Friday, Father Russell went to St. Celia Hospital to attend to the needs of one of his own older parishioners, who had broken her hip in a fall, and while he was there a nurse walked in and asked that he administer the sacrament of extreme unction to a man in the emergency room. He followed her down the hall and the stairs to the first floor, and while they walked she told him the man had suffered a heart attack, that he was already beyond help. She said this almost matter-of-factly, and Father Russell looked at the delicate curve of her ears, thinking about design. This was, of course, an odd thing to be thinking about now, but he cultivated it for just that reason. Early in his priesthood, he had learned to make his mind settle on other things during moments requiring him to look on sickness and death — small things, outside the province of questions of eternity and salvation, and the common doom. It was what he had always managed as a protection against too clear a memory of certain daily horrors — images that could blow through him in the night, like the very winds of fright and despair — and if over the years it had mostly worked, it had recently been in the process of failing him. Entering the crowded emergency room, he was concentrating on the coils of a young woman's ear as an instrument of hearing when he saw Tarmigian sitting on one of the chairs near the television, his hand in a bandage, his white face sunk over the pages of a magazine.

Tarmigian looked up, then smiled, held up the bandaged hand. There wasn't time for the two men to speak. Father Russell nodded at him and went on, following the nurse, feeling strangely precarious and weak. He looked over his shoulder at Tarmigian, who had simply gone back to reading the magazine, and then he was attending to what the nurse had brought him to see: she pulled a curtain aside to reveal a gurney with two people on it — a man and a woman of roughly the same late middle age, the woman cradling the man's head in her arms and whispering something to him.

"Mrs. Simpson," the nurse said, "here is the priest."

Father Russell stood there while the woman looked at him. She was perhaps fifty-five, with iron-gray hair and small, round wet eyes. "Mrs. Simpson," he said to her.

"He's my husband," she murmured, rising, letting the man's head down carefully. His eyes were wide, as was his mouth. "My Jack. Oh, Jack, Jack."

Father Russell stepped forward and took her hands, and she cried, staring down at her husband's face.

"He's gone," she said. "We were talking, you know. We were thinking about going down to see the kids. And he just put his head down. We were talking about how the kids never come to visit and we were going to surprise them."

"Mrs. Simpson," the nurse said, "would you like a sedative? Something to settle your nerves — "

"No," said Mrs. Simpson. "I'm fine."

Father Russell began to say the rite, and she stood by him, gazing down at the dead man.

"He just put his head down," she said. Her hands trembled over the cloth of her husband's shirt, which was open wide at the chest, and it was a moment before Father Russell understood that she was trying to button the shirt. But her hands were shaking too badly. She patted the shirt down, then bowed her head and sobbed. Somewhere in the jangled apparatus of the room something was beeping, and he heard air rushing through pipes; everything was obscured in the intricacies of procedure. He was simply staring at the dead man's blank countenance, all sound and confusion and movement falling away from him. It was as though he had never looked at anything like this before; he remained quite still, in a profound quiet, for some minutes before Mrs. Simpson got his attention again. She had taken him by the wrist.

"Father," she was saying. "Father, he was a good man. God has taken him home, hasn't He?"

Father Russell turned to face the woman, to take her hands into his own, and to whisper the words of hope.

"I think seeing you there, at the hospital — " he said to Tarmigian. "It upset me in a strange way."

"I cut my hand opening the paint jar," Tarmigian said. He was standing on a stepladder in the upstairs hallway of his rectory, painting the crown molding. Father Russell had walked out of his church in the chill of the first frost and made his way across the little stone bridge and up the incline to the old man's door, had knocked and been told to enter, and, entering, finding no one, had reached back and knocked again.

"Up here," came Tarmigian's voice.

And the priest had climbed the stairs in a kind of torpor, his heart beating in his neck and face. He had blurted out that he wasn't feeling right, hadn't slept at all well, and finally he'd begun to hint at what he could divine as to why. He was now sitting on the top step, hat in hand, still carrying with him the sense of the long night he had spent, lying awake in the dark, seeing not the dead face of poor Mrs. Simpson's husband but Tarmigian holding up the bandaged hand and smiling. The image had wakened him each time he had drifted toward sleep.

"Something's happening to me," he said now, unable to believe himself.

The other man was reaching high, concentrating. The ladder was rickety.

"Do you want me to hold the ladder?"

"Pardon me?"

"Nothing."

"Did you want to know if I wanted you to hold the ladder?"

"Well, do you?"

"You're worried I'll fall, right?"

"I would like to help."

"And did you say something was happening to you?"

Father Russell said nothing.

"Forget the ladder, son."

"I don't understand myself lately," said the priest.

"Are you making me your confessor or something there, Reverend?" Tarmigian asked.

"I — I can't — "

"I don't think I'm equipped."

"I've looked at the dead before," said Father Russell. "I've held them in my arms. I've never been very much afraid of it. I mean, I've never been morbid."

"Morbidity is an indulgence."

"Yes, I know."

"Simply refuse to indulge yourself."

"I'm forty-three — "

"A difficult age, you know, because you don't know whether you fit with the grown-ups or the children." Tarmigian paused to cough. He held the top step of the ladder with both hands, and his shoulders shook. Everything tottered. Then he stopped, breathed, wiped his mouth with the back of one hand.

Father Russell said, "I meant to say I don't think I'm worried about myself."

"Well, that's good."

"I'm going to call and make you an appointment with a doctor."

"I'm fine. I've got a cold. I've coughed like this all my life."

"Nevertheless."

Tarmigian smiled at him. "You're a good man, but you're learning a tendency."

No peace.

Father Russell had entered the priesthood without the sort of fervent sense of vocation that he believed others had. In fact, he had been troubled by serious doubts about it right up to the last year of seminary — doubts that, in spite of his confessor's reassurances to the contrary, he felt were more than the normal upsets of seminary life. In the first place, he had come to it against the wishes of his father, who had entertained dreams of a career in law for him; and while his mother applauded the decision, her own dream of grandchildren was visibly languishing in her eyes as the time of his final vows approached. Both parents had died within a month of each other during his last year of studies, and so there had been times when he'd also had to contend with an apprehension that he might unconsciously be learning to use his vocation as a form of refuge. But finally, nearing the end of his training, seeing the completion of the journey, something in him rejoiced, and he came to believe that this was what having a true vocation was: no extremes of emotion, no real sense of a break with the world, though the terms of his faith and the ancient ceremony that his training prepared him to celebrate spoke of just that. He was even-tempered and confident, and when he was ordained he set about the business of being a parish priest. There were things to involve himself in, and he found that he could be energetic and enthusiastic about most of them. The life was satisfying in ways he hadn't expected, and if in his less confident moments some part of him suspected that he was not progressing spiritually, he was also not the sort of man to go very deeply into such questions: there were things to do. He was not a contemplative.

Or hadn't been. Something was shifting in his soul.

Nights were awful. He couldn't even pray now. He stood at his rectory window and looked at the light in the old man's window, and his imagination presented him with the belief that he could hear the faint rattle of the deep cough, though he knew it was impossible across that distance. When he said the morning mass, he leaned down over the host, and had to work to remember the words. The stolid, calm faces of his parishioners were almost ugly in their absurd confidence in him, their smiles of happy expectation and welcome. He took their hospitality and their care of him as his due, and felt waves of despair at the ease of it, the habitual taste and lure of it, and all the time his body was aching in ways that filled him with dread, and reminded him of Tarmigian's ravaged features.

Sunday morning early, it began to rain. Someone called, then hung up before he could answer. He had been asleep; the loud ring at that hour frightened him, changed his heartbeat. He took his own pulse, then stood at his window and gazed at the darkened shape of Tarmigian's church. That morning, after the second mass, exhausted, miserable, he crossed the bridge in the rain and knocked on the old man's door. There wasn't any answer. He peered through the window on the porch and saw that there were dishes on the table in the kitchen, which was visible through the arched hallway off the living room. Tarmigian's Bible lay open on the arm of the easy chair. Father Russell knocked loudly, and then walked around the building, into the church itself. It was quiet. The wind stirred outside, and sounded like traffic whooshing by. Father Russell could feel his own heartbeat in the pit of his stomach. He sat down in the last pew of Tarmigian's church and tried to calm himself down. Perhaps ten minutes went by, and then he heard voices. The old man was coming up the walk outside, talking to someone. Father Russell stood, thought absurdly of trying to hide, but then the door was opened and Tarmigian walked in, accompanied by an old woman in a white woolen shawl. Tarmigian had a big umbrella, which he shook down and folded, breathing heavily from the walk and looking, as always, even in the pall of his decline, amused by something. He hadn't seen Father Russell yet, though the old woman had. She nodded, and smiled broadly, her hands folded neatly over a small black purse.

"Well," Tarmigian said, "to what do we owe this honor, Reverend?"

It struck Father Russell that they might be laughing at him. He dismissed this thought, and, clearing his throat, said, "I — I wanted to see you." His own voice sounded stiff and somehow foolish to him. He cleared his throat again.

"This is Father Russell," Tarmigian said, loud, to the old woman. Then he touched her shoulder and looked at the priest. "Mrs. Aldenberry."

"God bless you," Mrs. Aldenberry said.

"Mrs. Aldenberry wants a divorce," Tarmigian murmured.

"Eh?" she said. Then, turning to Father Russell: "I'm hard of hearing."

"She wants to have her own television set," Tarmigian whispered.

"Pardon me?"

"And her own room."

"I'm hard of hearing," she said cheerfully to the priest. "I'm deaf as a post."

"Irritates her husband," Tarmigian said.

"I'm sorry," said the woman. "I can't hear a thing."

Tarmigian guided her to the last row of seats, and she sat down there, still clutching the purse. She seemed quite content, quite trustful, and the old minister, beginning to stutter into a deep cough, winked at Father Russell — as if to say this was all very entertaining. "Now," he said, taking the priest by the elbow, "let's get to the flattering part of all this — you walking over here getting yourself all wet because you're worried about me."

"I just wanted to stop by," Father Russell said. He was almost pleading. The old man's face, in the dim light, looked appallingly bony and pale.

"Look at you," said Tarmigian. "You're shaking."

Father Russell could not speak.

"Are you all right now?"

The priest was assailed by the feeling that the older man found him somehow ridiculous — and he remembered the initial sense he'd had, when Tarmigian and Mrs. Aldenberry entered, that he was being laughed at. "I just wanted to see how you were doing," he said.

"I'm a little under the weather," Tarmigian said, smiling.

And it dawned on Father Russell, with the force of a physical blow, that the old man knew quite well he was dying.

Tarmigian indicated Mrs. Aldenberry with a nod of his head. "Now I have to attend to the depths of this lady's sorrow. You know, she says she should've listened to her mother and not married Mr. Aldenberry fifty-two years ago. Now, you think about that a little. Imagine her standing in a room slapping her forehead and saying, What a mistake! Fifty-two years! Oops! A mistake. She's glad she woke up in time. Think of it. And, I'll tell you, Reverend, I think she feels lucky."

Mrs. Aldenberry made a prim, throat-clearing sound, then turned in her seat, looking at them.

"Well," Tarmigian said, straightening, wiping the smile from his face. He offered his hand to the priest. "Shake hands. No, let's embrace. Let's give this poor woman an ecumenical thrill."

Father Russell shook hands, then walked into the old man's extended arms. It felt like a kind of collapse. He was breathing the odor of bay rum and talcum, and of something else, too, something indefinable and dark, and to his astonishment he found himself fighting back tears. The two men stood there while Mrs. Aldenberry watched, and Father Russell was unable to control the sputtering and trembling that took hold of him. When Tarmigian broke the embrace, the priest turned away, trying to compose himself. Tarmigian was coughing again.

"Excuse me," said Mrs. Aldenberry. She seemed a little confused.

Tarmigian held up one hand, still coughing; his eyes had grown wide with the effort.

"Hot toddy — honey with a touch of lemon and whiskey," she said, to no one in particular. "Works like a charm."

Father Russell thought about how someone her age would indeed learn to feel that small folk remedies were effective in stopping illness. It was logical, and reasonable, and he was surprised by the force of his own resentment of her for it. He stood there wiping his eyes and felt his heart constrict with hatred.

"There," Tarmigian said, getting his breath back.

"Hot toddy," said Mrs. Aldenberry. "Never knew it to fail." She was looking from one to the other of the two men, her expression taking on something of the look of tolerance. "Fix you up like new," she said, turning her attention to the priest, who could not stop blubbering. "What's — what's going on here?"

Father Russell had a moment of sensing that everything Tarmigian had done or said over the past year was somehow freighted with this one moment, and it took him a few seconds to recognize the implausibility of such a thing. No one could have planned it, or anticipated it: this one aimless gesture of humor — out of a habit of humorous gestures, and from a brave old man sick to death — that could feel so much like health, like the breath of new life.

He couldn't stop crying. He brought out a handkerchief and covered his face with it, then wiped his forehead. It was quiet. The other two were gazing at him. He straightened, caught his breath. "Excuse me."

"No excuse needed," Tarmigian said, looking down. His smile seemed tentative and sad now. Even a little afraid.

"What's going on here?" the old woman wanted to know.

"Why, nothing out of the ordinary," Tarmigian said, shifting the weight of his skeletal body, clearing his throat, managing to speak very loudly, very gently, so as to reassure her, but making certain, too, that she could hear him.

Mary Ward Brown

....

A New Life

THEY MEET BY CHANCE in front of the bank. Elizabeth is a recent widow, pale and dry-eyed, unable to cry. Paul, an old friend, old boyfriend, starts smiling the moment he sees her. He looks so *happy*, she thinks. She's never seen him look so happy. Under one arm he carries a wide farm checkbook, a rubber band around it so things won't fall out.

"Well. This is providential." He grips her hand and holds on, beaming, ignoring the distance he's long kept between them. Everything about him seems animated. Even his hair, thick, dark, shot with early gray, stands up slightly from his head instead of lying down flat. In the sunlight the gray looks electric. "We've been thinking about you," he says, still beaming. "Should have been to see you."

"But you *did* come." Something about him is different, she thinks, something major, not just the weight he's put on.

"We came when everyone else was there and you didn't need us. We should have been back long ago. How are you?"

"Fine," she says, to end it. "Thank you."

He studies her face, frowns. "You don't look fine," he says. "You're still grieving, when John is with God now. He's well again. Happy! Don't you know that?"

So that's it, she thinks. She's heard that Paul and his wife, Louise, are in a new religious group in town, something that has sprung up outside the church. They call themselves Keepers of the Vineyard. Like a rock band, someone said.

Small-town traffic moves up and down the street, a variety of mid-size cars and pickup trucks, plus an occasional big car or van. The newly remodeled bank updates a street of old redbrick buildings, some now painted white, green, gray. Around the corner the beauty shop is pink with white trim.

This is the southern Bible Belt, where people talk about God the way they talk about the weather, about His will and His blessings, about why He lets things happen. The Vineyard people claim that God also talks to them. Their meeting place is a small house on Green Street, where they meet, the neighbors say, all the time. Night and day.

Their leader is the new young pastor of the Presbyterian church, called by his first name, Steve. Regular church members look on the group with suspicion. They're all crazy, they go too far, the church people say.

When told, Steve had simply shrugged. "Some thought Jesus was a little crazy, too," he'd said.

He is a spellbinding preacher and no one moves or dozes while he speaks, but his church is split in two. Some are for him and some against him, but none are neutral. He is defined by extremes.

Paul opens the door to the bank for Elizabeth. "What are you doing tonight?" he asks, over his shoulder.

She looks back, surprised, and he winks.

"Louise and I could come over after supper," he says. "How about it?"

She understands his winks and jokes. They're cover-up devices, she'd discovered years ago, for all he meant to hide. New hurts, old wounds, the real Paul Dudley. Only once had she seen him show pain, ever. When his favorite dog, always with him, had been hit by a truck, he'd covered his face with his hands when he told her. But the minute she'd touched him, ready to cry, too, he'd stiffened. "I'll have to get another one," he'd said. And right away, he had. Another lemon-spotted pointer.

"You're turning down a good way of life, though," her mother had said, a little sadly, when she didn't take the ring. It had been his mother's diamond. He'd also inherited a large tract of land and a home in the country.

She'd never confessed one of her reasons, for fear that it might sound trivial. He'd simply made her nervous. Wherever they'd gone, to concerts, plays, movies, he hadn't been able to sit still and listen, but had had to look around and whisper, start conversations, pick up dropped programs. Go for more popcorn. He had rummaged through his hair, fiddled with his tie, jiggled keys in his pocket until it had been all she could do not to say, "Stop that, or I'll scream!"

He hadn't seemed surprised when she told him. Subdued at first, he had rallied and joked as he went out the door. But he'd cut her out of his life from then on, and ignored all her efforts to be friendly. Not until both were married, to other people, had he even stopped on the street to say hello.

Back home now in her clean, orderly kitchen, she has put away groceries and stored the empty bags. Without putting it off, she has subtracted the checks she'd just written downtown. Attention to detail has become compulsive with her. It is all that holds her together, she thinks.

Just before daylight-savings dark, Paul and Louise drive up in a white station wagon. Paul is wearing a fresh short-sleeved shirt, the top of its sleeves still pressed together like uncut pages in a book. In one hand he carries a Bible as worn as a wallet.

Louise, in her late forties like Elizabeth, is small and blond. Abandoned first by a father who had simply left home, then by a mother his leaving had destroyed, she'd been brought up by sad, tired grandparents. Her eyes are like those of an unspoiled pet, waiting for a sign to be friendly.

When Elizabeth asks if they'd like something to drink now or later, they laugh. It's a long-standing joke around Wakefield. "Mr. Paul don't drink nothing but sweetmilk," a worker on his place had said years ago.

"Now would be nice," he says, with his happy new smile.

Elizabeth leads the way to a table in her kitchen, a large light room with one end for dining. The table, of white wood with an airy glass top, overlooks her back lawn. While she fills glasses with tea and ice, Paul gazes out the window, humming to himself, drumming on the glass top. Louise admires the marigolds, snapdragons, and petunias in bloom. Her own flowers have been neglected this year, she says. Elizabeth brings out a pound cake still warm from the oven.

"Let's bless it," Paul says, when they're seated.

He holds out one hand to her and the other to Louise. His hand is trembling and so warm it feels feverish. Because of her?, Elizabeth thinks. No. Everyone knows he's been happy with his wife. Louise's hand is cool and steady.

He bows his head. "Lord, we thank you for this opportunity to witness in your name. We know that You alone can comfort our friend in her sorrow. Bring her, we pray, to the knowledge of your saving grace and give her your peace, which passes understanding. We ask it for your sake and in your name."

He smiles a benediction, and Elizabeth cuts the cake.

"The reason we're here, Elizabeth — " He pushes back the tea and cake before him, " — is that my heart went out to you this morning at the bank. You can't give John up, and it's tearing you apart."

What can she say? He's right. She can't give John up and she *is* torn apart, after more than a year.

"We have the cure for broken hearts," he says, as if stating a fact.

Louise takes a bite of cake, but when he doesn't she puts down her fork. On her left hand, guarded by the wedding band, is a ring that Elizabeth remembers.

"I have something to ask you, Elizabeth." Paul looks at her directly. "Are you saved?"

Elizabeth turns her tea glass slowly clockwise, wipes up the circle beneath it with her napkin. "I don't know how to answer that, Paul," she says, at last. "What happened to John did something to my faith. John didn't deserve all that suffering, or to die in his prime. I can't seem to accept it."

"Well, that's natural. Understandable. In my heart I was rebellious, too, at one time."

She frowns, trying to follow. He hadn't been religious at all when she'd known him. On the contrary, he'd worked on a tractor all day Sunday while everyone else went to church, had joked about people who were overly religious.

"But I had an encounter with Jesus Christ that changed my life," he says. "I kept praying, with all my heart, and He finally came to me. His presence was as real as yours is now!" His eyes fill up, remembering. "But you have to really want Him, first. Most people have to hit rock bottom, the way I did, before they do. You have to be down so low you say, 'Lord, I can't make it on my own. You'll have to help me. *You* take over!'"

Now he's lost her. Things had gone so well for him, she'd thought. He'd had everything he said he wanted out of life when they were dating — to have a big family and to live on his land. He'd been an only child whose parents had died young. Louise had been orphaned, too, in a way. So they'd had a child every year or two before they quit, a station wagon full of healthy, suntanned children. Some were driving themselves by now, she'd noticed.

As for her, rock bottom had been back in that hospital room with John, sitting in a chair by his bed. Six months maybe, a year at the most, they'd just told her out in the hall. She'd held his hand until the Demerol took effect and his hand had gone limp in hers. Then she'd leaned her head on the bed beside him and prayed, with all her heart. From hospital room to hospital room she had prayed, and at home in between.

"I've said that, too, Paul, many times," she says. "I prayed, and nothing happened. Why would He come to you and not me?"

"Because you were letting something stand in the way, my dear!" His smile is back, full force. "For Him to come in, you have to get rid of self — first of all your self-*will!* 'Not my will but Thine be done,' He said on the cross."

He breaks off, takes a quick sip of tea. With the first bite of cake, he shuts his eyes tight. A blissful smile melts over his face.

"Umh, umh!" He winks at Louise. "How about this pound cake, Mama!"

Late the next afternoon, Elizabeth is watering flowers in her backyard. Before, she grew flowers to bring in the house, zinnias for pottery pitchers, bulbs for clear glass vases. Now she grows them for themselves, and seldom cuts them. She has a new irrational notion that scissors hurt the stems. After what she's seen of pain, she wants to hurt nothing that lives.

From where she stands with the hose, she sees a small red car turn into her driveway. In front of the house, two young girls in sundresses get out.

"Mrs. North?" the first girl says, when Elizabeth comes up to meet them. "You probably don't remember me, but I'm Beth Woodall and this is Cindy Lewis. We're from The Vineyard."

Beth is blond and pretty. A young Louise, Elizabeth thinks. But Cindy has a limp and something is wrong with one arm. Elizabeth doesn't look at it directly.

"What can I do for you girls?"

"Oh, we just came to see you," Beth smiles brightly. "Paul and Louise thought we might cheer you up."

In the living room, Beth is the speaker. "We all knew your husband from the paper, Mrs. North. He was wonderful! My dad read every line he ever wrote, and says this town is lost without him." She pushes back her hair, anchors it behind one ear. Her nails, overlong, pale as sea-shells, seem to lag behind her fingers. "We've all been praying for you."

Elizabeth rubs a wet spot the hose has made on her skirt. "Thank you," she says, not looking up.

"I know how you feel," Beth says. "My boyfriend, Billy Moseley, was killed in a wreck last year. He'd been my boyfriend since grammar school, and we'd have gotten married someday, if he'd lived." Her eyes fill with tears. "We were just always . . . together."

Elizabeth remembers Billy. Handsome, polite. A star athlete killed by a drunk driver. She feels a quick stir of sympathy but, like every-thing painful since John died, it freezes before it can surface. Now it all seems packed in her chest, as in the top of a refrigerator so full the door will hardly shut. She looks back at Beth with dry, guilty eyes.

"Well, I'm all right now," Beth says. "But I thought it would kill me for a while. I didn't want to live without Billy, until I met the people at The Vineyard. They made me see it was God's will for him to die and me to live and serve the Lord. Now I know he's in heaven waiting for me, and it's not as bad as it was." She shrugs. "I try to help Billy's mother, but she won't turn it over to the Lord."

The room is growing dark. Elizabeth gets up to turn on more lights, which cast a roseate glow on their faces, delicate hands, slender feet in sandals.

"Would you girls like a Coke?" she asks.

Beth blinks to dry her eyes. "Yes, ma'am," she says. "Thank you. A Coke would be nice."

They follow Elizabeth to the kitchen, where she pours Coca-Cola into glasses filled with ice cubes.

"You must get lonesome here by yourself," Cindy says, looking around. "Are your children away from home or something?"

Elizabeth hands her a glass and paper napkin. "I don't have children, Cindy," she says. "My husband and I wanted a family, but couldn't have one. All we had was each other."

"Ah!" Beth says quickly. "*We'll* be your children, then. Won't we, Cindy?"

It is seven o'clock in the morning and Elizabeth is drinking instant coffee from an old, stained mug, staring dejectedly out the kitchen window. During the night, she'd had a dream about John. He'd been alive, not dead.

John had been editor-publisher of the *Wakefield Sun,* the town's weekly paper, had written most of the copy himself. In the dream, they'd been in bed for the night.

John had liked to work in bed, and she had liked to read beside him, so they'd gone to bed early as a rule. Propped up on pillows, he had worked on editorials, for which he'd been known throughout the state. At times, though, he had put aside his clipboard and taken off his glasses. When he turned her way, his eyes — blue-gray and rugged like the tweed jacket he'd worn so many winters — would take on a look that made the book fall from her hand. Later, sometimes, on to the floor.

In the dream, as he looked at her, the phone by their bed had rung. He'd forgotten a meeting, he said, throwing off covers. He had to get down there. It had already started, a meeting he couldn't afford to miss. Putting on his jacket, he'd stopped at the bedroom door.

"I'll be right back," he promised.

But he wasn't back and never would be, she'd been reminded, wide awake. In the dark, she had checked the space beside her with her hand to be sure, and her loss had seemed new again, more cruel than ever, made worse by time. If only she could cry, she'd thought, like other widows. Cry, everyone told her. Let the grief out! But she couldn't. It was frozen and locked up inside her, a mass that wouldn't move.

She had waked from the dream at two in the morning, and hasn't been back to sleep since. Now she's glad to be up with something to do, if it's only an appointment with her lawyer. She has sold John's business but kept the building, and the legalities are not yet over. She wants to be on time, is always on time. It is part of her fixation on detail, as if each thing attended to were somehow on a list that if ever completed would bring back meaning to her life.

In the fall she will go back to teaching school, but her heart is not in it as before. For twenty years she had been, first of all, John's wife — from deadline to deadline, through praise, blame, long stretches of indifference. He couldn't have done it without her, he'd said, with each award and honor he'd been given.

Now no other role seems right for her, which is her problem, she's thinking, when the front door bell rings.

Louise is there in a fresh summer dress, her clean hair shining in the sun. She smells of something lightly floral.

"May I come in?"

Still in a rumpled nightgown and robe, aware of the telltale look in her eyes, Elizabeth opens the door wider, steps back. "I have an appointment," she says, and smiles as best she can. "But come in. There's time for a cup of coffee."

At the white table, Louise takes the place she'd had before. "I won't stay long," she says.

Elizabeth puts on a pot of coffee, gets out cups and saucers, takes a seat across from Louise. Outside all is quiet. Stores and offices won't open until nine. So why is Louise in town at this hour?

"I was praying for you," she says, as if in answer. "But the Lord told me to come and see you instead."

Elizabeth stares at her. "God told you?"

Their eyes meet. Louise nods. "He wanted you to know that He loves you," she says. "He wanted to send you His love, by me." Her face turns a sudden bright pink that deepens and spreads.

Next door a car starts up and drives off. A dog barks. The coffee is ready and Elizabeth pours it. She's learned to drink hers black, but Louise adds milk and sugar.

"Come to The Vineyard with us next time, Elizabeth," Louise says suddenly. "Please."

This is what she came for, Elizabeth thinks, and it's more than an invitation. It's a plea, as from someone on the bank to a swimmer having trouble in the water.

"It could save your life!" Louise says.

The Vineyard is a narrow, shotgun-style house of the 1890s, last used as a dentist's office. It has one large front room, with two small rooms and a makeshift kitchen behind it. Having been welcomed and shown around, Elizabeth stands against the wall of the front room with Paul and Louise. The group is smaller than she'd expected and not all Presbyterian. Some are from other churches as well, all smiling and excited.

Everything revolves around Steve, a young man in jeans who looks like a slight, blond Jesus. When Elizabeth is introduced, he looks her deep in the eyes.

"Elizabeth!" he says, as if he knows her already. "We were hoping you'd come. Welcome to The Vineyard."

He says no more and moves on, but she has felt his power like the heat from a stove. She finds herself following him around the room with her eyes, wishing she could hear what he says to other people.

The night is hot and windows are open, but no breeze comes through. Rotary fans monotonously sweep away heat, in vain. Someone brings in a pitcher of Kool-Aid, which is passed around in paper cups.

"Okay, people." Steve holds up his cup and raises his voice for attention. "Let's have a song."

Everyone takes a seat on the floor, in a ring shaped by the long narrow room. A masculine girl with short dark hair stands up. She tests one key then another, low in her throat, and leads off. "We are one in the Spirit, we are one in the Lord. . . ."

Most of the singers are young, in shorts or jeans, but some are middle-aged or older. Of the latter, the majority are single women and widows like Elizabeth. The young people sit with folded legs, leaning comfortably forward, and the men draw up one leg or the other. But the women, in pastel pant suits and sleeveless dresses, sit up straight, like paper dolls bent in the middle.

The song gains momentum for the chorus, which ends, "Yes, they'll know-oh we are Christians by our love!"

"All *right*," Steve says. "Time to come to our Lord in prayer."

Someone clambers up to turn off the light switch and someone else lights a candle on the Kool-Aid table. In the dim light Steve reaches out to his neighbor on each side, and a chain of hands is quickly formed.

Without a hand to hold in her new single life, Elizabeth is glad to link in. She smiles at the young woman on her left and Paul on her right. Paul's hand no longer trembles but feels as it had in high school — not thrilling but dependable, a hand she could count on.

The room is suddenly hushed. "For the benefit of our visitor," Steve says, "we begin with sentence prayers around the circle, opening our hearts and minds to God."

Elizabeth feels a quick rush of misgiving. *Oh, no!* she thinks. *I can't do this!* She's never prayed out loud in her life except in unison, much less ad-libbed before a group.

But Steve has already started. "We thank you, Heavenly Father, for the privilege of being here. Guide us, we pray, in all we say and do, that it may be for the extension of your kingdom. We thank you again for each other, but above all for your blessed son Jesus, who is with us tonight, here in this circle."

On Steve's right, a young man with shoulder-length hair takes up at once. "I thank you, Lord, for turning me around. Until I found You, all I cared about was that bottle. But You had living water to satisfy my thirst. . . ."

Eagerly, one after the other, they testify, confess, ask help in bringing others to Jesus as Lord and Savior. They speak of the devil as if he's someone in town, someone they meet every day.

In her turn, a checkout girl from the supermarket starts to cry and can't stop. From around the circle come murmurs of "God bless you" and "We love you" until her weeping begins to subside.

"My heart's too full tonight," she chokes out, at last. "I have to pass."

On each side, Elizabeth's hands are gripped tighter. The back of her blouse is wet with sweat. The room begins to feel crowded and close.

"Praise God!" a man cries out in the middle of someone's prayer.

"Help me, Lord," a woman whimpers.

A teenage boy starts to pray, his words eerily unintelligible. Tongues?, Elizabeth wonders, electrified. They do it here, she's heard. But something nasal in his voice gives the clue, and she has a wild impulse to laugh. He's not speaking in tongues but is tongue-tied, from a cleft palate.

Too soon, she hears Paul's voice beside her, charged with emotion. He's praying about the sin of pride in his life, but she can't pay attention because she will be next. Heavy galloping hoofbeats seem to have taken the place of her heart.

When Paul is through, she says nothing. *I pass* flashes through her mind, but she doesn't say it. She is unable to decide on, much less utter, a word. Her hands are wet with cold perspiration. She tries to withdraw them, but Paul on one side and the young woman on the other hold on tight. Fans hum back and forth as her silence stretches out.

At last someone starts to pray out of turn, and the circle is mended. As the prayers move back toward Steve, she gives a sigh of relief and tries, without being obvious, to ease her position on the floor.

Steve gives a new directive. "We'll now lift up to God those with special needs tonight."

He allows them a moment to think, then leads off. "I lift up Ruth, in the medical center for diagnosis," he says. "Her tests begin in the morning."

They pray in silence for Ruth, for someone in the midst of divorce, for a man who's lost his job. An unnamed friend with an unidentified "problem" is lifted up.

Louise clears her throat for attention, then hesitates before speaking out. When she does, her voice is girlish and sweet as usual.

"I lift up Elizabeth," she says.

Elizabeth has avoided the telephone all day, though she's heard it ring many times. The weather is cloudy and cool, so she's spent the morning outside, weeding, hoeing, raking, and has come to one decision. She will not see the soul savers today.

Tomorrow, it may be, she can face them. Today, she will do anything not to. They were holding her up, she thinks, not for her sake but theirs. They refuse to look on the dark side of things, and they want her to blink it away, too. If she can smile in the face of loss, grief, and death, so can they. They're like children in a fairy tale, singing songs, holding hands. Never mind the dark wood, the wolves and witches. Or birds that eat up the bread crumbs.

During lunch she takes the phone off the hook, eats in a hurry, and goes back out with magazines and a book. For supper she will go to Breck's for a barbecue and visit with whoever's there. When she comes back, the day will be over. "One day at a time" is the new widow's motto.

She is drying off from a shower when the front door bell rings. She doesn't hurry, even when it rings again and someone's finger stays on the buzzer. The third time, she closes the bathroom door, little by little, so as not to be heard. Gingerly, as if it might shock her, she flips off the light switch.

Soon there is knocking on the back door, repeated several times. She can hear voices but not words. When she continues to keep quiet, hardly breathing for fear they will somehow know or divine that she's there, the knocking stops and the voices, jarred by retreating footsteps, fade away. At last, through a sneaked-back window curtain, she sees the small red car moving off.

And suddenly, in her mind's eye, she can also see herself as from a distance, towel clutched like a fig leaf, hiding from a band of Christians out to save her soul!

For the first time in her widowhood, she laughs when she's alone. It happens before she knows it, like a hiccough or a sneeze. With refound pleasure, she laughs again, more.

Still smiling, she dresses in a hurry and is about to walk out the back door when the front door bell rings.

This time she goes at once to face them. Beth and Cindy, plus Steve and two policemen, stare back at her. The policemen are in uniform, dark blue pants and lighter blue shirts, with badges, insignia, and guns on their belts. Obviously, they've been deciding how to get in the house without a key.

For a moment no one speaks. Then Beth, wide-eyed, bursts out, "You scared us to death, Mrs. North! We thought you had passed out or something. We knew you were in there because of your car."

"I didn't feel like seeing anyone today." Elizabeth's voice is calm and level. What has come over her?, she thinks. Where did it come from, that unruffled voice? She should be mad or upset, and she's not.

"Sorry we bothered you, Mrs. North," the older policeman says. "Your friends here were worried."

Out of the blue, Elizabeth is suffused all at once with what seems pure benevolence. For a split-second, and for no reason, she is sure that everything is overall right in the world, no matter what. And not just for her but for everyone, including the dead! The air seems rarefied, the light incandescent.

"It was no bother," she says, half-dazed. "I thank you."

Steve has said nothing. His eyes are as calm as ever, the eyes of a true believer blessed or cursed with certainty. His focus has been steadily on her, but now it breaks away.

"Let's go, people," he says lightly. "We're glad you're okay, Elizabeth. God bless you."

Elizabeth has slept all night, for once. As she sits down to coffee and cereal, she is sure of one thing. She has to start what everyone tells her must be "a whole new life" without John, and she has to do it now. Though frozen and numb inside still, she can laugh. And she has experienced, beyond doubt, a mystical moment of grace.

When a car door slams out front, not once but twice, she gets up without waiting for anyone to ring or knock. It is Paul and Louise, for the first time not smiling. Paul has on khaki work clothes. Louise has brushed her hair on top, but underneath sleep tangles show.

In the living room, they sit leaning forward on the sofa. Paul rocks one knee nervously from side to side, making his whole body shake from the tension locked inside him.

"They should have come to us instead of going to the police," he says at once. "They just weren't thinking."

"No, it was my fault," Elizabeth says. "I should have gone to the door."

"Why *didn't* you?" Louise asks.

"Well. . . ." She falls silent.

"Our meeting upset you?" Paul asks, in a moment.

Elizabeth's housecoat is old and too short. They catch her like this every time, she thinks. Why can't they call before they come, like everyone else? She begins to check snaps down her front.

"Level with us, honey," Paul says. "We're your friends. What upset you so much?"

Except for the faint click of a snap being snapped, the room is utterly quiet.

"We need to pray about this," Paul says. "Let's pray. . . ."

"No!" Elizabeth is on her feet without thinking. "No, Paul. I can't!" She's out of breath as from running. "This has got to stop! I can't be in your Vineyard. You'll have to find somebody else!"

He's silent for so long a countdown seems to start. Then he stands up slowly, Louise beside him as if joined. At the door, with his hand on the knob, he turns.

"Well, Elizabeth," he says. "I guess it's time to say good-bye."

Her heart slows down as if brakes had been applied. The beats become heavy, far apart. She can feel them in her ears, close to her brain.

"I'm sorry, Paul!" she says quickly. Before his accusing eyes, she says it again, like holding out a gift she knows to be inadequate. "I'm *sorry!*"

But this time he has no joke or smile. Without a word, he takes Louise by the arm and guides her through the doorway.

Elizabeth watches them walk to the car, side by side but not touching. Paul opens the door for Louise, quickly shuts her in, and gets behind the wheel himself. The station wagon moves out of sight down the driveway.

Elizabeth's cereal is soggy, her coffee cold. She pushes it all away, props her elbows on the table, and buries her face in her hands. Suddenly, as from a thaw long overdue, she's crying. Sobs shake her shoulders. Tears seep through her fingers and run down her wrists. One drop falls on the glass top where, in morning sunlight, it sparkles like a jewel.

Andre Dubus

....

A Father's Story

My NAME IS LUKE RIPLEY, and here is what I call my life: I own a stable of thirty horses, and I have young people who teach riding, and we board some horses too. This is in northeastern Massachusetts. I have a barn with an indoor ring, and outside I've got two fenced-in rings and a pasture that ends at a woods with trails. I call it my life because it looks like it is, and people I know call it that, but it's a life I can get away from when I hunt and fish, and some nights after dinner when I sit in the dark in the front room and listen to opera. The room faces the lawn and the road, a two-lane country road. When cars come around the curve northwest of the house, they light up the lawn for an instant, the leaves of the maple out by the road and the hemlock closer to the window. Then I'm alone again, or I'd appear to be if someone crept up to the house and looked through a window: a big-gutted gray-haired guy, drinking tea and smoking cigarettes, staring out at the dark woods across the road, listening to a grieving soprano.

My real life is the one nobody talks about anymore, except Father Paul LeBoeuf, another old buck. He has a decade on me: he's sixty-four, a big man, bald on top with gray at the sides; when he had hair, it was black. His face is ruddy, and he jokes about being a whiskey priest, though he's not. He gets outdoors as much as he can, goes for a long walk every morning, and hunts and fishes with me. But I can't get him on a horse anymore. Ten years ago I could badger him into a trail ride; I had to give him a Western saddle, and he'd hold the pommel and bounce through the woods with me, and be sore for days. He's looking at seventy with eyes that are younger than many I've seen in people in their twenties. I do not remember ever feeling the way they seem to; but I was lucky, because even as a child I knew that life would try me, and I must be strong to endure, though in those days I expected to be tortured and killed for my faith, like the saints I learned about in school.

Father Paul's family came down from Canada, and he grew up speaking more French than English, so he is different from the Irish priests who abound up here. I do not like to make general statements, or even to hold general beliefs, about people's blood, but the Irish do seem happiest when they're dealing with misfortune or guilt, either their own or somebody else's, and if you think you're not a victim of either one, you can count on certain Irish priests to try to change your mind. On Wednesday nights Father Paul comes to dinner. Often he comes on other nights too and once, in the old days when we couldn't eat meat on Fridays, we bagged our first ducks of the season on a Friday, and as we drove home from the marsh, he said: For the purposes of Holy Mother Church, I believe a duck is more a creature of water than land, and is not rightly meat. Sometimes he teases me about never putting anything in his Sunday collection, which he would not know about if I hadn't told him years ago. I would like to believe I told him so we could have philosophical talk at dinner, but probably the truth is I suspected he knew, and I did not want him to think I so loved money that I would not even give his church a coin on Sunday. Certainly the ushers who pass the baskets know me as a miser.

I don't feel right about giving money for buildings, places. This starts with the pope, and I cannot respect one of them till he sells his house and everything in it, and that church too, and uses the money to feed the poor. I have rarely, and maybe never, come across saintliness, but I feel certain it cannot exist in such a place. But I admit, also, that I know very little, and maybe the popes live on a different plane and are tried in ways I don't know about. Father Paul says his own church, St. John's, is hardly the Vatican. I like his church: it is made of wood, and has a simple altar and crucifix, and no padding on the kneelers. He does not have to lock its doors at night. Still it is a place. He could say Mass in my barn. I know this is stubborn, but I can find no mention by Christ of maintaining buildings, much less erecting them of stone or brick, and decorating them with pieces of metal and mineral and elements that people still fight over like barbarians. We had a Maltese woman taking riding lessons, she came over on the boat when she was ten, and once she told me how the nuns in Malta used to tell the little girls that if they wore jewelry, rings and bracelets and necklaces, in purgatory snakes would coil around their fingers and wrists and throats. I do not believe in frightening children or telling them lies, but if those nuns saved a few girls from devotion to things, maybe they were right. That Maltese woman laughed about it, but I noticed she wore only a watch, and that with a leather strap.

The money I give to the church goes in people's stomachs, and on their backs, down in New York City. I have no delusions about the worth of what I do, but I feel it's better to feed somebody than not. There's a priest in Times Square giving shelter to runaway kids, and some Franciscans who run a bread line; actually it's a morning line for coffee and a roll, and Father Paul calls it the continental breakfast for winos and bag ladies. He is curious about how much I am sending and I know why: he guesses I send a lot, he has said probably more than tithing, and he is right; he wants to know how much because he believes I'm generous and good, and he is wrong about that; he has never had much money and does not know how easy it is to write a check when you have everything you will ever need, and the figures are mere numbers, and represent no sacrifice at all. Being a real Catholic is too hard; if I were one, I would do with my house and barn what I want the pope to do with his. So I do not want to impress Father Paul, and when he asks me how much, I say I can't let my left hand know what my right is doing.

He came on Wednesday nights when Gloria and I were married, and the kids were young; Gloria was a very good cook (I assume she still is, but it is difficult to think of her in the present), and I liked sitting at the table with a friend who was also a priest. I was proud of my handsome and healthy children. This was long ago, and they were all very young and cheerful and often funny, and the three boys took care of their baby sister, and did not bully or tease her. Of course they did sometimes, with that excited cruelty children are prone to, but not enough so that it was part of her days. On the Wednesday after Gloria left with the kids and a U-Haul trailer, I was sitting on the front steps, it was summer, and I was watching cars go by on the road, when Father Paul drove around the curve and into the driveway. I was ashamed to see him because he is a priest and my family was gone, but I was relieved too. I went to the car to greet him. He got out smiling, with a bottle of wine, and shook my hand, then pulled me to him, gave me a quick hug, and said: "It's Wednesday, isn't it? Let's open some cans."

With arms about each other we walked to the house, and it was good to know he was doing his work but coming as a friend too, and I thought what good work he had. I have no calling. It is for me to keep horses.

In that other life, anyway. In my real one I go to bed early and sleep well and wake at four forty-five, for an hour of silence. I never want to get out of bed then, and every morning I know I can sleep for another four hours, and still not fail at any of my duties. But I get up, so have come to believe my life can be seen in miniature in that struggle in the dark of morning. While making the bed and boiling water for coffee, I talk to God: I offer Him my day, every act of my body and spirit, my thoughts and moods, as a prayer of thanksgiving, and for Gloria and my children and my friends and two women I made love with after Gloria left. This morning offertory is a habit from my boyhood in a Catholic school; or then it was a habit, but as I kept it and grew older it became a ritual. Then I say the Lord's Prayer, trying not to recite it, and one morning it occurred to me that a prayer, whether recited or said with concentration, is always an act of faith.

I sit in the kitchen at the rear of the house and drink coffee and smoke and watch the sky growing light before sunrise, the trees of the woods near the barn taking shape, becoming single pines and elms and oaks and maples. Sometimes a rabbit comes out of the treeline, or is already sitting there, invisible till the light finds him. The birds are awake in the trees and feeding on the ground and the little ones, the purple finches and titmice and chickadees, are at the feeder I rigged outside the kitchen window; it is too small for pigeons to get a purchase. I sit and give myself to coffee and tobacco, that get me brisk again, and I watch and listen. In the first year or so after I lost my family, I played the radio in the mornings. But I overcame that, and now I rarely play it at all. Once in the mail I received a questionnaire asking me to write down everything I watched on television during the week they had chosen. At the end of those seven days I wrote in *The Wizard of Oz* and returned it. That was in winter and was actually a busy week for my television, which normally sits out the cold months without once warming up. Had they sent the questionnaire during baseball season, they would have found me at my set. People at the stables talk about shows and performers I have never heard of, but I cannot get interested; when I am in the mood to watch television, I go to a movie or read a detective novel. There are always good detective novels to be found, and I like remembering them next morning with my coffee.

I also think of baseball and hunting and fishing, and of my children. It is not painful to think about them anymore, because even if we had lived together, they would be gone now, grown into their own lives, except Jennifer. I think of death too, not sadly, or with fear, though something like excitement does run through me, something more quickening than the coffee and tobacco. I suppose it is an intense interest, and an outright distrust: I never feel certain that I'll be here watching birds eating at tomorrow's daylight. Sometimes I try to think of other things, like the rabbit that is warm and breathing but not there till twilight. I feel on the brink of something about the life of the senses, but either am not equipped to go further, or am not interested enough to concentrate. I have called all of this thinking, but it is not, because it is unintentional; what I'm really doing is feeling the day, in silence, and that is what Father Paul is doing too on his five- to ten-mile walks.

When the hour ends I take an apple or carrot, and I go to the stable and tack up a horse. We take good care of these horses, and no one rides them but students, instructors, and me, and nobody rides the horses we board unless an owner asks me to. The barn is dark and I turn on lights and take some deep breaths, smelling the hay and horses and their manure, both fresh and dried, a combined odor that you either like or you don't. I walk down the wide space of dirt between stalls, greeting horses, joking with them about their quirks, and choose one for no reason at all other than the way it looks at me that morning. I get my old English saddle that has smoothed and darkened through the years, and go into the stall, talking to this beautiful creature who'll swerve out of a canter if a piece of paper blows in front of him, and if the barn catches fire and you manage to get him out he will, if he can get away from you, run back into the fire, to his stall. Like the smells that surround them, you either like them or you don't. I love them, so am spared having to try to explain why. I feed one the carrot or apple and tack up and lead him outside where I mount, and we go down the driveway to the road and cross it and turn northwest and walk then trot then canter to St. John's.

A few cars are on the road, their drivers looking serious about going to work. It is always strange for me to see a woman dressed for work so early in the morning. You know how long it takes them, with the makeup and hair and clothes, and I think of them waking in the dark of winter or early light of other seasons, and dressing as they might for an evening's entertainment. Probably this strikes me because I grew up seeing my father put on those suits he never wore on weekends or his two weeks off, and so am accustomed to the men, but when I see these women I think something went wrong, to send all those dressed-up people out on the road when the dew hasn't dried yet. Maybe it's because I so dislike getting up early, but am also doing what I choose to do, while they have no choice. At heart I am lazy, yet I find such peace and delight in it that I believe it is a natural state, and in what looks like my laziest periods I am closest to my center. The ride to St. John's is fifteen minutes. The horses and I do it in all weather; the road is well plowed in winter, and there are only a few days a year when ice makes me drive the pickup. People always look at someone on horseback, and for a moment their faces change and many drivers and I wave to each other. Then at St. John's, Father Paul and five or six regulars and I celebrate the Mass.

Do not think of me as a spiritual man whose every thought during those twenty-five minutes is at one with the words of the Mass. Each morning I try, each morning I fail, and know that always I will be a creature who, looking at Father Paul and the altar, and uttering prayers, will be distracted by scrambled eggs, the weather, and memories and daydreams that have nothing to do with the sacrament I am about to receive. I can receive, though: the Eucharist, and also, at Mass and at other times, moments and even minutes of contemplation. But I cannot achieve contemplation, as some can; and so, having to face and forgive my own failures, I have learned from them both the necessity and the wonder of ritual. For ritual allows those who cannot will themselves out of the secular to perform the spiritual as dancing allows the tongue-tied man a ceremony of love. And, while my mind dwells on breakfast, or Major or Duchess tethered under the church eave, there is, as I take the Host from Father Paul and place it on my tongue and return to the pew, a feeling that I am thankful I have not lost in the forty-eight years since my first Communion. At its center is excitement; spreading out from it is the peace of certainty. Or the certainty of peace. One night Father Paul and I talked about faith. It was long ago, and all I remember him saying: Belief is believing in God; faith is believing that God believes in you. That is the excitement, and the peace; then the Mass is over, and I go into the sacristy and we have a cigarette and chat, the mystery ends, we are two men talking like any two men on a morning in America, about baseball, plane crashes, presidents, governors, murders, the sun, the clouds. Then I go to the horse and ride back to the life people see, the one in which I move and talk, and most days I enjoy it.

It is late summer now, the time between fishing and hunting, but a good time for baseball. It has been two weeks since Jennifer left, to drive home to Gloria's after her summer visit. She is the only one who still visits; the boys are married and have children, and sometimes fly up for a holiday, or I fly down or west to visit one of them. Jennifer is twenty, and I worry about her the way fathers worry about daughters but not sons. I want to know what she's up to, and at the same time I don't. She looks athletic, and she is: she swims and runs and of course rides. All my children do. When she comes for six weeks in summer, the house is loud with girls, friends of hers since childhood, and new ones. I am glad she kept the girl friends. They have been young company for me and, being with them, I have been able to gauge her growth between summers. On their riding days, I'd take them back to the house when their lessons were over and they had walked the horses and put them back in the stalls, and we'd have lemonade or Coke, and cookies if I had some, and talk until their parents came to drive them home. One year their breasts grew, so I wasn't startled when I saw Jennifer in July. Then they were driving cars to the stable, and beginning to look like young women, and I was passing out beer and ashtrays and they were talking about college.

When Jennifer was here in summer, they were at the house most days. I would say generally that as they got older they became quieter, and though I enjoyed both, I sometimes missed the giggles and shouts. The quiet voices, just low enough for me not to hear from wherever I was, rising and falling in proportion to my distance from them, frightened me. Not that I believed they were planning or recounting anything really wicked, but there was a female seriousness about them, and it was secretive, and of course I thought: love, sex. But it was more than that: it was womanhood they were entering, the deep forest of it, and no matter how many women and men too are saying these days that there is little difference between us, the truth is that men find their way into that forest only on clearly marked trails while women move about in it like birds. So hearing Jennifer and her friends talking so quietly, yet intensely, I wanted very much to have a wife.

But not as much as in the old days, when Gloria had left but her presence was still in the house as strongly as if she had only gone to visit her folks for a week. There were no clothes or cosmetics, but potted plants endured my neglectful care as long as they could, and slowly died; I did not kill them on purpose, to exorcise the house of her, but I could not remember to water them. For weeks, because I did not use it much, the house was as neat as she had kept it, though dust layered the order she had made. The kitchen went first: I got the dishes in and out of the dishwasher and wiped the top of the stove, but did not return cooking spoons and potholders to their hooks on the wall, and soon the burners and oven were caked with spillings, the refrigerator had more space and was spotted with juices. The living room and my bedroom went next; I did not go into the children's rooms except on bad nights when I went from room to room and looked and touched and smelled, so they did not lose their order until a year later when the kids came for six weeks. It was three months before I ate the last of the food Gloria had cooked and frozen: I remember it was a beef stew, and very good. By then I had four cookbooks, and was boasting a bit, and talking about recipes with women at the stables, and looking forward to cooking for Father Paul. But I never looked forward to cooking at night only for myself, though I made myself do it; on some nights I gave in to my daily temptation, and took a newspaper or detective novel to a restaurant. By the end of the second year, though, I had stopped turning on the radio as soon as I woke in the morning, and was able to be silent and alone in the evening too, and then I enjoyed my dinners.

It was not hard to live through a day, if you can live through a moment. What creates despair is the imagination, that pretends there is a future, and insists on predicting millions of moments, thousands of days, and so drains you that you cannot live the moment at hand. That is what Father Paul told me in those first two years, on some of the bad nights when I believed I could not bear what I had to: the most painful loss was my children, then the loss of Gloria whom I still loved despite or maybe because of our long periods of sadness that rendered us helpless, so neither of us could break out of it to give a hand to the other. Twelve years later I believe ritual would have healed us more quickly than the repetitious talks we had, perhaps even kept us healed. Marriages have lost that, and I wish I had known then what I know now, and we had performed certain acts together every day, no matter how we felt, and perhaps then we could have subordinated feeling to action, for surely that is the essence of love. I know this from my distractions during Mass, and during everything else I do, so that my actions and feelings are seldom one. It does happen every day, but in proportion to everything else in a day, it is rare, like joy. The third most painful loss, which became second and sometimes first as months passed, was the knowledge that I could never marry again, and so dared not even keep company with a woman.

On some of the bad nights I was bitter about this with Father Paul, and I so pitied myself that I cried, or nearly did, speaking with damp eyes and breaking voice. I believe that celibacy is for him the same trial it is for me, not of the flesh, but the spirit: the heart longing to love. But the difference is he chose it, and did not wake one day to a life with thirty horses. In my anger I said I had done my service to love and chastity, and I told him of the actual physical and spiritual pain of practicing rhythm: nights of striking the mattress with a fist, two young animals lying side by side in heat, leaving the bed to pace, to smoke, to curse, and too passionate to question, for we were so angered and oppressed by our passion that we could see no further than our loins. So now I understand how people can be enslaved for generations before they throw down their tools or use them as weapons, the form of their slavery — the cotton fields, the shacks and puny cupboards and untended illnesses — absorbing their emotions and thoughts until finally they have little or none at all to direct their clarity and energy at the owners and legislators. And I told him of the trick of passion and its slaking: how during what we had to believe were safe periods, though all four children were conceived at those times, we were able with some coherence to question the tradition and reason and justice of the law against birth control, but not with enough conviction to soberly act against it, as though regular satisfaction in bed tempered our revolutionary as well as our erotic desires. Only when abstinence drove us hotly away from each other did we receive an urge so strong it lasted all the way to the drugstore and back; but always, after release, we threw away the remaining condoms; and after going through this a few times, we knew what would happen, and from then on we submitted to the calendar she so precisely marked on the bedroom wall. I told him that living two lives each month, one as celibates, one as lovers, made us tense and short-tempered, so we snapped at each other like dogs.

To have endured that, to have reached a time when we burned

slowly and could gain from bed the comfort of lying down at night with one who loves you and whom you love, could for weeks on end go to bed tired, and peacefully sleep after a kiss, a touch of the hands, and then to be thrown out of the marriage like a bundle from a moving freight car, was unjust, was intolerable, and I could not or would not muster the strength to endure it. But I did, a moment at a time, a day, a night, except twice, each time with a different woman and more than a year apart, and this was so long ago that I clearly see their faces in my memory, can hear the pitch of their voices, and the way they pronounced words, one with a Massachusetts accent, one midwestern, but I feel as though I only heard about them from someone else. Each rode at the stables and was with me for part of an evening; one was badly married, one divorced, so none of us was free. They did not understand this Catholic view, but they were understanding about my having it, and I remained friends with both of them until the married one left her husband and went to Boston, and the divorced one moved to Maine. After both those evenings, those good women, I went to Mass early while Father Paul was still in the confessional, and received his absolution. I did not tell him who I was, but of course he knew, though I never saw it in his eyes. Now my longing for a wife comes only once in a while, like a cold: on some late afternoons when I am alone in the barn then I lock up and walk to the house, daydreaming, then suddenly look at it and see it empty, as though for the first time, and all at once I'm weary and feel I do not have the energy to broil meat, and I think of driving to a restaurant, then shake my head and go on to the house, the refrigerator, the oven; and some mornings when I wake in the dark and listen to the silence and run my hand over the cold sheet beside me; and some days in summer when Jennifer is here.

Gloria left first me then the church, and that was the end of religion for the children, though on visits they went to Sunday Mass with me, and still do, out of a respect for my life that they manage to keep free of patronage. Jennifer is an agnostic, though I doubt she would call herself that, any more than she would call herself any other name that implied she had made a decision, a choice, about existence, death, and God. In truth she tends to pantheism, a good sign I think; but not wanting to be a father who tells his children what they ought to believe, I do not say to her that Catholicism includes pantheism, like onions in stew. Besides, I have no missionary instincts and do not believe everyone should or even could live with the Catholic faith. It is

Jennifer's womanhood that renders me awkward. And womanhood now is frank, not like when Gloria was twenty and there were symbols: high heels and cosmetics and dresses, a cigarette, a cocktail. I am glad that women are free now of false modesty and all its attention paid the flesh; but still it is difficult to see so much of your daughter, to face the deep and unabashed sensuality of women, with no tricks of the eyes and mouth to hide the pleasure she feels at having a strong young body. I am certain, with the way things are now, that she has very happily not been a virgin for years. That does not bother me. What bothers me is my certainty about it, just from watching her walk across a room or light a cigarette or pour milk on cereal.

She told me all of it, waking me that night when I had gone to sleep listening to the wind in the trees against the house, a wind so strong that I had to shut all but the lee windows, and still the house cooled; told it to me in such detail and so clearly that now, when she has driven the car to Florida, I remember it all as though I had been a passenger in the front seat, or even at the wheel. It started with a movie, then beer and driving to the sea to look at the waves in the night and the wind, Jennifer and Betsy and Liz. They drank a beer on the beach and wanted to go in naked but were afraid they would drown in the high surf. They bought another six-pack at a grocery store in New Hampshire, and drove home. I can see it now, feel it: the three girls and the beer and the ride on country roads where pines curved in the wind and the big deciduous trees swayed and shook as if they might leap from the earth. They would have some windows partly open so they could feel the wind; Jennifer would be playing a cassette, the music stirring them, as it does the young, to memories of another time, other people and places in what is for them the past.

She took Betsy home, then Liz, and sang with her cassette as she left the town west of us and started home, a twenty-minute drive on the road that passes my house. They each had four beers, but now there were twelve empty bottles in the bag on the floor at the passenger seat, and I keep focusing on their sound against each other when the car shifted speeds or changed directions. For I want to understand that one moment out of all her heart's time on earth, and whether her history had any bearing on it, or whether her heart was then isolated from all it had known, and the sound of those bottles urged it. She was just leaving town, accelerating past a nightclub on the right, gaining speed to climb a long gradual hill, then she went up it, singing, patting the beat on the steering wheel, the wind loud through her few inches of open window, blowing her hair as it did the high branches alongside the road, and she looked up at them and watched the top of the hill for someone drunk or heedless coming over it in part of her lane. She crested to an open black road, and there he was: a bulk, a blur, a thing running across her headlights, and she swerved left and her foot went for the brake and was stomping air above its pedal when she hit him, saw his legs and body in the air, flying out of her light, into the dark. Her brakes were screaming into the wind, bottles clinking in the fallen bag, and with the music and wind inside the car was his sound already a memory but as real as an echo, that car-shuddering thump as though she had struck a tree. Her foot was back on the accelerator. Then she shifted gears and pushed it. She ejected the cassette and closed the window. She did not start to cry until she knocked on my bedroom door, then called: "Dad?"

Her voice, her tears, broke through my dream and the wind I heard in my sleep, and I stepped into jeans and hurried to the door, thinking harm, rape, death. All were in her face, and I hugged her and pressed her cheek to my chest and smoothed her blown hair, then led her weeping to the kitchen and sat her at the table where still she could not speak, nor look at me; when she raised her face it fell forward again, as of its own weight, into her palms. I offered tea and she shook her head, so I offered beer twice then she shook her head, so I offered whiskey and she nodded. I had some rye that Father Paul and I had not finished last hunting season, and I poured some over ice and set it in front of her and was putting away the ice but stopped and got another glass and poured one for myself too, and brought the ice and bottle to the table where she was trying to get one of her long menthols out of the pack, but her fingers jerked like severed snakes, and I took the pack and lit one for her and took one for myself. I watched her shudder with her first swallow of rye, and push hair back from her face, it is auburn and gleamed in the overhead light, and I remembered how beautiful she looked riding a sorrel; she was smoking fast, then the sobs in her throat stopped, and she looked at me and said it, the words coming out with smoke: "I hit somebody. With the *car*."

Then she was crying and I was on my feet, moving back and forth, looking down at her asking Who? Where? Where? She was pointing at the wall over the stove, jabbing her fingers and cigarette at it, her other hand at her eyes, and twice in horror I actually looked at the wall. She finished the whiskey in a swallow and I stopped pacing and asking and poured another, and either the drink or the exhaustion of tears quieted her, even the dry sobs, and she told me; not as I tell it now, for that was later as again and again we relived it in the kitchen or living room, and if in daylight fled it on horseback out on the trails through the woods, and if at night walked quietly around in the moonlit pasture, walked around and around it, sweating through our clothes. She told it in bursts, like she was a child again, running to me, injured from play. I put on boots and a shirt and left her with the bottle and her streaked face and a cigarette twitching between her fingers, pushed the door open against the wind, and eased it shut. The wind squinted and watered my eyes as I leaned into it and went to the pickup.

When I passed St. John's I looked at it, and Father Paul's little white rectory in the rear, and wanted to stop, wished I could as I could if he were simply a friend who sold hardware or something. I had forgotten my watch but I always know the time within minutes, even when a sound or dream or my bladder wakes me in the night. It was nearly two; we had been in the kitchen about twenty minutes; she had hit him around one-fifteen. Or her. The road was empty and I drove between blowing trees; caught for an instant in my lights, they seemed to be in panic. I smoked and let hope play her tricks on me; it was neither man nor woman but an animal, a goat or calf or deer on the road; it was a man who had jumped away in time, the collision of metal and body glancing not direct, and he had limped home to nurse bruises and cuts. Then I threw the cigarette and hope both out the window and prayed that he was alive, while beneath that prayer, a reserve deeper in my heart, another one stirred: that if he were dead, they would not get Jennifer.

From our direction, east and a bit south, the road to that hill and the nightclub beyond it and finally the town is, for its last four or five miles, straight through farming country. When I reached that stretch I slowed the truck and opened my window for the fierce air; on both sides were scattered farmhouses and barns and sometimes a silo, looking not like shelters but like unsheltered things the wind would flatten. Corn bent toward the road from a field on my right, and always something blew in front of me: paper, leaves, dried weeds, branches. I slowed approaching the hill, and went up it in second, staring through my open window at the ditch on the left side of the road, its weeds alive, whipping, a mad dance with the trees above them. I went over the hill and down and, opposite the club, turned right onto a side street of houses, and parked there, in the leaping shadows of trees. I walked back across the road to the club's parking lot, the wind behind me, lifting me as I strode, and I could not hear my boots on pavement. I walked up the hill, on the shoulder, watching the branches above me, hearing their leaves and the creaking trunks and the wind. Then I was at the top, looking down the road and at the farms and fields; the night was clear, and I could see a long way; clouds scudded past the half-moon and stars, blown out to sea.

I started down, watching the tall grass under the trees to my right, glancing into the dark of the ditch, listening for cars behind me; but as soon as I cleared one tree, its sound was gone, its flapping leaves and rattling branches far behind me, as though the greatest distance I had at my back was a matter of feet, while ahead of me I could see a barn two miles off. Then I saw her skid marks: short, and going left and downhill, into the other lane. I stood at the ditch, its weeds blowing; across it were trees and their moving shadows, like the clouds. I stepped onto its slope, and it took me sliding on my feet then rump to the bottom where I sat still, my body gathered to itself, lest a part of me should touch him. But there was only tall grass, and I stood, my shoulders reaching the sides of the ditch, and I walked uphill, wishing for the flashlight in the pickup, walking slowly, and down in the ditch I could hear my feet in the grass and on the earth, and kicking cans and bottles. At the top of the hill I turned and went down, watching the ground above the ditch on my right, praying my prayer from the truck again, the first one, the one I would admit, that he was not dead, was in fact home, and began to hope again, memory telling me of lost pheasants and grouse I had shot, but they were small and the colors of their home, while a man was either there or not; and from that memory I left where I was and while walking the ditch under the wind was in the deceit of imagination with Jennifer in the kitchen, telling her she had hit no one, or at least had not badly hurt anyone, when I realized he could be in the hospital now and I would have to think of a way to check there, something to say on the phone. I see now that, once hope returned, I should have been certain what she prepared me for; ahead of me, in high grass and the shadows of trees, I saw his shirt. Or that is all my mind would allow itself: a shirt, and I stood looking at it for the moments it took my mind to admit the arm and head and the dark length covered by pants. He lay face down, the arm I could see near his side, his head turned from me, on its cheek.

"Fella?" I said. I had meant to call, but it came out quiet and high, lost inches from my face in the wind. Then I said, "Oh God," and felt Him in the wind and the sky moving past the stars and moon and the fields around me, but only watching me as He might have watched Cain or Job, I did not know which, and I said it again, and wanted to sink to the earth and weep until I slept there in the weeds. I climbed, scrambling up the side of the ditch, pulling at clutched grass, gained the top on hands and knees, and went to him like that, panting, moving through the grass as high and higher than my face, crawling under that sky, making sounds too like some animal, there being no words to let him know I was here with him now. He was long; that is the word that came to me, not tall. I kneeled beside him, my hands on my legs. His right arm was by his side, his left arm straight out from the shoulder, but turned, so his palm was open to the tree above us. His left cheek was clean shaven, his eye closed, and there was no blood. I leaned forward to look at his open mouth and saw the blood on it, going down into the grass. I straightened and looked ahead at the wind blowing past me through grass and trees to a distant light, and I stared at the light, imagining someone awake out there, wanting someone to be, a gathering of old friends, or someone alone listening to music or painting a picture, then I figured it was a night light at a farmyard whose house I couldn't see. *Going.* I thought. *Still going.* I leaned over again and looked at dripping blood.

So I had to touch his wrist, a thick one with a watch and expansion band that I pushed up his arm, thinking *he's left-handed,* my three fingers pressing his wrist and all I felt was my tough fingertips on that smooth underside flesh and small bones, then relief, then certainty. But against my will, or only because of it, I still don't know, I touched his neck, ran my fingers down it as if petting, then pressed and my hand sprang back as from fire. I lowered it again, held it there until it felt that faint beating that I could not believe. There was too much wind. Nothing could make a sound in it. A pulse could not be felt in it, nor could mere fingers in that wind feel the absolute silence of a dead man's artery. I was making sounds again; I grabbed his left arm and his waist, and pulled him toward me, and that side of him rose, turned, and I lowered him to his back, his face tilted up toward the tree that was groaning, the tree and I the only sounds in the wind. Turning my face from his, looking down the length of him at his sneakers, I placed my ear on his heart, and heard not that but something else, and I clamped a hand over my exposed ear, heard something liquid and alive, like when you pump a well and after a few strokes you hear air and water moving in the pipe, and I knew I must raise his legs and cover him and run to a phone, while still I listened to his chest, thinking *raise with what? cover with what?* and amid the liquid sound I heard the heart then lost it, and pressed my ear against bone, but his chest was quiet, and I did not know when the liquid had stopped, and do not know when I heard air, a faint rush of it, and whether under my ear or at his mouth or whether I heard it at all. I straightened and looked at the light, dim and yellow. Then I touched his throat, looking him full in the face. He was blond and young. He could have been sleeping in the shade of a tree, but for the smear of blood from his mouth to his hair, and the night sky, and the weeds blowing against his head, and the leaves shaking in the dark above us.

I stood. Then I kneeled again and prayed for his soul to join in peace and joy all the dead and living and doing so confronted my first sin against him, not stopping for Father Paul, who could have given him the last rites, and immediately then my second one, or, I saw then, my first, not calling an ambulance to meet me there, and I stood and turned into the wind, slid down the ditch and crawled out of it, and went up the hill and down it, across the road to the street of houses whose people I had left behind forever, so that I moved with stealth in the shadows to my truck.

When I came around the bend near my house, I saw the kitchen light at the rear. She sat as I had left her, the ashtray filled, and I looked at the bottle, felt her eyes on me, felt what she was seeing too: the dirt from my crawling. She had not drunk much of the rye. I poured some in my glass, with the water from melted ice, and sat down and swallowed some and looked at her and swallowed some more, and said: "He's dead."

She rubbed her eyes with the heels of her hands, rubbed the cheeks under them, but she was dry now.

"He was probably dead when he hit the ground. I mean, that's probably what killed — "

"Where was he?"

"Across the ditch, under a tree."

"Was he — did you see his face?"

"No. Not really. I just felt. For life, pulse. I'm going out to the car."

"What for? Oh."

I finished the rye, and pushed back the chair, then she was standing too.

"I'll go with you."

"There's no need."

"I'll go."

I took a flashlight from a drawer and pushed open the door and held it while she went out. We turned our faces from the wind. It was like on the hill, when I was walking, and the wind closed the distance behind me: after three or four steps I felt there was no house back there. She took my hand, as I was reaching for hers. In the garage we let go, and squeezed between the pickup and her little car, to the front of it, where we had more room, and we stepped back from the grill and I shone the light on the fender, the smashed headlight turned into it, the concave chrome staring to the right, at the garage wall.

"We ought to get the bottle," I said.

She moved between the garage and the car, on the passenger side, and had room to open the door and lift the bag. I reached out, and she gave me the bag and backed up and shut the door and came around the car. We sidled to the doorway, and she put her arm around my waist and I hugged her shoulders.

"I thought you'd call the police," she said.

We crossed the yard, faces bowed from the wind, her hair blowing away from her neck, and in the kitchen I put the bag of bottles in the garbage basket. She was working at the table: capping the rye and putting it away, filling the ice tray, washing the glasses, emptying the ashtray, sponging the table.

"Try to sleep now," I said.

She nodded at the sponge circling under her hand, gathering ashes. Then she dropped it in the sink and, looking me full in the face, as I had never seen her look, as perhaps she never had, being for so long a daughter on visits (or so it seemed to me and still does: that until then our eyes had never seriously met), she crossed to me from the sink, and kissed my lips, then held me so tightly I lost balance, and would have stumbled forward had she not held me so hard.

I sat in the living room, the house darkened, and watched the maple and the hemlock. When I believed she was asleep I put on *La Bohème*, and kept it at the same volume as the wind so it would not wake her. Then I listened to *Madame Butterfly*, and in the third act had to rise quickly to lower the sound: the wind was gone. I looked at the still maple near the window, and thought of the wind leaving farms and towns and the coast, going out over the sea to die on the waves. I smoked and gazed out the window. The sky was darker, and at daybreak the rain came. I listened to *Tosca,* and at six-fifteen went to the kitchen where Jennifer's purse lay on the table, a leather shoulder purse crammed with the things of an adult woman, things she had begun accumulating only a few years back, and I nearly wept, thinking of what sandy foundations they were: driver's license, credit card, disposable lighter, cigarettes, checkbook, ballpoint pen, cash, cosmetics, comb, brush, Kleenex, these the rite of passage from childhood, and I took one of them — her keys — and went out, remembering a jacket and hat when the rain struck me, but I kept going to the car, and squeezed and lowered myself into it, pulled the seat belt over my shoulder and fastened it and backed out, turning in the drive, going forward into the road, toward St. John's and Father Paul.

Cars were on the road, the workers, and I did not worry about any of them noticing the fender and light. Only a horse distracted them from what they drove to. In front of St. John's is a parking lot; at its far side, past the church and at the edge of the lawn, is an old pine, taller than the steeple now. I shifted to third, left the road, and aiming the right headlight at the tree, accelerated past the white blur of church, into the black trunk growing bigger till it was all I could see, then I rocked in that resonant thump she had heard, had felt, and when I turned off the ignition it was still in my ears, my blood, and I saw the boy flying in the wind. I lowered my forehead to the wheel. Father Paul opened the door, his face white in the rain.

"I'm all right."

"What happened?"

"I don't know. I fainted."

I got out and went around to the front of the car, looked at the smashed light, the crumpled and torn fender.

"Come to the house and lie down."

"I'm all right."

"When was your last physical?"

"I'm due for one. Let's get out of this rain."

"You'd better lie down."

"No. I want to receive."

That was the time to say I wanted to confess, but I have not and will not. Though I could now, for Jennifer is in Florida, and weeks have passed, and perhaps now Father Paul would not feel that he must tell me to go to the police. And, for that very reason, to confess now would be unfair. It is a world of secrets, and now I have one from my best, in truth my only, friend. I have one from Jennifer too, but that is the nature of fatherhood.

Most of that day it rained, so it was only in early evening, when the sky cleared, with a setting sun, that two little boys, leaving their confinement for some play before dinner, found him. Jennifer and I got that on the local news, which we listened to every hour, meeting at the radio, standing with cigarettes, until the one at eight o'clock; when she stopped crying, we went out and walked on the wet grass, around the pasture, the last of sunlight still in the air and trees. His name was Patrick Mitchell, he was nineteen years old, was employed by CETA, lived at home with his parents and brother and sister. The paper next day said he had been at a friend's house and was walking home, and I thought of that light I had seen, then knew it was not for him; he lived on one of the streets behind the club. The paper did not say then, or in the next few days, anything to make Jennifer think he was alive while she was with me in the kitchen. Nor do I know if we — if I — could have saved him.

In keeping her secret from her friends, Jennifer had to perform so often, as I did with Father Paul and at the stables, that I believe the acting, which took more of her than our daylight trail rides and our night walks in the pasture, was her healing. Her friends teased me about wrecking her car. When I carried her luggage out to the car on that last morning, we spoke only of the weather for her trip — the day was clear, with a dry cool breeze — and hugged and kissed, and I stood watching as she started the car and turned it around. But then she shifted to neutral and put on the parking brake and unclasped the belt, looking at me all the while, then she was coming to me, as she had that night in the kitchen, and I opened my arms.

I have said I talk with God in the mornings, as I start my day, and sometimes as I sit with coffee, looking at the birds, and the woods. Of course He has never spoken to me, but that is not something I require. Nor does He need to. I know Him, as I know the part of myself that knows Him, that felt Him watching from the wind and the night as I knelt over the dying boy. Lately I have taken to arguing with Him, as I can't with Father Paul who, when he hears my monthly confession, has not and will not hear anything of failure to do all that one can to save an anonymous life, of injustice to a family in their grief, of deepening their pain at the chance and mystery of death by giving them nothing — no one — to hate. With Father Paul, I feel lonely about this, but not with God. When I received the Eucharist while Jennifer's car sat twice-damaged, so redeemed, in the rain, I felt neither loneliness nor shame, but as though He were watching me, even from my tongue, intestines, blood, as I have watched my sons at times in their young lives when I was able to judge but without anger, and so keep silent while they, in the agony of their youth, decided how they must act; or found reasons, after their actions, for what they had done. Their reasons were never as good or as bad as their actions, but they needed to find them, to believe they were living by them, instead of the awful solitude of the heart.

I do not feel the peace I once did: not with God, nor the earth, or anyone on it. I have begun to prefer this state, to remember with fondness the other one as a period of peace I neither earned nor deserved. Now in the mornings while I watch purple finches driving larger titmice from the feeder, I say to Him: I would do it again. For when she knocked on my door then called me, she woke what had flowed dormant in my blood since her birth, so that what rose from the bed was not a stable owner or a Catholic or any other Luke Ripley I had lived with for a long time, but the father of a girl.

And He says: I am a Father too.

Yes, I say, as You are a Son Whom this morning I will receive; unless You kill me on the way to church, then I trust You will receive me. And as a Son You made Your plea.

Yes, He says, but I would not lift the cup.

True, and I don't want You to lift it from me either. And if one of my sons had come to me that night, I would have phoned the police and told them to meet us with an ambulance at the top of the hill.

Why? Do you love them less?

I tell Him no, it is not that I love them less, but that I could bear the pain of watching and knowing my sons' pain, could bear it with pride as they took the whip and nails. But You never had a daughter, and if You had, You could not have borne her passion.

So, He says, you love her more than you love Me.

I love her more than I love truth.

Then you love in weakness, He says.

As You love me, I say, and I go with an apple or carrot out to the barn.

Louise Erdrich

....

Satan: Hijacker of a Planet

O N   T H E   O U T S K I R T S   O F a small town in the West, on an afternoon when rain was promised, we sat upon the deck of our new subdivision ranchette and watched the sky pitch over Hungry Horse. It was a drought-dry summer, and in the suspension of rain everything seemed to flex. The trees stretched to their full length, each leaf open. I could almost feel the ground shake the timbers under my feet, as if the great searching taproots of the lodgepole pines all around trembled. Lust. Lust. Still, the rain held off. I left my mother sitting in her chair and went to the old field behind the house, up a hill. There the storm seemed even likelier. The wind came off the eastern mountains, smelling like a lake, and the grass reached for it, butter-yellow, its life concentrated in its fiber mat, the stalks so dry they gave off puffs of smoke when snapped. Grasshoppers sprang from each step I took, tripped off my arms, legs, glasses. I saw a small pile of stones halfway up the hill, which someone had cleared once, when this was orchard land. I sat down and continued to watch the sky as, out of nowhere, great solid-looking clouds built hot stacks and cotton cones. The trend was upward, upward, until you couldn't feel it anymore. I was sixteen years old.

I was looking down the hill, waiting for the rain to start, when his white car pulled into our yard. The driver was a big man, built long and square just like the Oldsmobile. He was wearing a tie and a shirt that was not yet sweaty. I noticed this as I was walking back down the hill. I was starting to notice these things about men — the way their hips moved when they hauled feed or checked fence lines. The way their forearms looked so tanned and hard when they rolled up their white sleeves after church. I was looking at men not with intentions, because

I didn't know yet what I would have done with one if I got him, but with a studious mind.

I was looking at them just to figure, for pure survival, the way a girl does. The way a farmer, which my dad was before he failed, gets to know the lay of the land. He loves his land, so he has to figure how to cultivate it — what it needs in each season, how much abuse it will sustain, what in the end it will yield.

And I, too, in order to increase my yield and use myself right, was taking my lessons. I never tried out my information, though, until the man arrived, pulled with a slow crackle into our lake-pebble driveway. He got out and looked at me where I stood in the shade of my mother's butterfly bush. I'm not saying that I flirted right off. I didn't know how to. I walked into the sunlight and looked him in the eye.

"What are you selling?" I smiled, and told him that my mother would probably buy it, since she had all sorts of things — a pruning saw you could use from the ground, a cherry pitter, a mechanical apple peeler that also removed the seeds and core, a sewing machine that remembered all the stitches it had sewed. He smiled back at me and walked with me to the steps of the house.

"You're a bright young lady," he said, though he was young himself. "Stand close. You'll see what I'm selling by looking into the middle of my eyes."

He pointed a finger between his eyebrows.

"I don't see a thing," I told him, as my mother came around the corner, off the deck out back, holding a glass of iced tea in her hand.

While they were talking, I didn't look at Stan Anderson. I felt challenged, as if I were supposed to make sense of what he did. At sixteen I didn't have perspective on the things men did. I'd never gotten a whiff of that odor that rolls off them like an acid. Later only a certain look was required, a tone of voice, a word, no more than a variation in the way he drew breath. A dog gets tuned that way, sensitized to an exquisite degree, but it wasn't like that in the beginning. I took orders from Stan as if I were doing him a favor — the way, since I'd hit my growth, I'd taken orders from my dad.

My dad, who was at the antiques store, gave orders only when he was tired. All other times he did the things he wanted done himself. My dad was not, in the end, the man I should have studied if I wanted to learn cold survival. He was too ineffective. All my life my parents had been splitting up. I lived in a no-man's-land between them, and the ground was pitted, scarred with ruts, useless. And yet no matter how hard they fought each other, they stuck together. He could not get away from my mother, somehow, nor she from him. So I couldn't look to my father for information on what a man was — nor could I look to my grandfather. Gramp was too nice a man. You should have seen him when he planted a tree.

"A ten-dollar hole for a two-bit seedling," he'd say. That was the way he dug, so as not to crowd the roots. He kept the little tree in water while he pried out any rocks that might be there, though our land was just as good as Creston soil, dirt that went ten feet down in that part of Montana, black as coal, rich as tar, fine as face powder. Gramp put the bare-root tree in and carefully, considerately even, sifted the soil around the roots, rubbing it to fine crumbs between his fingers. He packed the dirt in: he watered until the water pooled. Looking into my grandfather's eyes I would see the knowledge, tender and offhand, of the way roots took hold in the earth.

I saw no such knowledge in Stan's eyes. I watched him from behind my mother. I discovered what he had to sell.

"It's Bibles, isn't it?" I said.

"No fair." He put his hand across his heart and grinned at the two of us. He had seen my eyes flicker to the little gold cross in his lapel. "Something even better."

"What?" my mother asked.

"Spirit."

My mother turned and walked away. She had no time for conversion attempts. I was only intermittently religious, but I suppose I felt that I had to make up for her rudeness, and so I stayed a moment longer. I was wearing very short cutoff jeans and a little brown T-shirt, tight — old clothes for dirty work. I was supposed to help my mom clean out her hobby brooder house that afternoon, to set in new straw and wash down the galvanized feeders, to destroy the thick whorls of ground-spider cobwebs and shine the windows with vinegar and newspapers. All my stuff, rags and buckets, was scattered behind me on the steps. And, as I said, I was never all that religious.

"We'll be having a meeting tonight," he said. "I'm going to tell you where."

He always told in advance what he was going to say; that was the preaching habit in him. It made you wait and wonder in spite of yourself.

"Where?" I said finally.

As he told me the directions, how to get where the tent was pitched, as he spoke to me, looking full on with the whole intensity of his blue gaze, I was deciding that I would go, without anyone else in my family, to the fairground that evening. Just to study. Just to see.

I drove a small sledge and a tractor at the age of eleven, and a car back and forth into town, with my mother in the passenger seat, when I was fourteen. So I often went where I wanted to go. The storm had veered off. Disappointed, we watched rain drop across the valley. We got no more than a slash of moisture in the air, which dried before it fell. In town the streets were just on the edge of damp, but the air was still thin and dry. White moths fluttered in and out under the rolled flaps of the revival tent, but since the month of August was half spent, the mosquitoes were mainly gone. Too dry for them, too. Even though the tent was open-sided, the air within seemed close, compressed, and faintly salty with evaporated sweat. The space was three-quarters full of singing people, and I slipped into one of the rear rows. I sat on a gray metal folding chair, just sat there, keeping my eyes open and my mouth shut.

He was not the main speaker, I discovered, and I didn't see him until the one whom the others had come to hear finished a prayer. He called Stan to the front with a little preface. Stan was newly saved, endowed with a message from the Lord, and could play several musical instruments. We were to listen to what the Lord would reveal to us through Stan's lips. He took the stage. A white vest finished off his white suit, and a red-silk shirt with a pointed collar. He started talking. I can tell you what he said just about word for word, because after that night and long away into the next few years, sometimes four or five times in one day, I'd hear it over and over. You don't know preaching until you've heard Stan Anderson. You don't suffer with Christ, or fear loss of faith, a barbed wire ripped from your grasp, until you've heard it from Stan Anderson. You don't know subjection, the thorough happiness of letting go. You don't know how light and comforted you feel, how cherished.

I was too young to stand against it.

The stars are the eyes of God, and they have been watching us from the beginning of the world. Do you think there isn't an eye for each of us? Go on and count. Go on and look in The Book and add up all the nouns and adverbs, as if somehow you'd grasp the meaning of what you held if you did. You can't. The understanding is in you or it isn't. You can hide from the stars by daylight, but at night, under all of them, so many, you are pierced by the sight and by the vision.

Get under the bed!

Get under the sheet!

I say to you, Stand up, and if you fall, fall forward!

I'm going to go out blazing. I'm going to go out like a light. I'm going to burn in glory. I say to you, Stand up!

And so there's one among them. You have heard Luce, Light, Lucifer, the Fallen Angel. You have seen it with your own eyes, and you didn't know he came upon you. In the night, and in his own disguises, like the hijacker of a planet, he fell out of the air, he fell out of the dark leaves, he fell out of the fragrance of a woman's body, he fell out of you and entered you as though he'd reached through the earth.

Reached his hand up and pulled you down.

Fell into you with a jerk.

Like a hangman's noose.

Like nobody.

Like the slave of night.

Like you were coming home and all the lights were blazing and the ambulance sat out front in the driveway and you said, *Lord, which one?*

And the Lord said, *All of them.*

You, too, follow, follow, I'm pointing you down. In the sight of the stars and in the sight of the Son of Man. The grace is on me. Stand up, I say. *Stand.* Yes, and yes, I'm gonna scream, because I like it that way. Let yourself into the gate. Take it with you. In four years the earth will shake in its teeth.

Revelations. Face of the beast. In all fairness, in all fairness, let us quiet down and let us think.

Stan Anderson looked intently, quietly, evenly, at each person in the crowd and spoke to each one, proving things about the future that seemed complicated, like the way the Mideast had shaped up as such a trouble zone. How the Chinese armies were predicted in Tibet and that came true, and how they'll keep marching, moving, until they reach the Fertile Crescent. Stan Anderson told about the number. He slammed his forehead with his open hand and left a red mark. *There,* he yelled, gutshot, *there it will be scorched.* He was talking about the number of the beast, and said that they would take it from your Visa card, your Mastercard, your household insurance. That already, through these numbers, you are under the control of last things and you don't know it.

The Antichrist is among us.

He is the plastic in our wallets.

You want credit? Credit?

Then you'll burn for it, and you will starve. You'll eat sticks, you'll eat black bits of paper, your bills, and all the while you'll be screaming from the dark place, *Why the hell didn't I just pay cash?*

Because the number of the beast is a computerized number, and the computer is the bones, it is the guts, of the Antichrist, who is Lucifer, who is pure brain.

Pure brain got us to the moon, got us past the moon.

The voice of lonely humanity is in a space probe calling, *Anybody home? Anybody home out there?* The Antichrist will answer. The Antichrist is here, all around us in the tunnels and webs of radiance, in the microchips; the great mind of the Antichrist is fusing in a pattern, in a destiny, waking up nerve by nerve.

Serves us right. Don't it serve us right not to be saved?

It won't come easy. Not by waving a magic wand. You've got to close your eyes and hold out those little plastic cards.

Look at this!

He held a scissors high and turned it to every side so that the light gleamed off the blades.

The sword of Michael! Now I'm coming. I'm coming down the aisle. I'm coming with the sword that sets you free.

Stan Anderson started a hymn and walked down the rows of chairs, singing. Every person who held out a credit card he embraced, and then he plucked that card out of their fingers. He cut once, crosswise. Dedicated to the Lord! He cut again. He kept the song flowing, walked up and down the rows cutting, until the tough, trampled grass beneath the tent was littered with pieces of plastic. He came to me last of all, and noticed me, and smiled.

"You're too young to have established a line of credit," he said, "but I'm glad to see you here."

Then he stared at me, his eyes the blue of winter ice, cold in the warmth of his tanned blondness, so chilling I just melted.

"Stay," he said. "Stay afterward and join us in the trailer. We're going to pray over Ed's mother."

*   *   *

So I did stay. It didn't sound like a courting invitation, but that was the way I thought of it at the time, and I was right. Ed was the advertised preacher, and his mother was a sick, sick woman. She lay flat and still on a couch at the front of the house trailer, where she just fit end to end. The air around her was dim, close with the smell of sweat-out medicine and what the others had cooked and eaten — hamburger, burnt onions, coffee. The table was pushed to one side, and chairs were wedged around the couch. Ed's mother, poor old dying woman, was covered with a white sheet that her breathing hardly moved. Her face was caved in, sunken around the mouth and cheeks. She looked to me like a bird fallen out of its nest before it feathered, her shut eyelids bulging blue, wrinkled, beating with tiny nerves. Her head was covered with white wisps of hair. Her hands, just at her chest, curled like little pale claws. Her nose was a large and waxen bone.

I drew up a chair, the farthest to the back of the eight or so people who had gathered. One by one they opened their mouths, rolled their eyes or closed them tight, and let the words fly out until they began to garble and the sounds from their mouths resembled some ancient, dizzying speech. At first I was so uncomfortable with all the strangeness, and even a little faint from the airlessness and smells, that I breathed in with shallow gulps and shut the language out. Gradually, slowly, it worked its way in anyway, and I began to *feel* its effect — not hear, not understand, not listen.

The words are inside and outside of me, hanging in the air like small pottery triangles, broken and curved. But they are forming and crumbling so fast that I'm breathing dust, the sharp antibiotic bitterness, medicine, death, sweat. My eyes sting, and I'm starting to choke. All the blood goes out of my head and down along my arms into the ends of my fingers, and my hands feel swollen, twice as big as normal, like big puffed gloves. I get out of the chair and turn to leave, but he is there.

"Go on," he says. "Go on and touch her."

The others have their hands on Ed's mother. They are touching her with one hand and praying, the other palm held high, blind, feeling for the spirit like an antenna. Stan pushes me, not by making any contact, just by inching up behind me so I feel the forcefulness and move. Two people make room, and then I am standing over Ed's mother. She is absolutely motionless, as though she were a corpse, except that her pinched mouth has turned down at the edges so that she frowns into her own dark unconsciousness.

I put my hands out, still huge, prickling. I am curious to see what will happen when I do touch her — if she'll respond. But when I place my hands on her stomach, low and soft, she makes no motion at all. Nothing flows from me, no healing powers. Instead I am filled with the rushing dark of what she suffers. It fills me suddenly, as water from a faucet brims a jug, and spills over.

This is when it happens.

I'm not stupid; I have never been stupid. I have pictures. I can get a picture in my head at any moment, focus it so brilliant and detailed that it seems real. That's what I do, what I started when my mom and dad first went for each other. When I heard them downstairs, I always knew a moment would come. One of them would scream, tearing through the stillness. It would rise up, that howl, and fill the house, and then one would come running. One would come and get me and hold me. It would be my mother, smelling of smoked chicken, rice, and coffee grounds. It would be my father, sweat-soured, scorched with cigarette smoke from the garage, bitter with the dust of his fields. Then I would be somewhere in no-man's-land, between them, and that was the unsafest place in the world. So I would leave it. I would go limp and enter my pictures.

I have a picture. I go into it right off when I touch Ed's mother, veering off her thin pain. Here's a grainy mountain, a range of deep-blue Missions hovering off the valley in the west. Their foothills are blue, strips of dark-blue flannel, and their tops are cloudy walls. The sun strikes through once, twice, a pink radiance that dazzles patterns into their faces so that they gleam back, moon-pocked. Watch them, watch close, Ed's mother, and they start to walk. I keep talking until I know she is watching too. She is dimming her lights, she is turning as thin as tissue under my hands. She is dying until she goes into my picture with me, goes in strong, goes in willingly. And once she is in the picture, she gains peace from it, gains the rock strength, the power.

I was young. I was younger than I had a right to be. I was drawn the way a deer is drawn into the halogen lamplight, curious and calm. Heart about to explode. I wasn't helpless, though, not me. I had pictures.

"Show me what you did," Stan said that night, once Ed's mother was resting calmly.

We went into the room at the Red Lion that was Stan's, all carpet and deodorizer. All flocked paper on the walls. Black-red. Gold. Hilarious. Stan lay down on the king-size bed and patted the broad space beside him in a curious, not sexual, way. I lay down there and closed my eyes.

"Show me Milwaukee," Stan whispered. I breathed deep and let out the hems of my thoughts. After a while, then, I got the heft of it, the green medians in June, the way you felt entering your favorite restaurant with a dinner reservation, hungry, knowing that within fifteen minutes German food would start to fill you, German bread, German beer, German schnitzel. I got the neighborhood where Stan had lived, the powdery stucco, the old-board rotting infrastructure and the back yard, all shattered sun and shade, leaves; got Stan's mother lying on the ground full-length in a red suit, asleep; got the back porch, full of suppressed heat; and got the june bugs razzing indomitable against the night screens. Got the smell of Stan's river, got the first-day-of-school smell, the chalk and wax, the cleaned-and-stored, paper-towel scent of Milwaukee schools in the beginning of September. Got the milk cartons, got the straws. Got Stan's brother, thin and wiry arms holding Stan down. Got Stan a hot-dog stand, a nickel bag of peanuts, thirst.

"No," Stan said. "No more."

He could feel it coming, though I avoided it. I steered away from the burning welts, the scissors, pinched nerves, the dead eye, the strap, the belt, the spike-heeled shoe, the razor, the boiling-hot spilled tapioca, the shards of glass, the knives, the chinked armor, the small sister, the small sister, the basement, anything underground.

"Enough." Stan turned to me.

He didn't know what he wanted to see, and I don't mean to imply that he would see the whole of my picture anyway. I would walk the edge of his picture, and he'd walk the edge of mine, get the crumbs, the drops of water that flew off when a bird shook its feathers. That's how much I got across, but that was all it took. When you share like that, the rest of the earth shuts. You are locked in, twisted close, braided, born.

He smoothed his hands across my hair and closed me against him, and then we shut the door to everything and everyone but us. He stood me next to the bed, took off my clothing piece by piece, and made me climax just by brushing me, slowly, here, there, just by barely touching me until he forced apart my legs and put his mouth on me hard. Stood up. He came into me without a sound. I cried out. He pushed harder and then withdrew. It took more than an hour, by the bedside clock. It took a long time. He held my wrists behind my back and forced me down onto the carpet. Then he bent over me and gently, fast and slow, helplessly, without end or beginning, he went in and out until I grew bored, until I wanted to sleep, until I moaned, until I cried out, until I wanted nothing else, until I wanted him the way I always would from then on, since that first dry summer.

John Gardner

....

Redemption

ONE DAY IN APRIL — a clear, blue day when there were crocuses in bloom — Jack Hawthorne ran over and killed his brother, David. Even at the last moment he could have prevented his brother's death by slamming on the tractor brakes, easily in reach for all the shortness of his legs; but he was unable to think, or rather thought unclearly, and so watched it happen, as he would again and again watch it happen in his mind, with nearly undiminished intensity and clarity, all his life. The younger brother was riding, as both of them knew he should not have been, on the cultipacker, a two-ton implement lumbering behind the tractor, crushing new-ploughed ground. Jack was twelve, his brother, David, seven. The scream came not from David, who never got a word out, but from their five-year-old sister, who was riding on the fender of the tractor, looking back. When Jack turned to look, the huge iron wheels had reached his brother's pelvis. He kept driving, reacting as he would to a half-crushed farm animal, and imagining, in the same stab of thought, that perhaps his brother would survive. Blood poured from David's mouth.

Their father was nearly destroyed by it. Sometimes Jack would find him lying on the cow-barn floor, crying, unable to stand up. Dale Hawthorne, the father, was a sensitive, intelligent man, by nature a dreamer. It showed in old photographs, his smile coded, his eyes on the horizon. He loved all his children and would not consciously have been able to hate his son even if Jack had indeed been, as he thought himself, his brother's murderer. But he could not help sometimes seeming to blame his son, though consciously he blamed only his own unwisdom and — so far as his belief held firm — God. Dale Hawthorne's mind swung violently at this time, reversing itself almost hour by hour, from desperate faith to the most ferocious, black-hearted atheism. Every sickly calf, every sow that ate her litter, was a new, sure proof that the religion he'd followed all his life was a lie. Yet skeletons were orderly, as were, he thought, the stars. He was unable to decide, one moment full of rage at God's injustice, the next moment wracked by doubt of His existence.

Though he was not ordinarily a man who smoked, he would some-times sit up all night now, or move restlessly, hurriedly, from room to room, chain-smoking Lucky Strikes. Or he would ride away on his huge, darkly thundering Harley-Davidson 80, trying to forget, mor-bidly dwelling on what he'd meant to put behind him — how David had once laughed, cake in his fists; how he'd once patched a chair with precocious skill — or Dale Hawthorne would think, for the hundredth time, about suicide, hunting in mixed fear and anger for some reason not to miss the next turn, fly off to the right of the next iron bridge onto the moonlit gray rocks and black water below — discovering, invariably, no reason but the damage his suicide would do to his wife and the children remaining.

Sometimes he would forget for a while by abandoning reason and responsibility for love affairs. Jack's father was at this time still young, still handsome, well-known for the poetry he recited at local churches or for English classes or meetings of the Grange — recited, to loud applause (he had poems of all kinds, both serious and comic), for thrashing crews, old men at the V.A. Hospital, even the tough, flint-eyed orphans at the Children's Home. He was a celebrity, in fact, as much Romantic poet-hero as his time and western New York State could afford — and beyond all that, he was now so full of pain and unassuageable guilt that women's hearts flew to him unbidden. He became, with all his soul and without cynical intent — though aban-doning all law, or what he'd once thought law — a hunter of women, trading off his sorrow for the sorrows of wearied, unfulfilled country wives. At times he would be gone from the farm for days, abandoning the work to Jack and whoever was available to help — some neighbor or older cousin or one of Jack's uncles. No one complained, at least not openly. A stranger might have condemned him, but no one in the family did, certainly not Jack, not even Jack's mother, though her sor-row was increased. Dale Hawthorne had always been, before the accident, a faithful man, one of the most fair-minded, genial farmers in the county. No one asked that, changed as he was, he do more, for the moment, than survive.

As for Jack's mother, though she'd been, before the accident, a cheerful woman — one who laughed often and loved telling stories, sometimes sang anthems in bandanna and blackface before her husband recited poems — she cried now, nights, and did only as much as she had strength to do — so sapped by grief that she could barely move her arms. She comforted Jack and his sister, Phoebe — herself as well — by embracing them ferociously whenever new waves of guilt swept in, by constant reassurance and extravagant praise, frequent mention of how proud some relative would be — once, for instance, over a drawing of his sister's, "Oh, Phoebe, if only your great-aunt Lucy could see this!" Great-aunt Lucy had been famous, among the family and friends, for her paintings of families of lions. And Jack's mother forced on his sister and himself comforts more permanent: piano and, for Jack, French horn lessons, school and church activities, above all an endless, exhausting ritual of chores. Because she had, at thirty-four, considerable strength of character — except that, these days, she was always eating — and because, also, she was a woman of strong religious faith, a woman who, in her years of church work and teaching at the high school, had made scores of close, for the most part equally religious, friends, with whom she regularly corresponded, her letters, then theirs, half filling the mailbox at the foot of the hill and cluttering every table, desk, and niche in the large old house — friends who now frequently visited or phoned — she was able to move step by step past disaster and in the end keep her family from wreck. She said very little to her children about her troubles. In fact, except for the crying behind her closed door, she kept her feelings strictly secret.

But for all his mother and her friends could do for him — for all his father's older brothers could do, or, when he was there, his father himself — the damage to young Jack Hawthorne took a long while healing. Working the farm, ploughing, cultipacking, disking, dragging, he had plenty of time to think — plenty of time for the accident to replay, with the solidity of real time repeated, in his mind, his whole body flinching from the image as it came, his voice leaping up independent of him, as if a shout could perhaps drive the memory back into its cave. Maneuvering the tractor over sloping, rocky fields, dust whorling out like smoke behind him or, when he turned into the wind, falling like soot until his skin was black and his hair as thick and stiff as old clothes in an attic — the circle of foothills every day turning greener, the late spring wind flowing endless and sweet with the smell of coming rain — he had all the time in the world to cry and swear bitterly at himself, standing up to drive, as his father often did, Jack's sore hands clamped tight to the steering wheel, his shoes unsteady on the bucking axlebeam — for stones lay everywhere, yellowed in the sunlight, a field of misshapen skulls. He'd never loved his brother, he raged out loud, never loved anyone as well as he should have. He was incapable of love, he told himself, striking the steering wheel. He was inherently bad, a spiritual defective. He was evil.

So he raged and grew increasingly ashamed of his raging, reminded by the lengthening shadows across the field of the theatricality in all he did, his most terrible sorrow mere sorrow on a stage, the very thunderclaps above — dark blue, rushing sky, birds crazily wheeling — mere opera set, proper lighting for his rant. At once he would hush himself, lower his rear end to the tractor seat, lock every muscle to the stillness of a statue, and drive on, solitary, blinded by tears; yet even now it was theater, not life — mere ghastly posturing, as in that story of his father's, how Lord Byron once tried to get Shelley's skull to make a drinking cup. Tears no longer came, though the storm went on building. Jack rode on, alone with the indifferent, murderous machinery in the widening ten-acre field.

When the storm at last hit, he'd be driven up the lane like a dog in flight, lashed by gusty rain, chased across the tracks to the tractor shed and from there to the kitchen, steamy, full of food smells from his mother's work and Phoebe's, sometimes the work of some two or three friends who'd stopped by to look in on the family. Jack kept aloof, repelled by their bright, melodious chatter and absentminded humming, indignant at their pretense that all was well. "My, how you've grown!" the old friend or fellow teacher from the high school would say, and to his mother, "My, what big *hands* he has, Betty!" He would glare at his little sister, Phoebe, his sole ally, already half traitor — she would bite her lips, squinting, concentrating harder on the mixing bowl and beaters; she was forever making cakes — and he would retreat as soon as possible to the evening chores.

He had always told himself stories to pass the time when driving the tractor, endlessly looping back and forth, around and around, fitting the land for spring planting. He told them to himself aloud, taking all parts in the dialogue, gesturing, making faces, abandoning dignity, here where no one could see or overhear him, half a mile from the nearest house. Once all his stories had been of sexual conquest or of heroic battle with escaped convicts from the Attica Prison or kidnappers who, unbeknownst to anyone, had built a small shack where they kept their captives, female and beautiful, in the lush, swampy woods beside the field. Now, after the accident, his subject matter changed. His fantasies came to be all of self-sacrifice, pitiful stories in which he redeemed his life by throwing it away to save others more worthwhile. To friends and officials of his fantasy, especially to heroines — a girl named Margaret, at school, or his cousin Linda — he would confess his worthlessness at painful length, naming all his faults, granting himself no quarter. For a time this helped, but the lie was too obvious, the manipulation of shame to buy love, and in the end despair bled all color from his fantasies. The foulness of his nature became clearer and clearer in his mind until, like his father, he began to toy — dully but in morbid earnest now — with the idea of suicide. His chest would fill with anguish, as if he were dreaming some nightmare wide awake, or bleeding internally, and his arms and legs would grow shaky with weakness, until he had to stop and get down from the tractor and sit for a few minutes, his eyes fixed on some comforting object, for instance a dark, smooth stone.

Even from his father and his father's brothers, who sometimes helped with chores, he kept aloof. His father and uncles were not talkative men. Except for his father's comic poems, they never told jokes, though they liked hearing them; and because they had lived there all their lives and knew every soul in the county by name, nothing much surprised them or, if it did, roused them to mention it. Their wives might gossip, filling the big kitchen with their pealing laughter or righteous indignation, but the men for the most part merely smiled or compressed their lips and shook their heads. At the G.L.F. feedstore, occasionally, eating an ice cream while they waited for their grist, they would speak of the weather or the Democrats; but in the barn, except for "Jackie, shift that milker, will you?" or "You can carry this up to the milk house now," they said nothing. They were all tall, square men with deeply cleft chins and creases on their foreheads and muscular jowls; all Presbyterians, sometime deacons, sometime elders; and they

were all gentle-hearted, decent men who looked lost in thought, especially Jack's father, though on occasion they'd abruptly frown or mut-
ter, or speak a few words to a cow, or a cat, or a swallow. It was natural
that Jack, working with such men, should keep to himself, throwing
down ensilage from the pitch-dark, sweet-ripe crater of the silo or hay
bales from the mow, dumping oats in front of the cows' noses, or —
taking the long-handled, blunt wooden scraper from the whitewashed
wall — pushing manure into the gutters.

He felt more community with the cows than with his uncles or,
when he was there, his father. Stretched out flat between the two rows
of stanchions, waiting for the cows to be finished with their silage so
he could drive them out to pasture, he would listen to their chewing in
the dark, close barn, a sound as soothing, as infinitely restful, as waves
along a shore, and would feel their surprisingly warm, scented breath,
their bovine quiet, and for a while would find that his anxiety had left
him. With the cows, the barn cats, the half-sleeping dog, he could
forget and feel at home, feel that life was pleasant. He felt the same
when walking up the long, fenced lane at the first light of sunrise —
his shoes and pants legs sopping wet with dew, his ears full of birdcalls
— going to bring in the herd from the upper pasture. Sometimes on
the way he would step off the deep, crooked cow path to pick cherries
or red raspberries, brighter than jewels in the morning light. They
were sweeter then than at any other time, and as he approached,
clouds of sparrows would explode into flight from the branches, whir-
ring off to safety. The whole countryside was sweet, early in the morning — newly cultivated corn to his left, to his right, alfalfa and, beyond that, wheat. He felt at one with it all. It was what life ought to
be, what he'd once believed it was.

But he could not make such feelings last. *No,* he thought bitterly on
one such morning, throwing stones at the dull, indifferent cows, driving them down the lane. However he might hate himself and all his
race, a cow was no better, or a field of wheat. Time and again he'd
been driven half crazy, angry enough to kill, by the stupidity of cows
when they'd pushed through a fence and — for all his shouting, for all
the indignant barking of the dog — they could no longer locate the
gap they themselves had made. And no better to be grain, smashed flat
by the first rainy wind. So, fists clenched, he raged inside his mind,
grinding his teeth to drive out thought, at war with the universe. He
remembered his father, erect, eyes flashing, speaking Mark Antony's

angry condemnation from the stage at the Grange. His father had seemed to him, that night, a creature set apart. His extended arm, pointing, was the terrible warning of a god. And now, from nowhere, the black memory of his brother's death rushed over him again, mindless and inexorable as a wind or wave, the huge cultipacker lifting — only an inch or so — as it climbed toward the shoulders, then sank on the cheek, flattening the skull — and he heard, more real than the morning, his sister's scream.

One day in August, a year and a half after the accident, they were combining oats — Jack and two neighbors and two of his cousins — when Phoebe came out, as she did every day, to bring lunch to those who worked in the field. Their father had been gone, this time, for nearly three weeks, and since he'd left at the height of the harvest season, no one was sure he would return, though as usual they kept silent about it. Jack sat alone in the shade of an elm, apart from the others. It was a habit they'd come to accept as they accepted, so far as he knew, his father's ways. Phoebe brought the basket from the shade where the others had settled to the shade here on Jack's side, farther from the bright, stubbled field.

"It's chicken," she said, and smiled, kneeling.

The basket was nearly as large as she was — Phoebe was seven — but she seemed to see nothing unreasonable in her having to lug it up the hill from the house. Her face was flushed, and drops of perspiration stood out along her hairline, but her smile was not only uncomplaining but positively cheerful. The trip to the field was an escape from housework, he understood; even so, her happiness offended him.

"Chicken," he said, and looked down glumly at his hard, tanned arms black with oat-dust. Phoebe smiled on, her mind far away, as it seemed to him, and like a child playing house she took a dish towel from the basket, spread it on the grass, then set out wax-paper packages of chicken, rolls, celery, and salt, and finally a small plastic thermos, army green.

She looked up at him now. "I brought you a thermos all for yourself because you always sit alone."

He softened a little without meaning to. "Thanks," he said.

She looked down again, and for all his self-absorption he was touched, noticing that she bowed her head in the way a much older girl might do, troubled by thought, though her not quite clean, dimpled hands were a child's. He saw that there was something she wanted to say and, to forestall it, brushed flying ants from the top of the thermos, unscrewed the cap, and poured himself iced tea. When he drank, the tea was so cold it brought a momentary pain to his forehead and made him aware once more of the grating chaff under his collar, blackening all his exposed skin, gritty around his eyes — aware, too, of the breezeless, insect-filled heat beyond the shade of the elm. Behind him, just at the rim of his hearing, one of the neighbors laughed at some remark from the younger of his cousins. Jack drained the cup, brooding on his aching muscles. Even in the shade his body felt baked dry.

"Jack," his sister said, "did you want to say grace?"

"Not really," he said, and glanced at her.

He saw that she was looking at his face in alarm, her mouth slightly opened, eyes wide, growing wider, and though he didn't know why, his heart gave a jump. "I already said it," he mumbled. "Just not out loud."

"Oh," she said, then smiled.

When everyone had finished eating she put the empty papers, the jug, and the smaller thermos in the basket, grinned at them all and said goodbye — whatever had bothered her was forgotten as soon as that — and, leaning far over, balancing the lightened but still awkward basket, started across the stubble for the house. As he cranked the tractor she turned around to look back at them and wave. He nodded and, as if embarrassed, touched his straw hat.

Not till he was doing the chores that night did he grasp what her look of alarm had meant. If he wouldn't say grace, then perhaps there was no heaven. Their father would never get well, and David was dead. He squatted, drained of all strength again, staring at the hoof of the cow he'd been stripping, preparing her for the milker, and thought of his absent father. He saw the motorcycle roaring down a twisting mountain road, the clatter of the engine ringing like harsh music against shale. If what he felt was hatred, it was a terrible, desperate envy, too; his father all alone, uncompromised, violent, cut off as if by centuries from the warmth, chatter, and smells of the kitchen, the dimness of stained glass where he, Jack, sat every Sunday between his mother and sister, looking toward the pulpit where in the old days his father had sometimes read the lesson, soft-voiced but aloof from the timid-eyed flock, Christ's sheep.

Something blocked the light coming in through the cow barn window from the west, and he turned his head, glancing up.

"You all right there, Jackie?" his uncle Walt said, bent forward, near-sightedly peering across the gutter.

He nodded and quickly wiped his wrist across his cheeks. He moved his hands once more to the cow's warm teats.

A few nights later, when he went in from chores, the door between the kitchen and living room was closed, and the house was unnaturally quiet. He stood a moment listening, still holding the milk pail, absently fitting the heel of one boot into the bootjack and tugging until the boot slipped off. He pried off the other, then walked to the icebox in his stocking feet, opened the door, carried the pitcher to the table, and filled it from the pail. When he'd slid the pitcher into the icebox again and closed the door, he went without a sound, though not meaning to be stealthy, toward the living room. Now, beyond the closed door, he heard voices, his sister and mother, then one of his aunts. He pushed the door open and looked in, about to speak.

Though the room was dim, no light but the small one among the pictures on the piano, he saw his father at once, kneeling by the davenport with his face on his mother's lap. Phoebe was on the davenport beside their mother, hugging her and him, Phoebe's cheeks stained, like her mother's, with tears. Around them, as if reverently drawn back, Uncle Walt, Aunt Ruth, and their two children sat watching, leaning forward with shining eyes. His father's head, bald down the center, glowed, and he had his glasses off.

"Jackie," his aunt called sharply, "come in. It's all over. Your dad's come home."

He would have fled, but his knees had no strength in them and his chest was wild, churning as if with terror. He clung to the doorknob, grotesquely smiling — so he saw himself. His father raised his head. "Jackie," he said, and was unable to say more, all at once sobbing like a baby.

"Hi, Dad," he brought out, and somehow managed to go to him and get down on his knees beside him and put his arm around his back. He felt dizzy now, nauseated, and he was crying like his father. "I hate you," he whispered too softly for any of them to hear.

His father stayed. He worked long days, in control once more, though occasionally he smoked, pacing in his room nights, or rode off on his motorcycle for an hour or two, and seldom smiled. Nevertheless, in a month he was again reciting poetry for schools and churches and the Grange, and sometimes reading Scripture from the pulpit Sunday mornings. Jack, sitting rigid, hands over his face, was bitterly ashamed of those poems and recitations from the Bible. His father's eyes no longer flashed, he no longer had the style of an actor. Even his gestures were submissive, as pliant as the grass. Though tears ran down Jack Hawthorne's face — no one would deny that his father was still effective, reciting carefully, lest his voice should break, "Tomorrow's Bridge" and "This Too Will Pass" — Jack scorned the poems' opinions, scorned the way his father spoke directly to each listener, as if each were some new woman, his father some mere suffering sheep among sheep, and scorned the way Phoebe and his mother looked on smiling, furtively weeping, heads tipped. Sometimes his father would recite a poem that Jack himself had written, in the days when he'd tried to write poetry, a comic limerick or some maudlin piece about a boy on a hill. Though it was meant as a compliment, Jack's heart would swell with rage; yet he kept silent, more private than before. At night he'd go out to the cavernous haymow or up into the orchard and practice his French horn. One of these days, he told himself, they'd awaken and find him gone.

He used the horn more and more now to escape their herding warmth. Those around him were conscious of what was happening — his parents and Phoebe, his uncles, aunts, and cousins, his mother's many friends. But there was nothing they could do. "That horn's his whole world," his mother often said, smiling but clasping her hands together. Soon he was playing third horn with the Batavia Civic Orchestra, though he refused to play in church or when company came. He began to ride the Bluebus to Rochester, Saturdays, to take lessons from Arcady Yegudkin, "the General," at the Eastman School of Music.

Yegudkin was seventy. He'd played principal horn in the orchestra of Czar Nikolai and at the time of the Revolution had escaped, with his wife, in a dramatic way. At the time of their purge of Kerenskyites, the Bolsheviks had loaded Yegudkin and his wife, along with hundreds more, onto railroad flatcars, reportedly to carry them to Siberia. In a desolate place, machine guns opened fire on the people on the flatcars, then soldiers pushed the bodies into a ravine, and the train moved on. The soldiers were not careful to see that everyone was dead. Perhaps they did not relish their work; in any case, they must have believed that, in a place so remote, a wounded survivor would have no chance against wolves and cold weather. The General and his wife were among the few who lived, he virtually unmarked, she horribly crippled. Local peasants nursed the few survivors back to health, and in time the Yegudkins escaped to Europe. There Yegudkin played horn with all the great orchestras and received such praise — so he claimed, spreading out his clippings — as no other master of French horn had received, in all history. He would beam as he said it, his Tartar eyes flashing, and his smile was like a thrown-down gauntlet.

He was a big-bellied, solidly muscular man, hard as a boulder for all his age. His hair and moustache were as black as coal except for touches of silver, especially where it grew, with majestic indifference to ordinary taste, from his cavernous nostrils and large, dusty-looking ears. The sides of his moustache were carefully curled, in the fashion once favored by Russian dandies, and he was one of the last men in Rochester, New York, to wear spats. He wore formal black suits, a huge black overcoat, and a black fedora. His wife, who came with him and sat on the long maple bench outside his door, never reading or knitting or doing anything at all except that sometimes she would speak unintelligibly to a student — Yegudkin's wife, shriveled and twisted, watched him as if worshipfully, hanging on his words. She looked at least twice the old man's age. Her hair was snow white and she wore lumpy black shoes and long black shapeless dresses. The two of them would come, every Saturday morning, down the long marble hallway of the second floor of Killburn Hall, the General erect and imperatorial, like some sharp-eyed old Slavonic king, moving slowly, waiting for the old woman who crept beside him, gray claws on his coat sleeve, and seeing Jack Hawthorne seated on the bench, his books and French horn in its tattered black case on the floor beside him, the General would extend his left arm and boom, "Goot mworning!"

Jack, rising, would say, "Morning, sir."

"You have met my wife?" the old man would say then, bowing and taking the cigar from his mouth. He asked it each Saturday.

"Yes, sir. How do you do."

The old man was too deaf to play in orchestras anymore. "What's the difference?" he said. "Every symphony in America, they got Yegudkins. I have teach them all. Who teach you this? *The General!*" He would smile, chin lifted, triumphant, and salute the ceiling.

He would sit in the chair beside Jack's and would sing, with violent gestures and a great upward leap of the belly to knock out the high B's and C's — *Tee! Tee!* — as Jack read through Kopprasch, Gallay, and Kling, and when it was time to give Jack's lip a rest, the General would speak earnestly, with the same energy he put into his singing, of the United States and his beloved Russia that he would nevermore see. The world was at that time filled with Russophobes. Yegudkin, whenever he read a paper, would be so enraged he could barely contain himself. "In all my age," he often said, furiously gesturing with his black cigar, "if the Russians would come to this country of America, I would take up a rifle and shot at them — *boof!* But the newspapers telling you lies, all lies! You think they dumb fools, these Russians? You think they are big, fat bush-overs?" He spoke of mile-long parades of weaponry, spoke of Russian cunning, spoke with great scorn, a sudden booming laugh, of Napoleon. Jack agreed with a nod to whatever the General said. Nevertheless, the old man roared on, taking great pleasure in his rage, it seemed, sometimes talking like a rabid communist, sometimes like a fascist, sometimes like a citizen helplessly caught between mindless, grinding forces, vast, idiot herds. The truth was, he hated both Russians and Americans about equally, cared only for music, his students and, possibly, his wife. In his pockets, in scorn of the opinions of fools, he carried condoms, dirty pictures, and grimy, wadded-up dollar bills.

One day a new horn he'd ordered from Germany, an Alexander, arrived at his office — a horn he'd gotten for a graduate student. The old man unwrapped and assembled it, the graduate student looking on — a shy young man, blond, in a limp gray sweater — and the glint in the General's eye was like madness or at any rate lust, perhaps gluttony. When the horn was ready he went to the desk where he kept his clippings, his tools for the cleaning and repair of French horns, his cigars, photographs, and medals from the czar, and pulled open a wide, shallow drawer. It contained perhaps a hundred mouthpieces, of all sizes and materials, from raw brass to lucite, silver, and gold, from the shallowest possible cup to the deepest. He selected one, fitted it into the horn, pressed the rim of the bell into the right side of his large belly — the horn seemed now as much a part of him as his arm or leg — clicked the shining keys to get the feel of them, then played. In that large, cork-lined room, it was as if, suddenly, a creature from some other universe had appeared, some realm where feelings become birds and dark sky, and spirit is more solid than stone. The sound was not so much loud as large, too large for a hundred French horns, it seemed. He began to play now not single notes but, to Jack's astonishment, chords — two notes at a time, then three. He began to play runs. As if charged with life independent of the man, the horn sound fluttered and flew crazily, like an enormous trapped hawk hunting frantically for escape. It flew to the bottom of the lower register, the foundation concert F, and crashed below it, and on down and down, as if the horn in Yegudkin's hands had no bottom, then suddenly changed its mind and flew upward in a split-second run to the horn's top E, dropped back to the middle and then ran once more, more fiercely at the E, and this time burst through it and fluttered, manic, in the trumpet range, then lightly dropped back into its own home range and, abruptly, in the middle of a note, stopped. The room still rang, shimmered like a vision.

"Good horn," said Yegudkin, and held the horn toward the graduate student, who sat, hands clamped on his knees, as if in a daze.

Jack Hawthorne stared at the instrument suspended in space and at his teacher's hairy hands. Before stopping to think, he said, "You think I'll ever play like that?"

Yegudkin laughed loudly, his black eyes widening, and it seemed that he grew larger, beatific and demonic at once, like the music; overwhelming. "Play like *me?*" he exclaimed.

Jack blinked, startled by the bluntness of the thing, the terrible lack of malice, and the truth of it. His face tingled and his legs went weak, as if the life were rushing out of them. He longed to be away from there, far away, safe. Perhaps Yegudkin sensed it. He turned gruff, sending away the graduate student, then finishing up the lesson. He said nothing, today, of the stupidity of mankind. When the lesson was over he saw Jack to the door and bid him goodbye with a brief half-smile that was perhaps not for Jack at all but for the creature on the bench. "Next Saturday?" he said, as if there might be some doubt.

Jack nodded, blushing.

At the door opening on the street he began to breathe more easily, though he was weeping. He set down the horn case to brush away his tears. The sidewalk was crowded — dazed-looking Saturday-morning shoppers herding along irritably, meekly, through painfully bright light. Again he brushed tears away. He'd be late for his bus. Then the crowd opened for him and, with the horn cradled under his right arm, his music under his left, he plunged in, starting home.

Brendan Gill

....

The Knife

MICHAEL THREW HIMSELF DOWN, locked his hands over one of his father's knees, and began, in a loud whisper, "'Our Father, who art in heaven, hallowed be thy name, kingdom come, will be done, earth as it is in heaven, give us this day — '"

Carroll folded his newspaper. Michael should have been in bed an hour ago. "Take it easy, kid," he said. "Let's try it again, slow."

Michael repeated distinctly, "'Our Father, who art in heaven, hallowed . . .'" The boy's pajamas, Carroll saw, were dirty at the cuffs; probably he had not brushed his teeth. "'. . . as we forgive them, who trespass against us' — what does 'trespass' mean, Dad?"

"Why, hurting anybody."

"Do I trespass anybody?"

"Not much, I guess. Finish it up."

Michael drew a breath. "'And lead us not into temptation, but deliver us from evil. Amen.'"

"Now," his father said, brushing back Michael's tangled hair, "what about a good 'Hail, Mary'?"

"All right," Michael said. "'Hail, Mary, full of grace, the Lord is with thee, blessed art thou among women, and blessed is the fruit of thy womb, Jesus.'" Michael lifted his head to ask if a womb got fruit like a tree, but thought better of it. His father never answered questions seriously, the way his mother used to. Michael decided to wait and ask Mrs. Nolan. "Is Mrs. Nolan coming tomorrow?" he asked.

"She'll be here, all right," Carroll said. "I give you ten seconds to finish the prayer."

Michael grinned at the ultimatum. "I thought you wanted me to go slow. 'Holy Mary, Mother of God, pray for us sinners, now and at the hour of our death. Amen.'" He unlocked his fingers. "Will she?"

"Will she what?"

"Will she now and at the hour of our death, A-men?"

The words of Michael's prayer caught in Carroll's mind and stayed there, a long way beyond his smiling face. "Yes," he said, and set his pipe in the broken dish on the table beside him. He had not emptied the dish of ashes in two days. Mrs. Nolan would give him a piece of her mind tomorrow morning, as she did each week when she came in to give the apartment a general cleaning and to do the laundry.

"What good can she do?" Michael asked.

"Climb into bed, young ragamuffin," Carroll said sternly. "It's past nine."

"What *good* can she do?"

"She'll help you get anything you want. I suppose she'll help you climb up into heaven when the time comes. You know all about heaven, don't you?"

Michael felt himself on the defensive. "Of course."

"Well, then, get along with you."

But Michael had something difficult to say. "You mean she'll ask God for anything I want and He'll give it to her for me?"

"She's His mother."

Michael stood up and kissed his father carefully on the cheek. Then he walked from the room, and Carroll could hear his bare feet crossing the hall. The bed creaked as Michael lay down on it. Carroll opened the newspaper, read a paragraph, then dropped it in a white heap on the rug. He felt tired; perhaps tonight he might be able to get some sleep. He got up, slipped his suspenders from his shoulders, unknotted his tie, kicked off his shoes. He had learned to undress quickly in the last six months, since his wife had died.

His pajamas were hanging inside out in the bathroom, where he had left them that morning. When he had undressed he felt Michael's toothbrush with his thumb; it was dry. He should have explained to the child what happened to a person's teeth when he forgot to clean them every night and morning.

Carroll stared at his face in the mirror above the basin. He tried smiling. No one could honestly tell what a man was thinking by the way he smiled. Even Michael, who was like a puppy about sensing moods, could not tell. He entered the bedroom on tiptoe. Feeling the sheets bunched at the foot of the mattress, he remembered that he had made the beds in a hurry. The sheets felt fresh and cool only on Saturdays, when Mrs. Nolan changed them.

Michael was not asleep. "Dad?" he whispered.

"Go to sleep."

"I been asking Hail Mary for something."

"Tomorrow."

"No, I been asking her right now."

Carroll lay on his back with his hands over his eyes. "What've you been asking her for, Mickey?"

Michael hesitated. "I thought I'd better make it something easy first. To see what happened." He sat up in bed. "A jackknife."

A few blocks away the clock in the Metropolitan Life tower was striking ten. Michael was deep in the noisy middle of a dream. Carroll listened to his breathing. He tried matching his own breath to Michael's, to make sleep come, but it was no use. Every night Carroll pretended to himself he was just at the brink of falling off to sleep, but his eyes always widened with wakefulness in the dark. Now, as the clock stopped striking, Carroll got up and walked into the bathroom and dressed. Then he went into the living room, unlocked the outside door of the apartment, and then locked it again before he walked down the two flights of stairs to the sidewalk. Shops reached out of sight down both sides of Lexington Avenue. Carroll walked uptown as he always did. He stopped in front of each bright shop window, studying its contents for the fifth or sixth time. He knew by now the day on which each window was changed and by whom. Certain plaster models, certain fringed crêpe papers were old friends.

At the top of a long slope Carroll waited for the lights to change. On his left was a bar; on his right, across the street, a drugstore. Carroll waited a moment outside the bar. Between the slats of its cheap orange Venetian blinds he could see the gleaming mahogany counter, the stacked glasses, the barman slicing foam from a mug of beer. A man and a girl were sitting at a table by the window, a foot under Carroll's eyes. They did not seem to be speaking. The man's hands lay halfway across the table and the girl's black dress made her throat look soft and white. Carroll turned away and crossed the street to the drugstore. The owner, Sam Ramatsky, stood sniffing the night air under the painted sign bearing his name.

"Well, Mr. Carroll, nice night for March."

"Yes." Carroll wanted only to hear a voice. "How's business?" he asked.

"Can't complain." Sam grinned, shaking his head. "I take that back. It's *lousy*. I got to break myself of this old 'Can't complain.' I got to remember how serious it is. Business is lousy."

Carroll leaned back against Sam's window, which was crammed with hot-water bottles, perfumes, toys, and two cardboard girls in shorts and sandals. The girls had been there for two months. There was dust on their teeth and on their smooth brown legs. "You ought to brush their teeth, Sam," Carroll said, "and run your hand down their legs now and then."

"You walk a lot," Sam said. "I figure on you, ten or eleven, every night."

"I guess I do," Carroll said.

Sam patted his hard belly. "Nothing like exercise to keep a man in shape."

Carroll nodded impatiently. It was not Sam's voice he wanted to hear, after all. "Give me a milk shake, Sam."

They walked into the store. Carroll sat down on one of the round stools at the fountain and watched Sam pouring milk into the shaker. "Nothing like milk," Sam said, "keep a man's system clean." Carroll watched the hands of the electric clock above the door. Ten-forty-five. He could not go to bed before twelve. He glanced at the packed counters behind him. "Sell any jackknives, Sam?"

"Sure. I sell everything. That's what keeps me broke. Nothing like keeping a thing in stock to kill demand." Sam lifted a tray of jackknives from a counter, brought it over, and set it down on the fountain. "Beauties," Sam said. "Fifty cents up."

Carroll looked at several of them and finally picked up the biggest and shiniest one. "I'll take this one," he said.

"Such expensive taste! One buck."

Carroll paid for the milk shake and the knife, said "Good night, Sam," and walked out into the street. In another hour and a half he should have walked six miles. By that time his body would be tired enough so that he could sleep. By that time, he hoped, no voice could rouse him.

It was morning when Carroll awoke. He lay with his face on his hands, listening to the sound of the March rain against the windows. He remembered suddenly the absurd song that everyone used to sing: "Though April showers may come your way, they bring the flowers that bloom in May." March rains brought you nothing. March rains only shut you in your room without any hope of escape.

Michael and Mrs. Nolan were talking together in the kitchen. Michael's voice was high with excitement. "Look at it, Mrs. Nolan, look at it! Isn't it beautiful?"

"It is that," Mrs. Nolan said in her deep voice. Carroll sat up in bed. It was too late to give Mrs. Nolan warning.

"Do you ask for things when you say your prayers, Mrs. Nolan?" Michael demanded.

"I do." A pan clattered to the floor. "I've seen many a nice clean sty I'd swap for this dirty kitchen," Mrs. Nolan said. "You live like a couple of savages from week to week. God love you."

"Do you always get what you ask for?" Michael said.

"It all depends. I sort of try to guess what the good Lord wants to give me, and I ask for that."

"That's how I got this knife," Michael said. "It's got a big blade and a little blade and a screwdriver and a thing to punch holes in leather with and a file."

"You must have said yourself a fine prayer," Mrs. Nolan said. There was no hint of surprise in her voice.

"It was only a 'Hail, Mary,'" Michael said, "but I did it very slow, the way Dad told me to." Michael was silent for a moment. "But I'm asking for the real thing tonight. The knife was just to see. Someone's going to be here when you come next week."

Mrs. Nolan made a clucking sound in her mouth. "Someone instead of me?"

"She was here with Dad and me before you came," Michael said, his voice thin with its burden, "and she's coming back."

"Michael!" Carroll shouted.

Michael ran to the doorway. The knife gleamed in his fist. "Look what I got," he said. "I was showing Mrs. Nolan."

"Come here," Carroll said. When Michael reached the edge of the bed Carroll bent over and fastened his arms behind the child's back. There was only one thing to say, and one way to say it, and that was fast. "I'm glad you like it," he said. "I bought it for you at Ramatsky's last night. The biggest and shiniest one he had."

John Hersey

....

God's Typhoon

I N THE LOT NEXT TO OURS at the summer resort of Peitaiho, at the foot of the hill that swooped down toward Rocky
Point and the "American beach" and the sparkling North China
Sea, Dr. Wyman had planted his famous arboretum. It boasted every
conifer that could survive in that slice of the temperate zone. I was a
small boy; I didn't know the names of any of the trees, but I was in
awe of the grove. I did not dare go into it. Even Dr. Wyman's three
sons had been strictly ordered to stay out. Huge NO TRESPASSING
signs, in English and Chinese, capped its shoulder-high stone walls.
Only Dr. Wyman and his invited guests, who were few and far between, were allowed entry — besides, of course, Chinese coolies to
tend the grounds.

On days when I was bored, I used to sit on a boulder in our lot and
contemplate that exquisite little forest. Salty sea breezes off the Gulf of
Peichili had gnarled many of the pines and firs and spruces and cedars
and yews and had caused all their feather-bearing boles to tend to the
west, toward the plains and mountains beyond the hill, as if they
yearned for the bone-dry air that sometimes came all the way down
from the Gobi Desert. On foggy days even I could sense something of
the mystery in evergreen shapes that had entranced so many Chinese
painter-philosophers. Through the years the trees had woven a brown-
ish-green carpet on the ground, and after a rain a delicious fragrance
of resin and sweet gum spilled over onto our land.

Quite often I saw Dr. Wyman strolling alone along the paths among
the trees, with his head thrown back as if to drink. Sometimes I saw his
mouth moving. Possibly he was rehearsing his dreadful sermons.

His son Billy Wyman and I both had brothers who were old enough to be Boy Scouts, while we two were still only Wolf Cubs. North China reverberated that summer with the cannon fire of warlords' battles, and the Scouts were constantly being mobilized, in their insufferable (to us) uniforms with red kerchiefs and merit badges all up and down their arms and chests, to run errands for the 15th U.S. Infantry and the Royal Marines. Those troops were bivouacked to protect foreign persons and their property at this heavenly enclave on Chinese soil, where Chinese persons — except, naturally, for house servants and coolies and donkey tenders — were unwelcome.

Furious at being kept at home under our mothers' wings while the big boys were out defending us, Billy and I spent every minute we could in and around a pup tent, defending an imaginary world of our own. I played soldier and he, being a Brit, played marine. Our good guy was the warlord Wu Pei-fu, our sworn enemy the Japanese-supported Chang Tso-lin. We were very brave but not brave enough to pitch our tent near Billy's house. We were both scared of his father.

The Reverend Doctor Josephus P. Wyman had remarkable gifts of body and mind. He seemed as tall and broad and dangerous, coming along one of the resort's sandy roads, as a lorry, and when he ground his jaws in a grimace of effort, as he often did, his chin and throat muscles bulged so much that you expected a bullfrog's song to come out from between his huge, pipesmoke-tinted teeth. Billy said he had once scored six hundred and seventeen runs at one stretch as a cricketer for Oxford. His interminable sermons at the Union Church came at us in an insistent singsong, half whine, half roar, and my restlessness in the pews on those Sabbath mornings was edged with dread.

Dr. Wyman preached a God I couldn't quite see in my mind, and certainly couldn't love. I dimly pictured some kind of Grandfather, who dealt out to bad people their awful "just deserts," which I thought must be poisoned food at the end of delicious meals. Grandfathers seemed mysterious and rather awesome to me anyhow, because I had never seen my two, both of whom lived back in the States. The Grandfather Dr. Wyman talked about was suspicious and angry, for no reason I could perceive. Shouldn't He be wildly happy over having created, among other wondrous things, our ravishing summer resort? Yet this Grandfather apparently spent most of His time on the lookout for ways of punishing everybody's "trespasses" and "sins of pride." Dr. Wyman harped on sins of pride. After his sermons I gloomily wondered about mine. Something to do with merit badges? Skill in swimming the Australian crawl?

Dr. Wyman was a polymath; we could imagine no subject on which he could not bury an adversary under the ever-spreading lava of his knowledge. His house — a queer, ugly block of stone with a flat roof, which he had designed himself — was like an untidy museum, crammed with all sorts of tools and instruments invented by man in order to assist in the study of God's manifest ingenuities. Strewn about on work-benches, parlor chairs, the dining-room table, and even his poor wife's sewing machine and ironing board, were Bunsen burners, microscopes, several of the latest cameras, a delicate balance with tiny scalepans, a stereoscope, numerous magnifying glasses, racks of test tubes holding various ominous-looking fluids; scattered here and there were sets of pipettes and syringes and beakers, of scalpels and chisels and dissecting knives, slide rules and compasses and tape measures, electromagnets and inductor coils and Leyden jars. Only Dr. Wyman's Deity knew what else — but oh! also a crystal radio capable of picking up Peking, a telegraph key on which he had conversed in Morse code with Vladivostok, and, most majestic of all, right in the center of the parlor, causing some awkwardness in group conversation there, a seven-foot-long telescope that he sometimes lugged up onto the roof at night to make sure the spheres were still revolving in God's good order.

Though known for his brilliance, he was also a jovial man. My mother had said that his laughter was as loud as the roar of Niagara Falls. Adults agreed that he was conscientious and tender in his pastoral duties; he was wonderfully sweet to Mrs. Fenton, they said, a cranky old lady, whom Billy and I used to mimic, sitting on her veranda all day in a rocking chair, moaning. I had heard Billy's mother say that breathing the piny air in the arboretum was what made the Reverend, as she called him, so serene.

Yet I was afraid of him. The reason for this — beyond whatever it was in his marathon sermons that set my nerves twanging — was the kind of boy his son, my friend Billy, was turning out to be. Pale, thin, washed-out, obedient, with eyes as sad as those of a bloodhound, Billy wore shorts that hung down below his knees, and scuffed black shoes with no socks. He made a hopeless Royal Marine. He was a wonderful pal to have, though, because he would do anything I asked him to. But I pitied him, too, and blamed his flaccid condition entirely on his father. If Dr. Wyman could spend so much on a swarm of coolies to tend his conifers, why couldn't he buy Billy some decent clothes, instead of making him wear his older brothers' worn-out hand-me-downs? Couldn't he expend some of his renowned gentleness on his forlorn son? What I saw flicker in Billy's eyes whenever we came roistering into that cluttered house and found Dr. Wyman looming there over some foul-smelling chemicals in an experiment he was touchily conducting — the pain I glimpsed in Billy's eyes at such a moment — told me that he was mortally afraid of that big, kind man.

One day I had a thrilling idea: Billy and I would camp out overnight in the pup tent. I asked my mother if we could. "You'll have to ask your father," she said.

I waited until after he had won a tennis match, six–one, six–love, and then I did.

"Do you have your mother's permission?" he asked me.

"I haven't had a chance to check with her," I said.

"Come back when you have her permission," he said.

This was a game of shuttle diplomacy at which I had become adept, and before long I had my go-ahead. I announced the plan to Billy. He shook his head back and forth only about a quarter of an inch each way — an economical gesture that expressed an enormous negative. He would never get permission from his father. I suggested that, to begin with, we go to work on his mother.

Mrs. Wyman seemed at first glance to be one of those deeply wounded but resigned ladies — of whom there were so very many among missionary wives — who wore shapeless dresses and were always having to push back, with a sigh, stubborn stray tresses of their prematurely gray hair and refasten them any which way with one of a shoal of tortoiseshell hairpins. She had no territory of her own in her home. Dr. Wyman had considerately set aside a small oaken desk on which she might keep his accounts, but he had ruined its surface by spilling some acid during one of his explorations of God's marvelous secrets. Yet with my shrewd small-boy's eyes I had often observed the way she could balance the huge minister on the little finger of her left hand while her right hand was doing something that would have astonished if not outraged him, had he but noticed. She had Scottish blood and a residue of lake-country canniness in her makeup.

The long and the short of it was that we got permission from Wyman *mère* and later, with *mère*'s help but not without growls, from *père*. Protocols drawn up by Dr. Wyman required that the tent be pitched no more than twenty feet from the sleeping porch of our house, so that, if necessary, a yell would waken my parents. We were not to stir from inside the tent after sunset and before dawn. We could not sleep in our clothes but would have to wear pajamas. No foodstuffs, no matches, no loud talk.

It was dark in the tent, and we obeyed all the rules that first night.

For a while, the warlords having packed themselves off, Billy and I had to try to keep up with the energies of our older brothers. We galloped to East Cliff on donkeyback, left far behind by the big boys, in a paper chase — a simulated fox hunt, introduced at Peitaiho by British missionaries, in which the hunters followed a trail of torn-up bits of back issues of *The Peking and Tientsin Times,* which had been scattered earlier for miles across the country by an adult "master of hounds." We fished for puffers from Tiger Rocks, off the American beach, and under the pressure of dares from the bigger boys we dived in terror into mysterious boulder-rimmed depths off the high "forehead rock." They made us serve as ball boys for their tennis tournament, and allowed us to shag foul balls when they played baseball against the 15th Infantry team, which always beat the missionary kids by scores like 33–2, in five innings.

On some days our brothers refused to let "the brats" tag along, and we went howling to our mothers. A few of those days turned out to be the sweetest of the summer. Once, taking pity on us, Mrs. Wyman sent her Number One Boy down to the village to find an itinerant rice-paste sculptor, who came up the hill carrying the two cylindrical cases of his "studio" on a shoulder pole; in twenty minutes, for two coppers, mixing and tinting and molding the plasticene-like paste, he made for Billy and me a pair, each eight inches tall, of magnificently ferocious warriors of the era of the Three Kingdoms. The next time was my mother's turn, and she sent our Wang down to find a magician, who, also with his gear in two containers on a shoulder pole, dazzled us on our front veranda, pulling silk cloths out of his ear, and asking Billy and me to try to guess which shifting riceware cup the jade grasshopper was under, and even finding a live dove in my mother's hat, the one with red wax cherries on it, which she had left lying on the glider that day. Once we were entertained by child acrobats. Once we were allowed to make ice cream in midafternoon in the hand-turned freezer, with rock-salted ice, both of us licking the mixing blade at the same time.

The greatest treat of all for me — we had learned to redouble our howls when the big boys left us behind — was the day Dr. Wyman took us for a walk in the arboretum. My fear of him vanished, and I was glad to have him keep hold of my hand along the cavernous, deep-shaded paths. Birds were in ecstasy among the slivers of light overhead. The needle scent acted on me like opium, and I felt that I was floating, to the music of the Latin names of species that Dr. Wyman softly recited, in a kind of dream I had never even hoped to have.

A few days later news came that troops of Chang Tso-lin had shown up again near Shanhaikwan, only a few miles from us, where the Great Wall came down to the sea. The big boys were called up for guard duty, and Billy and I wheedled and whined until we were given permission to sleep out in the tent another time.

It was a full-moon night. The cloth of the tent glowed. I could not sleep. I don't know what time it was when something perverse surged up in me and I whispered, "Billy?"

He, too, was wide awake. "What?"

"Let's go down to the arboretum."

"Now?"

"Sure. It's a wizard night."

"It's against the rules," Billy said.

"Pshaw, Billy" — the closest I could come to swearing at that time — "don't be a spoilsport."

"I don't think Daddy would like it."

But Billy would do anything I asked him to, and soon we were two bright ghosts in our white PJs, slinking downhill along the three-foot-high border wall of my family's lot, both of us in a crouch, as if that would hide us from the searching light of the moon. The gate to the arboretum was locked. I had to help Billy up onto the wall and then, my heart beating wildly, I jumped up after him. We sat there on the curved plaster top quite a while, not daring to hurry down the other side. Finally I scrambled down. Billy still hesitated. I tugged at him, until finally his need for compliance overcame his fear, and he slithered down.

When our eyes had adjusted to the shadows, we started along the central path. I held Billy's hand. I had goose pimples all up and down my back and arms and legs. We did not speak.

Somewhere far away — not in the grove, I am now convinced — an owl suddenly hooted, and Billy and I turned and ran. He got over the wall this time without any help.

A British submarine cruised like a shark on the surface of the silver gulf and anchored in our bay, close enough to shore that boys even as small as Billy and I could swim out — nervous all the way — to look it over. Its presence lent a new naval arm to our daytime military operations in and around the pup tent. Since nothing naughty or dangerous appeared to have happened, our sleeping out in the tent on fair-weather nights had now come to be accepted by both mothers — and therefore had been sanctioned with doubtful glowers by the supposed final authorities, the fathers. The next three times after our adventure in the arboretum, we pitched the tent at sundown, crawled in, and more or less scrupulously followed the rules. But as I lay awake on the hard ground on those nights, something kept gnawing at me, filling me with delight and fear.

Finally, one afternoon, on the most delicious day of the summer, with a sky like the inside of a beautiful seedless Concord grape and air so calm that time seemed to have stopped, I waited until we were in a good mood after having routed Chang Tso-lin for the hundredth time, and then I said to Billy, "Tell you what, let's do something big."

"Oh, no," Billy said, the blood fleeing from his cheeks. "What now?"

I grabbed him by the shirt and whispered, "Tonight, after everyone's asleep, we'll strike the tent and take it down to the arboretum and pitch it in, you know, that open clearing. And sleep there. Wouldn't that be neat?"

Billy looked as if I had stabbed him. I kept whispering. I told him I'd take my new little alarm clock with us; we could get up at five and bring the tent back up, and no one would ever know. It would be easy. Sleeping so near the house had gotten boring.

"It's so dark down there," Billy said.

"I've thought about that," I said. "Listen, Billy, you know that coal miner's hat of your father's, the one with the little kerosene lamp fastened to it over the visor? I've noticed it's in that jumbled heap of stuff in the corner of your what-do-you-call-it, spare room? — where he just throws junk — you know? — that he's never going to use again? That he's completely forgotten about? We could borrow that."

I was pushing Billy into the very pith of danger, and I knew it. And I know now that this awareness was the knife-edge of my excitement.

Another thing I knew then was that Billy would in time come round to doing what I asked. It took a lot of whispering, but Billy came round.

It was about eleven o'clock, and the lights had long been out in both our houses, when we surreptitiously pulled up the tent pegs and collapsed the poles and folded the canvas. I had sneaked a tin of wick oil out to the tent and had filled the miner's lamp, and I had a box of wooden matches in the pocket of my shorts. (A couple of tent-nights ago we had given up changing into pajamas, though each time we would bundle them up and use them as pillows, so that our mothers could see the next day that they were wrinkled and soiled.) Of course we would wait until later to light the lamp, but I put the hat on Billy's head. There was a dim glow from a gibbous moon high in the sky. I looked up at it and shivered. It had a strange misty ring around it. It was like an eye in the sky, looking right at us. It knew everything. It must have been able to make out, as I could in its cold glare, that the miner's hat was too big for Billy's head but that it somehow stayed in place. He was going to be the one to wear it.

When we got the tent over the wall and had gone over ourselves, I lit the lamp. It created a magical sphere of soft visibility, into the fuzzy outer membrane of which, as we stole toward the glade, all the varieties of evergreens reached their feathery hands to greet us. I felt blissful, and even Billy was moved; he said in a trembling voice, "Say, this is keen." We pitched the tent with no trouble, crept in, snuffed the lamp, and bedded down on the fragrant carpet. We whispered awhile, but soon I drifted off into the deepest sleep I'd ever had on this earth.

I was having a frightful dream. The entire tent was snatched away from over us in a sudden swoop, like a single beat of the wings of a huge condor, and I heard a deep roaring, as of some great natural cataclysm. But no, no, I wasn't dreaming, I was all too awake. I sat up, my buttocks aprickle, and I sensed that Billy was sitting up beside me, whimpering. Dr. Wyman stood over us, glowing in the moonlight in his pajamas. The words of his rage broke on me like rough waves roiling me in the sand. With a grip on the ridgepole, he held the whole tent high in his right hand. "Up! Up!" he shouted. "Pick up your things!" he roared. As we scrambled about, he saw the miner's hat. "You brought a flame into my arboretum," he said in a kind of groan. "You lit matches under these trees." Then he leaned his huge face down toward me and shouted twice, "You little devil! You little devil!"

In my bed on our sleeping porch, much, much later, I could still hear, all the way from the Wymans' house, Billy crying out till I thought his lungs must burst.

The next afternoon I could only imagine that Mrs. Wyman felt her youngest duckling had been too severely punished in the night, and that she had begged the Reverend in the morning for Christian forgiveness. Because, to my astonishment, Billy was allowed to come over to play with me. The rims of his eyes were purple. I was sincere in my apologies to him and promised I would never get him in trouble again, and he, with his gentle, fragile nature, forgave me. But our play around the tent, which we repitched in its "safe" place twenty feet from our sleeping porch, was halfhearted. I didn't feel like singing out commands to Billy with my usual bravura. The day was sticky, and depressing. Despite a lack of wind on our cheeks, swift clouds scudded in from the sea, low overhead. We perspired. Chang Tso-lin languished in the enemy camp. I kept thinking that although Dr. Wyman had leaned down and spoken those last few words to me in sermon tones the night before, he must surely have meant the word "devil" only in a slangy sort of way, to be written in my heavenly record with a lowercase initial. Not the real thing. I sniffed my arm and could not smell burning sulfur. Billy was sympathetic. He saw how bad I felt, and to cheer me up he kept making suggestions: we could send a scouting party around the other side of the house, we could radio the sub to search toward Lighthouse Point. . . .

Later I was in the tent. "Hey," Billy said, "come out here."

I knew the various timbres of his voice, and I heard a ring in this summons that made me scramble out pell-mell on my hands and knees.

"Look," he said, pointing out to the gulf.

Above the horizon, along its whole span, rolled a cloud as black as charcoal, with a sickish viridian light between it and the sea, and then I saw what had alarmed Billy, as if the endless cloud itself weren't bad enough. On a bearing straight out from the submarine there hung down from the black cloud a slender conical tendril, equally black, which seemed at first to weave slightly back and forth. Then it grew longer, like a finger poking down, down. Next, in horror, as if we, too young, were watching a primal scene of unspeakable obscenity, sea mating with sky, we saw a cone rise up from the water and move in a wavering way toward the shore, dancing in response to the finger above, separate from it but following directly beneath it. With a sudden spurt, vapor and water flew together, and the sky began to suck up the sea.

Now we realized that the sinuous spout was coming close to the shore. Miraculously it took a detour around the submarine, which lay calmly at anchor at the rim of the vortex of violent whitecaps surrounding the column. I heard my mother screaming my name. The twister reached land, half a mile from us, and Billy and I saw a cottage seem to explode. Its roof — all the foreigners' cottages at Peitaiho had corrugated tin roofs — was ripped off in pieces, and huge sheets of metal and scraps of wood and branches of trees and a million fragments of everything rose and revolved and fell, until another house was hit, and after that . . . but Billy and I turned away and ran for it. My mother hugged me, and my father shouted, "You boys hold the sleeping-porch door shut!" We two, glad to have work to do, ran to that door, which, though it was latched, was already trembling. We braced ourselves against it. I was thinking how glad I was not to be able to see what was happening outside, when with a splitting sound the jamb gave way and the door flew open, throwing Billy and me to the floor halfway across the room. On hands and knees in the indoor gale, I looked up and saw the roof of the McAlisters' house, beyond and to the left of the Wymans', lifted off whole, almost exactly as the pup tent had been ripped from above us the night before, and I heard a roar that sounded to me just like Dr. Wyman's rage. The typhoon was calling me names. I closed my eyes. I heard a terrible crash but felt no pain. Then the ministerial roar seemed to move on toward other devils in other houses. The wind suddenly died. Torrents of water came down as the sky's buckets of salt sea fell back on us. Our house had held.

An hour after the wind subsided, but while it was still pouring, my oldest brother, Peter, the most adventurous of the three of us boys, rushed out of the house to scout the wreckage on our Rocky Point hill. My mother called to him to come back, but he ran on. He had not gone far when he noticed a knot of people in the Wymans' lot, and he ran to them and saw that they were standing in a soaked circle around Dr. Wyman's dead body. Of course Peter rushed back to tell us about it. He used to boast about the accuracy of his observations, and he described the cadaver to us in gruesome detail. A huge sheet of metal from the McAlisters' roof, skimming along over the ground "at a hundred miles an hour," Peter said, had cut Dr. Wyman in two at the waist and then had flipped away, leaving the two halves of the pastor prone in what still seemed to be something like a running position. The driving rain had washed away all the blood.

"And, oh, by the way," Peter said, "every single tree in the arboretum was uprooted. You should see the mess — trunks in all directions. It's a rat's nest."

Hearing these things, I experienced a surge of the greatest joy I had ever known. The Grandfather in Heaven was, after all, capable of love, and He loved me. He had brought this typhoon for me. The roar of the storm's rage had not been meant for me at all; it had been aimed at Billy's father. This God whom I welcomed at last was both merciful and angry, for He had forgiven me my trespasses and punished Dr. Wyman for his. I was sorry, deeply sorry, about the arboretum, but it seemed to me that in destroying it, God may have been pointing a finger at one of Dr. Wyman's sins of pride. From my Sunday-school lore I conjured up a dim sense that Dr. Wyman had tried to create — with only his coolies' help, not God's — a Garden of Eden of his own, which he had wanted to keep forever for Adam's own selfish use.

My joy, my conversion, my perfect faith, lasted only a day. The next morning, though the downpour was by no means over, my other brother, Amos, went across to the Wymans' house, and when he came back, he told me he'd heard Mrs. Wyman say that the reason the Reverend had been out there in the fury of the storm was that he had gone to look for Billy, to rescue him from danger. That changed everything. I began to have nightmares every night.

We had three solid days of torrential rain. Miraculously, our house had suffered only minor damage. A six-foot-square piece of roofing had struck our porch roof — the crash I had heard. The skirts of the twister must have swerved just enough to miss us; the McAlisters' house in one direction and two on the other side of us were hit hard. Dr. Wyman's little storm-proof box had taken the full force of the wind, with no damage but some broken windows. A few days later Amos found the canvas of the pup tent undamaged in a sorghum field a quarter of a mile from the house. The ridgepole was still in it but was broken; we never found the uprights.

I didn't see Billy for a fortnight. Because of the bad dreams I was having, my mother thought I should probably not go to the funeral. (After it, I overheard her scolding Peter for having told us all a fib the day of the storm: she had learned that Dr. Wyman had not been cut in two at all, though he had indeed been mortally wounded at the midriff.) The weather turned lovely. Our Number One Boy, Wang, was a clever carpenter, and he liked me; he made new poles and pegs for the tent, and I finally set it up in the "safe" place, but I had no fun playing around it alone.

The very next day Billy came over. I hardly recognized him. He had on brand-new white shorts, I could see his nubby knees, and he was wearing Keds. His hair was brushed. When we started our war game, he had some rather impertinent suggestions — they proved to be good ones, I had to admit — about maneuvers against Chang Tso-lin.

Before he left for home, he said, "Let's sleep in the arboretum tonight."

I was astonished at his taking that kind of initiative. "Gee, Billy," I said, "it's a ruin."

"I know," he said. "It belongs to me now. My brothers aren't interested. Mama said I could replant it."

"Replant it? What are you going to use for seeds?"

"Daddy has — I mean he had — masses of seeds. And I've already sent for some seedlings from Szechuan. One of the China Inland Missions advertises them in the *Recorder,* you know — jolly good cedars just like those in the Holy Land."

I slept poorly that night in what had been the clearing in the arboretum. Billy snored. In the morning he boiled water on a Sterno rack that he had brought in his knapsack, and made tea for us. Dr. Wyman's squad of coolies showed up with two-man saws. Billy had the key to the gate and let them in, and he told them where to start cutting up the trunks. He said he was going to try to right some of the very young trees, which still seemed to have life in them, and he asked me to help him with one of the smaller ones. He grabbed hold of the trunk with me and began straining, and I saw that his teeth were clenched and his pathetic jaw muscles and neck muscles were all tightened up.

William Hoffman

....

The Question of Rain

T HE REQUEST CAME from an unexpected source during the
dusty, choking summer. Wayland was in the back yard of the
white frame manse. His wife, Mims, called through the kitchen
screen door that Alex Bradner was on the way out. Oh damn, Wayland
thought, because he believed he had at last educated his congregation
not to bother him on Mondays except for illness or death.

Alex Bradner owned knitting mills, cinder-block plants which manu-
factured textured polyesters and spun down a fine, almost invisible lint
over the flat Virginia town. When the mills worked three shifts, a
person could look out at the early morning grass and believe it was
frosted even in July.

"We might have to close unless it rains," Alex said to Wayland.

Alex was a hard-driving man in his mid-fifties, his impatience held in
check only by his breeding. Even sitting in a lawn chair, Alex seemed in
motion, about to leap up to do a job, to wrench the world to the shape
his hands desired.

"I didn't know you used that much water," Wayland said.

"It's the dye," Alex explained. "We need water for our dyeing process, and if the river runs low, the discharge concentration is increased
to where the Water Control Board in Richmond can shut us down. I'd
like you to pray for rain."

Wayland almost smiled, because Alex Bradner had little spiritual
depth. He was generous with his pocketbook, but not himself. During
services, rather than sing the hymns, he studied them as if they were
corporate reports. He never recited The Apostles' Creed.

"Well, of course, I'll be happy to pray," Wayland said, the smile
twitching at his lips. "Would you like to right now, you and I together?"

"I think it ought to be in the church," Alex said. His green eyes were speckled and seemed lidless, they were so unblinking.

"All right, we'll walk over," Wayland said, prepared to stand. "Though I don't think it's necessary. I'm certain our prayers can be heard just as well from a back yard."

"I don't mean just us," Alex said. "I think you ought to make this Sunday a Special Prayer Day for Rain."

Wayland said nothing. He looked at Alex to see how serious he was. Alex wasn't frowning, but his face perpetually verged upon it.

"I don't think I'd care to alter our regular service," Wayland said.

"But wouldn't it be better?" Alex asked. "The more people we gather, the whole congregation, and in the church, would appear to make praying more productive."

Alex Bradner was playing divine odds. Four was better than two, a crowd more powerful than an individual. Wayland hoped he didn't sound peevish.

"God hears each of us," he said. "Efficacy doesn't require massing."

"I believe in covering all bases," Alex said.

"God knows our needs," Wayland explained. "He meets them out of His love for us. We don't pray to ask favors as if He's a rich uncle, but to have fellowship with Him, to achieve a feeling that we are close and in His care."

"Would it hurt to try?" Alex asked, pragmatic and relentless.

"I don't suppose it could hurt anything," Wayland said. "The question is whether or not our regular worship service ought to be used. I don't object to rain as part of the general prayer, but to make rain the point of an entire service not only might set a precedent whereby people would soon request snow on Christmas or cooling breezes in August, but would also presume on God's plans for us and this world. Loving and seeking Him is the great prayer, and He will order affairs so that we want nothing in any essential way."

"You won't do it, then?" Alex asked, and tightened his broad freckled hands on the aluminum chair arms to stand.

"I'm not speaking that strongly," Wayland said. "As I pray for the sick and the lost, I'll pray for rain, but not use the entire service."

"A lot of people are going to be out of work," Alex said.

Alex's visit soured the day for Wayland. He capped his paints, cleaned his brushes, and talked with Mims in the kitchen. She was thirty-three, four years younger than he, a small, fair-skinned woman with brown eyes and reddish-brown hair.

"But what can superdealer do?" she asked. She smelled of vinegar and linseed oil from her work of refinishing a pine washstand she had bought at a farm auction.

"I don't know, but I can tell you Alex won't let go," Wayland said.

On Tuesday night, as Wayland was about to close the deacons' meeting with a prayer, Harlan Henderson spoke. Harlan was chairman of the group, a weathered, square-jawed man who was the county agent.

"Are you going to take any action on the rain?" Harlan asked.

"You mean me personally?" Wayland asked, and got a laugh.

"There's sentiment among the congregation for a special day," Harlan persisted.

"I've winded that sentiment," Wayland said. "I have to tell you frankly I don't like the idea."

"We could sure God use a rain," Nelson Dunnavant said. Nelson had only one arm. He had lost the other to the claws of a mechanical corn picker. He owned both a dairy farm and a John Deere dealership.

"I want rain as much as anyone, but my feeling is rain is a lesser need," Wayland said. "If we're going to unite our voices, we should ask for grateful hearts, not put in a special order. I hope you see the distinction."

He looked into their faces, good faces, good men, his friends and helpers, men he loved and could rely on, but he observed that they did not see any distinction. They reminded him of cattle staring motionless in a pasture.

"I suggest some things have to be left to the minister's judgment," Wayland said.

As he walked home through the dry, abrasive darkness, he slapped at mosquitoes. Seared grass crackled under his shoes. Mims sat in the manse parlor playing the black upright piano. Barefoot, wearing white shorts and a blue halter, she was practicing hymns to be sung at Sunday School.

"You heard a weather report?" he asked.

"Rain?" she asked, brightening. Her fingers were still curved to the keys.

"I was hoping you'd listened and could tell me," he said.

"Sorry there, fellow. Failed once again by your trifling, weak-minded wife."

He laughed, crossed to sit by her on the piano bench, and kissed her neck, ear, and mouth. She wore perfume, but he still smelled the vinegar.

"Keep this up and you'll have to race me to the bedroom," she said.

When, on Wednesday morning, he walked to the post office, heat quivered above the gummy asphalt street. Lawns were a pale, kinky brown, scorched right to the soil. The soil itself had cracks in it, as if the earth would give up its dead. No flowers bloomed, no sprinklers spun.

Beyond the iron bridge over the shallow, dust-filmed river, cars were leaving the fenced parking lot at the mill. He first thought ten-forty was a strange time for a shift change. Then he understood that the men had been let go.

As he walked through the listless, sun-glazed town, he believed people were eyeing him. He might be imagining it. Ministers developed persecution feelings. The most intent eyes might be his own, peering at himself from within.

"Hear about the plant closings?" Spud Hogge, cashier and a member of the congregation, asked when Wayland stopped by the Planters & Merchants Bank to deposit his bimonthly salary check.

"Terrible for the men," Wayland said. Was he being criticized?

"Rough to have no beans for your family," Spud said, his lumpy face set. When the bell mechanism had broken in the church steeple, Spud had climbed through rafters and been stung by wasps in order to find the trouble and fix it.

"Spud, are you sending me a message?" Wayland asked, smiling.

"I think everybody has his Christian duty to help all he can in tight times," Spud said, his chin raised as if facing wind.

Wayland walked home, changed into shorts, and sat in his study. He intended to preach this Sunday on the sacrament of baptism. He would soon, obviously, have to work up a sermon on prayer, its nature.

Despite the open windows, no air moved in his study. It wasn't air at all, but a tormenting pressure which galled the skin. The mimosa, which stirred with even the slightest breeze, was immobile against a citrine sky, its dusty, drooping fronds tinged with yellow. No bird flew, no cloud floated. It would not rain today.

In this week's sermon he would emphasize that a man's being sprinkled or immersed symbolized drowning and the death of an old life and the emergence of a new person to a new life. It occurred to him that the subject of baptism might cause the congregation to think all the more about water and drought. He imagined some wag remarking that there wasn't enough river left to baptize even a dainty Episcopalian.

He was conscious of the weltering locusts, their chirring warping over the parched town. He scratched a bare shoulder. He switched on a radio which sat in his bookshelf. The Town Council was asking citizens to take as few baths as possible. His routine called for two showers a day. He considered which to deny himself.

He wrote pell-mell, having no thought for jarring transitions or even scriptural relevance, but just trying to get something on paper to work with. Afterward it would be polish, polish, polish until Saturday, when he taped the sermon in order that he and Mims could listen and judge how it would play in Peoria.

The ladies arrived at four, rang the bell — Bess Blakley, Ellen Boswer, and Caroline Devereaux, each an officer in the Women of the Church. Mims seated them in the parlor and came for Wayland. She rolled her eyes.

There was no way he could go past them and up the steps to change his clothes without being seen. He did pull on his red tank top and apologize for his bare feet. Caroline Devereaux looked at his legs, which were hairy and slightly bowed. Aware of his skin and the ladies' finery, he sat on a leatherette ottoman.

"I guess we're a delegation," Bess Blakley said. Oldest of the three, she had bluish-white hair. "The Women of the Church have gone on record as being in favor of a Special Prayer Day for Rain to end the drought."

Wayland almost sighed openly. The ladies were nearly always the problem. He loved, indeed honored them for being the most devout laborers in Christ's vineyard, but they also became too easily aroused and were regimental in their causes.

"Bess, to repeat my position, let me state that I'm strongly in favor of prayer, but I feel what people really want is a medicine man, and I never rattle bones, do a rain dance, or wear chicken feathers."

"All people want is for you to try," Caroline Devereaux said. She was a tanned, short-haired blond who annually won the town tennis tournament. She also taught the majorettes at the high school.

"Caroline, we can't twist God's arm," he explained. "All we have is given us by His grace, and we are undeserving of that."

"We could fill the church," said Ellen Boswer, the wife of Jamerson Boswer, the mayor, who was also in the tobacco export business. Ellen was tiny, hardly five feet tall, yet she had mothered six robust, rowdy children.

"Well, I'm sure we could, but the service would be a sideshow," Wayland said. "Somebody might suggest we serve popcorn and play bingo."

His sarcasm offended them. They had come to him with serious spiritual business, even if misguided, and he should have been patient and loving.

"It doesn't have to be a sideshow," Bess Blakley said. "I don't see why you and all of us couldn't pray with dignity."

"You're right, Bess, and I'm sorry," he said. "What I'm trying to tell you is, we can't force God's hand even with our most fervent prayers. In praying we shouldn't be talking at all, making demands, but listening, feeling, and receiving Him."

"Then you won't," Caroline Devereaux said. "We heard you were against it."

"Against it, not you," he said. "Refusing you ladies anything distresses me. I'd rather suffer toads and boils. Yet I know you wouldn't want me to do something I consider wrong for myself and the church."

They fidgeted, glanced at each other, and drew their pocketbooks higher on their laps. He walked them to the door, where Ellen Boswer turned to him.

"I hear cattle lowing," she said tearfully. "They sound hurt and mournful. They have no water or pasture. They stand by dry holes looking pitiful. I'd think a minister would be touched by that."

"Believe me, Ellen, I'm not in favor of pain and suffering," Wayland said, and for a moment he felt very near despair at the gap between them, their lives on one side of the theological divide, his life on the other, and so little possibility of ever reaching across and joining hands.

When they were gone, he walked musing to his study. He sat discouraged. He began to pray. Depression, rooted in self-pity, he considered a sin. To the Lord he gave thanks for tribulation, as the Epistle of

James suggested. All things truly worked for good to those who loved God. And Wayland did love God. When he lifted his head, Mims, hands folded, waited beyond the doorway.

"There wasn't time to warn you," she said. "I had to invite them in."

"It's okay," he said. "I'll be all right now. At least I hope I will."

"You'll feel better after your shower," she said.

"I'm not showering this afternoon," he said.

That night he had a telephone call from Henry Porter of the Danville *Bee*. Henry was nearly inactive in the church, a Christmas Christian.

"Richmond called me," Henry said. "They want a story about this Special Prayer Day for Rain."

"Wait just a second," Wayland said. "How would anybody in Richmond know?"

"I can't answer you," Henry said. "I can tell you they might send a reporter. You want to make a statement?"

"I'm definitely not holding a Special Prayer Day for Rain," Wayland said. "I'm having my regular Sunday service, though I will pray for rain in my pastoral prayer."

Wayland had trouble sleeping. He worried, and the heat chafed him. The locusts didn't cease their chirring until after ten o'clock. Then dogs started a monotonous, unrelieved barking. He attempted to lie still so as not to disturb Mims, but he sensed she wasn't sleeping either.

Finally, when he had nearly dropped off, the telephone rang. He snatched it from the night table.

"'O ye of little faith!'" a male voice said.

"What?" Wayland asked. "Who is this?"

But the person hung up. Wayland looked at Mims, who lay uncovered in the pearly glow from the bathroom night-light. Her dark eyes were open.

"I heard it," she said.

"Who'd do that to me?" Wayland asked. He lay beside her and held her moist hand.

"So many people have become irritable in this weather," she said. "The call could've come from a tavern."

He was up early Thursday to work on his sermon during the slight morning coolness. There was no dampness on the withered grass. He stayed at his desk until ten. He then drove his Plymouth to the community hospital, a modern brick and glass structure built on the town's only rise of ground. Stone visitor's benches were placed under shriveled locust and willow trees.

As he made his rounds to the sick and suffering, a voice calling his name echoed along the waxy, metallic corridor. The voice belonged to Lee Gordon, a young doctor whom Wayland had spoken the marriage vows over this past April.

"Margo tells me the phone lines are smoking," Lee said. Margo was his sultry Georgia wife. Lee laughed. "She tells me you're expected to perform miracles."

Slim and athletic, Lee, who had played for the Duke team, was a prowling shark on the golf course. He wore a starched white smock, wine slacks, and perforated black and white kilties. His good-humored assumption that he and Wayland were far more sophisticated about God and religion than anybody else in town disturbed Wayland.

"Miracles happen," Wayland said. "Even today they can happen." He did believe that, didn't he?

"But you wouldn't want to put your chips on the line, would you?" Lee asked, his outsized teeth gritted in a grin. "I mean right up there in front of everybody in church, to put your chips on the line for a miracle?"

How to make Lee and people understand it wasn't a question of chips on the line? God in His omnipotence could change the course of history by merely willing it, but the question was whether or not God was careless and ran the universe by whim and the seat of His divine trousers.

"Maybe you ought to break over and have a beer," Mims said that afternoon when Wayland, dejected, slumped in his study. She kept a few cans for him. Buying it was dangerous, never done locally, but only while she shopped in Danville or South Hill.

The telephone call came at ten minutes after five, not anonymous, but from Fred Pepper, chairman of the Board of Elders. They were holding a special meeting. Wayland had drunk two beers and was relaxed. He was forced to hurry his eating of Mims's cool shrimp salad and follow it with Listerine. He fought anger.

There were five elders, veteran Christians, important to the church and to the community. Fred Pepper owned a department store, yet was a man of the cross, always willing to attend presbytery and quick to reach for the check.

"We've been receiving calls," Fred said. He and the other elders sat on the same folding wooden chairs the diaconate used, chairs in a Sunday School room with a view of the thirsting cemetery. Fred wore a seersucker suit, a white shirt, and a narrow black tie. His gray hair had deep comb furrows in it.

"The ladies are in an uproar," Chap Bonney said. Chap, at least a hundred pounds overweight, was an attorney and on the board at the bank. "Do anything, face storms and earthquakes, lions and tigers, but not the fury of the aroused human female."

Wayland laughed with the others.

"Just what is the problem?" Reid Poindexter asked, slim, precise, mathematical Reid, a dispatcher for the Norfolk & Western Railroad.

"The problem with rain is, I'm in sales, not management," Wayland said.

That too got a laugh, though he still had to go through his explanation for refusing to hold the Special Prayer Day for Rain. He had given his reasons so many times he felt he was becoming practiced, smooth, like a sermon repeated until it possessed momentum of its own.

"It's God's world to do with what He will, and it falls to us to glorify His use of it," Wayland said.

"I thought the world belonged to Satan," Gaston Fervier said. Gaston was a tobacco planter and even now tightened his lip over a dip of snuff, though he was washed and handsome with his white hair, pale blue Palm Beach suit, and polished black shoes. If there was elder trouble, it usually came from Gaston, not because he intended to start it or was mischievous, but because Gaston had his own peculiar manner of seeing everything, including Scriptures.

"God created the world good," Wayland said. "When man sinned through pride, the world was wounded and broken, just as man himself, Adam, was wounded and broken in his relationship to God. In the end, however, all things are still God's to do with as He wills."

Gaston stared, his long face not hostile but serious, a trader calculating percentages.

"Maybe it's His will to have us meeting here tonight," Gaston said. "Maybe it's part of His plan to make us have a Special Prayer Day for Rain."

"Suppose it's not God's purpose to have rain at this time, for reasons we can't fathom?" Wayland said, seeing before them the endless convolutions of predestination, which Gaston loved. "Then it won't rain no matter how hard we pray. We'll have held the church and ourselves up to ridicule."

They were silent. When one spoke, it was Carson Puckett, a former superintendent of schools, now in his late seventies, bald, wasting; a deliberate, pious man, pious in the best sense of that misused word.

"Are we afraid to put our faith to the test?" Carson asked. "I believe the Lord will give us rain if we ask for it. He'll find a way."

Wayland hadn't expected it from Carson, a person he greatly respected. He knew the depths of Carson's spirituality. Carson was an Old Testament figure, a patriarch who could strike a rock for water, tread unravished among beasts, and stand unsinged in the fiery furnace. For the first time Wayland felt unsure, even shaken.

"And if we fail?" Wayland asked Carson.

"Then it's us, not God, who've failed," Carson said. "I think it ought to be tried. Pastor, I wish you'd at least consider it."

"I'll of course do that," Wayland said.

Walking home, he felt light-headed. Mims sat fanning herself on the screened porch. In the refrigerator was a glass of iced tea she had fixed for him.

"Maybe I'm wrong," Wayland said. "I could be behaving like one of these slick modern ministers who act as if Scriptures were private property. I've become so professional I've lost sight of the power of simple belief."

Early in the morning he drove to Richmond to see Dr. Hans Koppman, his friend and former teacher, at Union Theological. Dr. Koppman was a brusque and powerful man, one who, unlike many lecturers at the seminary, heaped work on his students because he believed the ministry was life's highest calling and more should be expected of those who aspired to it. He stormed around his classroom asking questions which were snares. He loved parable and paradox.

Dr. Koppman was in his office. From his ponderous head his graying black hair grew into tangled ovals, and hair curled from his porous nose. He whooped, laughed loudly, and repeatedly slapped his desk.

"Oh, brother, I'm glad it's you, not me!" he shouted. "I'd rather be roasted over hot coals. Lord, deliver my heifers from the drought!"

"Somehow it's not funny to me," Wayland said.

"So you've come to a foolish professor in a preacher factory and want him to tell you what to do," Dr. Koppman said. "Listen, the understanding of faith is not in the seminaries. Faith exists in the recesses of that mad place, the heart, and who knows the labyrinthine corridors of the heart?"

As Dr. Koppman discoursed, Wayland gazed out the mullioned window at tennis players, at the nets and lines on the green courts, at the patterns of white and green, the perfect little world of games. He longed for the certainty of rules.

"I'm reminded of the story about a holy young man who doubted the strength of his belief," Dr. Koppman said. "The young man thought that if he were really strong in the faith, he could walk on water. He traveled to the land's edge. Trembling, he set foot on the stormy depths. Lo, the waters held him! Joy welled in him as he walked over the thrashing waters like a tottering child, glorious, mind-blowing joy. He was fired by the ecstasy of knowing he was favored by God."

"Is that all the story?" Wayland asked.

"Not quite," Dr. Koppman said, his thick brows wagging. "In running for joy, he crossed a highway without due care, heard the blast of an air horn, looked up, and saw a bread truck which rolled over and killed him. His last vision was one of loaves."

Dr. Koppman laughed and laughed. Wayland drove home more muddled than ever. He sat in his study and stared at the yellowing mimosa and his desiccated rock garden. He slipped to his knees, rested his elbows on the swivel chair, and raised his face.

"Father, open me to Thy will so that what I do may be for Thy glory," he prayed.

Again he gave up his evening shower. After dinner he was unable to stop himself from studying the weather map in the Danville *Bee*. There was no mention of rain in the entire nation.

He returned to his study to work on the baptism sermon. The words wouldn't flow. He watched twilight settle like gauze over the dusty yard. He became fearful. Suppose his indecision indicated some mortal chink in his theological armor?

Scratching at his hot skin, he roamed the manse. In the kitchen Mims was pinching her rings from the windowsill where she always set them while washing dishes.

"I feel everybody in the country's taking a bite out of me," Wayland said.

"On suffocating days like these, people aren't themselves," she said.

"Who are they?" he asked. He saw she was tired — more than tired, worn.

"We can't expect them to be more than human," she said. Wilted, sweaty, carrying his worries as well as her own, she touched her forehead with the limp back of a hand. It was a beautiful gesture: patient, feminine, long-suffering. And then she served him up a smile to encourage him.

He was so moved he could only nod. Oh, he loved her! And her words, such simple, ordinary words, but there it was, the whole truth of prayer really, stripped of theology and man's encrustments. To plead when troubled, to go to one's father, was human. God knew our needs, sure, but He wouldn't expect anyone, not even a minister, to be more than human — just as no father would expect a son or daughter to be other than a child.

For an instant Wayland was tormented that he hadn't seen the truth, yet grateful that he saw it now.

"Would you consider your husband a weak, spineless creature if he reversed himself and decided to hold a rain service?" Wayland asked.

"Oh, I'd be so glad!" she said.

"You would?" he asked. He had believed she wholly supported his ideas on prayer.

"My husband, the good shepherd, wants to feed his flock," she said.

So Saturday he worked late writing and mimeographing a service for the Special Prayer Day, and on Sunday morning the church was full even to the balconies. Wayland had composed a responsive liturgy in order that the congregation might have a role. He spoke his part over the reverent, upturned faces.

"As Your children we come to ask of You," he intoned.

"Lord, bring us rain," the congregation responded.

After the service Wayland's fingers became sore from shaking hands. Men patted his shoulder. The ladies were gracious, and he and Mims received seven invitations to dinner. Only Gaston Fervier annoyed him.

"I see you didn't bring your umbrella," Gaston said. Gaston had his.

At the manse Mims fixed Wayland a sandwich. She was happy about the service, but he felt emptied. He lay down for a nap.

He would not anticipate. Rain wasn't necessary. He and the congregation had acknowledged God's fathership, which was the main thing.

He turned his back to the window so he wouldn't be tempted to judge the quality of the afternoon sunlight edging the drawn shade.

Yet he felt a stillness, the absolute hush of the day. Even the locusts were silent. A distant rumble had to be a truck. He stood, went downstairs, and walked out onto the screened porch where Mims sat. She wore her lavender church dress in case of visitors, but had pushed off her white pumps so that her heels were free.

The expression on her clean face was strange as she gazed upward. He looked at the sky and, tingling, saw the dazzling cloud growing, building rapidly into a thunderhead, the underside purplish, the crown of radiant whiteness seething as it mounted into a cathedral of a cloud. People came from their houses to stare. Then Wayland felt a coolness, a nudge of air, and knew rain must be close.

In wonder Mims watched the sky. Wayland's amazement gave way to rapture as the majestic thunderhead conquered the heavens. He realized his mouth had opened as if to catch the rain on his lips. The pressure of gratitude brought him near to weeping.

During the slashing, luminous rain, he put on his shorts to walk in the yard. With his face uplifted, he gave thanks. Children, despite lightning, ran in the streets and across glossy lawns. Adults too splashed through puddles. The artificial pond in his rock garden overflowed. The telephone rang so often that Mims, now wearing her pink bathing suit, took it off the hook.

Only later, during the wet night when he and Mims lay together, did he think of the holy young man who had walked on water. The story had to be just another of Dr. Koppman's pranks, but the truth is that for days Wayland not only looked in both directions with extreme care before crossing streets, even the least traveled ones, but also peered at ceilings, floors, the ground, tree limbs, and into shadows, as if something waited for him.

James Joyce

....

Grace

TWO GENTLEMEN who were in the lavatory at the time tried to lift him up: but he was quite helpless. He lay curled up at the foot of the stairs down which he had fallen. They succeeded in turning him over. His hat had rolled a few yards away and his clothes were smeared with the filth and ooze of the floor on which he had lain, face downwards. His eyes were closed and he breathed with a grunting noise. A thin stream of blood trickled from the corner of his mouth.

These two gentlemen and one of the curates carried him up the stairs and laid him down again on the floor of the bar. In two minutes he was surrounded by a ring of men. The manager of the bar asked everyone who he was and who was with him. No one knew who he was, but one of the curates said he had served the gentleman with a small rum.

"Was he by himself?" asked the manager.

"No, sir. There was two gentlemen with him."

"And where are they?"

No one knew; a voice said:

"Give him air. He's fainted."

The ring of onlookers distended and closed again elastically. A dark medal of blood had formed itself near the man's head on the tessellated floor. The manager, alarmed by the gray pallor of the man's face, sent for a policeman.

His collar was unfastened and his necktie undone. He opened his eyes for an instant, sighed and closed them again. One of the gentlemen who had carried him upstairs held a dinged silk hat in his hand. The manager asked repeatedly did no one know who the injured man was or where had his friends gone. The door of the bar opened and an immense constable entered. A crowd which had followed him down the laneway collected outside the door, struggling to look in through the glass panels.

The manager at once began to narrate what he knew. The constable, a young man with thick immobile features, listened. He moved his head slowly to right and left and from the manager to the person on the floor, as if he feared to be the victim of some delusion. Then he drew off his glove, produced a small book from his waist, licked the lead of his pencil and made ready to indite. He asked in a suspicious provincial accent:

"Who is the man? What's his name and address?"

A young man in a cycling-suit cleared his way through the ring of bystanders. He knelt down promptly beside the injured man and called for water. The constable knelt down also to help. The young man washed the blood from the injured man's mouth and then called for some brandy. The constable repeated the order in an authoritative voice until a curate came running with the glass. The brandy was forced down the man's throat. In a few seconds he opened his eyes and looked about him. He looked at the circle of faces and then, understanding, strove to rise to his feet.

"You're all right now?" asked the young man in the cycling-suit.

"Sha, 's nothing," said the injured man, trying to stand up.

He was helped to his feet. The manager said something about a hospital and some of the bystanders gave advice. The battered silk hat was placed on the man's head. The constable asked:

"Where do you live?"

The man, without answering, began to twirl the ends of his moustache. He made light of his accident. It was nothing, he said: only a little accident. He spoke very thickly.

"Where do you live?" repeated the constable.

The man said they were to get a cab for him. While the point was being debated, a tall agile gentleman of fair complexion, wearing a long yellow ulster, came from the far end of the bar. Seeing the spectacle, he called out:

"Hallo, Tom, old man! What's the trouble?"

"Sha, 's nothing," said the man.

The newcomer surveyed the deplorable figure before him and then turned to the constable, saying:

"It's all right, constable. I'll see him home."

The constable touched his helmet and answered:

"All right, Mr. Power!"

"Come now, Tom," said Mr. Power, taking his friend by the arm. "No bones broken. What? Can you walk?"

The young man in the cycling-suit took the man by the other arm and the crowd divided.

"How did you get yourself into this mess?" asked Mr. Power.

"The gentleman fell down the stairs," said the young man.

"I' 'ery 'uch o'liged to you, sir," said the injured man.

"Not at all."

"'an't we have a little . . .?"

"Not now. Not now."

The three men left the bar and the crowd sifted through the doors into the laneway. The manager brought the constable to the stairs to inspect the scene of the accident. They agreed that the gentleman must have missed his footing. The customers returned to the counter, and a curate set about removing the traces of blood from the floor.

When they came out into Grafton Street, Mr. Power whistled for an outsider. The injured man said again as well as he could:

"I' 'ery 'uch o'liged to you, sir. I hope we'll 'eet again. 'y na'e is Kernan."

The shock and the incipient pain had partly sobered him.

"Don't mention it," said the young man.

They shook hands. Mr. Kernan was hoisted on to the car and, while Mr. Power was giving directions to the carman, he expressed his gratitude to the young man and regretted that they could not have a little drink together.

"Another time," said the young man.

The car drove off towards Westmoreland Street. As it passed the Ballast Office the clock showed half-past nine. A keen east wind hit them, blowing from the mouth of the river. Mr. Kernan was huddled together with cold. His friend asked him to tell how the accident had happened.

"I 'an't 'an," he said, "'y 'ongue is hurt."

"Show."

The other leaned over the wheel of the car and peered into Mr. Kernan's mouth but he could not see. He struck a match and, sheltering it in the shell of his hands, peered again into the mouth which Mr.

Kernan opened obediently. The swaying movement of the car brought the match to and from the opened mouth. The lower teeth and gums were covered with clotted blood and a minute piece of the tongue seemed to have been bitten off. The match was blown out.

"That's ugly," said Mr. Power.

"Sha, 's nothing," said Mr. Kernan, closing his mouth and pulling the collar of his filthy coat across his neck.

Mr. Kernan was a commercial traveller of the old school which believed in the dignity of its calling. He had never been seen in the city without a silk hat of some decency and a pair of gaiters. By grace of these two articles of clothing, he said, a man could always pass muster. He carried on the tradition of his Napoleon, the great Blackwhite, whose memory he evoked at times by legend and mimicry. Modern business methods had spared him only so far as to allow him a little office in Crowe Street, on the window blind of which was written the name of his firm with the address — London, E.C. On the mantelpiece of this little office a little leaden battalion of canisters was drawn up and on the table before the window stood four or five china bowls which were usually half full of a black liquid. From these bowls Mr. Kernan tasted tea. He took a mouthful, drew it up, saturated his palate with it and then spat it forth into the grate. Then he paused to judge.

Mr. Power, a much younger man, was employed in the Royal Irish Constabulary Office in Dublin Castle. The arc of his social rise intersected the arc of his friend's decline, but Mr. Kernan's decline was mitigated by the fact that certain of those friends who had known him at his highest point of success still esteemed him as a character. Mr. Power was one of these friends. His inexplicable debts were a byword in his circle; he was a debonair young man.

The car halted before a small house on the Glasnevin road and Mr. Kernan was helped into the house. His wife put him to bed, while Mr. Power sat downstairs in the kitchen asking the children where they went to school and what book they were in. The children — two girls and a boy, conscious of their father's helplessness and of their mother's absence, began some horseplay with him. He was surprised at their manners and at their accents, and his brow grew thoughtful. After a while Mrs. Kernan entered the kitchen, exclaiming:

"Such a sight! Oh, he'll do for himself one day and that's the holy alls of it. He's been drinking since Friday."

Mr. Power was careful to explain to her that he was not responsible, that he had come on the scene by the merest accident. Mrs. Kernan, remembering Mr. Power's good offices during domestic quarrels, as well as many small, but opportune loans, said:

"O, you needn't tell me that, Mr. Power. I know you're a friend of his, not like some of the others he does be with. They're all right so long as he has money in his pocket to keep him out from his wife and family. Nice friends! Who was he with tonight, I'd like to know?"

Mr. Power shook his head but said nothing.

"I'm so sorry," she continued, "that I've nothing in the house to offer you. But if you wait a minute, I'll send round to Fogarty's, at the corner."

Mr. Power stood up.

"We were waiting for him to come home with the money. He never seems to think he has a home at all."

"O, now, Mrs. Kernan," said Mr. Power, "we'll make him turn over a new leaf. I'll talk to Martin. He's the man. We'll come here one of these nights and talk it over."

She saw him to the door. The carman was stamping up and down the footpath, and swinging his arms to warm himself.

"It's very kind of you to bring him home," she said.

"Not at all," said Mr. Power.

He got up on the car. As it drove off he raised his hat to her gaily.

"We'll make a new man of him," he said. "Good-night, Mrs. Kernan."

Mrs. Kernan's puzzled eyes watched the car till it was out of sight. Then she withdrew them, went into the house and emptied her husband's pockets.

She was an active, practical woman of middle age. Not long before she had celebrated her silver wedding and renewed her intimacy with her husband by waltzing with him to Mr. Power's accompaniment. In her days of courtship, Mr. Kernan had seemed to her a not ungallant figure: and she still hurried to the chapel door whenever a wedding was reported and, seeing the bridal pair, recalled with vivid pleasure how she had passed out of the Star of the Sea Church in Sandymount, leaning on the arm of a jovial well-fed man, who was dressed smartly in a frock-coat and lavender trousers and carried a silk hat gracefully balanced upon his other arm. After three weeks she had found a wife's life irksome and, later on, when she was beginning to find it unbearable, she had become a mother. The part of mother presented to her no insuperable difficulties and for twenty-five years she had kept house shrewdly for her husband. Her two eldest sons were launched. One was in a draper's shop in Glasgow and the other was clerk to a tea-merchant in Belfast. They were good sons, wrote regularly and sometimes sent home money. The other children were still at school.

Mr. Kernan sent a letter to his office next day and remained in bed. She made beef-tea for him and scolded him roundly. She accepted his frequent intemperance as part of the climate, healed him dutifully whenever he was sick and always tried to make him eat a breakfast. There were worse husbands. He had never been violent since the boys had grown up, and she knew that he would walk to the end of Thomas Street and back again to book even a small order.

Two nights after, his friends came to see him. She brought them up to his bedroom, the air of which was impregnated with a personal odor, and gave them chairs at the fire. Mr. Kernan's tongue, the occasional stinging pain of which had made him somewhat irritable during the day, became more polite. He sat propped up in the bed by pillows and the little color in his puffy cheeks made them resemble warm cinders. He apologized to his guests for the disorder of the room, but at the same time looked at them a little proudly, with a veteran's pride.

He was quite unconscious that he was the victim of a plot which his friends, Mr. Cunningham, Mr. M'Coy and Mr. Power had disclosed to Mrs. Kernan in the parlor. The idea had been Mr. Power's, but its development was entrusted to Mr. Cunningham. Mr. Kernan came of Protestant stock and, though he had been converted to the Catholic faith at the time of his marriage, he had not been in the pale of the Church for twenty years. He was fond, moreover, of giving side-thrusts at Catholicism.

Mr. Cunningham was the very man for such a case. He was an elder colleague of Mr. Power. His own domestic life was not very happy. People had great sympathy with him, for it was known that he had married an unpresentable woman who was an incurable drunkard. He had set up house for her six times; and each time she had pawned the furniture on him.

Everyone had respect for poor Martin Cunningham. He was a thoroughly sensible man, influential and intelligent. His blade of human knowledge, natural astuteness particularized by long association with cases in the police courts, had been tempered by brief immersions in the waters of general philosophy. He was well informed. His friends bowed to his opinions and considered that his face was like Shakespeare's.

When the plot had been disclosed to her, Mrs. Kernan had said: "I leave it all in your hands, Mr. Cunningham."

After a quarter of a century of married life, she had very few illusions left. Religion for her was a habit, and she suspected that a man of her husband's age would not change greatly before death. She was tempted to see a curious appropriateness in his accident and, but that she did not wish to seem bloody-minded, she would have told the gentlemen that Mr. Kernan's tongue would not suffer by being shortened. However, Mr. Cunningham was a capable man; and religion was religion. The scheme might do good and, at least, it could do no harm. Her beliefs were not extravagant. She believed steadily in the Sacred Heart as the most generally useful of all Catholic devotions and approved of the sacraments. Her faith was bounded by her kitchen, but, if she was put to it, she could believe also in the banshee and in the Holy Ghost.

The gentlemen began to talk of the accident. Mr. Cunningham said that he had once known a similar case. A man of seventy had bitten off a piece of his tongue during an epileptic fit and the tongue had filled in again, so that no one could see a trace of the bite.

"Well, I'm not seventy," said the invalid.

"God forbid," said Mr. Cunningham.

"It doesn't pain you now?" asked Mr. M'Coy.

Mr. M'Coy had been at one time a tenor of some reputation. His wife, who had been a soprano, still taught young children to play the piano at low terms. His line of life had not been the shortest distance between two points and for short periods he had been driven to live by his wits. He had been a clerk in the Midland Railway, a canvasser for advertisements for *The Irish Times* and for *The Freeman's Journal*, a town traveller for a coal firm on commission, a private inquiry agent, a clerk in the office of the Sub-Sheriff, and he had recently become secretary to the City Coroner. His new office made him professionally interested in Mr. Kernan's case.

"Pain? Not much," answered Mr. Kernan. "But it's so sickening. I feel as if I wanted to retch off."

"That's the booze," said Mr. Cunningham firmly.

"No," said Mr. Kernan. "I think I caught cold on the car. There's something keeps coming into my throat, phlegm or — "

"Mucus," said Mr. M'Coy.

"It keeps coming like from down in my throat; sickening thing."

"Yes, yes," said Mr. M'Coy, "that's the thorax."

He looked at Mr. Cunningham and Mr. Power at the same time with an air of challenge. Mr. Cunningham nodded his head rapidly and Mr. Power said:

"Ah, well, all's well that ends well."

"I'm very much obliged to you, old man," said the invalid.

Mr. Power waved his hand.

"Those other two fellows I was with — "

"Who were you with?" asked Mr. Cunningham.

"A chap. I don't know his name. Damn it now, what's his name? Little chap with sandy hair. . . ."

"And who else?"

"Harford."

"Hm," said Mr. Cunningham.

When Mr. Cunningham made that remark, people were silent. It was known that the speaker had secret sources of information. In this case the monosyllable had a moral intention. Mr. Harford sometimes formed one of a little detachment which left the city shortly after noon on Sunday with the purpose of arriving as soon as possible at some public house on the outskirts of the city where its members duly qualified themselves as bona fide travellers. But his fellow-travellers had never consented to overlook his origin. He had begun life as an obscure financier by lending small sums of money to workmen at usurious interest. Later on he had become the partner of a very fat, short gentleman, Mr. Goldberg, in the Liffey Loan Bank. Though he had never embraced more than the Jewish ethical code, his fellow-Catholics, whenever they had smarted in person or by proxy under his exactions, spoke of him bitterly as an Irish Jew and an illiterate, and saw divine disapproval of usury made manifest through the person of his idiot son. At other times they remembered his good points.

"I wonder where did he go to," said Mr. Kernan.

He wished the details of the incident to remain vague. He wished his friends to think there had been some mistake, that Mr. Harford and he had missed each other. His friends, who knew quite well Mr. Harford's manners in drinking, were silent. Mr. Power said again:

"All's well that ends well."

Mr. Kernan changed the subject at once.

"That was a decent young chap, that medical fellow," he said. "Only for him — "

"O, only for him," said Mr. Power, "it might have been a case of seven days, without the option of a fine."

"Yes, yes," said Mr. Kernan, trying to remember. "I remember now there was a policeman. Decent young fellow, he seemed. How did it happen at all?"

"It happened that you were peloothered, Tom," said Mr. Cunningham gravely.

"True bill," said Mr. Kernan, equally gravely.

"I suppose you squared the constable, Jack," said Mr. M'Coy.

Mr. Power did not relish the use of his Christian name. He was not straight-laced, but he could not forget that Mr. M'Coy had recently made a crusade in search of valises and portmanteaus to enable Mrs. M'Coy to fulfil imaginary engagements in the country. More than he resented the fact that he had been victimized, he resented such low playing of the game. He answered the question, therefore, as if Mr. Kernan had asked it.

The narrative made Mr. Kernan indignant. He was keenly conscious of his citizenship, wished to live with his city on terms mutually honorable and resented any affront put upon him by those whom he called country bumpkins.

"Is this what we pay rates for?" he asked. "To feed and clothe these ignorant bostooms . . . and they're nothing else."

Mr. Cunningham laughed. He was a Castle official only during office hours.

"How could they be anything else, Tom?" he said.

He assumed a thick, provincial accent and said in a tone of command:

"65, catch your cabbage!"

Everyone laughed. Mr. M'Coy, who wanted to enter the conversation by any door, pretended that he had never heard the story. Mr. Cunningham said:

"It is supposed — they say, you know — to take place in the depot where they get these thundering big country fellows, omadhauns, you know, to drill. The sergeant makes them stand in a row against the wall and hold up their plates." He illustrated the story by grotesque gestures.

"At dinner, you know. Then he has a bloody big bowl of cabbage before him on the table and a bloody big spoon like a shovel. He takes up a wad of cabbage on the spoon and pegs it across the room and the poor devils have to try and catch it on their plates: *65, catch your cabbage.*"

Everyone laughed again: but Mr. Kernan was somewhat indignant still. He talked of writing a letter to the papers.

"These yahoos coming up here," he said, "think they can boss the people. I needn't tell you, Martin, what kind of men they are."

Mr. Cunningham gave a qualified assent.

"It's like everything else in this world," he said. "You get some bad ones and you get some good ones."

"O yes, you get some good ones, I admit," said Mr. Kernan, satisfied.

"It's better to have nothing to say to them," said Mr. M'Coy. "That's my opinion!"

Mrs. Kernan entered the room and, placing a tray on the table, said: "Help yourselves, gentlemen."

Mr. Power stood up to officiate, offering her his chair. She declined it, saying she was ironing downstairs, and, after having exchanged a nod with Mr. Cunningham behind Mr. Power's back, prepared to leave the room. Her husband called out to her:

"And you have nothing for me, duckie?"

"O, you! The back of my hand to you!" said Mrs. Kernan tartly.

Her husband called after her:

"Nothing for poor little hubby!"

He assumed such a comical face and voice that the distribution of the bottles of stout took place amid general merriment.

The gentlemen drank from their glasses, set the glasses again on the table and paused. Then Mr. Cunningham turned towards Mr. Power and said casually:

"On Thursday night, you said, Jack?"

"Thursday, yes," said Mr. Power.

"Righto!" said Mr. Cunningham promptly.

"We can meet in M'Auley's," said Mr. M'Coy. "That'll be the most convenient place."

"But we mustn't be late," said Mr. Power earnestly, "because it is sure to be crammed to the doors."

"We can meet at half-seven," said Mr. M'Coy.

"Righto!" said Mr. Cunningham.

"Half-seven at M'Auley's be it!"

There was a short silence. Mr. Kernan waited to see whether he would be taken into his friends' confidence. Then he asked:

"What's in the wind?"

"O, it's nothing," said Mr. Cunningham. "It's only a little matter that we're arranging about for Thursday."

"The opera, is it?" said Mr. Kernan.

"No, no," said Mr. Cunningham in an evasive tone, "it's just a little . . . spiritual matter."

"Oh," said Mr. Kernan.

There was silence again. Then Mr. Power said, point-blank:

"To tell you the truth, Tom, we're going to make a retreat."

"Yes, that's it," said Mr. Cunningham, "Jack and I and M'Coy here — we're all going to wash the pot."

He uttered the metaphor with a certain homely energy and, encouraged by his own voice, proceeded:

"You see, we may as well all admit we're a nice collection of scoundrels, one and all. I say, one and all," he added with gruff charity and turning to Mr. Power. "Own up now!"

"I own up," said Mr. Power.

"And I own up," said Mr. M'Coy.

"So we're going to wash the pot together," said Mr. Cunningham.

A thought seemed to strike him. He turned suddenly to the invalid and said:

"D'ye know what, Tom, has just occurred to me? You might join in and we'd have a four-handed reel."

"Good idea," said Mr. Power. "The four of us together."

Mr. Kernan was silent. The proposal conveyed very little meaning to his mind, but, understanding that some spiritual agencies were about to concern themselves on his behalf, he thought he owed it to his dignity to show a stiff neck. He took no part in the conversation for a long while, but listened, with an air of calm enmity, while his friends discussed the Jesuits.

"I haven't such a bad opinion of the Jesuits," he said, intervening at length. "They're an educated order. I believe they mean well, too."

"They're the grandest order in the Church, Tom," said Mr. Cunningham, with enthusiasm. "The General of the Jesuits stands next to the Pope."

"There's no mistake about it," said Mr. M'Coy, "if you want a thing well done and no flies about, you go to a Jesuit. They're the boyos have influence. I'll tell you a case in point . . ."

"The Jesuits are a fine body of men," said Mr. Power.

"It's a curious thing," said Mr. Cunningham, "about the Jesuit Order. Every other order of the Church had to be reformed at some time or other, but the Jesuit Order was never once reformed. It never fell away."

"Is that so?" asked Mr. M'Coy.

"That's a fact," said Mr. Cunningham. "That's history."

"Look at their church, too," said Mr. Power. "Look at the congregation they have."

"The Jesuits cater for the upper classes," said Mr. M'Coy.

"Of course," said Mr. Power.

"Yes," said Mr. Kernan. "That's why I have a feeling for them. It's some of those secular priests, ignorant, bumptious — "

"They're all good men," said Mr. Cunningham, "each in his own way. The Irish priesthood is honored all the world over."

"O yes," said Mr. Power.

"Not like some of the other priesthoods on the continent," said Mr. M'Coy, "unworthy of the name."

"Perhaps you're right," said Mr. Kernan, relenting.

"Of course I'm right," said Mr. Cunningham. "I haven't been in the world all this time and seen most sides of it without being a judge of character."

The gentlemen drank again, one following another's example. Mr. Kernan seemed to be weighing something in his mind. He was impressed. He had a high opinion of Mr. Cunningham as a judge of character and as a reader of faces. He asked for particulars.

"O, it's just a retreat, you know," said Mr. Cunningham. "Father Purdon is giving it. It's for businessmen, you know."

"He won't be too hard on us, Tom," said Mr. Power persuasively.

"Father Purdon? Father Purdon?" said the invalid.

"O, you must know him, Tom," said Mr. Cunningham, stoutly. "Fine, jolly fellow! He's a man of the world like ourselves."

"Ah, . . . yes. I think I know him. Rather red face; tall."

"That's the man."

"And tell me, Martin . . . Is he a good preacher?"

"Munno . . . It's not exactly a sermon, you know. It's just a kind of friendly talk, you know, in a commonsense way."

Mr. Kernan deliberated. Mr. M'Coy said:

"Father Tom Burke, that was the boy!"

"O, Father Tom Burke," said Mr. Cunningham, "that was a born orator. Did you ever hear him, Tom?"

"Did I ever hear him!" said the invalid, nettled. "Rather! I heard him . . ."

"And yet they say he wasn't much of a theologian," said Mr. Cunningham.

"Is that so?" said Mr. M'Coy.

"O, of course, nothing wrong, you know. Only sometimes, they say, he didn't preach what was quite orthodox."

"Ah! . . . he was a splendid man," said Mr. M'Coy.

"I heard him once," Mr. Kernan continued. "I forget the subject of his discourse now. Crofton and I were in the back of the . . . pit, you know . . . the — "

"The body," said Mr. Cunningham.

"Yes, in the back near the door. I forget now what . . . O yes, it was on the Pope, the late Pope. I remember it well. Upon my word it was magnificent, the style of the oratory. And his voice! God! hadn't he a voice! *The Prisoner of the Vatican,* he called him. I remember Crofton saying to me when we came out — "

"But he's an Orangeman, Crofton, isn't he?" said Mr. Power.

"'Course he is," said Mr. Kernan, "and a damned decent Orangeman, too. We went into Butler's in Moore Street — faith, I was genuinely moved, tell you the God's truth — and I remember well his very words. *Kernan,* he said, *we worship at different altars,* he said, *but our belief is the same.* Struck me as very well put."

"There's a good deal in that," said Mr. Power. "There used always be crowds of Protestants in the chapel where Father Tom was preaching."

"There's not much difference between us," said Mr. M'Coy. "We both believe in — "

He hesitated for a moment.

". . . in the Redeemer. Only they don't believe in the Pope and in the mother of God."

"But, of course," said Mr. Cunningham quietly and effectively, "our religion is *the* religion, the old, original faith."

"Not a doubt of it," said Mr. Kernan warmly.

Mrs. Kernan came to the door of the bedroom and announced:

"Here's a visitor for you!"

"Who is it?"

"Mr. Fogarty."

"O, come in! come in!"

A pale, oval face came forward into the light. The arch of its fair trailing moustache was repeated in the fair eyebrows looped above pleasantly astonished eyes. Mr. Fogarty was a modest grocer. He had failed in business in a licensed house in the city because his financial condition had constrained him to tie himself to second-class distillers and brewers. He had opened a small shop on Glasnevin Road where, he flattered himself, his manners would ingratiate him with the house-wives of the district. He bore himself with a certain grace, compli-mented little children and spoke with a neat enunciation. He was not without culture.

Mr. Fogarty brought a gift with him, a half-pint of special whisky. He inquired politely for Mr. Kernan, placed his gift on the table and sat down with the company on equal terms. Mr. Kernan appreciated the gift all the more since he was aware that there was a small account for groceries unsettled between him and Mr. Fogarty. He said:

"I wouldn't doubt you, old man. Open that, Jack, will you?"

Mr. Power again officiated. Glasses were rinsed and five small meas-ures of whisky were poured out. This new influence enlivened the con-versation. Mr. Fogarty, sitting on a small area of the chair, was spe-cially interested.

"Pope Leo XIII," said Mr. Cunningham, "was one of the lights of the age. His great idea, you know, was the union of the Latin and Greek Churches. That was the aim of his life."

"I often heard he was one of the most intellectual men in Europe," said Mr. Power. "I mean, apart from his being Pope."

"So he was," said Mr. Cunningham, "if not *the* most so. His motto, you know, as Pope, was *Lux upon Lux* — *Light upon Light*."

"No, no," said Mr. Fogarty eagerly. "I think you're wrong there. It was *Lux in Tenebris*, I think — *Light in Darkness*."

"O yes," said Mr. M'Coy, "*Tenebrae.*"

"Allow me," said Mr. Cunningham positively, "it was *Lux upon Lux*. And Pius IX his predecessor's motto was *Crux upon Crux* — that is, *Cross upon Cross* — to show the difference between their two pontifi-cates."

The inference was allowed. Mr. Cunningham continued.

"Pope Leo, you know, was a great scholar and poet."

"He had a strong face," said Mr. Kernan.

"Yes," said Mr. Cunningham. "He wrote Latin poetry."

"Is that so?" said Mr. Fogarty.

Mr. M'Coy tasted his whisky contentedly and shook his head with a double intention, saying:

"That's no joke, I can tell you."

"We didn't learn that, Tom," said Mr. Power, following Mr. M'Coy's example, "when we went to the penny-a-week school."

"There was many a good man went to the penny-a-week school with a sod of turf under his oxter," said Mr. Kernan sententiously. "The old system was the best: plain honest education. None of your modern trumpery. . . ."

"Quite right," said Mr. Power.

"No superfluities," said Mr. Fogarty.

He enunciated the word and then drank gravely.

"I remember reading," said Mr. Cunningham, "that one of Pope Leo's poems was on the invention of the photograph — in Latin, of course."

"On the photograph!" exclaimed Mr. Kernan.

"Yes," said Mr. Cunningham.

He also drank from his glass.

"Well, you know," said Mr. M'Coy, "isn't the photograph wonderful when you come to think of it?"

"O, of course," said Mr. Power, "great minds can see things."

"As the poet says: *Great minds are very near to madness,*" said Mr. Fogarty.

Mr. Kernan seemed to be troubled in mind. He made an effort to recall the Protestant theology on some thorny points and in the end addressed Mr. Cunningham.

"Tell me, Martin," he said. "Weren't some of the popes — of course, not our present man, or his predecessor, but some of the old popes — not exactly . . . you know . . . up to the knocker?"

There was a silence. Mr. Cunningham said:

"O, of course, there were some bad lots . . . But the astonishing thing is this. Not one of them, not the biggest drunkard, not the most . . . out-and-out ruffian, not one of them ever preached *ex cathedra* a word of false doctrine. Now isn't that an astonishing thing?"

"That is," said Mr. Kernan.

"Yes, because when the Pope speaks *ex cathedra,*" Mr. Fogarty explained, "he is infallible."

"Yes," said Mr. Cunningham.

"O, I know about the infallibility of the Pope. I remember I was younger then . . . Or was it that — ?"

Mr. Fogarty interrupted. He took up the bottle and helped the others to a little more. Mr. M'Coy, seeing that there was not enough to go round, pleaded that he had not finished his first measure. The others accepted under protest. The light music of whisky falling into glasses made an agreeable interlude.

"What's that you were saying, Tom?" asked Mr. M'Coy.

"Papal infallibility," said Mr. Cunningham, "that was the greatest scene in the whole history of the Church."

"How was that, Martin?" asked Mr. Power.

Mr. Cunningham held up two thick fingers.

"In the sacred college, you know, of cardinals and archbishops and bishops there were two men who held out against it while the others were all for it. The whole conclave except these two was unanimous. No! They wouldn't have it!"

"Ha!" said Mr. M'Coy.

"And they were a German cardinal by the name of Dolling . . . or Dowling . . . or — "

"Dowling was no German, and that's a sure five," said Mr. Power, laughing.

"Well, this great German cardinal, whatever his name was, was one; and the other was John MacHale."

"What?" cried Mr. Kernan. "Is it John of Tuam?"

"Are you sure of that now?" asked Mr. Fogarty dubiously. "I thought it was some Italian or American."

"John of Tuam," repeated Mr. Cunningham, "was the man."

He drank and the other gentlemen followed his lead. Then he resumed: "There they were at it, all the cardinals and bishops and archbishops from all the ends of the earth and these two fighting dog and devil until at last the Pope himself stood up and declared infallibility a dogma of the Church *ex cathedra*. On the very moment John MacHale, who had been arguing and arguing against it, stood up and shouted out with the voice of a lion: '*Credo!*'"

"*I believe!*" said Mr. Fogarty.

"*Credo!*" said Mr. Cunningham. "That showed the faith he had. He submitted the moment the Pope spoke."

"And what about Dowling?" asked Mr. M'Coy.

"The German cardinal wouldn't submit. He left the Church."

Mr. Cunningham's words had built up the vast image of the Church in the minds of his hearers. His deep, raucous voice had thrilled them as it uttered the word of belief and submission. When Mrs. Kernan came into the room, drying her hands, she came into a solemn company. She did not disturb the silence, but leaned over the rail at the foot of the bed.

"I once saw John MacHale," said Mr. Kernan, "and I'll never forget it as long as I live."

He turned towards his wife to be confirmed.

"I often told you that?"

Mrs. Kernan nodded.

"It was at the unveiling of Sir John Gray's statue. Edmund Dwyer Gray was speaking, blathering away, and here was this old fellow, crabbed-looking old chap, looking at him from under his bushy eyebrows."

Mr. Kernan knitted his brows and, lowering his head like an angry bull, glared at his wife.

"God!" he exclaimed, resuming his natural face, "I never saw such an eye in a man's head. It was as much as to say: *I have you properly taped, my lad.* He had an eye like a hawk."

"None of the Grays was any good," said Mr. Power.

There was a pause again. Mr. Power turned to Mrs. Kernan and said with abrupt joviality:

"Well, Mrs. Kernan, we're going to make your man here a good holy pious and God-fearing Roman Catholic."

He swept his arm round the company inclusively.

"We're all going to make a retreat together and confess our sins — and God knows we want it badly."

"I don't mind," said Mr. Kernan, smiling a little nervously.

Mrs. Kernan thought it would be wiser to conceal her satisfaction. So she said:

"I pity the poor priest that has to listen to your tale."

Mr. Kernan's expression changed.

"If he doesn't like it," he said bluntly, "he can . . . do the other thing. I'll just tell him my little tale of woe. I'm not such a bad fellow — "

Mr. Cunningham intervened promptly.

"We'll all renounce the devil," he said, "together, not forgetting his works and pomps."

"Get behind me, Satan!" said Mr. Fogarty, laughing and looking at the others.

Mr. Power said nothing. He felt completely outgeneralled. But a pleased expression flickered across his face.

"All we have to do," said Mr. Cunningham, "is to stand up with lighted candles in our hands and renew our baptismal vows."

"O, don't forget the candle, Tom," said Mr. M'Coy, "whatever you do."

"What?" said Mr. Kernan. "Must I have a candle?"

"O yes," said Mr. Cunningham.

"No, damn it all," said Mr. Kernan sensibly, "I draw the line there. I'll do the job right enough. I'll do the retreat business and confession, and . . . all that business. But . . . no candles! No, damn it all, I bar the candles!"

He shook his head with farcical gravity.

"Listen to that!" said his wife.

"I bar the candles," said Mr. Kernan, conscious of having created an effect on his audience and continuing to shake his head to and fro. "I bar the magic-lantern business."

Everyone laughed heartily.

"There's a nice Catholic for you!" said his wife.

"No candles!" repeated Mr. Kernan obdurately. "That's off!"

The transept of the Jesuit Church in Gardiner Street was almost full; and still at every moment gentlemen entered from the side door and, directed by the lay brother, walked on tiptoe along the aisles until they found seating accommodation. The gentlemen were all well dressed and orderly. The light of the lamps of the church fell upon an assembly of black clothes and white collars, relieved here and there by tweeds, on dark mottled pillars of green marble and on lugubrious canvases. The gentlemen sat in the benches, having hitched their trousers slightly above their knees and laid their hats in security. They sat well back and gazed formally at the distant speck of red light which was suspended before the high altar.

In one of the benches near the pulpit sat Mr. Cunningham and Mr. Kernan. In the bench behind sat Mr. M'Coy alone: and in the bench behind him sat Mr. Power and Mr. Fogarty. Mr. M'Coy had tried unsuccessfully to find a place in the bench with the others, and, when the party had settled down in the form of a quincunx he had tried unsuccessfully to make comic remarks. As these had not been well received, he had desisted. Even he was sensible of the decorous atmosphere and even he began to respond to the religious stimulus. In a whisper, Mr. Cunningham drew Mr. Kernan's attention to Mr. Harford, the moneylender, who sat some distance off, and to Mr. Fanning, the registration agent and mayor maker of the city, who was sitting immediately under the pulpit beside one of the newly elected councillors of the ward. To the right sat old Michael Grimes, the owner of three pawnbroker's shops, and Dan Hogan's nephew, who was up for the job in the Town Clerk's office. Farther in front sat Mr. Hendrick, the chief reporter of *The Freeman's Journal,* and poor O'Carroll, an old friend of Mr. Kernan's, who had been at one time a considerable commercial figure. Gradually, as he recognized familiar faces, Mr. Kernan began to feel more at home. His hat, which had been rehabilitated by his wife, rested upon his knees. Once or twice he pulled down his cuffs with one hand while he held the brim of his hat lightly, but firmly, with the other hand.

A powerful-looking figure, the upper part of which was draped with a white surplice, was observed to be struggling up into the pulpit. Simultaneously the congregation unsettled, produced handkerchiefs and knelt upon them with care. Mr. Kernan followed the general example. The priest's figure now stood upright in the pulpit, two-thirds of its bulk, crowned by a massive red face, appearing above the balustrade.

Father Purdon knelt down, turned towards the red speck of light and, covering his face with his hands, prayed. After an interval, he uncovered his face and rose. The congregation rose also and settled again on its benches. Mr. Kernan restored his hat to its original position on his knee and presented an attentive face to the preacher. The preacher turned back each wide sleeve of his surplice with an elaborate large gesture and slowly surveyed the array of faces. Then he said:

"For the children of this world are wiser in their generation than the children of light. Wherefore make unto yourselves friends out of the mammon of iniquity so that when you die they may receive you into everlasting dwellings."

Father Purdon developed the text with resonant assurance. It was one of the most difficult texts in all the Scriptures, he said, to interpret properly. It was a text which might seem to the casual observer at variance with the lofty morality elsewhere preached by Jesus Christ. But, he told his hearers, the text had seemed to him specially adapted for the guidance of those whose lot it was to lead the life of the world and who yet wished to lead that life not in the manner of worldlings. It was a text for businessmen and professional men. Jesus Christ, with His divine understanding of every cranny of our human nature, understood that all men were not called to the religious life, that by far the vast majority were forced to live in the world, and, to a certain extent, for the world: and in this sentence He designed to give them a word of counsel, setting before them as exemplars in the religious life those very worshippers of Mammon who were of all men the least solicitous in matters religious.

He told his hearers that he was there that evening for no terrifying, no extravagant purpose; but as a man of the world speaking to his fellow-men. He came to speak to businessmen and he would speak to them in a businesslike way. If he might use the metaphor, he said, he was their spiritual accountant; and he wished each and every one of his hearers to open his books, the books of his spiritual life, and see if they tallied accurately with conscience.

Jesus Christ was not a hard taskmaster. He understood our little failings, understood the weakness of our poor fallen nature, understood the temptations of this life. We might have had, we all had from time to time, our temptations: we might have, we all had, our failings. But one thing only, he said, he would ask of his hearers. And that was: to be straight and manly with God. If their accounts tallied in every point to say:

"Well, I have verified my accounts. I find all well."

But if, as might happen, there were some discrepancies, to admit the truth, to be frank and say like a man:

"Well, I have looked into my accounts. I find this wrong and this wrong. But, with God's grace, I will rectify this and this. I will set right my accounts."

Bernard Malamud

....

Idiots First

THE THICK TICKING of the tin clock stopped. Mendel, dozing in the dark, awoke in fright. The pain returned as he listened. He drew on his cold embittered clothing, and wasted minutes sitting at the edge of the bed.

"Isaac," he ultimately sighed.

In the kitchen, Isaac, his astonished mouth open, held six peanuts in his palm. He placed each on the table. "One . . . two . . . nine."

He gathered each peanut and appeared in the doorway. Mendel, in loose hat and long overcoat, still sat on the bed. Isaac watched with small eyes and ears, thick hair graying the sides of his head.

"Schlaf," he nasally said.

"No," muttered Mendel. As if stifling he rose. "Come, Isaac."

He wound his old watch though the sight of the stopped mechanism nauseated him.

Isaac wanted to hold it to his ear.

"No, it's late." Mendel put the watch carefully away. In the drawer he found the little paper bag of crumpled ones and fives and slipped it into his overcoat pocket. He helped Isaac on with his coat.

Isaac looked at one dark window, then at the other. Mendel stared at both blank windows.

They went slowly down the darkly lit stairs, Mendel first, Isaac watching the moving shadows on the wall. To one long shadow he offered a peanut.

"Hungrig."

In the vestibule the old man gazed through the thin glass. The November night was cold and bleak. Opening the door, he cautiously thrust his head out. Though he saw nothing he quickly shut the door.

"Ginzburg, that he came to see me yesterday," he whispered in Isaac's ear.

Isaac sucked air.

"You know who I mean?"

Isaac combed his chin with his fingers.

"That's the one, with the black whiskers. Don't talk to him or go with him if he asks you."

Isaac moaned.

"Young people he don't bother so much," Mendel said in after-thought.

It was suppertime and the street was empty, but the store windows dimly lit their way to the corner. They crossed the deserted street and went on. Isaac, with a happy cry, pointed to the three golden balls. Mendel smiled but was exhausted when they got to the pawnshop.

The pawnbroker, a red-bearded man with black horn-rimmed glasses, was eating a whitefish at the rear of the store. He craned his head, saw them, and settled back to sip his tea.

In five minutes he came forward, patting his shapeless lips with a large white handkerchief.

Mendel, breathing heavily, handed him the worn gold watch. The pawnbroker, raising his glasses, screwed in his eyepiece. He turned the watch over once. "Eight dollars."

The dying man wet his cracked lips. "I must have thirty-five."

"So go to Rothschild."

"Cost me myself sixty."

"In 1905." The pawnbroker handed back the watch. It had stopped ticking. Mendel wound it slowly. It ticked hollowly.

"Isaac must go to my uncle that he lives in California."

"It's a free country," said the pawnbroker.

Isaac, watching a banjo, snickered.

"What's the matter with him?" the pawnbroker asked.

"So let be eight dollars," muttered Mendel, "but where will I get the rest till tonight?"

"How much for my hat and coat?" he asked.

"No sale." The pawnbroker went behind the cage and wrote out a ticket. He locked the watch in a small drawer but Mendel still heard it ticking.

In the street he slipped the eight dollars into the paper bag, then searched in his pockets for a scrap of writing. Finding it, he strained to read the address by the light of the street lamp.

As they trudged to the subway, Mendel pointed to the sprinkled sky. "Isaac, look how many stars are tonight."

"Eggs," said Isaac.

"First we will go to Mr. Fishbein, after we will eat."

They got off the train in upper Manhattan and had to walk several blocks before they located Fishbein's house.

"A regular palace," Mendel murmured, looking forward to a moment's warmth.

Isaac stared uneasily at the heavy door of the house.

Mendel rang. The servant, a man with long sideburns, came to the door and said Mr. and Mrs. Fishbein were dining and could see no one.

"He should eat in peace but we will wait till he finishes."

"Come back tomorrow morning. Tomorrow morning Mr. Fishbein will talk to you. He don't do business or charity at this time of the night."

"Charity I am not interested — "

"Come back tomorrow."

"Tell him it's life or death — "

"Whose life or death?"

"So if not his, then mine."

"Don't be such a big smart aleck."

"Look me in my face," said Mendel, "and tell me if I got time till tomorrow morning?"

The servant stared at him, then at Isaac, and reluctantly let them in.

The foyer was a vast high-ceilinged room with many oil paintings on the walls, voluminous silken draperies, a thick flowered rug on the floor, and a marble staircase.

Mr. Fishbein, a paunchy bald-headed man with hairy nostrils and small patent-leather feet, ran lightly down the stairs, a large napkin tucked under a tuxedo coat button. He stopped on the fifth step from the bottom and examined his visitors.

"Who comes on Friday night to a man that he has guests to spoil him his supper?"

"Excuse me that I bother you, Mr. Fishbein," Mendel said. "If I didn't come now I couldn't come tomorrow."

"Without more preliminaries, please state your business. I'm a hungry man."

"Hungrig," wailed Isaac.

Fishbein adjusted his pince-nez. "What's the matter with him?"

"This is my son Isaac. He is like this all his life."

Isaac mewled.

"I am sending him to California."

"Mr. Fishbein don't contribute to personal pleasure trips."

"I am a sick man and he must go tonight on the train to my Uncle Leo."

"I never give to unorganized charity," Fishbein said, "but if you are hungry I will invite you downstairs in my kitchen. We having tonight chicken with stuffed derma."

"All I ask is thirty-five dollars for the train to my uncle in California. I have already the rest."

"Who is your uncle? How old a man?"

"Eighty-one years, a long life to him."

Fishbein burst into laughter. "Eighty-one years and you are sending him this halfwit."

Mendel, flailing both arms, cried, "Please, without names."

Fishbein politely conceded.

"Where is open the door there we go in the house," the sick man said. "If you will kindly give me thirty-five dollars, God will bless you. What is thirty-five dollars to Mr. Fishbein? Nothing. To me, for my boy, is everything."

Fishbein drew himself up to his tallest height.

"Private contributions I don't make — only to institutions. This is my fixed policy."

Mendel sank to his creaking knees on the rug.

"Please, Mr. Fishbein, if not thirty-five, give maybe twenty."

"Levinson!" Fishbein angrily called.

The servant with the long sideburns appeared at the top of the stairs.

"Show this party where is the door — unless he wishes to partake food before leaving the premises."

"For what I got chicken won't cure it," Mendel said.

"This way if you please," said Levinson, descending.

Isaac assisted his father up.

"Take him to an institution," Fishbein advised over the marble balustrade. He ran quickly up the stairs and they were at once outside, buffeted by winds.

The walk to the subway was tedious. The wind blew mournfully. Mendel, breathless, glanced furtively at shadows. Isaac, clutching his peanuts in his frozen fist, clung to his father's side. They entered a small park to rest for a minute on a stone bench under a leafless two-branched tree. The thick right branch was raised, the thin left one hung down. A very pale moon rose slowly. So did a stranger as they approached the bench.

"Gut yuntif," he said hoarsely.

Mendel, drained of blood, waved his wasted arms. Isaac yowled sickly. Then a bell chimed and it was only ten. Mendel let out a piercing anguished cry as the bearded stranger disappeared into the bushes. A policeman came running and, though he beat the bushes with his nightstick, could turn up nothing. Mendel and Isaac hurried out of the little park. When Mendel glanced back the dead tree had its thin arm raised, the thick one down. He moaned.

They boarded a trolley, stopping at the home of a former friend, but he had died years ago. On the same block they went into a cafeteria and ordered two fried eggs for Isaac. The tables were crowded except where a heavyset man sat eating soup with kasha. After one look at him they left in haste, although Isaac wept.

Mendel had another address on a slip of paper but the house was too far away, in Queens, so they stood in a doorway shivering.

What can I do, he frantically thought, in one short hour?

He remembered the furniture in the house. It was junk but might bring a few dollars. "Come, Isaac." They went once more to the pawnbroker's to talk to him, but the shop was dark and an iron gate — rings and gold watches glinting through it — was drawn tight across his place of business.

They huddled behind a telephone pole, both freezing. Isaac whimpered.

"See the big moon, Isaac. The whole sky is white."

He pointed but Isaac wouldn't look.

Mendel dreamed for a minute of the sky lit up, long sheets of light in all directions. Under the sky, in California, sat Uncle Leo drinking tea with lemon. Mendel felt warm but woke up cold.

Across the street stood an ancient brick synagogue.

He pounded on the huge door but no one appeared. He waited till he had breath and desperately knocked again. At last there were footsteps within, and the synagogue door creaked open on its massive brass hinges.

A darkly dressed sexton, holding a dripping candle, glared at them.

"Who knocks this time of night with so much noise on the synagogue door?"

Mendel told the sexton his troubles. "Please, I would like to speak to the rabbi."

"The rabbi is an old man. He sleeps now. His wife won't let you see him. Go home and come back tomorrow."

"To tomorrow I said goodbye already. I am a dying man."

Though the sexton seemed doubtful he pointed to an old wooden house next door. "In there he lives." He disappeared into the synagogue with his lit candle casting shadows around him.

Mendel, with Isaac clutching his sleeve, went up the wooden steps and rang the bell. After five minutes a big-faced, gray-haired, bulky woman came out on the porch with a torn robe thrown over her nightdress. She emphatically said the rabbi was sleeping and could not be waked.

But as she was insisting, the rabbi himself tottered to the door. He listened a minute and said, "Who wants to see me let them come in."

They entered a cluttered room. The rabbi was an old skinny man with bent shoulders and a wisp of white beard. He wore a flannel nightgown and black skullcap; his feet were bare.

"Vey is mir," his wife muttered. "Put on shoes or tomorrow comes sure pneumonia." She was a woman with a big belly, years younger than her husband. Staring at Isaac, she turned away.

Mendel apologetically related his errand. "All I need is thirty-five dollars."

"Thirty-five?" said the rabbi's wife. "Why not thirty-five thousand? Who has so much money? My husband is a poor rabbi. The doctors take away every penny."

"Dear friend," said the rabbi, "if I had I would give you."

"I got already seventy," Mendel said, heavy-hearted. "All I need more is thirty-five."

"God will give you," said the rabbi.

"In the grave," said Mendel. "I need tonight. Come, Isaac."

"Wait," called the rabbi.

He hurried inside, came out with a fur-lined caftan, and handed it to Mendel.

"Yascha," shrieked his wife, "not your new coat!"

"I got my old one. Who needs two coats for one old body?"

"Yascha, I am screaming — "

"Who can go among poor people, tell me, in a new coat?"

"Yascha," she cried, "what can this man do with your coat? He needs tonight the money. The pawnbrokers are asleep."

"So let him wake them up."

"No." She grabbed the coat from Mendel.

He held onto a sleeve, wrestling her for the coat. Her I know, Mendel thought. "Shylock," he muttered. Her eyes glittered.

The rabbi groaned and tottered dizzily. His wife cried out as Mendel yanked the coat from her hands.

"Run," cried the rabbi.

"Run, Isaac."

They ran out of the house and down the steps.

"Stop, you thief," called the rabbi's wife.

The rabbi pressed both hands to his temples and fell to the floor. "Help!" his wife wept. "Heart attack! Help!"

But Mendel and Isaac ran through the streets with the rabbi's new fur-lined caftan. After them noiselessly ran Ginzburg.

It was very late when Mendel bought the train ticket in the only booth open.

There was no time to stop for a sandwich so Isaac ate his peanuts and they hurried to the train in the vast deserted station.

"So in the morning," Mendel gasped as they ran, "there comes a man that he sells sandwiches and coffee. Eat but get change. When reaches California the train, will be waiting for you on the station Uncle Leo. If you don't recognize him he will recognize you. Tell him I send best regards."

But when they arrived at the gate to the platform it was shut, the light out.

"Too late," said the uniformed ticket collector, a bulky, bearded man with hairy nostrils and a fishy smell.

He pointed to the station clock. "Already past twelve."

"But I see standing there still the train," Mendel said, hopping in his grief.

"It just left — in one more minute."

"A minute is enough. Just open the gate."

"Too late I told you."

Mendel socked his bony chest with both hands. "With my whole heart I beg you this little favor."

"Favors you had enough already. For you the train is gone. You shoulda been dead already at midnight. I told you that yesterday. This is the best I can do."

"Ginzburg!" Mendel shrank from him.

"Who else?" The voice was metallic, eyes glittered, the expression amused.

"For myself," the old man begged, "I don't ask a thing. But what will happen to my boy?"

Ginzburg shrugged slightly. "What will happen happens. This isn't my responsibility. I got enough to think about without worrying about somebody on one cylinder."

"What then is your responsibility?"

"To create conditions. To make happen what happens. I ain't in the anthropomorphic business."

"Whichever business you in, where is your pity?"

"This ain't my commodity. The law is the law."

"Which law is this?"

"The cosmic, universal law, goddamn it, the one I got to follow myself."

"What kind of a law is it?" cried Mendel. "For God's sake, don't you understand what I went through in my life with this poor boy? Look at him. For thirty-nine years, since the day he was born, I wait for him to grow up, but he don't. Do you understand what this means in a father's heart? Why don't you let him go to his uncle?" His voice had risen and he was shouting.

Isaac mewled loudly.

"Better calm down or you'll hurt somebody's feelings," Ginzburg said, with a wink toward Isaac.

"All my life," Mendel cried, his body trembling, "what did I have? I was poor. I suffered from my health. When I worked I worked too hard. When I didn't work was worse. My wife died a young woman. But I didn't ask from anybody nothing. Now I ask a small favor. Be so kind, Mr. Ginzburg."

The ticket collector was picking his teeth with a matchstick.

"You ain't the only one, my friend, some got it worse than you. That's how it goes."

"You dog you." Mendel lunged at Ginzburg's throat and began to choke. "You bastard, don't you understand what it means human?"

They struggled nose to nose. Ginzburg, though his astonished eyes bulged, began to laugh. "You pipsqueak nothing. I'll freeze you to pieces."

His eyes lit in rage, and Mendel felt an unbearable cold like an icy dagger invading his body, all of his parts shriveling.

Now I die without helping Isaac.

A crowd gathered. Isaac yelped in fright.

Clinging to Ginzburg in his last agony, Mendel saw reflected in the ticket collector's eyes the depth of his terror. Ginzburg, staring at himself in Mendel's eyes, saw mirrored in them the extent of his own awful wrath. He beheld a shimmering, starry, blinding light that produced darkness.

Ginzburg looked astounded. "Who, me?"

His grip on the squirming old man loosened, and Mendel, his heart barely beating, slumped to the ground.

"Go," Ginzburg muttered, "take him to the train."

"Let pass," he commanded a guard.

The crowd parted. Isaac helped his father up and they tottered down the steps to the platform where the train waited, lit and ready to go.

Mendel found Isaac a coach seat and hastily embraced him. "Help Uncle Leo, Isaakl. Also remember your father and mother."

"Be nice to him," he said to the conductor. "Show him where everything is."

He waited on the platform until the train began slowly to move. Isaac sat at the edge of his seat, his face strained in the direction of his journey. When the train was gone, Mendel ascended the stairs to see what had become of Ginzburg.

Bobbie Ann Mason

....

The Retreat

GEORGEANN HAS PUT OFF packing for the annual church retreat. "There's plenty of time," she tells Shelby when he bugs her about it. "I can't do things that far ahead."

"Don't you want to go?" he asks her one evening. "You used to love to go."

"I wish they'd do something different, just once. Something besides pray and yack at each other." Georgeann is basting facings on a child's choir robe, and she looks at him testily as she bites off a thread.

Shelby says, "You've been looking peaked lately. I believe you've got low blood."

"There's nothing wrong with me."

"I think you better get a checkup before we go. Call Dr. Armstrong in the morning."

When Georgeann married Shelby Pickett, her mother warned her about the disadvantages of marrying a preacher. Delinquents who suddenly get saved always make the worst kind of preachers, her mother said — just like former drug addicts in their zealousness. Shelby was never that bad, though. In high school, when Georgeann first knew him, he was on probation for stealing four cases of Sundrop cola and a ham from Kroger's. There was something charismatic about him even then, although he frightened her at first with his gloomy countenance — a sort of James Dean brooding — and his tendency to contradict whatever the teachers said. But she admired the way he argued so smoothly and professionally in debate class. He always had a smart answer that left his opponent speechless. He was the type of person who could get away with anything. Georgeann thought he seemed a little dangerous — he was always staring people down, as though he held a deep grudge — but when she started going out with him, at the end of her senior year, she was surprised to discover how serious he was. He had spent a month studying the life of Winston Churchill. It wasn't even a class assignment. No one she knew would have thought of doing that. When the date of the senior prom approached, Shelby said he couldn't take her because he didn't believe in dancing. Georgeann suspected that he was just embarrassed and shy. On a Friday night, when her parents were away at the movies, she put on a Kinks album and tried to get him to loosen up, to get in shape for the prom. It was then that he told her of his ambition to be a preacher. Georgeann was so moved by his sense of atonement and his commitment to the calling — he had received the call while hauling hay for an uncle — that she knew she would marry him. On the night of the prom, they went instead to the Burger King, and he showed her the literature on the seminary while she ate a Double Whopper and french fries.

The ministry is not necessarily a full-time calling, Georgeann discovered. The pay is too low. While Shelby attended seminary, he also went to night school to learn a trade, and Georgeann supported him by working at Kroger's — the same one her husband had robbed. Georgeann had wanted to go to college, but they were never able to afford for her to go.

Now they have two children, Tamara and Jason. During the week, Shelby is an electrician, working out of his van. In ten years of marriage, they have served in three different churches. Shelby dislikes the rotation system and longs for a church he can call his own. He says he wants to grow with a church, so that he knows the people and doesn't have to preach only the funerals of strangers. He wants to perform the marriages of people he knew as children. Shelby lives by many little rules, some of which come out of nowhere. For instance, for years he has rubbed baking soda onto his gums after brushing his teeth, but he cannot remember who taught him to do this, or exactly why. Shelby comes from a broken home, so he wants things to last. But the small country churches in western Kentucky are dying, as people move to town or simply lose interest in the church. The membership at the Grace United Methodist Church is seventy-five, but attendance varies between thirty and seventy. The day it snowed this past winter, only three people came. Shelby was so depressed afterward that he couldn't eat Sunday dinner. He was particularly upset because he had prepared a special sermon aimed at Hoyt Jenkins, who somebody said had begun drinking, but Hoyt did not appear. Shelby had to deliver the sermon anyway, on the evils of alcohol, to old Mr. and Mrs. Elbert Flood and Miss Addie Stone, the president of the WCTU chapter.

"Even the best people need a little reinforcement," Shelby said half-heartedly to Georgeann.

She said, "Why didn't you just save that sermon? You work yourself half to death. With only three people there, you could have just talked to them, like a conversation. You didn't have to waste a big sermon like that."

"The church isn't for just a conversation," said Shelby.

The music was interesting that snowy day. Georgeann plays the piano at church. As she played, she listened to the voices singing — Shelby booming out like Bert Parks; the weak, shaky voices of the Floods; and Miss Stone, with a surprisingly clear and pretty little voice. She sounded like a folk singer. Georgeann wanted to hear more, so she abruptly switched hymns and played "Joy to the World," which she knew the Floods would have trouble with. Miss Stone sang out, high above Shelby's voice. Later, Shelby was annoyed that Georgeann had changed the program because he liked for the church bulletins that she typed and mimeographed each week before the Sunday service to be an accurate record of what went on that day. Georgeann made corrections on the bulletin and filed it in Shelby's study. She penciled in a note, "Three people showed up." She even listed their names. Writing this, Georgeann felt peculiar, as though a gear had shifted inside her.

Even then, back in the winter, Shelby had been looking forward to the retreat, talking about it like a little boy anticipating summer camp.

Georgeann has been feeling disoriented. She can't think about the packing for the retreat. She's not finished with the choir robes for Jason and Tamara, who sing in the youth choir. On the Sunday before the retreat, Georgeann realizes that it is Communion Sunday and she has forgotten to buy grape juice. She has to race into town at the last minute to buy it. It is overpriced at the Kwik-Pik, but that is the only place open on Sunday. Waiting in line, she discovers that she still has hair clips in her hair. As she stands there, she watches two teenage boys in everyday clothes playing an electronic video game. One boy is pressing buttons, his fingers working rapidly and a look of rapture on his face. The other boy is watching and murmuring "Gah!" Georgeann holds her hand out automatically for the change when the salesgirl rings up the grape juice. She stands by the door a few minutes, watching the boys. The machine makes tom-tom sounds, and blips fly across the screen. When she gets to the church, she is so nervous that she sloshes the grape juice while pouring it into the tray of tiny Communion glasses. Two of the glasses are missing because she broke them last month while washing them after Communion service. She has forgotten to order replacements. Shelby will notice, but she will say that it doesn't matter, because there won't be that many people at church anyway.

"You spilled some," says Tamara.

"You forgot to let us have some," Jason says, taking one of the little glasses and holding it out. Tamara takes one of the glasses too. This is something they do every Communion Sunday.

"I'm in a hurry," says Georgeann. "This isn't a tea party."

They are still holding the glasses out to her.

"Do you want one too?" Jason asks.

"No, I don't have time."

Both children look disappointed, but they drink the sip of grape juice, and Tamara takes the glasses to wash them.

"Hurry," says Georgeann.

Shelby doesn't mention the missing glasses. But over Sunday dinner, they quarrel about her going to a funeral he has to preach that afternoon.

"Why should I go? I didn't even know the man."

"Who is he?" Tamara wants to know.

Shelby says, "No one you know. Hush."

Jason says, "I'll go with you. I like to go to funerals."

"I'm not going," says Georgeann. "They give me nightmares, and I didn't even know the guy."

Shelby glares at her icily for talking like this in front of the children. He agrees to go alone, and promises Jason he can go to the next one. Today the children are going to Georgeann's sister's to play with their cousins. "You don't want to disappoint Jeff and Lisa, do you?" Shelby asks Jason.

As he is getting ready to leave, Shelby asks Georgeann, "Is there something about the way I preach funerals that bothers you?"

"No. Your preaching's fine. I like the weddings. And the piano and everything. But just count me out when it comes to funerals." Georgeann suddenly bangs a skillet in the sink. "Why do I have to tell you that ten times a year?"

They quarrel infrequently, but after they do, Georgeann always does something spiteful. Today, while Shelby and the kids are away, she cleans out the hen-house. It gives her pleasure to put on her jeans and shovel manure into a cart. She wheels it to the garden, not caring who sees. People drive by and she waves. There's the preacher's wife, cleaning out her hen-house on Sunday, they are probably saying. Georgeann puts down new straw in the hen-house and gathers the eggs. She sees a hen looking droopy in a corner. "Perk up," she says. "You look like you've got low blood." After she finishes with the chore, she sits down to read the Sunday papers, feeling relieved that she is alone and can relax. She gets very sleepy, but in a few minutes she has to get up and change clothes. She is getting itchy under the waistband, probably from chicken mites.

She turns the radio on and finds a country-music station.

When Shelby comes in, with the children, she is asleep on the couch. They tiptoe around her and she pretends to sleep on. "Sunday is a day of rest," Shelby is saying to the children. "For everybody but preachers, that is." Shelby turns off the radio.

"Not for me," says Jason. "That's my day to play catch with Jeff."

When Georgeann gets up, Shelby gives her a hug, one of his proper Sunday embraces. She apologizes for not going with him. "How was the funeral?"

"The usual. You don't really want to know, do you?"

"No."

Georgeann plans for the retreat. She makes a doctor's appointment for Wednesday. She takes Shelby's suits to the cleaners. She visits some shut-ins she neglected to see on Sunday. She arranges with her mother to keep Tamara and Jason. Although her mother still believes Georgeann married unwisely, she now promotes the sanctity of the union. "Marriage is forever, but a preacher's marriage is longer than that," she says.

Today, Georgeann's mother sounds as though she is making excuses for Shelby. She knows that Georgeann is unhappy, but she says, "I never gave him much credit at first, but Lord knows he's ambitious. I'll say that for him. And practical. He knew he had to learn a trade so he could support himself in his dedication to the church."

"You make him sound like a junkie supporting a habit."

Georgeann's mother laughs uproariously. "It's the same thing! The same thing." She is a stout, good-looking woman who loves to drink at parties. She and Shelby have never had much to say to each other, and Georgeann gets very sad whenever she realizes that her mother treats her marriage like a joke. It isn't fair.

When Georgeann feeds the chickens, she notices the sick hen unable to get up on its feet. Its comb is turning black. She picks it up and sets it in the hen-house. She puts some mash in a Crisco can and sets it in front of the chicken. It pecks indifferently at the mash. Georgeann goes to the house and finds a margarine tub and fills it with water. There is nothing to do for a sick chicken, except to let it die. Or kill it, to keep disease from spreading to the others. She won't tell Shelby the chicken is sick, because Shelby will get the ax and chop its head off. Shelby isn't being cruel. He believes in the necessities of things.

Shelby will have a substitute in church next Sunday, while he is at the retreat, but he has his sermon ready for the following Sunday. On Tuesday evening, Georgeann types it for him. He writes in longhand on yellow legal pads, the way Nixon wrote his memoirs, and after ten years Georgeann has finally mastered his corkscrew handwriting. The sermon is on sex education in the schools. When Georgeann comes to a word she doesn't know, she goes downstairs.

"There's no such word as 'pucelage,'" she says to Shelby, who is at the kitchen table, trying to fix a gun-shaped hair-dryer. Parts are scattered all over the table.

"Sure there is," he said. "'Pucelage' means virginity."

"Why didn't you say so! Nobody will know what it means."

"But it's just the word I want."

"And what about this word in the next paragraph? 'Maturescent'? Are you kidding?"

"Now don't start in on how I'm making fun of you because you haven't been to college," Shelby says.

Georgeann doesn't answer. She goes back to the study and continues typing. Something pinches her on the stomach. She raises her blouse and scratches a bite. She sees a tiny brown speck scurrying across her flesh. Fascinated, she catches it by moistening a fingertip. It drowns in her saliva. She puts it on a scrap of yellow legal paper and folds it up. Something to show the doctor. Maybe the doctor will let her look at it under a microscope.

The next day, Georgeann goes to the doctor, taking the speck with her. "I started getting these bites after I cleaned out the hen-house," she tells the nurse. "And I've been handling a sick chicken."

The nurse scrapes the speck onto a slide and instructs Georgeann to get undressed and put on a paper robe so that it opens in the back. Georgeann piles her clothes in a corner behind a curtain and pulls on the paper robe. As she waits, she twists and stretches a corner of the robe, but the paper is tough, like the "quicker picker-upper" paper towel she has seen in TV ads. When the doctor bursts in, Georgeann gets a whiff of strong cologne.

The doctor says, "I'm afraid we can't continue with the examination until we treat you for that critter you brought in." He looks alarmed.

"I was cleaning out the hen-house," Georgeann explains. "I figured it was a chicken mite."

"What you have is a body louse. I don't know how you got it, but we'll have to treat it completely before we can look at you further."

"Do they carry diseases?"

"This *is* a disease," the doctor says. "What I want you to do is take off that paper gown and wad it up very tightly into a ball and put it in the wastebasket. Whatever you do, don't shake it! When you get dressed, I'll tell you what to do next."

Later, after prescribing a treatment, the doctor lets her look at the louse through the microscope. It looks like a bloated tick from a dog; it is lying on its back and its legs are flung around crazily.

"I just brought it in for fun," Georgeann says. "I had no idea."

At the library, she looks up "louse" in a medical book. There are three kinds, and to her relief she has the kind that won't get in the hair. The book says that body lice are common only in alcoholics and indigent elderly persons who rarely change their clothes. Georgeann cannot imagine how she got lice. When she goes to the drugstore to get her prescription filled, a woman brushes close to her, and Georgeann sends out a silent message: I have lice. She is enjoying this.

"I've got lice," she announces when Shelby gets home. "I have to take a fifteen-minute hot shower and put this cream on all over, and then I have to wash all the clothes and curtains and everything — and what's more, the same goes for you and Tamara and Jason. You're incubating them, the doctor said. They're in the bedcovers and the mattresses and the rugs. Everywhere." Georgeann makes creepy-crawling motions with her fingers.

The pain on Shelby's face registers with her after a moment. "What about the retreat?" he asks.

"I don't know if I'll have time to get all this done first."

"This sounds fishy to me. Where would you get lice?"

Georgeann shrugs. "He asked me if I'd been to a motel room lately. I probably got them from one of those shut-ins. Old Mrs. Speed, maybe. That filthy old horsehair chair of hers."

Shelby looks really depressed, but Georgeann continues brightly, "I thought sure it was chicken mites because I'd been cleaning out the hen-house? But he let me look at it in the microscope and he said it was a body louse."

"Those doctors don't know everything," Shelby says. "Why don't you call a vet? I bet that doctor you went to wouldn't know a chicken mite if it crawled up his leg."

"He said it was lice."

"I've been itching ever since you brought this up."

"Don't worry. Why don't we just get you ready for the retreat — clean clothes and hot shower — and then I'll stay here and get the rest of us fumigated?"

"You don't really want to go to the retreat, do you?"

Georgeann doesn't answer. She gets busy in the kitchen. She makes a pork roast for supper, with fried apples and mashed potatoes. For dessert she makes Jell-O and peaches with Dream Whip. She is really hungry. While she peels potatoes, she sings a song to herself. She doesn't know the name of it, but it has a haunting melody. It is either a song her mother used to sing to her or a jingle from a TV ad.

They decide not to tell Tamara and Jason that the family has lice. Tamara was inspected for head lice once at school, but there is no reason to make a show of this, Shelby tells Georgeann. He gets the children to take long baths by telling them it's a ritual cleansing, something like baptism. That night in bed, after long showers, Georgeann and Shelby don't touch each other. Shelby lies flat with his hands behind his head, looking at the ceiling. He talks about the value of spiritual renewal. He wants Georgeann to finish washing all the clothes so that she can go to the retreat. He says, "Every person needs to stop once in a while and take a look at what's around him. Even preaching wears thin."

"Your preaching's up-to-date," Georgeann says. "You're more up-to-date than a lot of those old-timey preachers who haven't even been to seminary." Georgeann is aware that she sounds too perky.

"You know what's going to happen, don't you? This little church is falling off so bad they're probably going to close it down and re-assign me to Deep Springs."

"Well, you've been expecting that for a long time, haven't you?"

"It's awful," Shelby says. "These people depend on this church. They don't want to travel all the way to Deep Springs. Besides, everybody wants their own home church." He reaches across Georgeann and turns out the light.

The next day, after Shelby finishes wiring a house, he consults with a veterinarian about chicken mites. When he comes home, he tells Georgeann that in the veterinarian's opinion, the brown speck was a chicken mite. "The vet just laughed at that doctor," Shelby says. "He said the mites would leave of their own accord. They're looking for chickens, not people."

"Should I wash all these clothes or not? I'm half finished."

"I don't itch anymore, do you?"

Shelby has brought home a can of roost paint, a chemical to kill chicken mites. Georgeann takes the roost paint to the hen-house and applies it to the roosts. It smells like fumes from a paper mill, and almost makes her gag. When she finishes, she gathers eggs, and then sees that the sick hen has flopped outside again and can't get up on her feet. Georgeann carries the chicken into the hen-house and sets her down by the food. She examines the chicken's feathers. Suddenly she notices that the chicken is covered with moving specks. Georgeann backs out of the hen-house and looks at her hands in the sunlight. The specks are swarming all over her hands. She watches them head up her arms, spinning crazily, disappearing on her.

The retreat is at a lodge at Kentucky Lake. In the mornings, a hundred people eat a country-ham breakfast on picnic tables, out of doors by the lake. The dew is still on the grass. Now and then a speedboat races by, drowning out conversation. Georgeann wears a badge with her name on it and "BACK TO BASICS," the theme of the gathering, in Gothic lettering. After the first day, Shelby's spirit seems renewed. He talks and laughs with old acquaintances, and during social hour, he seems cheerful and relaxed. At the workshops and lectures, he takes notes like mad on his yellow legal paper, which he carries on a clipboard. He already has fifty ideas for new sermons, he tells Georgeann happily. He looks handsome in his clean suit. She has begun to see him as someone remote, like a meter-reader. Georgeann thinks: He is not the same person who once stole a ham.

On the second day, she skips silent prayers after breakfast and stays in the room watching Phil Donahue. Donahue is interviewing parents of murdered children; the parents have organized to support each other in their grief. There is an organization for everything, Georgeann realizes. When Shelby comes in, before the noon meal, she is asleep and the farm-market report is blaring from the TV. As she wakes up, he turns off the TV. Shelby is a kind and good man, she says to herself. He still thinks she has low blood. He wants to bring her food on a tray, but Georgeann refuses.

"I'm alive," she says. "There's a workshop this afternoon I want to go to. On marriage. Do you want to go to that one?"

"No, I can't make that one," says Shelby, consulting his schedule. "I have to attend The Changing Role of the Country Pastor."

"It will probably be just women," says Georgeann. "You wouldn't enjoy it." When he looks at her oddly, she says, "I mean the one on marriage."

Shelby winks at her. "Take notes for me."

The workshop concerns Christian marriage. A woman leading the workshop describes seven kinds of intimacy, and eleven women volunteer their opinions. Seven of the women present are ministers' wives. Georgeann isn't counting herself. The women talk about marriage enhancement, a term that is used five times.

A fat woman in a pink dress says, "God made man so that he can't resist a woman's adoration. She should treat him as a priceless treasure, for man is the highest form of creation. A man is born of God — and, just think, *you* get to live with him."

"That's so exciting I can hardly stand it," says a young woman, giggling, then looking around innocently with an expansive smile.

"Christians are such beautiful people," says the fat woman. "And we have such nice-looking young people. We're not dowdy at all."

"People just get that idea," someone says.

A tall woman with curly hair stands up and says, "The world has become so filled with the false, the artificial — we have gotten so phony that we think the First Lady doesn't have smelly feet. Or the Pope doesn't go to the bathroom."

"Leave the Pope out of this," says the fat woman in pink. "He can't get married." Everyone laughs.

Georgeann stands up and asks a question. "What do you do if the man you're married to — this is just a hypothetical question — say, he's the cream of creation and all, and he's sweet as can be, but he turns out to be the wrong one for you? What do you do if you're just simply mismatched?"

Everyone looks at her.

Shelby stays busy with the workshops and lectures, and Georgeann wanders in and out of them, as though she is visiting someone else's dreams. She and Shelby pass each other casually on the path, hurrying along between the lodge and the conference building. They wave hello like friendly acquaintances. In bed she tells him, "Christella Simmons told me I looked like Mindy on *Mork & Mindy*. Do you think I do?"

Shelby laughs. She expects him to lecture her on false women and all their finery. "Don't be silly," he says. When he reaches for her, she turns away.

The next day, Georgeann walks by the lake. She watches sea gulls flying over the water. It amazes her that sea gulls have flown this far inland, as though they were looking for something, the source of all that water. They arc above the water, flying away from her. She expects them to return, like hurled boomerangs. The sky changes as she watches, puffy clouds thinning out into threads, a jet contrail intersecting them and spreading, like something melting: an icicle. The sun pops out. Georgeann walks past a family of picnickers. The family is having an argument over who gets to use an inner tube first. The father says threateningly, "I'm going to get me a switch!" Georgeann feels a stiffening inside her. Instead of letting go, loosening up, relaxing, she is tightening up. But this means she is growing stronger.

Georgeann goes to the basement of the lodge to buy a Coke from a machine, but she finds herself drawn to the electronic games along the wall. She puts a quarter in one of the machines, the Galaxians. She is a Galaxian, with a rocket ship something like the *Enterprise* on *Star Trek*, firing at a convoy of fleeing, multi-colored aliens. When her missiles hit them, they make satisfying little bursts of color. Suddenly, as she is firing away, three of them — two red ships and one yellow ship — zoom down the screen and blow up her ship. She loses her three ships one right after the other and the game is over. Georgeann runs upstairs to the desk and gets change for a dollar. She puts another quarter in the machine and begins firing. She likes the sound of the firing and the siren-wail of the diving formation. She is beginning to get the hang of it. The hardest thing is controlling the left and right movements of her ship with her left hand as she tries to aim or to dodge the formation. The aliens keep returning and she keeps on firing and firing until she goes through all her quarters.

After supper, Georgeann removes her name badge and escapes to the basement again. Shelby has gone to the evening service, but she told him she had a headache. She has five dollars' worth of quarters, and she loses two of them before she can regain her control. Her game improves and she scores 3,660. The high score of the day, according to the machine, is 28,480. The situation is dangerous and thrilling, but Georgeann feels in control. She isn't running away; she is chasing the aliens. The basement is dim, and some men are playing at the other machines. One of them begins watching her game, making her nervous. When the game ends, he says, "You get 800 points when you get those three zonkers, but you have to get the yellow one last or it ain't worth as much."

"You must be an expert," says Georgeann, looking at him skeptically.

"You catch on after a while."

The man says he is a trucker. He wears a yellow billed cap and a denim jacket lined with fleece. He says, "You're good. Get a load of them fingers."

"I play the piano."

"Are you with them church people?"

"Uh-huh."

"You don't look like a church lady."

Georgeann plugs in another quarter. "This could be an expensive habit," she says idly. It has just occurred to her how good-looking the man is. He has curly sideburns that seem to match the fleece inside his jacket.

"I'm into Space Invaders myself," the trucker says. "See, in Galaxians, you're attacking from behind. It's a kind of cowardly way to go at things."

"Well, they turn around and get you," says Georgeann. "And they never stop coming. There's always more of them."

The man takes off his cap and tugs at his hair, then puts his cap back on. "I'd ask you out for a beer, but I don't want to get in trouble with the church." He laughs. "Do you want a Coke? I'll buy you a Co'-Cola."

Georgeann shakes her head no. She starts the new game. The aliens

are flying in formation. She begins the chase. When the game ends —
her best yet — she turns to look for the man, but he has left.

Georgeann spends most of the rest of the retreat in the basement,
playing Galaxians. She doesn't see the trucker again. Eventually, Shelby
finds her in the basement. She has lost track of time, and she has spent
all their reserve cash. Shelby is treating her like a mental case. When
she tries to explain to him how it feels to play the game, he looks at her
indulgently, the way he looks at shut-ins when he takes them baskets of
fruit. "You forget everything but who you are," Georgeann tells him.
"Your mind leaves your body." Shelby looks depressed.

As they drive home, he says, "What can I do to make you happy?"

Georgeann doesn't answer at first. She's still blasting aliens off a
screen in her mind. "I'll tell you when I can get it figured out," she says
slowly. "Just let me work on it."

Shelby lets her alone. They drive home in silence. As they turn off
the main highway toward the house, she says suddenly, "I was happy
when I was playing that game."

"We're not children," says Shelby. "What do you want — toys?"

At home, the grass needs cutting. The brick house looks small and
shabby, like something abandoned. In the mailbox, Shelby finds his
re-assignment letter. He has been switched to the Deep Springs church,
sixty miles away. They will probably have to move. Shelby folds up the
letter and puts it back in the envelope, then goes to his study. The
children are not home yet, and Georgeann wanders around the house,
pulling up the shades, looking for things that have changed in her
absence. A short while later, she goes to Shelby's study, and knocks on
the door. One of his little rules. She says, "I can't go to Deep Springs.
I'm not going with you."

Shelby stands up, blocking the light from the windows. "I don't want
to move either," he says. "But it's too awful far to commute."

"You don't understand. I don't want to go at all. I want to stay here
by myself so I can think straight."

"What's got into you lately, girl? Have you gone crazy?" Shelby
draws the blind on the window so the sun doesn't glare in. He says,
"You've got me so confused. Here I am in this big crisis and you're not
standing by me."

"I don't know how."

Shelby snaps his fingers. "We can go to a counselor."

"I went to that marriage workshop and it was a lot of hooey."

Shelby's face has a pallor, Georgeann notices. He is distractedly thumbing through some papers, his notes from the conference. Georgeann realizes that Shelby is going to compose a sermon directed at her. "We're going to have to pray over this," he says quietly.

"Later," says Georgeann. "I have to go pick up the kids."

Before leaving, she goes to check on the chickens. A neighbor has been feeding them. The sick chicken is still alive, but it doesn't move from a corner under the roost. Its eyelids are half shut, and its comb is dark and crusty. The hen-house still smells of roost paint. Georgeann gathers eggs and takes them to the kitchen. Then, without stopping to reflect, she gets the ax from the shed and returns to the hen-house. She picks up the sick chicken and takes it outside to a stump behind the hen-house. She sets the chicken on the stump and examines its feathers. She doesn't see any mites on it now. Taking the hen by the feet, she lays it on its side, its head pointing away from her. She holds its body down, pressing its wings. The chicken doesn't struggle. When the ax crashes down blindly on its neck, Georgeann feels nothing, but knows she has done her duty.

Alice Munro

....

Pictures of the Ice

THREE WEEKS BEFORE HE DIED — drowned in a boating accident in a lake whose name nobody had heard him mention — Austin Cobbett stood deep in the clasp of a three-way mirror in Crawford's Men's Wear, in Logan, Ontario, looking at himself in a burgundy sports shirt and a pair of cream, brown, and burgundy plaid pants. Both pants and shirt permanent press.

"Listen to me," Jerry Crawford said to him, "with the darker shirt and the lighter pants you can't go wrong. It's youthful."

Austin cackled. "Did you ever hear that expression — mutton dressed as lamb?"

"Referred to ladies," Jerry said. "Anyway, it's all changed now. There's no old-men's clothes, no old-ladies' clothes, anymore. Style applies to everybody."

Once Austin got used to what he had on, Jerry was going to talk him into a neck scarf of complementary colors and a cream pullover. Austin needed all the cover-up he could get. Since his wife had died, about a year ago, and they had finally got a new minister at the United Church (Austin, who was over seventy, was officially retired but had been hanging on and filling in while they haggled over whom to hire as a replacement and what they would pay him), he had lost weight, his muscles had shrunk, and he was getting the pot-bellied, caved-in shape of an old man. His neck was corded and his nose lengthened and his cheeks drooped; he was a stringy old rooster — stringy but tough, and game enough to gear up for a second marriage.

"The pants are going to have to be taken in," Jerry said. "You can give us time for that, can't you? When's the big day?"

Austin was going to be married in Hawaii, where his wife-to-be lived. He named a date a couple of weeks ahead.

Phil Stadelman, from the Toronto Dominion Bank, came in then and did not recognize Austin from the back, though Austin was his former minister. He'd never seen Cobbett in clothes like that.

Phil told his AIDS joke: Jerry couldn't stop him.

Why did the Newfie put condoms on his ears?

Because he didn't want to get hearing aids.

Then Austin turned around, and instead of saying, *Well, I don't know about you fellows but I find it hard to think of* AIDS *as a laughing matter,* or, *I wonder what kind of jokes they tell in Newfoundland about the folks from Huron County?* he said, "That's rich." He laughed.

That's rich. Then he asked Phil's opinion of his clothes. "Do you think they're going to laugh when they see me coming, in Hawaii?"

Karin heard about this when she went into Logan's most crowded doughnut place to drink a cup of coffee, after finishing her afternoon stint as a crossing guard. She sat at the counter and heard the men talking at a table behind her. She swung around on the stool and said, "Listen, I could have told you, he's changed. I see him every day and I could have told you."

Karin is a tall, thin woman with rough skin and a hoarse voice and long blonde hair, dark for a couple of inches at the roots. She's letting it grow out, and it's gotten to where she could cut it short, but she doesn't. She used to be a lanky blonde girl, shy and pretty, who rode around on the back of her husband's motorcycle. She has gone a little strange — not too much so, or she wouldn't be a crossing guard, not even on the strength of Austin Cobbett's recommendation. She interrupts conversations. She never seems to wear anything but her jeans and an old navy-blue duffle coat. She has a hard and suspicious expression, and she has a public grudge against her ex-husband. She will write things on his car with her finger. *Fake Christian. Kiss arse Phony. Brent Duprey is a snake.* Nobody knows that she is the one who wrote *Lazarus Sucks,* because she went back (she does her writing at night) and rubbed it off with her sleeve. Why? It seemed dangerous, something that might get her into trouble — the trouble being of a vaguely supernatural kind, not a talk with the chief of police — and she has nothing against Lazarus in the Bible, only against Lazarus House, which is the place Brent runs, and where he lives now.

Karin lives where she and Brent lived together for the last few months — upstairs over the hardware store, at the back, in a big room with an alcove (the baby's) and a kitchen at one end. She spends a lot of her time over at Austin's, cleaning out his house, getting everything ready for his departure to Hawaii. The house he lives in, still, is the old parsonage, on Pondicherry Street. The church has built the new minister a new house, quite nice, with a patio and a double garage — ministers' wives often work now, as nurses or teachers, and then you need two cars. The old parsonage is a grayish-white brick house, with blue-painted trim on the veranda and the gables. It needs a lot of work: insulating, sandblasting, new paint, new window frames, new tiles in the bathroom. Walking back to her own place at night, Karin sometimes thinks about what she'd do to that place, if it were hers and she had the money.

Austin shows her a picture of Sheila Brothers, the woman he is to marry. Actually it's a picture of three people: Austin, the woman who used to be his wife, and Sheila Brothers, in front of a log building and some pine trees. A retreat, where he — they — first met Sheila. Austin has his minister's black shirt and turned collar on: he looks shifty, with his apologetic, ministerial smile. His wife is looking away from him, but the big bow of her flowered scarf flutters against his neck. Fluffy white hair, trim figure. Chic. Sheila Brothers — Mrs. Brothers, a widow — is looking straight ahead, and she is the only one who seems really cheerful. She has short fair hair, combed around her face in a businesslike way, brown slacks, a white sweat shirt, with the fairly large bumps of her breasts and stomach plain to see; she meets the camera head-on, and doesn't seem worried about what it will make of her.

"She looks happy," Karin says.

"Well. She didn't know she was going to marry me, at the time."

He shows Karin a postcard picture of the town where Sheila lives, the town where he will live, in Hawaii. Also a photograph of her house. The town's main street has a row of palm trees down the middle; it has low white or pinkish buildings, lampposts with brimming flower baskets, and over all a sky of deep turquoise in which the town's name — a Hawaiian name no one can pronounce or remember — is written in flowing letters like silk ribbon. The name floating in the sky looks as real as anything else in the picture. As for the house, you can hardly make it out at all — just a bit of balcony among the red and pink and gold flowering trees and bushes. But the beach is there in front of the house, the sand as pure as cream and the jewel-bright waves breaking. This is where Austin Cobbett will walk with friendly Sheila. No wonder he needs all new clothes.

Austin wants Karin to clear everything out. Even his books, his old typewriter, the pictures of his wife and children. His son lives in Denver, his daughter in Montreal. He has written to them, he has talked to them on the phone, he has asked them to claim anything they want. His son wants the dining-room furniture, which a moving truck will pick up next week. His daughter says she doesn't want anything. (Karin thinks she's likely to reconsider; people always want *something*.) All the furniture, books, pictures, curtains, rugs, dishes, pots and pans, are to go to the Auction Barn. Austin's car will be auctioned as well, along with his power mower and the snowblower his son gave him last Christmas. Everything will be sold after Austin leaves for Hawaii, and the money will go to Lazarus House. Austin started Lazarus House, when he was a minister. Only he didn't call it that; he called it Turnaround House. Now they have decided — Brent Duprey has decided — they'd rather have a name that is more religious, more Christian.

At first Austin was going to give them all these things, to use in or around Lazarus House. Then he thought that he would be showing more respect if he gave them money, to buy things they liked, instead of using his wife's dishes and sitting on his wife's chintz sofa.

"What if they take the money and buy lottery tickets with it?" Karin asks him. "Won't they be tempted?"

"You don't get anywhere in life without temptations," Austin says, with his maddening little smile. "What if they *won* the lottery?"

"Brent Duprey is a snake."

Brent has taken control of Lazarus House. It was a place to stay for people who wanted to stop drinking or some other troublesome way of life: now it's a born-again sort of place, with night-long sessions of praying and singing and groaning and confessing. That's how Brent got hold of it — by becoming more religious than Austin. Austin got Brent to stop drinking; he pulled and pulled on Brent until he pulled him right out of the life he was leading and into a new life of running this house with money from the church, and the government, and so on, and he made a big mistake, Austin did, in thinking he could hold Brent there. Once started on the holy road, Brent went shooting on past. He got past Austin's careful, quiet kind of religion in no time and cut Austin out with the people in his own church who wanted a stricter, more ferocious kind of Christianity. Austin was shifted out of Lazarus House and the church at about the same time, and Brent bossed the new minister around without difficulty. In spite of this, or perhaps because of it, Austin wants to give Lazarus House the money.

"Who's to say whether Brent's way isn't closer to God than mine is, after all?" he says.

Karin says just about anything to anybody now. She says to Austin, "Don't make me puke."

Austin says she must be sure to keep a record of her time, so that she will be paid for all this work, and also, if she sees anything here she would particularly like, to tell him, so that they can discuss it.

"Within reason," he says. "If you said you'd like the car or the snowblower, I guess I'd be obliged to say no, because that would be cheating the folks over at Lazarus House. But how about the vacuum cleaner?"

Is that how he sees her — as somebody who's always thinking about cleaning houses? The vacuum cleaner is practically an antique, anyway.

"I bet I know what Brent said when you told him I was going to be in charge of all this," she says. "I bet he said, Are you going to get a lawyer to check up on her? He did, didn't he?"

Instead of answering that, Austin says, "Why would I trust a lawyer any more than I trust you?"

"Is that what you said to him?"

"I'm saying it to you. You either trust or you don't trust, in my opinion. When you decide you're going to trust, you have to start where you are."

Austin rarely mentions God. Nevertheless, you feel the mention of God hovering on the edge of sentences like these, and it makes you so uneasy — Karin gets a crumbly feeling along her spine — that you wish he'd say it and get it over with.

Four years ago Karin and Brent were still married, and they hadn't had the baby yet or moved to their place above the hardware store. They were living in a cheap apartment building belonging to Morris Fordyce that had at one time been a slaughterhouse. In wet weather Karin could smell pig, and always she smelled another smell that she thought was blood. Brent sniffed around the walls, and got down and sniffed the floor, but he couldn't smell what she was smelling. How could he smell anything other than the clouds of boozy breath that rose from his own gut? Brent was a drunk then, but not a sodden drunk. He played hockey on the O.T. (over-thirty, old-timers) hockey team — he was quite a bit older than Karin — and he claimed that he had never played sober. He worked for Fordyce Construction for a while, and then he worked for the town, cutting up trees. He drank on the job when he could, and after work he drank at the Fish and Game Club or at the Green Haven Motel Bar, called the Greasy Heaven. One night he started up a bulldozer that was sitting outside the Greasy Heaven and drove it across town to the Fish and Game Club. Of course he was caught, and charged with impaired driving of a bulldozer — a big joke all over town. But nobody who laughed at the joke came around to pay the fine. And Brent just kept getting wilder. Another night he took down the stairs that led to their apartment. He didn't bash the steps out in a fit of temper; he removed them thoughtfully and methodically, steps and uprights, one by one, backing downstairs as he did so, and leaving Karin cursing at the top. First she laughed at him — she had had a few beers herself by that time. Then, when she realized he was in earnest and she was being marooned, she started cursing. Cowardly neighbors peeped out of the doors behind him.

Brent came home the next afternoon and was amazed, or pretended to be. What happened to the steps? he yelled. He stomped around the hall, his lined, exhausted face working, his blue eyes snapping, his smile innocent and conniving. God damn that Morris. Goddamn steps caved in. I'm going to sue him. God damn *fuck*. Karin was upstairs, with nothing to eat but half a box of Rice Krispies, no milk, and a can of yellow beans. She had thought of phoning somebody to come with a ladder, but she was too mad and stubborn. If Brent wanted to starve her, she would show him. She would starve.

That time was the beginning of the end, the change. Brent went around to see Morris Fordyce, to beat him up and tell him about how he was going to be sued, and Morris talked to Brent in a reasonable, sobering way, until Brent decided not to sue or beat up Morris but to commit suicide instead. Morris called Austin Cobbett, because Austin had a reputation for knowing how to deal with people who were in a desperate way. Austin didn't talk Brent out of drinking, or into the church, but he did talk him out of suicide. Then, a couple of years later, when the baby died, Austin was the only minister they knew to call. By the time he came to see them, to talk about the funeral, Brent had drunk everything in the house and had gone out looking for more. Austin went after him and spent the next five days — with a brief time out for burying the baby — just staying with him on a bender. He spent the next week nursing him out of it, and the next month talking to him or sitting with him until Brent decided he would not drink anymore, that he had been put in touch with God. Austin said that Brent meant that he had been put in touch with the fullness of his own life and the power of his innermost self. Brent said it was God.

Karin went to Austin's church with Brent for a while; she didn't mind that. She could see, though, that the church wasn't going to be enough to hold Brent. She saw him bouncing up to sing the hymns, swinging his arms and clenching his fists, his whole body primed. He was the same as he was after three or four beers, when he couldn't stop himself from going for more. He was bursting. Soon he burst out of Austin's hold, and took a good part of the church with him. A lot of people had wanted that loosening, more noise and praying and sing-ing, and not so much quiet persuading, talking. They'd been wanting it for a long while.

None of it surprised her. She wasn't surprised that Brent learned to fill out papers and make the right impression and get government money, that he took over Turnaround House and kicked Austin out. He'd always been full of possibilities. She wasn't really surprised that he got as mad at her now for drinking one beer and smoking one cigarette as he used to do when she wanted to stop partying and go to bed at two o'clock. He said he was giving her a week to decide. No more drinking, no more smoking, Christ as her savior. One week. Karin said, Don't bother with the week. After Brent was gone, she quit smoking, she almost quit drinking, and she also quit going to Austin's church. She gave up everything but a slow, smoldering grudge against Brent, which grew and grew. One day Austin stopped her on the street, and she thought he was going to say some gentle, personal, condemn-ing thing to her, because of her grudge or her quitting church, but all he did was ask her to come and help him look after his wife, who was getting home from the hospital that week.

Austin is talking on the phone to his daughter in Montreal. Her name is Megan. She is around thirty, unmarried, a television producer. "Life has a lot of surprises up its sleeve," Austin says. "You know this has nothing to do with your mother. This is a new life, entirely. But I regret. No, no. I just mean you can love God in more than one way, and taking pleasure in the world is surely one of them. That's a revelation that's come to me rather late. Too late to be of any use to your mother. No. Guilt is a sin and a seduction. I've said that to many a poor soul who liked to wallow in it. Regret's another matter. How could you get through a long life and escape it?"

I was right, Karin is thinking. Megan does want something. But after a little more talk — Austin says that he might take up golf, don't laugh, and that Sheila belongs to a play-reading club; he expects he'll be a star at that, after all his pulpit haranguing — the conversation ends. Austin walks out to the kitchen — the phone is in the front hall; this is an old-fashioned house — and looks up at Karin, who is cleaning out the high cupboards.

"Parents and children, Karin," he says, sighing, sighing, looking humorous. "Oh, what a tangled web we weave, when first we — have children. Then they always want us to be the same, they want us to be parents. They are shaken up dreadfully if we do anything they didn't think we'd do. Dreadfully."

"I guess she'll get used to it," Karin says, without much sympathy.

"Oh, she will, she will. Poor Megan."

Then he says he's going uptown to have his hair cut. He doesn't want to postpone it any longer because he always looks and feels so foolish with a fresh haircut. His mouth turns down as he smiles — first up, then down. That downward slide is what's noticeable on him everywhere — face slipping down into neck wattles, chest emptied out and mounded into that abrupt, queer little belly. The flow has left dry channels, deep lines. Yet Austin speaks — perversely — as if out of a body that was light and ready and a pleasure to carry around.

In a short time the phone rings again, and Karin has to climb down and answer it.

"Karin? Is that you, Karin? It's Megan!"

"Your father's just gone up to get a haircut."

"Good. Good. I'm glad. That gives me a chance to talk to you. I've been hoping I'd get a chance to talk to you."

"Oh," Karin says.

"Karin. Now, listen. I know I'm behaving just the way adult children seem always to behave in this situation. I don't like it. I don't like that in myself. But I can't help it. I'm suspicious. I wonder what's going on. Is he all right? What do you think of it? What do you think of this woman he's going to marry?"

"All I ever saw of her is her picture," Karin says.

"I am terribly busy right now, and I can't just drop everything and come home and have a real heart-to-heart with him. Anyway, he's very difficult to talk to. He makes all the right noises, he seems so open, but in reality he's very closed. He's never been at all a personal kind of person, do you know what I mean? He's never done anything before for a *personal* kind of reason. He always did things *for* somebody. He always liked to find people who *needed* things done for them, a lot. Well, you know that. Even bringing you into the house, you know, to look after Mother — it wasn't exactly for Mother's sake or his sake he did that."

Karin can picture Megan — the long, dark, smooth hair, parted in the middle and combed over her shoulders, the heavily made-up eyes and tanned skin and pale-pink lip-sticked mouth, the handsomely clothed, plump body. Wouldn't her voice bring such looks to mind even if you'd never seen her? Such smoothness, such rich sincerity. A fine gloss on every word, and little appreciative spaces in between. She talks as if listening to herself. A little too much that way, really. Could she be drunk?

"Let's face it, Karin, Mother was a snob." Yes, she is drunk. "Well, she had to have something. Dragged around from one dump to another, always doing good. Doing good wasn't her thing at all. So now, *now*, he gives it all up, he's off to the easy life. In Hawaii! Isn't it bizarre?"

Bizarre. Karin has heard that word on television and heard people, mostly teenagers, say it, and she knows it is not the church bazaar that Megan's talking about. Nevertheless, that's what the word makes her think of — the church bazaars that Megan's mother used to organize, always trying to give them some style and make things different. Striped umbrellas and a sidewalk café one year, Devonshire teas and a rose arbor the next. Then she thinks of Megan's mother on the chintz-covered sofa in the living room, weak and yellow after her chemotherapy, one of those padded, perky kerchiefs around her nearly bald head. Still, she could look up at Karin with faint, formal surprise when Karin came into the room. *Was there something you wanted, Karin?* The thing that Karin was supposed to ask her, she would ask Karin.

Bizarre. Bazaar. Snob. When Megan got in that dig, Karin should have said, at least, "I know that." All she can think to say is, "Megan. This is costing you money."

"Money, Karin! We're talking about my *father*. We're talking about whether my father is sane or whether he has flipped his wig, Karin!"

A day later a call from Denver. Don, Austin's son, is calling to tell his father that they should forget about the dining-room furniture; the cost of shipping it is too high. Austin agrees with him. The money could be better spent, he says. What's furniture? Then Austin is called upon to explain about the Auction Barn and what Karin is doing.

"Of course, of course, no trouble," he says. "They'll list everything they get and what it sold for. They can easily send a copy. They've got a computer, I understand. No longer the Dark Ages up here."

Austin listens to Don and then he says, "That's true. I had hoped you'd see it that way about the money. It's a project close to my heart. And you and your sister are providing well for yourselves. I'm very fortunate in my children."

He listens some more. "The old-age pension and my own pension, whatever more could I want? And this lady, this lady, I can tell you, Sheila — she is not short of money, if I can put it that way." He laughs, rather mischievously, at something his son says.

After he hangs up, he says to Karin, "Well, my son is worried about my finances and my daughter is worried about my mental state. My mental-emotional state. The male and female ways of looking at things. The male and female ways of expressing anxiety. Underneath, it's the same thing. The old order changeth, yielding place to the new."

Don wouldn't remember everything that was in the house anyway. How could he? He was here the day of the funeral, but his wife wasn't with him, she was too pregnant to come. He wouldn't have her to rely on. Men don't remember that sort of thing well. He just asked for the list so that he would seem to be keeping track of everything, and nobody better try to hoodwink him. Or hoodwink his father.

Karin is going to get some things from the house, and nobody need know where she has gotten them. Nobody comes up to her place anyway. A willow-pattern plate. The blue-and-gray flowered curtains. A little fat jug of ruby-colored glass with a silver lid. A white damask cloth, a tablecloth, that she ironed until it shone like a frosted snowfield, and the enormous napkins that go with it. The tablecloth alone weighs as much as a child, and the napkins flop out of wineglasses like lilies — if you have wineglasses. She has already taken home six silver spoons, in her coat pocket. She knows enough not to disturb the silver tea service or the good dishes. But some pink glass dishes for dessert, with long stems, have caught her eye. She can see her place transformed, with these things in it. More than that, she can feel the quiet and contentment they would extend to her. Sitting in a room so furnished, she wouldn't need to go out. She would never need to think of Brent and imagine ways to torment him. A person sitting in such a room could turn and floor anybody trying to intrude. *Was there something you wanted?*

On Monday of Austin's last week — he is supposed to fly to Hawaii on Saturday — the first big storm of the winter began. The wind came in from the west, over the lake, and the snow blew furiously all day and night. Monday and Tuesday the schools were closed, so Karin didn't have to work as a guard. But she couldn't stand staying indoors. She put on her duffle coat, wrapped her head and half her face in a wool scarf, and plowed through the snow-filled streets to the parsonage.

The house is cold; the wind is coming in around the doors and windows. In the kitchen cupboard along the west wall the dishes feel like ice. Austin is dressed but lying down on the living-room sofa, wrapped in various quilts and blankets. He is not reading or watching television or dozing, so far as she can tell — just staring. She makes him a cup of instant coffee.

"Do you think this'll stop by Saturday?" she says. She has the feeling that if he doesn't go Saturday, he may not go at all — the whole thing could be called off, all plans could falter.

"It'll stop in due time," he says. "I'm not worried."

Karin's baby died in a snowstorm. In the afternoon, when Brent was drinking with his friend Rob and watching television. Karin said that the baby was sick and she needed money for a taxi to take him to the hospital. Brent told her to fuck off. He thought she was just trying to bother him. And partly she was — the baby had thrown up only once, and whimpered, and he didn't seem very hot. Then, about suppertime, with Rob gone, Brent went to pick up the baby and play with him, forgetting that he was sick. This baby's like a hot coal, he yelled at Karin, and wanted to know why she hadn't called the doctor, why she hadn't taken the baby to the hospital. You tell me why, Karin said, and they started to fight. You said he didn't need to go, Karin said. Okay, so he doesn't need to go. Brent called the taxi company, but the taxis weren't going out because of the storm, which up to then neither he nor Karin had noticed. He called the hospital and asked them what to do, and they said to get the fever down by wrapping the baby in wet towels. So they did that, and by midnight the storm had quieted down, the snowplows were out on the streets, and they got the baby to the hospital. But he died. He probably would have died no matter what they'd done — he had meningitis. Even if he'd been a fussed-over, precious little baby in a home where the father didn't get drunk and the mother and father didn't have fights, he might have died; he probably would have died anyway.

Brent wanted it to be his fault, though. Sometimes he wanted it to be their fault. It was like sucking candy to him, that confession. Karin told him to shut up, she told him to *shut up*. She said, "He would have died anyway."

When the storm is over, Tuesday afternoon, Karin puts on her coat and goes out and shovels the parsonage walk. The temperature seems to be dropping even lower and the sky is clear. Austin says they're going to go down to the lake, to look at the ice. If a big storm like this comes fairly early in the year, the wind drives the waves up on the shore and they freeze there. Ice is everywhere, in unlikely formations. People go down and take pictures. The paper often prints the best of them. Austin wants to take some pictures too. He says they'll be something to show people in Hawaii. So Karin shovels the car out, and off they go, Austin driving with great care. Nobody else is down there. The wind is too cold. Austin hangs on to Karin as they struggle along the boardwalk — or where they think the boardwalk must be, under the snow. Sheets of ice drop from the burdened branches of the willow trees to the ground, and the sun shines through them from the west; they're like walls of pearl. Ice is woven through the wire of the high fence, which makes it look like a honeycomb. Waves have frozen as they hit the shore, making mounds and caves, a crazy landscape, out to the rim of the open water. And all the playground equipment, the children's swings and climbing bars, has been transformed by ice, hung with organ pipes or buried in what look like half-carved statues, shapes of ice that seem meant to be people, animals, angels, monsters, left unfinished.

Karin is nervous when Austin stands alone to take pictures. He seems shaky to her, and what if he fell? He could break a leg, a hip. Old people break a hip and that's the end of them. Even taking off his gloves to work the camera seems risky. A frozen thumb might be enough to keep him here, make him miss his plane.

Back in the car he does have to rub and blow on his hands. He lets her drive. If something dire happened to him, would Sheila Brothers come here, take over his care, settle into the parsonage, countermand his orders?

"This is strange weather," he says. "Up in northern Ontario it's balmy, even the little lakes are open, temperatures above freezing. And here we are in the grip of the ice, and the wind straight off the Great Plains."

"It'll be all the same to you when you get there," Karin says firmly. "Northern Ontario or the Great Plains or here, you'll be glad to be out of it. Doesn't she ever call you?"

"Who?" Austin says.

"*Her.* Mrs. Brothers."

"Oh, Sheila. She calls me late at night. The time's so much earlier in Hawaii."

The phone rings with Karin alone in the house the morning before Austin is to leave. A man's voice, uncertain and sullen-sounding.

"He isn't here right now," Karin says. Austin has gone to the bank. "I could get him to call you when he comes in."

"Well, it's long distance," the man says. "It's Shaft Lake."

"Shaft Lake," Karin repeats, feeling around on the phone shelf for a pencil.

"We were just wondering. Like we were just checking. That we got the right time that he gets in. Somebody's got to drive down and meet him. So, he gets in to Thunder Bay at three o'clock, is that right?"

Karin has stopped looking for a pencil. She finally says, "I guess that's right. As far as I know. If you called back around noon, he'd be here."

"I don't know for sure I can get to a phone around noon. I'm at the hotel here, but then I got to go someplace else. I'd just as soon leave him the message. Somebody's going to meet him at the airport in Thunder Bay three o'clock tomorrow. Okay?"

"Okay," Karin says.

"You could tell him we got him a place to live, too."

"Oh. Okay."

"It's a trailer. He said he wouldn't mind a trailer. See, we haven't had a minister here in a long time."

"Oh," Karin says. "Okay. Yes. I'll tell him."

As soon as she has hung up, she finds Megan's number on the list above the phone and dials it. It rings three or four times and then she hears Megan's voice, sounding brisker than the last time Karin heard it.

"I am very sorry that I cannot take your call at the moment, but if you would leave your name and phone number I will get back to you as soon as possible."

Karin has already started to say she is sorry but this is important when she is interrupted by a beep and realizes it's one of those machines. She starts again, speaking quickly but distinctly after a deep breath.

"I just wanted to tell you. I just wanted you to know. Your father is fine. He is in good health, and mentally he is fine. So you don't have to worry. He is off to Hawaii tomorrow. I was just thinking about — I was just thinking about our conversation on the phone. So I thought I'd tell you not to worry. This is Karin speaking."

And she has just gotten all that said when she hears Austin at the door. Before he can ask or wonder what she's doing there in the hall, she fires a series of questions at him. Did he get to the bank? Did the cold make his chest hurt? When was the Auction Barn truck coming? When did the people from the board want the parsonage keys? Was he going to phone Don and Megan before he left or after he got there or what?

Yes. No. Monday for the truck. Tuesday for the keys, but no rush — if she wasn't finished then. Wednesday would be okay. No more phone calls. He and his children have said all they need to say to each other. Once he's there, he will write them a letter. Write each of them a letter.

"After you're married?"

Yes. Well. Maybe sooner than that.

He has laid his coat across the banister railing. Then she sees him put out a hand, to steady himself, holding on to the railing. He pretends to be fiddling around with his coat.

"You okay?" she says. "You want a cup of coffee?"

For a moment he doesn't say anything. His eyes swim past her. How did anybody believe that this tottery old man, whose body looked to be shriveling day by day, was on his way to marry a comforting widow and spend the rest of his life walking on a sunny beach? It wasn't in him to do such a thing, ever. He meant to wear himself out, quick, quick, on people as thankless as possible, thankless as Brent. Meanwhile fooling all of them into thinking he'd changed his spots. Otherwise somebody might stop him from going. Slipping out from under, fooling them, enjoying it.

But he really is after something in the coat. He brings out a pint of whiskey.

"Put a little of that in a glass for me," he says. "Never mind the coffee. Just a precaution. Against weakness. From the cold."

He is sitting on the steps when she brings him the whiskey. He drinks it. He wags his head back and forth, as if trying to get it clear. He stands up. "Much better," he says. "Oh, very much better. Now, about those pictures of the ice, Karin. I was wondering, could you pick them up next week? If I left you the money? They're not ready yet."

Even though he's just in from the cold, he's white. If you put a candle behind his face, it would shine through as if he were wax or thin china.

"You'll have to leave me your address," she says. "Where to send them."

"Just hang on to them till I write you. That'd be best."

So she has ended up with a whole roll of pictures of the ice, along with all those other things she had her mind set on. The pictures show the sky bluer than it ever was, but the weaving in the fence, the shape of the organ pipes, is not so plain to see. A human figure needs to be there also, to show what size things were. She should have taken the camera and captured Austin — who has vanished even more completely than the ice, unless his body washes up somewhere in the spring. A thaw, a drowning, and they're altogether gone. But Karin looks so often at these pictures that Austin took — the blue sky, the pale, lumpy ice monstrosities — she looks at them so often that she gets the feeling that he is in them after all. He's a blank in them, but the blank is bright.

She thinks now that he knew. Right at the last, he knew that she'd caught on to him, she understood what he was up to. No matter how alone you are, and how tricky and determined, don't you need one person to know? She could be the one for him. Each of them knew what the other was up to, and didn't let on, and that was a link beyond the usual. Every time she thinks of it she feels approved of — a most unexpected thing.

She puts one of the pictures in an envelope and sends it to Megan.

(She tore the list of addresses and phone numbers off the wall, just in case.) She sends another to Don, and another, stamped and addressed, across town to Brent. She doesn't write anything on the pictures or enclose any note. She won't be bothering any of these people again, not even Brent. (The fact is, it's not long till she'll be leaving here.) She just wants to make them wonder.

Flannery O'Connor

·····························

Parker's Back

PARKER'S WIFE was sitting on the front porch floor, snapping beans. Parker was sitting on the step, some distance away, watching her sullenly. She was plain, plain. The skin on her face was thin and drawn as tight as the skin on an onion and her eyes were gray and sharp like the points of two icepicks. Parker understood why he had married her — he couldn't have got her any other way — but he couldn't understand why he stayed with her now. She was pregnant and pregnant women were not his favorite kind. Nevertheless, he stayed as if she had him conjured. He was puzzled and ashamed of himself.

The house they rented sat alone save for a single tall pecan tree on a high embankment overlooking a highway. At intervals a car would shoot past below and his wife's eyes would swerve suspiciously after the sound of it and then come back to rest on the newspaper full of beans in her lap. One of the things she did not approve of was automobiles. In addition to her other bad qualities, she was forever sniffing up sin. She did not smoke or dip, drink whiskey, use bad language or paint her face, and God knew some paint would have improved it, Parker thought. Her being against color, it was the more remarkable she had married him. Sometimes he supposed that she had married him because she meant to save him. At other times he had a suspicion that she actually liked everything she said she didn't. He could account for her one way or another; it was himself he could not understand.

She turned her head in his direction and said, "It's no reason you can't work for a man. It don't have to be a woman."

"Aw shut your mouth for a change," Parker muttered.

If he had been certain she was jealous of the woman he worked for he would have been pleased but more likely she was concerned with the sin that would result if he and the woman took a liking to each other. He had told her that the woman was a hefty young blonde; in fact she was nearly seventy years old and too dried up to have an interest in anything except getting as much work out of him as she could. Not that an old woman didn't sometimes get an interest in a young man, particularly if he was as attractive as Parker felt he was, but this old woman looked at him the same way she looked at her old tractor — as if she had to put up with it because it was all she had. The tractor had broken down the second day Parker was on it and she had set him at once to cutting bushes, saying out of the side of her mouth to the nigger, "Everything he touches, he breaks." She also asked him to wear his shirt when he worked; Parker had removed it even though the day was not sultry; he put it back on reluctantly.

This ugly woman Parker married was his first wife. He had had other women but he had planned never to get himself tied up legally. He had first seen her one morning when his truck broke down on the highway. He had managed to pull it off the road into a neatly swept yard on which sat a peeling two-room house. He got out and opened the hood of the truck and began to study the motor. Parker had an extra sense that told him when there was a woman nearby watching him. After he had leaned over the motor a few minutes, his neck began to prickle. He cast his eye over the empty yard and porch of the house. A woman he could not see was either nearby beyond a clump of honeysuckle or in the house, watching him out the window.

Suddenly Parker began to jump up and down and fling his hand about as if he had mashed it in the machinery. He doubled over and held his hand close to his chest. "God dammit!" he hollered, "Jesus Christ in hell! Jesus God Almighty damm! God dammit to hell!" he went on, flinging out the same few oaths over and over as loud as he could.

Without warning a terrible bristly claw slammed the side of his face and he fell backwards on the hood of the truck. "You don't talk no filth here!" a voice close to him shrilled.

Parker's vision was so blurred that for an instant he thought he had been attacked by some creature from above, a giant hawk-eyed angel wielding a hoary weapon. As his sight cleared, he saw before him a tall raw-boned girl with a broom.

"I hurt my hand," he said. "I HURT my hand." He was so incensed that he forgot that he hadn't hurt his hand. "My hand may be broke," he growled although his voice was still unsteady.

"Lemme see it," the girl demanded.

Parker stuck out his hand and she came closer and looked at it. There was no mark on the palm and she took the hand and turned it over. Her own hand was dry and hot and rough and Parker felt himself jolted back to life by her touch. He looked more closely at her. I don't want nothing to do with this one, he thought.

The girl's sharp eyes peered at the back of the stubby reddish hand she held. There emblazoned in red and blue was a tattooed eagle perched on a cannon. Parker's sleeve was rolled to the elbow. Above the eagle a serpent was coiled about a shield and in the spaces be-tween the eagle and the serpent there were hearts, some with arrows through them. Above the serpent there was a spread hand of cards. Every space on the skin of Parker's arm, from wrist to elbow, was covered in some loud design. The girl gazed at this with an almost stupefied smile of shock, as if she had accidentally grasped a poisonous snake; she dropped the hand.

"I got most of my other ones in foreign parts," Parker said. "These here I mostly got in the United States. I got my first one when I was only fifteen year old."

"Don't tell me," the girl said, "I don't like it. I ain't got any use for it."

"You ought to see the ones you can't see," Parker said and winked.

Two circles of red appeared like apples on the girl's cheeks and softened her appearance. Parker was intrigued. He did not for a minute think that she didn't like the tattoos. He had never yet met a woman who was not attracted to them.

Parker was fourteen when he saw a man in a fair, tattooed from head to foot. Except for his loins which were girded with a panther hide, the man's skin was patterned in what seemed from Parker's distance — he was near the back of the tent, standing on a bench — a single intricate design of brilliant color. The man, who was small and sturdy, moved about on the platform, flexing his muscles so that the arabesque of men and beasts and flowers on his skin appeared to have a subtle motion of its own. Parker was filled with emotion, lifted up as some people are when the flag passes. He was a boy whose mouth habitually hung open. He was heavy and earnest, as ordinary as a loaf of bread. When the show was over, he had remained standing on the bench, staring where the tattooed man had been, until the tent was almost empty.

Parker had never before felt the least motion of wonder in himself. Until he saw the man at the fair, it did not enter his head that there was anything out of the ordinary about the fact that he existed. Even then it did not enter his head, but a peculiar unease settled in him. It was as if a blind boy had been turned so gently in a different direction that he did not know his destination had been changed.

He had his first tattoo some time after — the eagle perched on the cannon. It was done by a local artist. It hurt very little, just enough to make it appear to Parker to be worth doing. This was peculiar too for before he had thought that only what did not hurt was worth doing. The next year he quit school because he was sixteen and could. He went to the trade school for a while, then he quit the trade school and worked for six months in a garage. The only reason he worked at all was to pay for more tattoos. His mother worked in a laundry and could support him, but she would not pay for any tattoo except her name on a heart, which he had put on, grumbling. However, her name was Betty Jean and nobody had to know it was his mother. He found out that the tattoos were attractive to the kind of girls he liked but who had never liked him before. He began to drink beer and get in fights. His mother wept over what was becoming of him. One night she dragged him off to a revival with her, not telling him where they were going. When he saw the big lighted church, he jerked out of her grasp and ran. The next day he lied about his age and joined the navy.

Parker was large for the tight sailor's pants but the silly white cap, sitting low on his forehead, made his face by contrast look thoughtful and almost intense. After a month or two in the navy, his mouth ceased to hang open. His features hardened into the features of a man. He stayed in the navy five years and seemed a natural part of the gray mechanical ship, except for his eyes, which were the same pale slate-color as the ocean and reflected the immense spaces around him as if they were a microcosm of the mysterious sea. In port Parker wandered about comparing the run-down places he was in to Birmingham, Alabama. Everywhere he went he picked up more tattoos.

He had stopped having lifeless ones like anchors and crossed rifles. He had a tiger and a panther on each shoulder, a cobra coiled about a torch on his chest, hawks on his thighs, Elizabeth II and Philip over where his stomach and liver were respectively. He did not care much what the subject was so long as it was colorful; on his abdomen he had a few obscenities but only because that seemed the proper place for them. Parker would be satisfied with each tattoo about a month, then something about it that had attracted him would wear off. Whenever a decent-sized mirror was available, he would get in front of it and study his overall look. The effect was not of one intricate arabesque of colors but of something haphazard and botched. A huge dissatisfaction would come over him and he would go off and find another tattooist and have another space filled up. The front of Parker was almost completely covered but there were no tattoos on his back. He had no desire for one anywhere he could not readily see it himself. As the space on the front of him for tattoos decreased, his dissatisfaction grew and became general.

After one of his furloughs, he didn't go back to the navy but remained away without official leave, drunk, in a rooming house in a city he did not know. His dissatisfaction, from being chronic and latent, had suddenly become acute and raged in him. It was as if the panther and the lion and the serpents and the eagles and the hawks had penetrated his skin and lived inside him in a raging warfare. The navy caught up with him, put him in the brig for nine months and then gave him a dishonorable discharge.

After that Parker decided that country air was the only kind fit to breathe. He rented the shack on the embankment and bought the old truck and took various jobs which he kept as long as it suited him. At the time he met his future wife, he was buying apples by the bushel and selling them for the same price by the pound to isolated homesteaders on back country roads.

"All that there," the woman said, pointing to his arm, "is no better than what a fool Indian would do. It's a heap of vanity." She seemed to have found the word she wanted. "Vanity of vanities," she said.

Well what the hell do I care what she thinks of it? Parker asked himself, but he was plainly bewildered. "I reckon you like one of these better than another anyway," he said, dallying until he thought of something that would impress her. He thrust the arm back at her. "Which you like best?"

"None of them," she said, "but the chicken is not as bad as the rest."

"What chicken?" Parker almost yelled.

She pointed to the eagle.

"That's an eagle," Parker said. "What fool would waste their time having a chicken put on themself?"

"What fool would have any of it?" the girl said and turned away. She went slowly back to the house and left him there to get going. Parker remained for almost five minutes, looking agape at the dark door she had entered.

The next day he returned with a bushel of apples. He was not one to be outdone by anything that looked like her. He liked women with meat on them, so you didn't feel their muscles, much less their old bones. When he arrived, she was sitting on the top step and the yard was full of children, all as thin and poor as herself; Parker remembered it was Saturday. He hated to be making up to a woman when there were children around, but it was fortunate he had brought the bushel of apples off the truck. As the children approached him to see what he carried, he gave each child an apple and told it to get lost; in that way he cleared out the whole crowd.

The girl did nothing to acknowledge his presence. He might have been a stray pig or goat that had wandered into the yard and she too tired to take up the broom and send it off. He set the bushel of apples down next to her on the step. He sat down on a lower step.

"Hep yourself," he said, nodding at the basket; then he lapsed into silence.

She took an apple quickly as if the basket might disappear if she didn't make haste. Hungry people made Parker nervous. He had always had plenty to eat himself. He grew very uncomfortable. He reasoned he had nothing to say so why should he say it? He could not think now why he had come or why he didn't go before he wasted another bushel of apples on the crowd of children. He supposed they were her brothers and sisters.

She chewed the apple slowly but with a kind of relish of concentration, bent slightly but looking out ahead. The view from the porch stretched off across a long incline studded with iron weed and across the highway to a vast vista of hills and one small mountain. Long views depressed Parker. You look out into space like that and you begin to feel as if someone were after you, the navy or the government or religion.

"Who them children belong to, you?" he said at length.

"I ain't married yet," she said. "They belong to momma." She said it as if it were only a matter of time before she would be married.

Who in God's name would marry her? Parker thought.

A large barefooted woman with a wide gap-toothed face appeared in the door behind Parker. She had apparently been there for several minutes.

"Good evening," Parker said.

The woman crossed the porch and picked up what was left of the bushel of apples. "We thank you," she said and returned with it into the house.

"That your old woman?" Parker muttered.

The girl nodded. Parker knew a lot of sharp things he could have said like "You got my sympathy," but he was gloomily silent. He just sat there, looking at the view. He thought he must be coming down with something.

"If I pick up some peaches tomorrow I'll bring you some," he said.

"I'll be much obliged to you," the girl said.

Parker had no intention of taking any basket of peaches back there but the next day he found himself doing it. He and the girl had almost nothing to say to each other. One thing he did say was, "I ain't got any tattoo on my back."

"What you got on it?" the girl said.

"My shirt," Parker said. "Haw."

"Haw, haw," the girl said politely.

Parker thought he was losing his mind. He could not believe for a minute that he was attracted to a woman like this. She showed not the least interest in anything but what he brought until he appeared the third time with two cantaloups. "What's your name?" she asked.

"O. E. Parker," he said.

"What does the O.E. stand for?"

"You can just call me O.E.," Parker said. "Or Parker. Don't nobody call me by my name."

"What's it stand for?" she persisted.

"Never mind," Parker said. "What's yours?"

"I'll tell you when you tell me what them letters are the short of," she said. There was just a hint of flirtatiousness in her tone and it went rapidly to Parker's head. He had never revealed the name to any man or woman, only to the files of the navy and the government, and it was on his baptismal record which he got at the age of a month; his mother was a Methodist. When the name leaked out of the navy files, Parker narrowly missed killing the man who used it.

"You'll go blab it around," he said.

"I'll swear I'll never tell nobody," she said. "On God's holy word I swear it."

Parker sat for a few minutes in silence. Then he reached for the girl's neck, drew her ear close to his mouth and revealed the name in a low voice.

"Obadiah," she whispered. Her face slowly brightened as if the name came as a sign to her. "Obadiah," she said.

The name still stank in Parker's estimation.

"Obadiah Elihue," she said in a reverent voice.

"If you call me that aloud, I'll bust your head open," Parker said. "What's yours?"

"Sarah Ruth Cates," she said.

"Glad to meet you, Sarah Ruth," Parker said.

Sarah Ruth's father was a Straight Gospel preacher but he was away, spreading it in Florida. Her mother did not seem to mind his attention to the girl so long as he brought a basket of something with him when he came. As for Sarah Ruth herself, it was plain to Parker after he had visited three times that she was crazy about him. She liked him even though she insisted that pictures on the skin were vanity of vanities and even after hearing him curse, and even after she had asked him if he was saved and he had replied that he didn't see it was anything in particular to save him from. After that, inspired, Parker had said, "I'd be saved enough if you was to kiss me."

She scowled. "That ain't being saved," she said.

Not long after that she agreed to take a ride in his truck. Parker parked it on a deserted road and suggested to her that they lie down together in the back of it.

"Not until after we're married," she said — just like that.

"Oh, that ain't necessary," Parker said and as he reached for her, she thrust him away with such force that the door of the truck came off and he found himself flat on his back on the ground. He made up his mind then and there to have nothing further to do with her.

They were married in the County Ordinary's office because Sarah Ruth thought churches were idolatrous. Parker had no opinion about that one way or the other. The Ordinary's office was lined with cardboard file boxes and record books with dusty yellow slips of paper hanging on out of them. The Ordinary was an old woman with red hair who had held office for forty years and looked as dusty as her books. She married them from behind the iron-grill of a stand-up desk and when she finished, she said with a flourish, "Three dollars and fifty cents and till death do you part!" and yanked some forms out of a machine.

Marriage did not change Sarah Ruth a jot and it made Parker gloomier than ever. Every morning he decided he had had enough and would not return that night; every night he returned. Whenever Parker couldn't stand the way he felt, he would have another tattoo, but the only surface left on him now was his back. To see a tattoo on his own back he would have to get two mirrors and stand between them in just the correct position and this seemed to Parker a good way to make an idiot of himself. Sarah Ruth who, if she had had better sense, could have enjoyed a tattoo on his back, would not even look at the ones he had elsewhere. When he attempted to point out especial details of them, she would shut her eyes tight and turn her back as well. Except in total darkness, she preferred Parker dressed and with his sleeves rolled down.

"At the judgment seat of God, Jesus is going to say to you, 'What you been doing all your life besides have pictures drawn all over you?'" she said.

"You don't fool me none," Parker said, "you're just afraid that hefty girl I work for'll like me so much she'll say, 'Come on, Mr. Parker, let's you and me . . .'"

"You're tempting sin," she said, "and at the judgment seat of God you'll have to answer for that too. You ought to go back to selling the fruits of the earth."

Parker did nothing much when he was at home but listen to what the judgment seat of God would be like for him if he didn't change his ways. When he could, he broke in with tales of the hefty girl he worked for. "'Mr. Parker,'" he said she said, "'I hired you for your brains.'" (She had added, "So why don't you use them?")

"And you should have seen her face the first time she saw me without my shirt," he said. "'Mr. Parker,' she said, 'you're a walking panner-rammer!'" This had, in fact, been her remark but it had been delivered out of one side of her mouth.

Dissatisfaction began to grow so great in Parker that there was no containing it outside of a tattoo. It had to be his back. There was no help for it. A dim half-formed inspiration began to work in his mind. He visualized having a tattoo put there that Sarah Ruth would not be able to resist — a religious subject. He thought of an open book with HOLY BIBLE tattooed under it and an actual verse printed on the page. This seemed just the thing for a while; then he began to hear her say, "Ain't I already got a real Bible? What you think I want to read the same verse over and over for when I can read it all?" He needed something better even than the Bible! He thought about it so much that he began to lose sleep. He was already losing flesh — Sarah Ruth just threw food in the pot and let it boil. Not knowing for certain why he continued to stay with a woman who was both ugly and pregnant and no cook made him generally nervous and irritable, and he developed a little tic in the side of his face.

Once or twice he found himself turning around abruptly as if someone were trailing him. He had had a granddaddy who had ended in the state mental hospital, although not until he was seventy-five, but as urgent as it might be for him to get a tattoo, it was just as urgent that he get exactly the right one to bring Sarah Ruth to heel. As he continued to worry over it, his eyes took on a hollow preoccupied expression. The old woman he worked for told him that if he couldn't keep his mind on what he was doing, she knew where she could find a fourteen-year-old colored boy who could. Parker was too preoccupied even to be offended. At any time previous, he would have left her then and there, saying drily, "Well, you go ahead on and get him then."

Two or three mornings later he was baling hay with the old woman's sorry baler and her broken down tractor in a large field, cleared save for one enormous old tree standing in the middle of it. The old woman was the kind who would not cut down a large old tree because it was a large old tree. She had pointed it out to Parker as if he didn't have eyes and told him to be careful not to hit it as the machine picked up hay near it. Parker began at the outside of the field and made circles inward toward it. He had to get off the tractor every now and then and untangle the baling cord or kick a rock out of the way. The old woman had told him to carry the rocks to the edge of the field, which he did when she was there watching. When he thought he could make it, he ran over them. As he circled the field his mind was on a suitable design for his back. The sun, the size of a golf ball, began to switch regularly from in front to behind him, but he appeared to see it both places as if he had eyes in the back of his head. All at once he saw the tree reaching out to grasp him. A ferocious thud propelled him into the air, and he heard himself yelling in an unbelievably loud voice, "GOD ABOVE!"

He landed on his back while the tractor crashed upside-down into the tree and burst into flame. The first thing Parker saw were his shoes, quickly being eaten by the fire; one was caught under the tractor, the other was some distance away, burning by itself. He was not in them. He could feel the hot breath of the burning tree on his face. He scrambled backwards, still sitting, his eyes cavernous, and if he had known how to cross himself he would have done it.

His truck was on a dirt road at the edge of the field. He moved toward it, still sitting, still backwards, but faster and faster; halfway to it he got up and began a kind of forward-bent run from which he collapsed on his knees twice. His legs felt like two old rusted rain gutters. He reached the truck finally and took off in it, zigzagging up the road. He drove past his house on the embankment and straight for the city, fifty miles distant.

Parker did not allow himself to think on the way to the city. He only knew that there had been a great change in his life, a leap forward into a worse unknown, and that there was nothing he could do about it. It was for all intents accomplished.

The artist had two large cluttered rooms over a chiropodist's office on a back street. Parker, still barefooted, burst silently in on him at a little after three in the afternoon. The artist, who was about Parker's own age — twenty-eight — but thin and bald, was behind a small drawing table, tracing a design in green ink. He looked up with an annoyed glance and did not seem to recognize Parker in the hollow-eyed creature before him.

"Let me see the book you got with all the pictures of God in it," Parker said breathlessly. "The religious one."

The artist continued to look at him with his intellectual, superior stare. "I don't put tattoos on drunks," he said.

"You know me!" Parker cried indignantly. "I'm O. E. Parker! You done work for me before and I always paid!"

The artist looked at him another moment as if he were not altogether sure. "You've fallen off some," he said. "You must have been in jail."

"Married," Parker said.

"Oh," said the artist. With the aid of mirrors the artist had tattooed on the top of his head a miniature owl, perfect in every detail. It was about the size of a half-dollar and served him as a show piece. There were cheaper artists in town but Parker had never wanted anything but the best. The artist went over to a cabinet at the back of the room and began to look over some art books. "Who are you interested in?" he said, "saints, angels, Christs or what?"

"God," Parker said.

"Father, Son or Spirit?"

"Just God," Parker said impatiently. "Christ. I don't care. Just so it's God."

The artist returned with a book. He moved some papers off another table and put the book down on it and told Parker to sit down and see what he liked. "The up-to-date ones are in the back," he said.

Parker sat down with the book and wet his thumb. He began to go through it, beginning at the back where the up-to-date pictures were. Some of them he recognized — The Good Shepherd, Forbid Them Not, The Smiling Jesus, Jesus the Physician's Friend, but he kept turning rapidly backwards and the pictures became less and less reassuring. One showed a gaunt green dead face streaked with blood. One was yellow with sagging purple eyes. Parker's heart began to beat faster and faster until it appeared to be roaring inside him like a great generator. He flipped the pages quickly, feeling that when he reached the one ordained, a sign would come. He continued to flip through until he had almost reached the front of the book. On one of the pages a pair of eyes glanced at him swiftly. Parker sped on, then stopped. His heart too appeared to cut off; there was absolute silence. It said as plainly as if silence were a language itself, GO BACK.

Parker returned to the picture — the haloed head of a flat stern Byzantine Christ with all-demanding eyes. He sat there trembling; his heart began slowly to beat again as if it were being brought to life by a subtle power.

"You found what you want?" the artist asked.

Parker's throat was too dry to speak. He got up and thrust the book at the artist, opened at the picture.

"That'll cost you plenty," the artist said. "You don't want all those little blocks though, just the outline and some better features."

"Just like it is," Parker said, "just like it is or nothing."

"It's your funeral," the artist said, "but I don't do that kind of work for nothing."

"How much?" Parker asked.

"It'll take maybe two days work."

"How much?" Parker said.

"On time or cash?" the artist asked. Parker's other jobs had been on time, but he had paid.

"Ten down and ten for every day it takes," the artist said.

Parker drew ten dollar bills out of his wallet; he had three left in.

"You come back in the morning," the artist said, putting the money in his own pocket. "First I'll have to trace that out of the book."

"No, no!" Parker said. "Trace it now or gimme my money back," and his eyes blared as if he were ready for a fight.

The artist agreed. Any one stupid enough to want a Christ on his back, he reasoned, would be just as likely as not to change his mind the next minute, but once the work was begun he could hardly do so.

While he worked on the tracing, he told Parker to go wash his back at the sink with the special soap he used there. Parker did it and returned to pace back and forth across the room, nervously flexing his shoulders. He wanted to go look at the picture again but at the same time he did not want to. The artist got up finally and had Parker lie down on the table. He swabbed his back with ethyl chloride and then began to outline the head on it with his iodine pencil. Another hour passed before he took up his electric instrument. Parker felt no particular pain. In Japan he had had a tattoo of the Buddha done on his upper arm with ivory needles; in Burma, a little brown root of a man had made a peacock on each of his knees using thin pointed sticks, two feet long; amateurs had worked on him with pins and soot. Parker was usually so relaxed and easy under the hand of the artist that he often went to sleep, but this time he remained awake, every muscle taut.

At midnight the artist said he was ready to quit. He propped one mirror, four feet square, on a table by the wall and took a smaller mirror off the lavatory wall and put it in Parker's hands. Parker stood with his back to the one on the table and moved the other until he saw a flashing burst of color reflected from his back. It was almost completely covered with little red and blue and ivory and saffron squares; from them he made out the lineaments of the face — a mouth, the beginning of heavy brows, a straight nose, but the face was empty; the eyes had not yet been put in. The impression for the moment was almost as if the artist had tricked him and done the Physician's Friend.

"It don't have eyes," Parker cried out.

"That'll come," the artist said, "in due time. We have another day to go on it yet."

Parker spent the night on a cot at the Haven of Light Christian Mission. He found these the best places to stay in the city because they were free and included a meal of sorts. He got the last available cot and because he was still barefooted, he accepted a pair of second-hand shoes which, in his confusion, he put on to go to bed; he was still shocked from all that had happened to him. All night he lay awake in the long dormitory of cots with lumpy figures on them. The only light was from a phosphorescent cross glowing at the end of the room. The tree reached out to grasp him again, then burst into flame; the shoe burned quietly by itself; the eyes in the book said to him distinctly G O B A C K and at the same time did not utter a sound. He wished that he were not in this city, not in this Haven of Light Mission, not in a bed by himself. He longed miserably for Sarah Ruth. Her sharp tongue and icepick eyes were the only comfort he could bring to mind. He decided he was losing it. Her eyes appeared soft and dilatory compared with the eyes in the book, for even though he could not summon up the exact look of those eyes, he could still feel their penetration. He felt as though, under their gaze, he was as transparent as the wing of a fly.

The tattooist had told him not to come until ten in the morning, but when he arrived at that hour, Parker was sitting in the dark hallway on the floor, waiting for him. He had decided upon getting up that, once the tattoo was on him, he would not look at it, that all his sensations of the day and night before were those of a crazy man and that he would return to doing things according to his own sound judgment.

The artist began where he left off. "One thing I want to know," he said presently as he worked over Parker's back, "why do you want this on you? Have you gone and got religion? Are you saved?" he asked in a mocking voice.

Parker's throat felt salty and dry. "Naw," he said, "I ain't got no use for none of that. A man can't save his self from whatever it is he don't deserve none of my sympathy." These words seemed to leave his mouth like wraiths and to evaporate at once as if he had never uttered them.

"Then why . . ."

"I married this woman that's saved," Parker said. "I never should have done it. I ought to leave her. She's done gone and got pregnant."

"That's too bad," the artist said. "Then it's her making you have this tattoo."

"Naw," Parker said, "she don't know nothing about it. It's a surprise for her."

"You think she'll like it and lay off you a while?"

"She can't hep herself," Parker said. "She can't say she don't like the looks of God." He decided he had told the artist enough of his business. Artists were all right in their place but he didn't like them poking their noses into the affairs of regular people. "I didn't get no sleep last night," he said. "I think I'll get some now."

That closed the mouth of the artist but it did not bring him any sleep. He lay there, imagining how Sarah Ruth would be struck speechless by the face on his back and every now and then this would be interrupted by a vision of the tree of fire and his empty shoe burning beneath it.

The artist worked steadily until nearly four o'clock, not stopping to have lunch, hardly pausing with the electric instrument except to wipe the dripping dye off Parker's back as he went along. Finally he finished. "You can get up and look at it now," he said.

Parker sat up but he remained on the edge of the table.

The artist was pleased with his work and wanted Parker to look at it at once. Instead Parker continued to sit on the edge of the table, bent forward slightly but with a vacant look. "What ails you?" the artist said. "Go look at it."

"Ain't nothing ail me," Parker said in a sudden belligerent voice. "That tattoo ain't going nowhere. It'll be there when I get there." He reached for his shirt and began gingerly to put it on.

The artist took him roughly by the arm and propelled him between the two mirrors. "Now *look*," he said, angry at having his work ignored.

Parker looked, turned white and moved away. The eyes in the reflected face continued to look at him — still, straight, all-demanding, enclosed in silence.

"It was your idea, remember," the artist said. "I would have advised something else."

Parker said nothing. He put on his shirt and went out the door while the artist shouted, "I'll expect all of my money!"

Parker headed toward a package shop on the corner. He bought a pint of whiskey and took it into a nearby alley and drank it all in five minutes. Then he moved on to a pool hall nearby which he frequented when he came to the city. It was a well-lighted barn-like place with a bar up one side and gambling machines on the other and pool tables in the back. As soon as Parker entered, a large man in a red and black checkered shirt hailed him by slapping him on the back and yelling, "Yeyyyyyy boy! O. E. Parker!"

Parker was not yet ready to be struck on the back. "Lay off," he said, "I got a fresh tattoo there."

"What you got this time?" the man asked and then yelled to a few at the machines. "O.E.'s got him another tattoo."

"Nothing special this time," Parker said and slunk over to a machine that was not being used.

"Come on," the big man said, "let's have a look at O.E.'s tattoo," and while Parker squirmed in their hands, they pulled up his shirt. Parker felt all the hands drop away instantly and his shirt fell again like a veil over the face. There was a silence in the pool room which seemed to Parker to grow from the circle around him until it extended to the foundations under the building and upward through the beams in the roof.

Finally some one said, "Christ!" Then they all broke into noise at once. Parker turned around, an uncertain grin on his face.

"Leave it to O.E.!" the man in the checkered shirt said, "That boy's a real card!"

"Maybe he's gone and got religion," some one yelled.

"Not on your life," Parker said.

"O.E.'s got religion and is witnessing for Jesus, ain't you, O.E.?" a little man with a piece of cigar in his mouth said wryly. "An o-riginal way to do it if I ever saw one."

"Leave it to Parker to think of a new one!" the fat man said.

"Yyeeeeeeyyyyyyy boy!" someone yelled and they all began to whistle and curse in compliment until Parker said, "Aaa shut up."

"What'd you do it for?" somebody asked.

"For laughs," Parker said. "What's it to you?"

"Why ain't you laughing then?" somebody yelled. Parker lunged into the midst of them and like a whirlwind on a summer's day there began a fight that raged amid overturned tables and swinging fists until two of them grabbed him and ran to the door with him and threw him out. Then a calm descended on the pool hall as nerve shattering as if the long barn-like room were the ship from which Jonah had been cast into the sea.

Parker sat for a long time on the ground in the alley behind the pool hall, examining his soul. He saw it as a spider web of facts and lies that was not at all important to him but which appeared to be necessary in spite of his opinion. The eyes that were now forever on his back were eyes to be obeyed. He was as certain of it as he had ever been of anything. Throughout his life, grumbling and sometimes cursing, often afraid, once in rapture, Parker had obeyed whatever instinct of this kind had come to him — in rapture when his spirit had lifted at the sight of the tattooed man at the fair, afraid when he had joined the navy, grumbling when he had married Sarah Ruth.

The thought of her brought him slowly to his feet. She would know what he had to do. She would clear up the rest of it, and she would at least be pleased. It seemed to him that, all along, that was what he wanted, to please her. His truck was still parked in front of the building where the artist had his place, but it was not far away. He got in it and drove out of the city and into the country night. His head was almost clear of liquor and he observed that his dissatisfaction was gone, but he felt not quite like himself. It was as if he were himself but a stranger to himself, driving into a new country though everything he saw was familiar to him, even at night.

He arrived finally at the house on the embankment, pulled the truck under the pecan tree and got out. He made as much noise as possible to assert that he was still in charge here, that his leaving her for a night without word meant nothing except it was the way he did things. He slammed the car door, stamped up the two steps and across the porch and rattled the door knob. It did not respond to his touch. "Sarah Ruth!" he yelled, "let me in."

There was no lock on the door and she had evidently placed the back of a chair against the knob. He began to beat on the door and rattle the knob at the same time.

He heard the bed springs screak and bent down and put his head to the keyhole, but it was stopped up with paper. "Let me in!" he hollered, bamming on the door again. "What you got me locked out for?"

A sharp voice close to the door said, "Who's there?"

"Me," Parker said, "O.E."

He waited a moment.

"Me," he said impatiently, "O.E."

Still no sound from inside.

He tried once more. "O.E.," he said, bamming the door two or three more times. "O. E. Parker. You know me."

There was a silence. Then the voice said slowly, "I don't know no O.E."

"Quit fooling," Parker pleaded. "You ain't got any business doing me this way. It's me, old O.E., I'm back. You ain't afraid of me."

"Who's there?" the same unfeeling voice said.

Parker turned his head as if he expected someone behind him to give him the answer. The sky had lightened slightly and there were two or three streaks of yellow floating above the horizon. Then as he stood there, a tree of light burst over the skyline.

Parker fell back against the door as if he had been pinned there by a lance.

"Who's there?" the voice from inside said and there was a quality about it now that seemed final. The knob rattled and the voice said peremptorily, "Who's there, I ast you?"

Parker bent down and put his mouth near the stuffed keyhole. "Obadiah," he whispered and all at once he felt the light pouring through him, turning his spider web soul into a perfect arabesque of colors, a garden of trees and birds and beasts.

"Obadiah Elihue!" he whispered.

The door opened and he stumbled in. Sarah Ruth loomed there, hands on her hips. She began at once, "That was no hefty blonde woman you was working for and you'll have to pay her every penny on her tractor you busted up. She don't keep insurance on it. She came here and her and me had us a long talk and I . . ."

Trembling, Parker set about lighting the kerosene lamp.

"What's the matter with you, wasting that keresene this near day-light?" she demanded. "I ain't got to look at you."

A yellow glow enveloped them. Parker put the match down and began to unbutton his shirt.

"And you ain't going to have none of me this near morning," she said.

"Shut your mouth," he said quietly. "Look at this and then I don't want to hear no more out of you." He removed the shirt and turned his back to her.

"Another picture," Sarah Ruth growled. "I might have known you was off after putting some more trash on yourself."

Parker's knees went hollow under him. He wheeled around and cried, "Look at it! Don't just say that! *Look* at it!"

"I done looked," she said.

"Don't you know who it is?" he cried in anguish.

"No, who is it?" Sarah Ruth said. "It ain't anybody I know."

"It's him," Parker said.

"Him who?"

"God!" Parker cried.

"God? God don't look like that!"

"What do you know how he looks?" Parker moaned. "You ain't seen him."

"He don't *look*," Sarah Ruth said. "He's a spirit. No man shall see his face."

"Aw listen," Parker groaned, "this is just a picture of him."

"Idolatry!" Sarah Ruth screamed. "Idolatry! Enflaming yourself with idols under every green tree! I can put up with lies and vanity but I don't want no idolator in this house!" and she grabbed up the broom and began to thrash him across the shoulders with it.

Parker was too stunned to resist. He sat there and let her beat him until she had nearly knocked him senseless and large welts had formed on the face of the tattooed Christ. Then he staggered up and made for the door.

She stamped the broom two or three times on the floor and went to the window and shook it out to get the taint of him off it. Still gripping it, she looked toward the pecan tree and her eyes hardened still more. There he was — who called himself Obadiah Elihue — leaning against the tree, crying like a baby.

Cynthia Ozick

....

Rosa

OSA LUBLIN, A MADWOMAN and a scavenger, gave up
her store — she smashed it up herself — and moved to Miami.
It was a mad thing to do. In Florida she became a dependent.
Her niece in New York sent her money and she lived among the
elderly, in a dark hole, a single room in a "hotel." There was an ancient
dresser-top refrigerator and a one-burner stove. Over in a corner a
round oak table brooded on its heavy pedestal, but it was only for
drinking tea. Her meals she had elsewhere, in bed or standing at the
sink — sometimes toast with a bit of sour cream and half a sardine, or
a small can of peas heated in a Pyrex mug. Instead of maid service
there was a dumbwaiter on a shrieking pulley. On Tuesdays and Fridays it swallowed her meager bags of garbage. Squads of dying flies
blackened the rope. The sheets on her bed were just as black — it was
a five-block walk to the laundromat. The streets were a furnace, the
sun an executioner. Every day without fail it blazed and blazed, so
she stayed in her room and ate two bites of a hard-boiled egg in bed,
with a writing board on her knees; she had lately taken to composing
letters.

She wrote sometimes in Polish and sometimes in English, but her
niece had forgotten Polish; most of the time Rosa wrote to Stella in
English. Her English was crude. To her daughter Magda she wrote in
the most excellent literary Polish. She wrote on the brittle sheets of
abandoned stationery that inexplicably turned up in the cubbyholes of
a blistered old desk in the lobby. Or she would ask the Cuban girl in the
receptionist's cage for a piece of blank billing paper. Now and then she
would find a clean envelope in the lobby bin; she would meticulously

rip its seams and lay it out flat: it made a fine white square, the fresh face of a new letter.

The room was littered with these letters. It was hard to get them mailed — the post office was a block farther off than the laundromat, and the hotel lobby's stamp machine had been marked OUT OF ORDER for years. There was an oval tin of sardines left open on the sink counter since yesterday. Already it smelled vomitous. She felt she was in hell. "Golden and beautiful Stella," she wrote to her niece. "Where I put myself is in hell. Once I thought the worst was the worst, after that nothing could be the worst. But now I see, even after the worst there's still more." Or she wrote: "Stella, my angel, my dear one, a devil climbs into you and ties up your soul and you don't even know it."

To Magda she wrote: "You have grown into a lioness. You are tawny and you stretch apart your furry toes in all their power. Whoever steals you steals her own death."

Stella had eyes like a small girl's, like a doll's. Round, not big but pretty, bright skin underneath, fine pure skin above, tender eyebrows like rainbows, and lashes as rich as embroidery. She had the face of a little bride. You could not believe from all this beauty, these doll's eyes, these buttercup lips, these baby's cheeks, you could not believe in what harmless containers the bloodsucker comes.

Sometimes Rosa had cannibal dreams about Stella: she was boiling her tongue, her ears, her right hand, such a fat hand with plump fingers, each nail tended and rosy, and so many rings, not modern rings but old-fashioned junk-shop rings. Stella liked everything from Rosa's junk shop, everything used, old, lacy with other people's history. To pacify Stella, Rosa called her Dear One, Lovely, Beautiful; she called her Angel; she called her all these things for the sake of peace, but in reality Stella was cold. She had no heart. Stella, already nearly fifty years old, the Angel of Death.

The bed was black, as black as Stella's will. After a while Rosa had no choice, she took a bundle of laundry in a shopping cart and walked to the laundromat. Though it was only ten in the morning, the sun was killing. Florida, why Florida? Because here they were shells like herself, already fried from the sun. All the same she had nothing in common with them. Old ghosts, old socialists: idealists. The Human Race was all they cared for. Retired workers, they went to lectures, they frequented the damp and shadowy little branch library. She saw them walking with Tolstoy under their arms, with Dostoevsky. They knew good material. Whatever you wore they would feel between their fingers and give a name to: faille, corduroy, shantung, jersey, worsted, velours, crepe. She heard them speak of bias, grosgrain, the "season," the "length." Yellow they called mustard. What was pink to everyone else to them was sunset; orange was tangerine; red was hot tomato. They were from the Bronx, from Brooklyn, lost neighborhoods, burned out. A few were from West End Avenue. Once she met a former vegetable-store owner from Columbus Avenue; his store was on Columbus Avenue, his residence not far, on West Seventieth Street, off Central Park. Even in the perpetual garden of Florida, he reminisced about his flowery green heads of romaine lettuce, his glowing strawberries, his sleek avocados.

It seemed to Rosa Lublin that the whole peninsula of Florida was weighted down with regret. Everyone had left behind a real life. Here they had nothing. They were all scarecrows, blown about under the murdering sunball with empty ribcages.

In the laundromat she sat on a cracked wooden bench and watched the round porthole of the washing machine. Inside, the surf of detergent bubbles frothed and slapped her underwear against the pane.

An old man sat cross-legged beside her, fingering a newspaper. She looked over and saw that the headlines were all in Yiddish. In Florida the men were of higher quality than the women. They knew a little more of the world, they read newspapers, they lived for international affairs. Everything that happened in the Israeli Knesset they followed. But the women only recited meals they used to cook in their old lives — kugel, pirogen, latkes, blintzes, herring salad. Mainly the women thought about their hair. They went to hairdressers and came out into the brilliant day with plantlike crowns the color of zinnias. Seagreen paint on their eyelids. One could pity them: they were in love with rumors of their grandchildren, Katie at Bryn Mawr, Jeff at Princeton. To the grandchildren Florida was a slum, to Rosa it was a zoo.

She had no one but her cold niece in Queens, New York.

"Imagine this," the old man next to her said. "Just look, first he has Hitler, then he has Siberia, he's in a camp in Siberia! Next thing he gets away to Sweden, then he comes to New York and he peddles. He's a peddler, by now he's got a wife, he's got kids, so he opens a little store — just a little store, his wife is a sick woman, it's what you call a bargain store — "

"What?" Rosa said.

"A bargain store on Main Street, a place in Westchester, not even the Bronx. And they come in early in the morning, he didn't even hang out his shopping bags yet, robbers, muggers, and they choke him, they finish him off. From Siberia he lives for this day!"

Rosa said nothing.

"An innocent man alone in his store. Be glad you're not up there anymore. On the other hand, here it's no paradise neither. Believe me, when it comes to muggers and stranglers there's no utopia nowhere."

"My machine's finished," Rosa said. "I have to put in the dryer." She knew about newspapers and their evil reports: a newspaper item herself. WOMAN AXES OWN BIZ. Rosa Lublin, 59, owner of a second-hand furniture store on Utica Avenue, Brooklyn, yesterday afternoon deliberately demolished . . . The *News* and the *Post*. A big photograph, Stella standing near with her mouth stretched and her arms wild. In the *Times*, six lines.

"Excuse me, I notice you speak with an accent."

Rosa flushed. "I was born somewhere else, not here."

"I also was born somewhere else. You're a refugee? Berlin?"

"Warsaw."

"I'm also from Warsaw! Nineteen-twenty I left. Nineteen-six I was born."

"Happy birthday," Rosa said. She began to pull her things out of the washing machine. They were twisted into each other like mixed-up snakes.

"Allow me," said the old man. He put down his paper and helped her untangle. "Imagine this," he said. "Two people from Warsaw meet in Miami, Florida. In nineteen-ten I didn't dream of Miami, Florida."

"My Warsaw isn't your Warsaw," Rosa said.

"As long as your Miami, Florida, is my Miami, Florida." Two whole rows of glinting dentures smiled at her; he was proud to be a flirt. Together they shoved the snarled load into the dryer. Rosa put in two quarters and the thundering hum began. They heard the big snaps on the belt of her dress with the blue stripes, the one that was torn in the armpit, under the left sleeve, clanging against the caldron's metal sides.

"You read Yiddish?" the old man said.

"No."

"You can speak a few words maybe?"

"No." My Warsaw isn't your Warsaw. But she remembered her grandmother's cradle-croonings: her grandmother was from Minsk.

Unter Reyzls vigele shteyt a klor-vays tsigele. How Rosa's mother despised those sounds! When the drying cycle ended, Rosa noticed that the old man handled the clothes like an expert. She was ashamed for him to touch her underpants. *Under Rosa's cradle there's a clear-white little goat* . . . But he knew how to find a sleeve, wherever it might be hiding.

"What is it," he asked, "you're bashful?"

"No."

"In Miami, Florida, people are more friendly. What," he said, "you're still afraid? Nazis we ain't got, even Ku Kluxers we ain't got. What kind of person are you, you're still afraid?"

"The kind of person," Rosa said, "is what you see. Thirty-nine years ago I was somebody else."

"Thirty-nine years ago I wasn't so bad myself. I lost my teeth without a single cavity," he bragged. "Everything perfect. Periodontal disease."

"*I* was a chemist almost. A physicist," Rosa said. "You think I wouldn't have been a scientist?" The thieves who took her life! All at once the landscape behind her eyes fell out of control: a bright field flashed; then a certain shadowy corridor leading to the laboratory-supplies closet. The closet opened in her dreams also. Retorts and microscopes were ranged on the shelves. Once, walking there, she was conscious of the coursing of her own ecstasy — her new brown shoes, laced and sober, her white coat, her hair cut short in bangs: a serious person of seventeen, ambitious, responsible, a future Marie Curie! One of her teachers in the high school praised her for what he said was a "literary style" — oh, lost and kidnapped Polish! — and now she wrote and spoke English as helplessly as this old immigrant. From Warsaw! Born 1906! She imagined what bitter ancient alley, dense with stalls, cheap clothes strung on outdoor racks, signs in jargoned Yiddish. Anyhow they called her refugee. The Americans couldn't tell her apart from this fellow with his false teeth and his dewlaps and his rakehell reddish toupee bought God knows when or where — Delancey Street, the lower East Side. A dandy. Warsaw! What did he know? In school she had read Tuwim: such delicacy, such loftiness, such *Polishness.* The Warsaw of her girlhood: a great light: she switched it on, she wanted to live inside her eyes. The curve of the legs of her mother's bureau. The strict leather smell of her father's desk. The white tile tract of the kitchen floor, the big pots breathing, a narrow tower stair next to the attic . . . the house of her girlhood laden with a thousand books. Polish, German, French; her father's Latin books; the shelf of shy literary periodicals her mother's poetry now and then wandered through, in short lines like heated telegrams. Cultivation, old civilization, beauty, history! Surprising turnings of streets, shapes of venerable cottages, lovely aged eaves, unexpected and gossamer turrets, steeples, the gloss, the antiquity! Gardens. Whoever speaks of Paris has never seen Warsaw. Her father, like her mother, mocked at Yiddish; there was not a particle of ghetto left in him, not a grain of rot. Whoever yearns for an aristocratic sensibility, let him switch on the great light of Warsaw.

"Your name?" her companion said.

"Lublin, Rosa."

"A pleasure," he said. "Only why backwards? I'm an application form? Very good. You apply, I accept." He took command of her shopping cart. "Wherever is your home is my direction that I'm going anyhow."

"You forgot to take your laundry," Rosa said.

"Mine I did day before yesterday."

"So why did you come here?"

"I'm devoted to nature. I like the sound of a waterfall. Wherever it's cool it's a pleasure to sit and read my paper."

"What a story!"

"All right, so I go to have a visit with the ladies. Tell me, you like concerts?"

"I like my own room, that's all."

"A lady what wants to be a hermit!"

"I got my own troubles," Rosa said.

"Unload on me."

In the street she plodded beside him dumbly, a led animal. Her shoes were not nice; she should have put on the other ones. The sunlight was smothering — cooked honey dumped on their heads: one lick was good, too much could drown you. She was glad to have someone to pull the cart.

"You got internal warnings about talking to a stranger? If I say my name, no more a stranger. Simon Persky. A third cousin to Shimon Peres, the Israeli politician. I have different famous relatives, plenty of family pride. You ever heard of Betty Bacall, who Humphrey Bogart the movie star was married to, a Jewish girl? Also a distant cousin. I could tell you the whole story of my life experience, beginning with Warsaw. Actually it wasn't Warsaw, it was a little place a few miles out of town. In Warsaw I had uncles."

Rosa said again, "Your Warsaw isn't my Warsaw."

He stopped the cart. "What is this? A song with one stanza? You think I don't know the difference between generations? I'm seventy-one, and you, you're only a girl."

"Fifty-eight." Though in the papers, when they told how she smashed up her store, it came out fifty-nine. Stella's fault, Stella's black will, the Angel of Death's arithmetic.

"You see? I told you! A girl!"

"I'm from an educated family."

"Your English ain't better than what any other refugee talks."

"Why should I learn English? I didn't ask for it, I got nothing to do with it."

"You can't live in the past," he advised. Again the wheels of the cart were squealing. Like a calf, Rosa followed. They were approaching a self-service cafeteria. The smells of eggplant, fried potatoes, mushrooms blew out as if pumped. Rosa read the sign: KOLLINS KO-SHER KAMEO: EVERYTHING ON YOUR PLATE AS PRETTY AS A PICTURE: REMEMBRANCES OF NEW YORK AND THE PARADISE OF YOUR MATERNAL KITCHEN: DELICIOUS DISHES OF AMBROSIA AND NOSTALGIA: AIR CONDITIONED THRU-OUT.

"I know the owner," Persky said. "He's a big reader. You want tea?"

"Tea?"

"Not iced. The hotter the better. This is physiology. Come in, you'll cool off. You got some red face, believe me."

Rosa looked in the window. Her bun was loose, strings dangling on either side of her neck. The reflection of a ragged old bird with worn feathers. Skinny, a stork. Her dress was missing a button, but maybe the belt buckle covered this shame. What did she care? She thought of her room, her bed, her radio. She hated conversation.

"I got to get back," she said.

"An appointment?"

"No."

"Then have an appointment with Persky. So come, first tea. If you take with an ice cube, you're involved in a mistake."

They went in and chose a tiny table in a corner — a sticky disc on a wobbly plastic pedestal. "You'll stay, I'll get," Persky said.

She sat and panted. Silverware tapped and clicked all around. No one here but old people. It was like the dining room of a convalescent home. Everyone had canes, dowager's humps, acrylic teeth, shoes cut out for bunions. Everyone wore an open collar showing mottled skin, ferocious clavicles, the wrinkled foundations of wasted breasts. The air conditioning was on too high; she felt the cooling sweat licking from around her neck down, down her spine into the crevice of her bottom. She was afraid to shift; the chair had a wicker back and a black plastic seat. If she moved even a little, an odor would fly up: urine, salt, old woman's fatigue. She left off panting and shivered. What do I care? I'm used to everything. Florida, New York, it doesn't matter. All the same, she took out two hairpins and caught up the hanging strands; she shoved them into the core of her gray knot and pierced them through. She had no mirror, no comb, no pocketbook; not even a handkerchief. All she had was a Kleenex pushed into her sleeve and some coins in the pocket of her dress.

"I came out only for the laundry," she told Persky. With a groan he set down a loaded tray: two cups of tea, a saucer of lemon slices, a dish of eggplant salad, bread on what looked like a wooden platter but was really plastic, another plastic platter of Danish. "Maybe I didn't bring enough to pay."

"Never mind, you got the company of a rich retired taxpayer. I'm a well-off man. When I get my Social Security, I spit on it."

"What line of business?"

"The same what I see you got one lost. At the waist. Buttons. A shame. That kind's hard to match, as far as I'm concerned we stopped making them around a dozen years ago. Braided buttons is out of style."

"Buttons?" Rosa said.

"Buttons, belts, notions, knickknacks, costume jewelry. A factory. I thought my son would take it over but he wanted something different. He's a philosopher, so he became a loiterer. Too much education makes fools. I hate to say it, but on account of him I had to sell out. And the girls, whatever the big one wanted, the little one also. The big one found a lawyer, that's what the little one looked for. I got one son-in-law in business for himself, taxes, the other's a youngster, still on Wall Street."

"A nice family," Rosa bit off.

"A loiterer's not so nice. Drink while it's hot. Otherwise it won't reach to your metabolism. You like eggplant salad on top of bread and butter? You got room for it, rest assured. Tell me, you live alone?"

"By myself," Rosa said, and slid her tongue into the tea. Tears came from the heat.

"My son is over thirty, I still support him."

"My niece, forty-nine, not married, she supports me."

"Too old. Otherwise I'd say let's make a match with my son, let her support him too. The best thing is independence. If you're able-bodied, it's a blessing to work." Persky caressed his chest. "I got a bum heart."

Rosa murmured, "I had a business, but I broke it up."

"Bankruptcy?"

"Part with a big hammer," she said meditatively, "part with a piece of construction metal I picked up from the gutter."

"You don't look that strong. Skin and bones."

"You don't believe me? In the papers they said an axe, but where would I get an axe?"

"That's reasonable. Where would you get an axe?" Persky's finger removed an obstruction from under his lower plate. He examined it: an eggplant seed. On the floor near the cart there was something white, a white cloth. Handkerchief. He picked it up and stuffed it in his pants pocket. Then he said, "What kind of business?"

"Antiques. Old furniture. Junk. I had a specialty in antique mirrors. Whatever I had there, I smashed it. See," she said, "*now* you're sorry you started with me!"

"I ain't sorry for nothing," Persky said. "If there's one thing I know to understand, it's mental episodes. I got it my whole life with my wife."

"You're not a widower?"

"In a manner of speaking."

"Where is she?"

"Great Neck, Long Island. A private hospital, it don't cost me peanuts." He said, "She's in a mental condition."

"Serious?"

"It used to be once in a while, now it's a regular thing. She's mixed up that she's somebody else. Television stars. Movie actresses. Different people. Lately my cousin, Betty Bacall. It went to her head."

"Tragic," Rosa said.

"You see? I unloaded on you, now you got to unload on me."

"Whatever I would say, you would be deaf."

"How come you smashed up your business?"

"It was a store. I didn't like who came in it."

"Spanish? Colored?"

"What do I care who came? Whoever came, they were like deaf people. Whatever you explained to them, they didn't understand." Rosa stood up to claim her cart. "It's very fine of you to treat me to the Danish, Mr. Persky. I enjoyed it. Now I got to go."

"I'll walk you."

"No, no, sometimes a person feels to be alone."

"If you're alone too much," Persky said, "you think too much."

"Without a life," Rosa answered, "a person lives where they can. If all they got is thoughts, that's where they live."

"You ain't got a life?"

"Thieves took it."

She toiled away from him. The handle of the cart was a burning rod. A hat, I ought to have worn a hat! The pins in her bun scalded her scalp. She panted like a dog in the sun. Even the trees looked exhausted: every leaf face downward under a powder of dust. Summer without end, a mistake!

In the lobby she waited before the elevator. The "guests" — some had been residents for a dozen years — were already milling around, groomed for lunch, the old women in sundresses showing their thick collarbones and the bluish wells above them. Instead of napes they had rolls of wide fat. They wore no stockings. Brazen blue-marbled sinews strangled their squarish calves; in their reveries they were again young women with immortal pillar legs, the white legs of strong goddesses; it was only that they had forgotten about impermanence. In their faces, too, you could see everything they were not noticing about themselves — the red gloss on their drawstring mouths was never meant to restore youth. It was meant only to continue it. Flirts of seventy. Everything had stayed the same for them: intentions, actions, even expectations — they had not advanced. They believed in the seamless continuity of the body. The men were more inward, running their lives in front of their eyes like secret movies.

A syrup of cologne clogged the air. Rosa heard the tearing of envelopes, the wing-shudders of paper sheets. Letters from children: the

guests laughed and wept, but without seriousness, without belief. Re-
port-card marks, separations, divorces, a new coffee table to match the
gilt mirror over the piano, Stuie at sixteen learning to drive, Millie's
mother-in-law's second stroke, rumors of the cataracts of half-remem-
bered acquaintances, a cousin's kidney, the rabbi's ulcer, a daughter's
indigestion, burglary, perplexing news of East Hampton parties, psy-
choanalysis . . . the children were rich, how was this possible from such
poor parents? It was real and it was not real. Shadows on a wall; the
shadows stirred, but you could not penetrate the wall. The guests were
detached; they had detached themselves. Little by little they were
forgetting their grandchildren, their aging children. More and more
they were growing significant to themselves. Every wall of the lobby a
mirror. Every mirror hanging thirty years. Every table surface a mirror. In these mirrors the guests appeared to themselves as they used to
be, powerful women of thirty, striving fathers of thirty-five, mothers
and fathers of dim children who had migrated long ago, to other con-
tinents, inaccessible landscapes, incomprehensible vocabularies. Rosa
made herself brave; the elevator gate opened, but she let the empty
car ascend without her and pushed the cart through to where the
black Cuban receptionist sat, maneuvering clayey sweat balls up from
the naked place between her breasts with two fingers.

"Mail for Lublin, Rosa," Rosa said.

"Lublin, you lucky today. Two letters."

"Take a look where you keep packages also."

"You a lucky dog, Lublin," the Cuban girl said, and tossed an object
into the pile of wash.

Rosa knew what was in that package. She had asked Stella to send it;
Stella did not easily do what Rosa asked. She saw immediately that the
package was not registered. This angered her: Stella the Angel of
Death! Instantly she plucked the package out of the cart and tore the
wrapping off and crumpled it into a standing ashtray. Magda's shawl!
Suppose, God forbid, it got lost in the mail, what then? She squashed
the box into her breasts. It felt hard, heavy; Stella had encased it in
some terrible untender rind; Stella had turned it to stone. She wanted
to kiss it, but the maelstrom was all around her, pressing toward the
dining room. The food was monotonous and sparse and often stale;
still, to eat there increased the rent. Stella was all the time writing that
she was not a millionaire; Rosa never ate in the dining room. She kept
the package tight against her bosom and picked through the crowd, a
sluggish bird on ragged toes, dragging the cart.

In her room she breathed noisily, almost a gasp, almost a squeal, left the laundry askew in the tiny parody of a vestibule, and carried the box and the two letters to the bed. It was still unmade, fish-smelling, the covers knotted together like an umbilical cord. A shipwreck. She let herself down into it and knocked off her shoes — oh, they were scarred; that Persky must have seen her shame, first the missing button, afterward the used-up shoes. She turned the box round and round — a rectangular box. Magda's shawl! Magda's swaddling cloth. Magda's shroud. The memory of Magda's smell, the holy fragrance of the lost babe. Murdered. Thrown against the fence, barbed, thorned, electrified; grid and griddle; a furnace; the child on fire! Rosa put the shawl to her nose, to her lips. Stella did not want her to have Magda's shawl all the time, she had such funny names for having it — trauma, fetish, God knows what: Stella took psychology courses at the New School at night, looking for marriage among the flatulent bachelors in her classes.

One letter was from Stella and the other was one of those university letters, still another one, another sample of the disease. But in the box, Magda's shawl! The box would be last, Stella's fat letter first (fat meant trouble), the university letter did not matter. A disease. Better to put away the laundry than to open the university letter.

Dear Rosa [Stella wrote]:
   All right, I've done it. Been to the post office and mailed it. Your idol is on its way, separate cover. Go on your knees to it if you want. You make yourself crazy, everyone thinks you're a crazy woman. Whoever goes by your old store still gets glass in their soles. You're the older one, I'm the niece, I shouldn't lecture, but my God! It's thirty years, forty, who knows, give it a rest. It isn't as if I don't know just exactly how you do it, what it's like. What a scene, disgusting! You'll open the box and take it out and cry, and you'll kiss it like a crazy person. Making holes in it with kisses. You're like those people in the Middle Ages who worshipped a piece of the True Cross, a splinter from some old outhouse as far as anybody knew, or else they fell down in front of a single hair supposed to be some saint's. You'll kiss, you'll pee tears down your face, and so what? Rosa, by now, believe me, it's time, you have to have a life.

Out loud Rosa said, "Thieves took it."
And she said, "And you, Stella, *you* have a life?"

If I were a millionaire I'd tell you the same thing: get a job. Or else, come back and move in here. I'm away the whole day, it will be like living alone if that's what you want. It's too hot to look around down there, people get like vegetables. With everything you did for me I don't mind keeping up this way maybe another year or so, you'll think I'm stingy for saying it like that, but after all I'm not on the biggest salary in the world.

Rosa said, "Stella! Would you be alive if I didn't take you out from there? Dead. You'd be dead! So don't talk to me how much an old woman costs! I didn't give you from my store? The big gold mirror, you look in it at your bitter face — I don't care how pretty, even so it's bitter — and you forget who gave you presents!"

> And as far as Florida is concerned, well, it doesn't solve anything. I don't mind telling you now that they would have locked you up if I didn't agree to get you out of the city then and there. One more public outburst puts you in the bughouse. No more public scandals! For God's sake, don't be a crazy person! Live your life!

Rosa said again, "Thieves took it," and went, scrupulously, meticulously, as if possessed, to count the laundry in the cart.

A pair of underpants was missing. Once more Rosa counted everything: four blouses, three cotton skirts, three brassieres, one half-slip and one regular, two towels, eight pairs of underpants . . . nine went into the washing machine, the exact number. Degrading. Lost bloomers — dropped God knows where. In the elevator, in the lobby, in the street even. Rosa tugged, and the dress with the blue stripes slid like a coarse colored worm out of twisted bedsheets. The hole in the armpit was bigger now. Stripes, never again anything on her body with stripes! She swore it, but this, fancy and with a low collar, was Stella's birthday present, Stella bought it. As if innocent, as if ignorant, as if *not there*. Stella, an ordinary American, indistinguishable! No one could guess what hell she had crawled out of until she opened her mouth and up coiled the smoke of accent.

Again Rosa counted. A fact, one pair of pants lost. An old woman who couldn't even hang on to her own underwear.

She decided to sew up the hole in the stripes. Instead she put water on to boil for tea and made the bed with the clean sheets from the cart. The box with the shawl would be the last thing. Stella's letter she pushed under the bed next to the telephone. She tidied all around. Everything had to be nice when the box was opened. She spread jelly on three crackers and deposited a Lipton's tea bag on the Welch's lid. It was grape jelly, with a picture of Bugs Bunny elevating an officious finger. In spite of Persky's Danish, empty insides. Always Stella said: Rosa eats little by little, like a tapeworm in the world's belly.

Then it came to her that Persky had her underpants in his pocket.

Oh, degrading. The shame. Pain in the loins. Burning. Bending in the cafeteria to pick up her pants, all the while tinkering with his teeth. Why didn't he give them back? He was embarrassed. He had thought a handkerchief. How can a man hand a woman, a stranger, a piece of her own underwear? He could have shoved it right back into the cart, how would that look? A sensitive man, he wanted to spare her. When he came home with her underpants, what then? What could a man, half a widower, do with a pair of female bloomers? Nylon-plus-cotton, the long-thighed kind. Maybe he had filched them on purpose, a sex maniac, a wife among the insane, his parts starved. According to Stella, Rosa also belonged among the insane, Stella had the power to put her there. Very good, they would become neighbors, confidantes, she and Persky's wife, best friends. The wife would confess all of Persky's sexual habits. She would explain how it is that a man of this age comes to steal a lady's personal underwear. Whatever stains in the crotch are nobody's business. And not only that: a woman with children, Persky's wife would speak of her son and her married lucky daughters. And Rosa too, never mind how Stella was sour over it, she would tell about Magda, a beautiful young woman of thirty, thirty-one: a doctor married to a doctor; large house in Mamaroneck, New York; two medical offices, one on the first floor, one in the finished basement. Stella was alive, why not Magda? Who was Stella, coarse Stella, to insist that Magda was not alive? Stella the Angel of Death. Magda alive, the pure eyes, the bright hair. Stella, never a mother, who was Stella to mock the kisses Rosa put in Magda's shawl? She meant to crush it into her mouth. Rosa, a mother the same as anyone, no different from Persky's wife in the crazy house.

This disease! The university letter, like all of them — five, six postmarks on the envelope. Rosa imagined its pilgrimage: first to the *News,* the *Post,* maybe even the *Times,* then to Rosa's old store, then to the store's landlord's lawyers, then to Stella's apartment, then to Miami, Florida. A Sherlock Holmes of a letter. It had struggled to find its victim, and for what? More eating alive.

DEPARTMENT OF CLINICAL SOCIAL PATHOLOGY
UNIVERSITY OF KANSAS-IOWA

April 17, 1977

Dear Ms. Lublin:

Though I am not myself a physician, I have lately begun to amass survivor data as rather a considerable specialty. To be concrete: I am presently working on a study, funded by the Minew Foundation of the Kansas-Iowa Institute for Humanitarian Context, designed to research the theory developed by Dr. Arthur R. Hidgeson and known generally as Repressed Animation. Without at this stage going into detail, it may be of some preliminary use to you to know that investigations so far reveal an astonishing generalized minimalization during any extended period of stress resulting from incarceration, exposure, and malnutrition. We have turned up a wide range of neurological residues (including, in some cases, acute cerebral damage, derangement, disorientation, premature senility, etc.), as well as hormonal changes, parasites, anemia, thready pulse, hyperventilation, etc.; in children especially, temperatures as high as 108°, ascitic fluid, retardation, bleeding sores on the skin and in the mouth, etc. What is remarkable is that these are all *current conditions* in survivors and their families.

Disease, disease! Humanitarian Context, what did it mean? An excitement over other people's suffering. They let their mouths water up. Stories about children running blood in America from sores, what muck. Consider also the special word they used: *survivor.* Something new. As long as they didn't have to say *human being.* It used to be *refugee,* but by now there was no such creature, no more refugees, only survivors. A name like a number — counted apart from the ordinary swarm. Blue digits on the arm, what difference? They don't call you a woman anyhow. *Survivor.* Even when your bones get melted into the grains of the earth, still they'll forget *human being.* Survivor and survivor and survivor; always and always. Who made up these words, parasites on the throat of suffering!

For some months teams of medical paraphrasers have been conducting interviews with survivors, to contrast current medical paraphrase with conditions found more than three decades ago, at the opening of the camps. This, I confess, is neither my field nor my interest. My own concern, both as a scholar of social pathology and as a human being . . .

Ha! For himself it was good enough, for himself he didn't forget this word *human being!*

. . . is not with medical nor even with psychological aspects of survivor data.

Data. Drop in a hole!

What particularly engages me for purposes of my own participation in the study (which, by the way, is intended to be definitive, to close the books, so to speak, on this lamentable subject) is what I can only term the "metaphysical" side of Repressed Animation (R.A.). It begins to be evident that prisoners gradually came to Buddhist positions. They gave up craving and began to function in terms of non-functioning, i.e., nonattachment. The Four Noble Truths in Buddhist thought, if I may remind you, yield a penetrating summary of the fruit of craving: pain. "Pain" in this view is defined as ugliness, age, sorrow, sickness, despair, and, finally, birth. Nonattachment is attained through the Eightfold Path, the highest stage of which is the cessation of all human craving, the loftiest rapture, one might say, of consummated indifference.

It is my hope that these speculations are not displeasing to you. Indeed, I further hope that they may even attract you, and that you would not object to joining our study by means of an in-depth interview to be conducted by me at, if it is not inconvenient, your home. I should like to observe survivor syndroming within the natural setting.

Home! Where, where?

As you may not realize, the national convention of the American Association of Clinical Social Pathology has this year, for reasons of fairness to our East Coast members, been moved from Las Vegas to Miami Beach. The convention will take place at a hotel in your vicinity about the middle of next May, and I would be deeply grateful if you could receive me during that period. I have noted via a New York City newspaper (we are not so provincial out here as some may think!) your recent removal to Florida; consequently you are ideally circumstanced to make a contribution to our R.A. study. I look forward to your consent at your earliest opportunity.

> Very sincerely yours,
> James W. Tree, Ph.D.

Drop in a hole! Disease! It comes from Stella, everything! Stella saw what this letter was, she could see from the envelope — Dr. Stella! Kansas-Iowa Clinical Social Pathology, a fancy hotel, this is the cure for the taking of a life! Angel of Death!

With these university letters Rosa had a routine: she carried the scissors over to the toilet bowl and snipped little bits of paper and flushed. In the bowl going down, the paper squares whirled like wedding rice.

But this one: drop in a hole with your Four Truths and your Eight Paths together! Nonattachment! She threw the letter into the sink; also its crowded envelope ("Please forward," Stella's handwriting instructed, pretending to be American, leaving out the little stroke that goes across the 7); she lit a match and enjoyed the thick fire. Burn, Dr. Tree, burn up with your Repressed Animation! The world is full of Trees! The world is full of fire! Everything, everything is on fire! Florida is burning!

Big flakes of cinder lay in the sink: black foliage, Stella's black will. Rosa turned on the faucet, and the cinders spiraled down and away. Then she went to the round oak table and wrote the first letter of the day to her daughter, her healthy daughter, her daughter who suffered neither from thready pulse nor anemia, her daughter who was a professor of Greek philosophy at Columbia University in New York City, a stone's throw — the philosopher's stone that prolongs life and transmutes iron to gold — from Stella in Queens!

Magda, my Soul's Blessing [Rosa wrote],
Forgive me, my yellow lioness. Too long a time since the last writing. Strangers scratch at my life; they pursue, they break down the bloodstream's sentries. Always there is Stella. And so half a day passes without my taking up my pen to speak to you. A pleasure, the deepest pleasure, home bliss, to speak in our own language. Only to you. I am always having to write to Stella now, like a dog paying respects to its mistress. It's my obligation. She sends me money. She, whom I plucked out of the claws of all those Societies that came to us with bread and chocolate after the liberation! Despite everything, they were selling sectarian ideas; collecting troops for their armies. If not for me they would have shipped Stella with a boatload of orphans to Palestine, to become God knows what, to live God knows how. A field worker jabbering Hebrew. It would serve her right. Americanized airs. My father was never a Zionist. He used to call himself a "Pole by right." The Jews, he said, didn't put a thousand years of brains and blood into Polish soil in order to have to prove themselves to anyone. He was the wrong sort of idealist, maybe, but he had the instincts of a natural nobleman. I could laugh at that now — the whole business — but I don't, because I feel too vividly what he was, how substantial, how not given over to any light-mindedness whatever. He had Zionist

friends in his youth. Some left Poland early and lived. One is a book-
seller in Tel Aviv. He specializes in foreign texts and periodicals. My
poor little father. It's only history — an ad hoc instance of it, you might
say — that made the Zionist solution. My father's ideas were more
logical. He was a Polish patriot on a temporary basis, he said, until the
time when nation should lie down beside nation like the lily and the
lotus. He was at bottom a prophetic creature. My mother, you know,
published poetry. To you all these accounts must have the ring of pure
legend.

Even Stella, who *can* remember, refuses. She calls me a parable-
maker. She was always jealous of you. She has a strain of dementia, and
resists you and all other reality. Every vestige of former existence is an
insult to her. Because she fears the past she distrusts the future — it,
too, will turn into the past. As a result she has nothing. She sits and
watches the present roll itself up into the past more quickly than she
can bear. That's why she never found the one thing she wanted more
than anything, an American husband. I'm immune to these pains and
panics. Motherhood — I've always known this — is a profound distrac-
tion from philosophy, and all philosophy is rooted in suffering over the
passage of time. I mean the *fact* of motherhood, the physiological fact.
To have the power to create another human being, to be the instrument
of such a mystery. To pass on a whole genetic system. I don't believe in
God, but I believe, like the Catholics, in mystery. My mother wanted so
much to convert; my father laughed at her. But she was attracted. She
let the maid keep a statue of the Virgin and Child in the corner of the
kitchen. Sometimes she used to go in and look at it. I can even remember the words of a poem she wrote about the heat coming up from the
stove, from the Sunday pancakes —

> Mother of God, how you shiver
> in these heat-ribbons!
> Our cakes rise to you
> and in the trance of His birthing
> you hide.

Something like that. Better than that, more remarkable. Her Polish was
very dense. You had to open it out like a fan to get at all the meanings.
She was exceptionally modest, but she was not afraid to call herself a
symbolist.

I know you won't blame me for going astray with such tales. After
all, you're always prodding me for these old memories. If not for you, I
would have buried them all, to satisfy Stella. Stella Columbus! She
thinks there's such a thing as the New World. Finally — at last, at last —
she surrenders this precious vestige of your sacred babyhood. Here it is

in a box right next to me as I write. She didn't take the trouble to send it by registered mail! Even though I told her and told her. I've thrown out the wrapping paper, and the lid is plastered down with lots of Scotch tape. I'm not hurrying to open it. At first my hunger was unrestrained and I couldn't wait, but nothing is nice now. I'm saving you; I want to be serene. In a state of agitation one doesn't split open a diamond. Stella says I make a relic of you. She has no heart. It would shock you if I told you even one of the horrible games I'm made to play with her. To soothe her dementia, to keep her quiet, I pretend you died. Yes! It's true! There's nothing, however crazy, I wouldn't say to her to tie up her tongue. She slanders. Everywhere there are slanders, and sometimes — my bright lips, my darling! — the slanders touch even you. My purity, my snow queen!

I'm ashamed to give an example. Pornography. What Stella, that pornographer, has made of your father. She thieves all the truth, she robs it, she steals it, the robbery goes unpunished. She lies, and it's the lying that's rewarded. The New World! That's why I smashed up my store! Because here they make up lying theories. Even the professors — they take human beings for specimens. In Poland there used to be justice; here they have social theories. Their system inherits almost nothing from the Romans, that's why. Is it a wonder that the lawyers are no better than scavengers who feed on the droppings of thieves and liars? Thank God you followed your grandfather's bent and studied philosophy and not law.

Take my word for it, Magda, your father and I had the most ordinary lives — by "ordinary" I mean respectable, gentle, cultivated. Reliable people of refined reputation. His name was Andrzej. Our families had status. Your father was the son of my mother's closest friend. She was a converted Jew married to a Gentile: you can be a Jew if you like, or a Gentile, it's up to you. You have a legacy of choice, and they say choice is the only true freedom. We were engaged to be married. We would have been married. Stella's accusations are all Stella's own excretion. Your father was not a German. I was forced by a German, it's true, and more than once, but I was too sick to conceive. Stella has a naturally pornographic mind, she can't resist dreaming up a dirty sire for you, an SS man! Stella was with me the whole time, she knows just what I know. They never put me in their brothel either. Never believe this, my lioness, my snow queen! No lies come out of me to you. You are pure. A mother is the source of consciousness, of conscience, the ground of being, as philosophers say. I have no falsehoods for you. Otherwise I don't deny some few tricks: the necessary handful. To those who don't deserve the truth, don't give it. I tell Stella what it pleases her to hear. My child, perished. Perished. She always wanted it. She was always jealous of you. She has no heart. Even now she believes in my loss of you: and you a stone's throw from her door in New York! Let her think whatever she thinks; her mind is awry, poor thing; in me the strength of your being consumes my joy. Yellow blossom! Cup of the sun!

What a curiosity it was to hold a pen — nothing but a small pointed stick, after all, oozing its hieroglyphic puddles: a pen that speaks, miraculously, Polish. A lock removed from the tongue. Otherwise the tongue is chained to the teeth and the palate. An immersion into the living language: all at once this cleanliness, this capacity, this power to make a history, to tell, to explain. To retrieve, to reprieve!

To lie.

The box with Magda's shawl was still on the table. Rosa left it there. She put on her good shoes, a nice dress (polyester, "wrinkle-free" on the inside label); she arranged her hair, brushed her teeth, poured mouthwash on the brush, sucked it up through the nylon bristles, gargled rapidly. As an afterthought she changed her bra and slip; it meant getting out of her dress and into it again. Her mouth she reddened very slightly — a smudge of lipstick rubbed on with a finger.

Perfected, she mounted the bed on her knees and fell into folds. A puppet, dreaming. Darkened cities, tombstones, colorless garlands, a black fire in a gray field, brutes forcing the innocent, women with their mouths stretched and their arms wild, her mother's voice calling. After hours of these pitiless tableaux, it was late afternoon; by then she was certain that whoever put her underpants in his pocket was a criminal capable of every base act. Humiliation. Degradation. Stella's pornography!

To retrieve, to reprieve. Nothing in the elevator; in the lobby, nothing. She kept her head down. Nothing white glimmered up.

In the street a neon dusk was already blinking. Gritty mixture of heat and toiling dust. Cars shot by like large bees. It was too early for headlights: in the lower sky two strange competing lamps — a scarlet sun, round and brilliant as a blooded egg yolk; a silk-white moon, gray-veined with mountain ranges. These hung simultaneously at either end of the long road. The whole day's burning struck upward like a moving weight from the sidewalk. Rosa's nostrils and lungs were cautious: burning molasses air. Her underpants were not in the road.

In Miami at night no one stays indoors. The streets are clogged with wanderers and watchers; everyone in search, bedouins with no fixed paths. The foolish Florida rains spray down — so light, so brief and fickle, no one pays attention. Neon alphabets, designs, pictures, flashing undiminished right through the sudden small rain. A quick lick of lightning above one of the balconied hotels. Rosa walked. Much Yiddish. Caravans of slow old couples, linked at the elbows, winding down to the cool of the beaches. The sand never at rest, always churning, always inhabited; copulation under blankets at night, beneath neon-radiant low horizons.

She had never been near the beach; why should her underpants be lost in the sand?

On the sidewalk in front of the KOLLINS KOSHER KAMEO, nothing. Shining hungry smell of boiled potatoes in sour cream. The pants were not necessarily in Persky's pocket. Dented garbage barrels, empty near the curb. Pants already smoldering in an ash heap, among blackened tomato cans, kitchen scrapings, conflagrations of old magazines. Or: a simple omission, an accident, never transferred from the washing machine to the dryer. Or, if transferred, never removed. Overlooked. Persky unblemished. The laundromat was locked up for the night, with a metal accordion gate stretched across the door and windows. What marauders would seek out caldrons, giant washtubs? Property misleads, brings false perspectives. The power to smash her own. A kind of suicide. She had murdered her store with her own hands. She cared more for a missing pair of underpants, lost laundry, than for business. She was ashamed; she felt exposed. What was her store? A cave of junk.

On the corner across the street from the laundromat a narrow newspaper store, no larger than a stall. Persky might have bought his paper there. Suppose later in the day he had come down for an afternoon paper, her pants in his pocket, and dropped them?

Mob of New York accents. It was a little place, not air-conditioned.

"Lady? You're looking for something?"

A newspaper? Rosa had enough of the world.

"Look, it's like sardines in here. Buy something or go out."

"My store used to be six times the size of this place," Rosa said.

"So go to your store."

"I don't have a store." She reconsidered. If someone wanted to hide — to hide, not destroy — a pair of underpants, where would he put them? Under the sand. Rolled up and buried. She thought what a weight of sand would feel like in the crotch of her pants, wet heavy sand, still hot from the day. In her room it was hot, hot all night. No air. In Florida there was no air, only this syrup seeping into the esophagus. Rosa walked; she saw everything, but as if out of invention, out of imagination; she was unconnected to anything. She came to a gate; a mottled beach spread behind it. It belonged to one of the big hotels. The latch opened. At the edge of the waves you could look back and see black crenelated forms stretching all along the shore. In the dark, in silhouette, the towered hotel roofs held up their merciless teeth. Impossible that any architect pleasurably dreamed these teeth. The sand was only now beginning to cool. Across the water the sky breathed a starless black; behind her, where the hotels bit down on the city, a dusty glow of brownish red lowered. Mud clouds. The sand was littered with bodies. Photograph of Pompeii: prone in the volcanic ash. Her pants were under the sand; or else packed hard with sand, like a piece of torso, a broken statue, the human groin detached, the whole soul gone, only the loins left for kicking by strangers. She took off her good shoes to save them and nearly stepped on the sweated faces of two lovers plugged into a kiss. A pair of water animals in suction. The same everywhere, along the rim of every continent, this gurgling, foaming, trickling. A true smasher, a woman whose underpants have been stolen, a woman who has murdered her business with her own hands, would know how to step cleanly into the sea. A horizontal tunnel. You can fall into its pull just by entering it upright. How simple the night sea; only the sand is unpredictable, with its hundred burrowings, its thousand buryings.

When she came back to the gate, the latch would not budge. A cunning design, it trapped the trespasser.

She gazed up, and thought of climbing; but there was barbed wire on top.

So many double mounds in the sand. It was a question of choosing a likely sentinel: someone who would let her out. She went back down onto the beach again and tapped a body with the tip of her dangling shoe. The body jerked as if shot: it scrambled up.

"Mister? You know how to get out?"

"Room key does it," said the second body, still flat in the sand. It was a man. They were both men, slim and coated with sand; naked. The one lying flat — she could see what part of him was swollen.

"I'm not from this hotel," Rosa said.

"Then you're not allowed here. This is a private beach."

"Can you let me out?"

"Lady, please. Just buzz off," the man in the sand said.

"I can't get out," Rosa pleaded.

The man who was standing laughed.

Rosa persisted. "If you have a key — "

"Believe me, lady, not for you" — muffled from below.

She understood. Sexual mockery. "Sodom!" she hissed, and stumbled away. Behind her their laughter. They hated women. Or else they saw she was a Jew; they hated Jews; but no, she had noticed the circumcision, like a jonquil, in the dim sand. Her wrists were trembling. To be locked behind barbed wire! No one knew who she was; what had happened to her; where she came from. Their gates, the terrible ruse of their keys, wire brambles, men lying with men . . . She was afraid to approach any of the other mounds. No one to help. Persecutors. In the morning they would arrest her.

She put on her shoes again, and walked along the cement path that followed the fence. It led her to light; voices of black men. A window. Vast deep odors: kitchen exhaust, fans stirring soup smells out into the weeds. A door wedged open by a milk-can lid. Acres of counters, stoves, steamers, refrigerators, percolators, bins, basins. The kitchen of a castle. She fled past the black cooks in their meat-blooded aprons, through a short corridor; a dead end facing an elevator. She pushed the button and waited. The kitchen people had seen her; would they pursue? She heard their yells, but it was nothing to do with her — they were calling Thursday, Thursday. On Thursday no more new potatoes. A kind of emergency maybe. The elevator took her to the main floor, to the lobby; she emerged, free.

This lobby was the hall of a palace. In the middle a real fountain. Water springing out of the mouths of emerald-green dolphins. Skirted cherubs, gilded. A winged mermaid spilling gold flowers out of a gold pitcher. Lofty plants — a forest — palms sprayed dark blue and silver and gold, leafing out of masses of green marble vessels at the lip of the fountain. The water flowed into a marble channel, a little indoor brook. A royal carpet for miles around, woven with crowned birds. Well-dressed men and women sat in lion-clawed gold thrones, smoking. A golden babble. How happy Stella would be, to stroll in a place like this! Rosa kept close to the walls.

She saw a man in a green uniform.

"The manager," she croaked. "I have to tell him something."

"Office is over there." He shrugged toward a mahogany desk behind a glass wall. The manager, wearing a red wig, was making a serious mark on a crested letterhead. Persky, too, had a red wig. Florida was glutted with fake fire, burning false hair! Everyone a piece of impostor. "Ma'am?" the manager said.

"Mister, you got barbed wire by your beach."

"Are you a guest here?"

"I'm someplace else."

"Then it's none of your business, is it?"

"You got barbed wire."

"It keeps out the riffraff."

"In America it's no place for barbed wire on top of fences."

The manager left off making his serious marks. "Will you leave?" he said. "Will you please just leave?"

"Only Nazis catch innocent people behind barbed wire," Rosa said.

The red wig dipped. "My name is Finkelstein."

"Then you should know better!"

"Listen, walk out of here if you know what's good for you."

"Where were you when we was there?"

"Get out. So far I'm asking nicely. Please get out."

"Dancing in the pool in the lobby, that's where. Eat your barbed wire, Mr. Finkelstein, chew it and choke on it!"

"Go home," Finkelstein said.

"You got Sodom and Gomorrah in your back yard! You got gays and you got barbed wire!"

"You were trespassing on our beach," the manager said. "You want me to call the police? Better leave before. Some important guests have come in, we can't tolerate the noise and I can't spare the time for this."

"They write me letters all the time, your important guests. Conventions," Rosa scoffed. "Clinical Social Pathology, right? You got a Dr. Tree staying?"

"Please go," Finkelstein said.

"Come on, you got a Dr. Tree? No? I'll tell you, if not today you'll get him later on, he's on the way. He's coming to investigate specimens. I'm the important one! It's me he's interviewing, Finkelstein, not you! I'm the study!"

The red wig dipped again.

"Aha!" Rosa cried. "I see you got Tree! You got a whole bunch of Trees!"

"We protect the privacy of our guests."

"With barbed wire you protect. It's Tree, yes? I can see I'm right! It's Tree! You got Tree staying here, right! Admit you got Tree! Finkelstein, you SS, admit it!"

The manager stood up. "Out," he said. "Get out now. Immediately."

"Don't worry, it's all right. It's my business to keep away. Tree I don't need. With Trees I had enough, you don't have to concern your-self —"

"*Leave,*" said the red wig.

"A shame," Rosa said, "a Finkelstein like you." Irradiated, trium-phant, cleansed, Rosa marched through the emerald glitter, toward the illuminated marquee in front. HOTEL MARIE LOUISE, in green neon. A doorman like a British admiral, gold braid cascading from his shoulders. They had trapped her, nearly caught her; but she knew how to escape. Speak up, yell. The same way she saved Stella, when they were pressing to take her on the boat to Palestine. She had no fear of Jews; sometimes she had — it came from her mother, her father — a certain contempt. The Warsaw swarm, shut off from the grandeur of the true world. Neighborhoods of a particular kind. Persky and Finkelstein. "Their" synagogues — balconies for the women. Primi-tive. Her own home, her own upbringing — how she had fallen. A loathsome tale of folk sorcery: nobility turned into a small dun rodent. Cracking her teeth on the poison of English. Here they were shallow, they knew nothing. Light-minded. Stella looking, on principle, to be light-minded. Blue stripes, barbed wire, men embracing men . . . what-ever was dangerous and repugnant they made prevalent, frivolous.

Lost. Lost. Nowhere. All of Miami Beach, empty; the sand, empty. The whole wild hot neon night city: an empty search. In someone's pocket.

Persky was waiting for her. He sat in the torn brown plastic wing chair near the reception desk, one leg over the side, reading a news-paper.

He saw her come in and jumped up. He wore only a shirt and pants; no tie, no jacket. Informal.

"Lublin, Rosa!"

Rosa said, "How come you're here?"

"Where you been the whole night? I'm sitting hours."

"I didn't tell you where I stay," Rosa accused.

"I looked in the telephone book."

"My phone's disconnected, I don't know nobody. My niece, she writes, she saves on long distance."

"All right. You want the truth? This morning I followed you, that's all. A simple walk from my place. I sneaked in the streets behind you. I found out where you stay, here I am."

"Very nice," Rosa said.

"You don't like it?"

She wanted to tell him he was under suspicion; he owed her a look in his jacket pocket. A self-confessed sneak who follows women. If not his jacket, his pants. But it wasn't possible to say a thing like this. Her pants in his pants. Instead she said, "What do you want?"

He flashed his teeth. "A date."

"You're a married man."

"A married man what ain't got a wife."

"You got one."

"In a manner of speaking. She's crazy."

Rosa said, "I'm crazy, too."

"Who says so?"

"My niece."

"What does a stranger know?"

"A niece isn't a stranger."

"My own son is a stranger. A niece definitely. Come on, I got my car nearby. Air-conditioned, we'll take a spin."

"You're not a kid, I'm not a kid," Rosa said.

"You can't prove it by me," Persky said.

"I'm a serious person," Rosa said. "It isn't my kind of life, to run around noplace."

"Who said noplace? I got a place in mind." He reflected. "My Senior Citizens. Very nice pinochle."

"Not interested," Rosa said. "I don't need new people."

"Then a movie. You don't like new ones, we'll find dead ones. Clark Gable. Jean Harlow."

"Not interested."

"A ride to the beach. A walk on the shore, how about it?"

"I already did it," Rosa said.

"When?"

"Tonight. Just now."

"Alone?"

Rosa said, "I was looking for something I lost."

"Poor Lublin, what did you lose?"

"My life."

She was all at once not ashamed to say this outright. Because of the missing underwear she had no dignity before him. She considered Persky's life: how trivial it must always have been: buttons, himself no more significant than a button. It was plain he took her to be another button like himself, battered now and out of fashion, rolled into Florida. All of Miami Beach, a box for useless buttons!

"This means you're tired. Tell you what," Persky said. "Invite me upstairs. A cup of tea. We'll make a conversation. You'll see, I got other ideas up my sleeve — tomorrow we'll go someplace and you'll like it."

Her room was miraculously ready: tidy, clarified. It was sorted out: you could see where the bed ended and the table commenced. Sometimes it was all one jumble, a highway of confusion. Destiny had clarified her room just in time for a visitor. She started the tea. Persky put his newspaper down on the table, and on top of it an oily paper bag. "Crullers!" he announced. "I bought them to eat in the car, but this is very nice, cozy. You got a cozy place, Lublin."

"Cramped," Rosa said.

"I work from a different theory. For everything there's a bad way of describing, also a good way. You pick the good way, you get along better."

"I don't like to give myself lies," Rosa said.

"Life is short, we all got to lie. Tell me, you got paper napkins? Never mind, who needs them. Three cups! That's a lucky thing, usually when a person lives alone they don't keep so many. Look, vanilla icing, chocolate icing. Two plain also. You prefer with icing or plain? Such fine tea bags, they got style. Now, you see, Lublin? Everything's nice!"

He had set the table. To Rosa this made the corner of the room look new, as if she had never seen it before.

"Don't let the tea cool off. Remember what I told you this morning, the hotter the better," Persky said; he clanged his spoon happily. "Here, let's make more elbow room — "

His hand, greasy from the crullers, was on Magda's box.

"Don't touch!"

"What's the matter? It's something alive in there? A bomb? A rabbit? It's squashable? No, I got it — a lady's hat!"

Rosa hugged the box; she was feeling foolish, trivial. Everything was frivolous here, even the deepest property of being. It seemed to her someone had cut out her life organs and given them to her to hold. She walked the little distance to the bed — three steps — and set the box down against the pillow. When she turned around, Persky's teeth were persisting in their independent bliss.

"The fact is," he said, "I didn't expect nothing from you tonight. You got to work things through, I can see that. You remind me of my son. Even to get a cup of tea from you is worth something, I could do worse. Tomorrow we'll have a real appointment. I'm not inquiring, I'm not requesting. I'll be the boss, what do you say?"

Rosa sat. "I'm thinking, I should get out and go back to New York to my niece — "

"Not tomorrow. Day after tomorrow you'll change your life, and tomorrow you'll come with me. We got six meetings to pick from."

Rosa said doubtfully, "Meetings?"

"Speakers. Lectures for fancy people like yourself. Something higher than pinochle."

"I don't play," Rosa acknowledged.

Persky looked around. "I don't see no books neither. You want me to drive you to the library?"

A thread of gratitude pulled in her throat. He almost understood what she was: no ordinary button. "I read only Polish," she told him. "I don't like to read in English. For literature you need a mother tongue."

"*Literature*, my my. Polish ain't a dime a dozen. It don't grow on trees neither. Lublin, you should adjust. Get used to it!"

She was wary: "I'm used to everything."

"Not to being a regular person."

"My niece Stella," Rosa slowly gave out, "says that in America cats have nine lives, but we — we're less than cats, so we got three. The life before, the life during, the life after." She saw that Persky did not follow. She said, "The life after is now. The life before is our *real* life, at home, where we was born."

"And during?"

"This was Hitler."

"Poor Lublin," Persky said.

"You wasn't there. From the movies you know it." She recognized that she had shamed him; she had long ago discovered this power to shame. "After, after, that's all Stella cares. For me there's one time only, there's no after."

Persky speculated. "You want everything the way it was before."

"No, no, no," Rosa said. "It can't be. I don't believe in Stella's cats. Before is a dream. After is a joke. Only during stays. And to call it a life is a lie."

"But it's over," Persky said. "You went through it, now you owe yourself something."

"This is how Stella talks. Stella — " Rosa halted; then she came on the word. "Stella is self-indulgent. She wants to wipe out memory."

"Sometimes a little forgetting is necessary," Persky said, "if you want to get something out of life."

"Get something! Get *what*?"

"You ain't in a camp. It's finished. Long ago it's finished. Look around, you'll see human beings."

"What I see," Rosa said, "is bloodsuckers."

Persky hesitated. "Over there, they took your family?"

Rosa held up all the fingers of her two hands. Then she said, "I'm left. Stella's left." She wondered if she dared to tell him more. The box on the bed. "Out of so many, three."

Persky asked, "Three?"

"Evidence," Rosa said briskly. "I can show you."

She raised the box. She felt like a climber on the margin of a precipice. "Wipe your hands."

Persky obeyed. He rubbed the last of the cruller crumbs on his shirt front.

"Unpack and look in. Go ahead, lift up what's inside."

She did not falter. What her own hands longed to do she was yielding to a stranger, a man with pockets; she knew why. To prove herself pure: a madonna. Supposing he had vile old man's thoughts: let him see her with the eye of truth. A mother.

But Persky said, "How do you count three — "

"Look for yourself."

He took the cover off and reached into the box and drew out a sheet of paper and began to skim it.

"That has to be from Stella. Throw it out, never mind. More scolding, how I'm a freak — "

"Lublin, you're a regular member of the intelligentsia! This is quite some reading matter. It ain't in Polish neither." His teeth danced. "On such a sad subject, allow me a little joke. Who came to America was one, your niece Stella; Lublin, Rosa, this makes two; and Lublin's brain — three!"

Rosa stared. "I'm a mother, Mr. Persky," she said, "the same as your wife, no different." She received the paper between burning palms. "Have some respect," she commanded the bewildered glitter of his plastic grin. And read:

Dear Ms. Lublin:

I am taking the liberty of sending you, as a token of my good faith, this valuable study by Hidgeson (whom, you may recall, I mentioned in passing in my initial explanatory letter), which more or less lays the ethological groundwork for our current structures. I feel certain that — in preparation for our talks — you will want to take a look at it. A great deal of our work has been built on these phylogenetic insights. You may find some of the language a bit too technical; nevertheless I believe that simply having this volume in your possession will go far toward reassuring you concerning the professionalism of our endeavors, and of your potential contribution toward them.

Of special interest, perhaps, is Chapter Six, entitled "Defensive Group Formation: The Way of the Baboons."

Gratefully in advance,
James W. Tree, Ph.D.

Persky said, "Believe me, I could smell with only one glance it wasn't from Stella."

She saw that he was holding the thing he had taken out of the box. "Give me that," she ordered.

He recited, "By A. R. Hidgeson. And listen to the title, something fancy — 'Repressed Animation: A Theory of the Biological Ground of Survival.' I told you fancy! This isn't what you wanted?"

"Give it to me."

"You didn't want? Stella sent you what you didn't want?"

"Stella sent!" She tore the book from him — it was heavier than she had guessed — and hurled it at the ceiling. It slammed down into Persky's half-filled teacup. Shards and droplets flew. "The way I smashed up my store, that's how I'll smash Tree!"

Persky was watching the tea drip to the floor.

"Tree?"

"Dr. Tree! Tree the bloodsucker!"

"I can see I'm involved in a mistake," Persky said. "I'll tell you what, you eat up the crullers. You'll feel better and I'll come tomorrow when the mistake is finished."

"I'm not your button, Persky! I'm nobody's button, not even if they got barbed wire everywhere!"

"Speaking of buttons, I'll go and push the elevator button. Tomorrow I'll come back."

"Barbed wire! You took my laundry, you think I don't know that? Look in your dirty pockets, you thief Persky!"

In the morning, washing her face — it was swollen, nightmares like weeds, the bulb of her nose pale — Rosa found, curled inside a towel, the missing underwear.

She went downstairs to the desk; she talked over having her phone reconnected. Naturally they would charge more, and Stella would squawk. All the same, she wanted it.

At the desk they handed her a package; this time she examined the wrapping. It had come by registered mail and it was from Stella. It was not possible to be hoodwinked again, but Rosa was shocked, depleted, almost as if yesterday's conflagration hadn't been Tree but really the box with Magda's shawl.

She lifted the lid of the box and looked down at the shawl; she was indifferent. Persky too would have been indifferent. The colorless cloth lay like an old bandage; a discarded sling. For some reason it did not instantly restore Magda, as usually happened, a vivid thwack of restoration, like an electric jolt. She was willing to wait for the sensation to surge up whenever it would. The shawl had a faint saliva smell, but it was more nearly imagined than smelled.

Under the bed the telephone vibrated: first a sort of buzz, then a real ring. Rosa pulled it out.

The Cuban's voice said, "Missus Lublin, you connected now."

Rosa wondered why it was taking so long for Magda to come alive. Sometimes Magda came alive with a brilliant swoop, almost too quickly, so that Rosa's ribs were knocked on their insides by copper hammers, clanging and gonging.

The instrument, still in her grip, drilled again. Rosa started: it was as if she had squeezed a rubber toy. How quickly a dead thing can come to life! Very tentatively, whispering into a frond, Rosa said, "Hello?" It was a lady selling frying pans.

"No," Rosa said, and dialed Stella. She could hear that Stella had been asleep. Her throat was softened by a veil. "Stella," Rosa said, "I'm calling from my own room."

"Who is this?"

"Stella, you don't recognize me?"

"Rosa! Did anything happen?"

"Should I come back?"

"My God," Stella said, "is it an emergency? We could discuss this by mail."

"You wrote me I should come back."

"I'm not a millionaire," Stella said. "What's the point of this call?"

"Tree's here."

"Tree? What's that?"

"*Doctor* Tree. You sent me his letter, he's after me. By accident I found out where he stays."

"No one's after you," Stella said grimly.

Rosa said, "Maybe I should come back and open up again."

"You're talking nonsense. You *can't*. The store's finished. If you come back it has to be a new attitude absolutely, recuperated. The end of morbidness."

"A very fancy hotel," Rosa said. "They spend like kings."

"It's none of your business."

"A Tree is none of my business? He gets rich on our blood! Prestige! People respect him! A professor with specimens! He wrote me baboons!"

"You're supposed to be recuperating," Stella said; she was wide awake. "Walk around. Keep out of trouble. Put on your bathing suit. Mingle. How's the weather?"

"In that case you come here," Rosa said.

"Oh my God, I can't afford it. You talk like I'm a millionaire. What would I do down there?"

"I don't like it alone. A man stole my underwear."

"Your *what*?" Stella squealed.

"My panties. There's plenty perverts in the streets. Yesterday in the sand I saw two naked men."

"Rosa," Stella said, "if you want to come back, come back. I wrote you that, that's all I said. But you could get interested in something down there for a change. If not a job, a club. If it doesn't cost too much, I wouldn't mind paying for a club. You could join some kind of group, you could walk, you could swim — "

"I already walked."

"Make friends." Stella's voice tightened. "Rosa, this is long *distance*."

On that very phrase, "long *distance*," Magda sprang to life. Rosa took the shawl and put it over the knob of the receiver: it was like a little doll's head then. She kissed it, right over Stella's admonitions. "Good-bye," she told Stella, and didn't care what it had cost. The whole room was full of Magda: she was like a butterfly, in this corner and in that corner, all at once. Rosa waited to see what age Magda was going to be: how nice, a girl of sixteen, girls in their bloom move so swiftly that their blouses and skirts balloon, they are always butterflies at sixteen. There was Magda, all in flower. She was wearing one of Rosa's dresses from high school. Rosa was glad: it was the sky-colored dress, a middling blue with black buttons seemingly made of round chips of coal, like the unlit shards of stars. Persky could never have been acquainted with buttons like that, they were so black and so sparkling; original, with irregular facets like bits of true coal from a vein in the earth or some other planet. Magda's hair was still as yellow as buttercups, and so slippery and fine that her two barrettes, in the shape of cornets, kept sliding down toward the sides of her chin — that chin which was the marvel of her face; with a different kind of chin it would have been a much less explicit face. The jaw was ever so slightly too long, a deepened oval, so that her mouth, especially the lower lip, was not crowded but rather made a definite mark in the middle of spaciousness. Consequently the mouth seemed as significant as a body arrested in orbit, and Magda's sky-filled eyes, nearly rectangular at the corners, were like two obeisant satellites. Magda could be seen with great clarity. She had begun to resemble Rosa's father, who had also had a long oval face anchored by a positive mouth. Rosa was enraptured by Magda's healthy forearms. She would have given everything to set her before an easel, to see whether she could paint in watercolors; or to have her seize a violin, or a chess queen; she knew little about Magda's mind at this age, or whether she had any talents; even what her intelligence tended toward. And also she was always a little suspicious of Magda, because of the other strain, whatever it was, that ran in her. Rosa herself was not truly suspicious, but Stella was, and that induced perplexity in Rosa. The other strain was ghostly, even dangerous. It was as if the peril hummed out from the filaments of Magda's hair, those narrow bright wires.

My Gold, my Wealth, my Treasure, my Hidden Sesame, my Paradise, my Yellow Flower, my Magda! Queen of Bloom and Blossom!

When I had my store I used to "meet the public," and I wanted to tell everybody — not only our story but other stories as well. Nobody knew anything. This amazed me, that nobody remembered what happened only a little while ago. They didn't remember because they didn't know. I'm referring to certain definite facts. The tramcar in the Ghetto, for instance. You know they took the worst section, a terrible slum, and they built a wall around it. It was a regular city neighborhood, with rotting old tenements. They pushed in half a million people, more than double the number there used to be in that place. Three families, including all their children and old folks, into one apartment. Can you imagine a family like us — my father who had been the director-general of the Bank of Warsaw, my sheltered mother, almost Japanese in her shyness and refinement, my two young brothers, my older brother, and me — all of us, who had lived in a tall house with four floors and a glorious attic (you could touch the top of the house by sticking your arm far out its window; it was like pulling the whole green ribbon of summer indoors) — imagine confining *us* with teeming Mockowiczes and Rabinowiczes and Perskys and Finkelsteins, with all their bad-smelling grandfathers and their hordes of feeble children! The children were half-dead, always sitting on boxes in tatters with such sick eyes, pus on the lids and the pupils too wildly lit up. All these families used up their energies with walking up and down, and bowing, and shaking and quaking over old rags of prayer books, and their children sat on the boxes and yelled prayers, too. We thought they didn't know how to organize themselves in adversity, and, besides that, we were furious: because the same sort of adversity was happening to *us* — my father was a person of real importance, and my tall mother had so much delicacy and dignity that people would bow automatically, even before they knew who she was. So we were furious in every direction, but most immediately we were furious because we had to be billeted with such a class, with these old Jew peasants worn out from their rituals and superstitions, phylacteries on their foreheads sticking up so stupidly, like unicorn horns, every morning. And in the most repulsive slum, deep in slops and vermin and a toilet not fit for the lowest criminal. We were not of a background to show our fury, of course, but my father told my brothers and me that my mother would not be able to live through it, and he was right.

In my store I didn't tell this to everyone; who would have the patience to hear it all out? So I used to pick out one little thing here, one little thing there, for each customer. And if I saw they were in a hurry — most of them were, after I began — I would tell just about the tramcar. When I told about the tramcar, no one ever understood that it ran on tracks! Everybody always thought of buses. Well, they couldn't tear up the tracks, they couldn't get rid of the overhead electric wire, could they? The point is they couldn't reroute the whole tram system; so, you know, they didn't. The tramcar came right through the middle of the Ghetto. What they did was build a sort of overhanging pedestrian bridge for the Jews — they couldn't get near the tramcar to escape on it into the other part of Warsaw. The other side of the wall.

The most astonishing thing was that the most ordinary streetcar, bumping along on the most ordinary trolley tracks, and carrying the most ordinary citizens going from one section of Warsaw to another, ran straight into the place of our misery. Every day, and several times a day, we had these witnesses. Every day they saw us — women with shopping sacks, and once I noticed a head of lettuce sticking up out of the top of a sack. Green lettuce! I thought my salivary glands would split with aching for that leafy greenness. And girls wearing hats. They were all the sort of plain people of the working class with slovenly speech who ride tramcars, but they were considered better than we, because no one regarded us as Poles anymore. And we, my father, my mother — we had so many pretty jugs on the piano and shining little tables, replicas of Greek vases, and one an actual archeological find that my father had dug up on a school vacation in his teens, on a trip to Crete — it was all pieced together, and the missing parts, which broke up the design of a warrior with a javelin, filled in with reddish clay. And on the walls, up and down the corridors and along the stairs, we had wonderful ink drawings, the black so black and miraculous, how it measured out a hand and then the shadow of the hand. And with all this — especially our Polish, the way my parents enunciated Polish in soft calm voices with the most precise articulation, so that every syllable struck its target — the people in the tramcar were regarded as Poles — well, they *were*, I don't take it away from them, though they took it away from us — and we were not! They, who couldn't read one line of Tuwim, never mind Virgil, and my father, who knew nearly the whole first half of the Aeneid by heart. And in this place now I am like the woman who held the lettuce in the tramcar. I said all this in my store, talking to the deaf. How I became like the woman with the lettuce.

Rosa wanted to explain to Magda still more about the jugs and the drawings on the walls, and the old things in the store, things that nobody cared about, broken chairs with carved birds, long strings of glass beads, gloves and wormy muffs abandoned in drawers. But she was tired from writing so much, even though this time she was not using her regular pen, she was writing inside a blazing flying current, a terrible beak of light bleeding out a kind of cuneiform on the underside of her brain. The drudgery of reminiscence brought fatigue, she felt glazed, lethargic. And Magda! Already she was turning away. Away. The blue of her dress was now only a speck in Rosa's eye. Magda did not even stay to claim her letter: there it flickered, unfinished, like an ember, and all because of the ringing from the floor near the bed. Voices, sounds, echoes, noise — Magda collapsed at any stir, fearful as a phantom. She behaved at these moments as if she were ashamed, and hid herself. Magda, my beloved, don't be ashamed! Butterfly, I am not ashamed of your presence: only come to me, come to me again, if no longer now, then later, always come. These were Rosa's private words; but she was stoic, tamed; she did not say them aloud to Magda. Pure Magda, head as bright as a lantern.

The shawled telephone, little grimy silent god, so long comatose — now, like Magda, animated at will, ardent with its cry. Rosa let it clamor once or twice and then heard the Cuban girl announce — oh, "announce"! — Mr. Persky: should he come up or would she come down? A parody of a real hotel! — of, in fact, the MARIE LOUISE, with its fountains, its golden thrones, its thorned wire, its burning Tree!

"He's used to crazy women, so let him come up," Rosa told the Cuban. She took the shawl off the phone.

Magda was not there. Shy, she ran from Persky. Magda was away.

Peggy Payne

....

The Pure in Heart

H E WOULD NOT HAVE SAID that he was ever "called" to
the ministry. It wasn't like that. Instead, he grew up knowing that it would be so. The church was Swain Hammond's
future — unofficially. He got his doctorate at Yale. Then, after one
brief stint as an associate minister, he became the pastor at Westside,
a good choice for — as he had become — a man of rational, ethical
orientation.

The church, in Chapel Hill, North Carolina, is Presbyterian. It is
fairly conventional, though influenced, certainly, by the university
community. Swain is happy here. Westside suits him. But it is clearly
not the best place to hold the pastorate if you're the sort who's inclined
to hear the actual voice of God. Up until recently, this would not have
been a problem for Swain. But about eight weeks ago, the situation
changed. At that time, Swain did indeed hear God.

He and his wife Julie were grilling skewers of pork and green pep-
pers on the back patio of the stone house they chose themselves as the
manse. They have no children. Julie works. She is a medical librarian at
the hospital, though if you met her you would never think of libraries.
You might think of Hayley Mills in some of those movies from her
teenage years. She has the same full features and thick red hair. On this
particular night, Julie is turning a shish ke-bab, which seems to be
falling apart. Swain, bare-footed — it is June — is drinking a beer and
squinting up the slight hill of their backyard, which they have kept
wooded.

"Isn't that a lady slipper?" he says. "Was that out yesterday?" But
Julie is busy; she doesn't look. Swain, his long white feet still bare,

carefully picks his way up the hill to examine the flower. It is then, as he stops yards away from the plant — clearly not a lady slipper — that he hears God for the first time.

The sound comes up and over the hill. One quick cut. Like a hugely amplified PA system, blocks away, switched on for a moment by mistake. "Know that there is truth. Know this." The last vowel, the 'i' of this, lies quivering on the air like a note struck on a wineglass.

The voice is unmistakable. At the first intonation, the first rolling syllable, Swain wakes, feeling the murmuring life of each of a million cells. Each of them all at once. He feels the line where his two lips touch, the fingers of his left hand pressed against his leg, the spears of wet grass against the flat soles of his feet, the gleaming half-circles of tears that stand in his eyes. His own bone marrow hums inside him like colonies of bees. He feels the breath pouring in and out of him, through the damp red passages of his skull. Then in the slow way that fireworks die, the knowledge fades. He is left again with his surfaces and the usual vague darkness within. He turns back around to see if Julie has heard.

She has not. Her back turned to him, she is serving the two plates that he has set on the patio table. A breeze is moving the edge of the outdoor tablecloth. She turns back around toward him, looking up the hill. "Soup's on," she says, smiling. "Come eat." She stands and waits for him, as he walks, careful still of his feet and the nettles, back down to her. Straight to her. He takes her in his arms, ignoring her surprise, the half-second of her resistance. He pulls her close, tight against him, one hand laced now in her hair, one arm around her hips. He is as close as he can get. He has gathered all of her to him that he can hold.

He puts the side of his face against her cheek, so he will not have to see her eyes when he says: "Julie, over there on the grass, I heard something. A voice."

She pulls back from him, forcing him to see her. She raises her eyebrows, half-smiling, searching his face for the signs of a joke. "A voice?" she says. There is laughter ready in her tone.

"God," he says. His mouth is dry. "God's voice."

She watches him carefully now, her eyes scanning his eyes, ever-so-slightly moving. The trace of a smile is gone. "What do you mean?"

"Standing up there on the hill," he says, almost irritably. "I heard God. That's what I mean." He watches her, his own face blank. Hers is struggling. Let her question it if she wants to. He doesn't know how to explain.

"So what happened?" she says. "Tell me some more." She pauses. "What did it — what did the voice sound like?"

Swain repeats the words he heard. He does not say then what happened to him: that hearing the voice, he had felt the mortality of his every cell.

They stand apart from each other now. She reaches over and touches his hair, strokes it. If one of us was to hear God, it should have been Julie, he thinks. But a different God — the one he has believed in until today.

She is looking at him steadily. "I don't think you're crazy, if that's what you're worried about." Her uncertainty has left her. "It's all right," she says. "It is."

"For you it would be," he says. He means it as a compliment. He has envied her her imaginings, felt left behind sometimes by the unfocused look of her eyes. Though she will tell him where she is: that she goes back, years back, to particular days with particular weathers. That she plays in the backyard of her grandparents' house, shirtless, in seersucker shorts, breathing the heavy summer air, near the blue hydrangeas. Swain wants to be with her then. He wants to go: "Except ye become as little children, ye shall not enter. . . ." He wants, and yet he doesn't want.

She glances at the food on the plates. They move toward the table. The sweat that soaked his shirt has started to chill him.

"I'm going to get a sweater," he says. "Do you want anything?" She shakes her head no. She sits, begins to eat her cooling dinner.

There are no lights on inside the house, only the yellowish glow of the patio light through the window, shining on one patch of floor in the hall. He goes to the hall closet, looking for something to put on. He finds a light windbreaker. He has his hand in the closet, reaching for the jacket, when he hears the voice again. One syllable. "Son." The sound unfurls down the long hall toward him. He feels the sound and its thousand echoes hit him all at once. He holds onto the wooden bar where the coat hangs, while the shock washes over his back.

He stays where he is, his back and neck bent, his hand bracing him, waiting. Nothing else happens. Again, it is over. Again he is wet with sweat. He straightens, painfully, as if he had held the position for hours. He walks again out onto the patio. Julie, at the table, squints to see his face against the light beside the door.

"Are you all right?" she says.

He sits, looks down at his plate. He holds the jacket, lays it across his lap like a napkin. He shakes his head. A sob is starting low in his chest, dry like a cough. He feels it coming, without tears. He has not cried since he tore a ligament playing school soccer. He has had no reason. Now he is crying, his own voice tearing and breaking through him. Inside him, walls are falling. Interior walls cave like old plaster, fall away to dust. He feels it like the breaking of living bones. In the last cool retreat of his reason, he thinks: I am seeing my own destruction. Then that cool place is invaded too. He feels the violent tide of whatever is in him flooding his last safe ground. He holds himself with both arms; Julie, on her knees beside his chair, holds him. God has done this to him. This is God. Tears drip from his face and trickle down his neck.

Two days later Swain sits alone in his office at the church. He has a sermon to write. Should he tell the congregation what happened to him? His note pad is blank. He has put down his pen. It is an afternoon with all the qualities of a sleepless night: hot, restless, unending. There are no distractions from what he is unable to do. The secretary is holding his calls. The couple who were to come in with marital difficulties cancelled. The window behind his desk is open; he stares out into the shimmery heat and listens to the churning of a lawn mower. He has already been through the literature and found nothing to reassure him.

Son. He keeps coming back to that one word in his mind. It was not Swain's own father talking. That was clear. His father would never have been so definite, so terse. The elder Dr. Hammond would have interspersed his words, and there would have been more of them, with long moments of musing and probably the discreet small noises of his dyspepsia. He would have asked Swain to consider whether there was indeed 'a truth.' Swain would have considered this, as he was asked. And possibly at some later time they would have discussed it, without conclusion.

Swain, twisting in his chair, resettling his legs, knows he did not create the voice. He did not broadcast that sound out through the pines of his own backyard. He sees again the reddish gold light of the late sun on the bark of those backyard trees. He did not imagine it. His mind does not play tricks.

Though the whole thing seems like a bad trick, a bad dream — divine revelation, coming now. He imagines himself in the pulpit, staring out at the congregation, telling them. He sees the horror waking on their faces, as they understand him. He sees them exchanging glances, glances that cut diagonally across the pews. He would be out. It would cost him the church. Leaders of the congregation would gradually, lovingly ease him out, help him make 'other arrangements.' He tries to imagine those other arrangements: churches with marquees that tally up the number saved on a Sunday, churches with buses and all-white congregations. Appalling. It makes him shudder.

He turns his chair away from the window, back to his desk. It is too soon. He has nothing to say. Know that there is truth? A half-sentence? He at least needs time to think about it. Then perhaps he can make some sense out of it. Of course he will make public confession finally. He will witness. He has to. "Whoever shall confess me before men, him shall the Son of Man also confess before the angels of God." There is no question. ". . . He that denieth me before men . . ." It is his mission — to speak. A man could not remain a minister with such a secret.

On Saturday, he has a wedding. He has already put on his robe. His black shoes gleam. He sits at his desk, ready early, signing letters left here in his box by the secretary. Routine business. His sermon for Sunday is written, typed in capital letters. It makes no direct reference to hearing the voice of God.

He does like marrying couples, thinks of it, in fact, as an important part of his ministry. When a couple gets together within the church, it always seems to him a sort of personal victory. As the boy said two weeks ago at the junior high retreat, "Human relations is where it's at."

The pair this afternoon is interesting to him in a more particular way. He has been counseling them since Louise, the bride-to-be, found out she was pregnant. She is thirty-eight, roughly his own age. She and Alphonse, a Colombian, have lived together for about three years. They have planned for today a fairly traditional, almost formal ceremony. She is not yet showing. He remembers her when she was alone. He could see her on Sunday mornings canvassing the congregation with her eyes, picking out the occasional male visitor holding his hymnbook alone. Watching her in those years, he wondered what his own life would be like, without Julie. Whether he would show that same hunger so plainly on his face. He is glad for Louise, pregnant as she is. He caps his pen and stands. It's time to go in.

The feel is different now in the sanctuary, more relaxed than the eleven o'clock. Maybe it's only the afternoon light, filtered as it is by stained glass. He stands at the chancel steps, the ceremony begins. Alphonse comes to stand beside him. They face the aisle where Louise is to enter on the arm of her sister's husband. Swain tests the sound of their names, rehearses them in silence — Louise Elizabeth Berryman, Alphonse Martinez Vasconcellos. The twang and the beat of the Spanish — he has resolved to get it right, not to anglicize. He runs through the name again — and a scene unwinds like a scroll inside him. Gerona.

Louise, coming down the aisle now, slowly, slowly, moves in her long pale dress behind the clear shapes of his sudden unsought memory. He is twenty years old, standing in a stone-walled room in Spain. The straps of his backpack pull at his shoulders. It is quiet here, blocks away from the narrow river and the arched bridges. In this room — he read it in his guidebook — there was a revelation. He stands, with his two friends, in a medieval landmark of the kabbalah. It is the moment, unplanned, when all three become quiet, when he can only hear the muted traffic from the street. He is looking for something in this room. He lays his hand on the grainy stone of the wall. Standing now in the sanctuary, he feels the damp grit of rock against the flat of his palm. He can't escape it, he can't shake it off. He wears it — this slight tingling pressure — like a glove. A wet glove that clings to his skin. Louise is now at the front before him.

The couple turns to him. They wait. "Dearly beloved," he hears himself say. Faces stretch in a blur to the back of the church. He hears his voice — it must be his — float out to those faces, saying, "We are gathered here today. . . ."

He has told Julie everything, about hearing the voice. Not just the words, but how it felt. He has told her about the intrusion of the scene from Spain at the wedding this afternoon. "That was the last thing I needed," he says. "For that to happen while I'm actually standing at the front." They are sitting at the kitchen table. It's late.

She shrugs. The look on her face is the one he tries to cultivate in counseling. She is not shocked. Yet she does not diminish what happened to him. The look is one of sympathy and respect at once. She does it, he knows, without thinking.

She nods toward the typewriter, his old one, standing in its case near the bookshelves. They both use it for letters, neither one of them has a legible handwriting. "You've always set the margins so narrow," she says. "On yourself, on what's real. You don't give yourself much room."

She waits. He thinks about it.

"True," he says, nodding, looking away from her. "And you give yourself that kind of — 'room' you're talking about." He looks at her, her chin propped on one hand, her face pushed slightly out of shape. "But do you actually believe in it," he says, "in what you see and hear, in the things you imagine? You don't. Of course you don't."

She puts her hand down, on the table, away from her face. She takes a breath and holds it a second before she speaks. The look she has had, of authority, is gone. "In a way," she says. She searches his face. "I don't think too much about it. But — yes, in a way, I do."

There is no joy in it. That's what bothers him. He is lying on the living room floor, still thinking about it, though he hasn't mentioned any of it, even to Julie, for almost a week. Maybe silence will make the whole thing go away. Julie is in the armchair reading, her feet in old white tennis shoes, her ankles crossed near his head. He watches her feet move, very slightly, in a rhythm, as if she were listening to music instead of reading. Maybe she hears music and never mentions it. She likes music. Maybe she's hearing Smetana's *Moldau*, close enough to the orchestra to hear between the movements the creakings of musicians' chairs. She would do this and think nothing of it. She has been patient with his days of silent turmoil.

As a kid, he wanted something like this to happen. Some sign. He did imagine though that it would bring with it pleasure — great happiness, in fact. He had a daydream of how it would be, set in the halls and classrooms of his elementary school, where he first imagined it. A column of warm pink light would pour over him, overpowering him with a sensation so intensely sweet it was unimaginable. He tried and tried to feel how it would feel. The warmth would wrap around his heart inside his chest, like two hands cradling him there. He would be full of happiness, completely at peace. The notion stayed with him past childhood, though, certainly in his earlier years, he didn't talk about it.

But he did what he could to have that experience. Divine revelation. He wanted it. He lay on the floor of his bedroom at home, later his dorm room at Brown, and waited. He stared at rippling creeks and wind-blown leaves and the deep chalky green of blackboards until his mind was lulled into receptive quiet. The quietness always passed, though, without interruption, at least by anything divine.

The search must have ended finally. Only now does he realize it, lying here with the front door standing open and moths batting against the screen. He doesn't recall any such preoccupation during divinity school, though there was that one thing that happened in his last year. It hardly qualified him as a mystic, though it was reassuring at the time.

He was sitting out on the balcony of his apartment, a second-floor place he shared with two other students. He and Julie, not married then, were in one of their off times. He was feeling bad. The concordance, the notepad had slid off his lap. His legs were sprawled, completely motionless, in front of him, hanging off the end of the butt-sagged recliner. He had lost Julie; he was bone-tired of school, he wouldn't have cared if he died.

He was staring at the scrubby woods behind the apartment complex, behind the parking lot and a weedy patch of mud and three dumpsters. Nothing mattered. Nothing at all. Then while he watched, everything — without motion or shift of light — everything he saw changed. He stared at the painted stripes on the asphalt, at water standing on the yellowish mud. It was all alive. Alive and sharing one life. The parking lot, the bare ground had become the varied skin of one living being. In the stillness, he waited for the huge creature to move, to take a breath. Nothing stirred. Yet he felt the benevolence of the animal, its power, rising off the surface before him like waves of heat.

What he felt then was a lightness, a sort of happiness. This was so important. It was at least a hint of what he had once imagined.

That afternoon he was buoyed. He finished the work he had sat with the whole afternoon. He fried himself a hamburger and ate it and was still hungry. He watched a few minutes of the news. He did not die or think further of dying that day, other than for the purposes of sermons, counseling, and facing the inevitable facts.

Facts. He is lying on the floor of his living room. Julie is reading in the chair. God has spoken to him, in English, clearly, in an unmistakable voice. He is not glad.

"What would you do, Julie?" he says. He is looking at the ceiling, he does not turn his head. "Would you stand up in that pulpit and tell them, 'I have heard the voice of God'? Would you do it?" He rolls over on his side and looks at her. Her foot has stopped moving. She has put her book down.

"I've been thinking about that," she says.

"What did you decide?"

"Probably," she says. "I think I would." She is not smiling. She looks at him steadily. Her eyes are tired.

"Oh?" he says. There is an edge in his voice. "What else would you say? How would you explain it? Explain to me, if you understand so well." He pauses, waits.

"Say as much as you know," she says.

"What is that? One piece of a sentence: know that there is truth. It isn't enough. I have nothing to say."

"It's your job, isn't it?" she says. "To tell them. Isn't it?" He sees the fear flickering across her face now. She needs to say it, but she's scared. It's the way he would be, standing before his incredulous congregation. Fearing the cost. What could it cost her to say this?

"You're afraid to tell me," he says. His voice is weary, dull.

She nods.

"Why?"

She swallows, looks away from him. "Because I'm saying you need to do something that may turn out bad. It would be the most incredible irony — but it could happen. They might decide you're losing your marbles. They might call it that, when really they don't want a minister who says this kind of stuff — about hearing God. It's not that kind of church. You know?"

He ignores the question. "We could have to move," he says. "We could wind up somewhere we would hate. Is that what you're worried about?"

"Some," she says. "But mostly that you would blame me, if it happened — that you would always feel like I pushed you into it."

"And then the marriage would fall apart," he says.

"Yeah," she says. Her voice shakes. Her mouth has the soft forgotten look it gets when all of her is concentrated elsewhere. In this case, on fear. He is not in the mood to reassure her.

"And what if I don't do it?" he says. "What if I never say a word and you spend the rest of your life thinking I'm a shit — a minister who denies God? What happens to us then?"

She shakes her head. She is close to tears. "I don't think that will happen," she says. It comes out in an uneven whisper.

Swain stands, straightens his pants legs. He looks at her once with-out sympathy, but her face is averted, she doesn't see. He leaves the room, goes into the kitchen. He gets out a small tub of Häagen-Dazs and a spoon, stands near the fridge, eating from the container. There is no sound from her in the other room. Pink light — what a joke. "Suppose ye that I am come to give peace on earth? I tell you, Nay; but rather division." The voice didn't warn him, didn't remind him. He shakes his head. He digs and scrapes at the ice cream.

He is turning his car into the church parking lot when it happens again. He hears God. His window is open. The car is lurched upward onto the incline of the pavement. The radio is on, but low. From the hedge, a few feet from his elbow on the window frame, a sound emerges. It clearly comes from there: a burst, a jumble of phrases, scripture, dis-tortions of scripture: "He that heareth and doeth not . . . for there is nothing hid . . . the word is sown on stony ground . . . why reason ye . . . seeketh his own glory . . . he that hath ears . . . he that hath. . . ." A nightmare. A nightmare after a night of too much reading. A spilling of accusation, reproach. Swain is staring straight ahead. A hot weight presses into him, into the soft vee beneath the joining of his ribs. It hurts, it pins him to the seat. It passes like cramp, leaving only a shadow, a distrust of those muscles.

Another car is waiting behind him, easing toward his fender. He pulls into the parking lot, into a space. He does it automatically. His face feels as hot as the sun-baked plastic car seat. He looks at the hedge, running between the sidewalk and the street. Tear it out — that's what he wants to do. Pull it up, plant by plant, with his hands. He is a pastor. Not a prophet. Not a radio evangelist. He does not believe in gods that quote the King James version out of bushes and trees.

He gets out of the car, goes into the church, into his office. He kicks the door shut behind him. He tosses a new yellow legal pad onto the bare center of his desk. There has to be something in this room to smash. He looks around: at the small panes of the window; at the veneer on the side of his desk; at the cluster of family pictures, framed; at the bud vase Julie gave him, that now holds two wilting daisies and a home-grown rose. Something to break. He grabs the vase by the neck and slings it, overarm, dingy water spilling, into a pillow of the sofa. A soft thump, and the stain of water spreads on the dark upholstery. He looks away from it, looks at the yellow pad on his desk. His career.

That's what he'll smash. That ought to be enough. He walks around behind the desk, sits, red-faced, breathing audibly through parted lips. He stares at the lined paper with the pen in his hand. Say as much as you know. He begins to write. Beyond writing it down, he tells himself, he has made no decision.

On the following Sunday, he walks forward into the pulpit. He has received the offering. He has performed the preliminary duties with a detached methodical calm. Now he stands with his hands on the wooden rail, his fingers finding their familiar places along the tiered wood. "Friends," he says. He looks at no one in particular. "I have struggled with what I have to say to you today." They are waiting, with no more than their routine interest. "I have come to say to you that I have heard the voice of God." He says it to the rosette of stained glass at the back of the sanctuary. He cannot look at Julie in the third row. He cannot look at the McDougalls or Sam Bagdikian or Mary Elgar, as he says it. In the ensuing silence, his eyes sweep forward again, from the window back across three hundred faces. They are blank, waiting still, mildly interested. No one is alarmed. They have not understood.

He begins again. As much as he knows. "I think you know that I believe in an immanent God. I think you know that I believe in the presence and power of God in all our lives. I have come to tell you today that something has happened to me in recent days which I do not understand.

"A voice has spoken to me. I know that it is God. A voice has spoken to me that was a chorus of voices. I know that they are God." He pauses. "My wife Julie and I were cooking dinner on the grill on our back patio. . . ." The faces grow taut with attention. Sudden stillness falls over the church to the back pews of the balcony. There is no flutter of church bulletins. There are no averted faces. It is not a metaphor, not a parable he is telling. His wife Julie, the back patio — they are listening. He proceeds, with a trembling deep in his gut. He begins with the lady slipper and voice that came over the hill.

He tells them about the word "son" and the windbreaker and his own tears. "I asked myself whether I should bring this to you on a Sunday morning," he says. He looks from face to face in the rows in front of him. What are they thinking? It's impossible to tell. The shaking inside him has moved outward, to his hands. He feels them damp against the wood of the pulpit rail. He does not trust his voice.

"I asked myself how you, the members of this congregation, would react. Would you think that I've — " he tries to say this lightly, with a wry laugh — "that maybe I've been under too much stress lately." The laugh is not convincing. He himself hears its false ring. "But I will tell you," he says, "that that is not what has happened. I have not taken leave of my senses."

He looks at Julie. He can see her wrists, before the back of the pew breaks his vision. He knows her hands are knotted together, moving one against the other. He pulls his eyes away.

"I asked myself whether you would want a pastor who hears voices. Or even whether some of you might come to expect wisdom from me, because of what has happened, that I do not have." He pauses. "I don't know what to expect," he says, "from you or — " he hesitates — "from God. But I will tell you that my heart is now open. I will listen." He steps back, hearing as he does so the first note of the organ; reliable Miss Bateman is playing. The congregation stands, hymnbooks in hands. The service ends without incident. Swain stands as usual at the front steps afterwards to shake hands and greet people. Three of all those who file past tell him that the Lord works in wondrous ways, or something to that effect. Miss Frances Eastwood squeezes his elbow and tells him to trust. Ed Fitzgerald lays one hand on his shoulder, close to his collar, and says, "I like what you did here today." The rest make no mention of what has occurred. The line moves quickly past him, handshakes, heartiness, veiled eyes.

It is not over, of course. Julie keeps her hand on his knee as he drives home, though they say little. During the afternoon, he receives several phone calls at home, of an encouraging and congratulatory nature. Coming back into the kitchen, where Julie is cleaning out drawers to keep busy, he says, "It's the ones who don't call, who are calling each other. . . ."

What does occur happens gradually. Swain is given no answer, no sense of having-got-it-over on that Sunday afternoon. First, as he surmises, conversations buzz back and forth, on the telephone, at get-togethers, in chance meetings on the street. People inside and outside the church talk about what happened, about Swain Hammond's sermon.

The night the church operations committee meets, Swain and Julie stay home and play Scrabble. Swain can't concentrate, but Julie protests every time he wants to quit. The call comes at 11:15. It's Joe

Morris. "Between you and me," Joe reminds him, "this is an unoffi-
cial. . . ."

The upshot of it is that the committee voted five-to-four to privately recommend that Swain get professional help. The chairman, Bill
Bartholomew, who made the motion, comes to Swain's office to tell
him. "Of course," he says, "this is something which is not easy to say.
But we all go through times when we need. . . ."

"Thank you for your prayers and concern," Swain says. He is accustomed to assuming a look of gratitude when it is called for. It only fails
him in the last minutes of the conversation.

"Are you so sure I'm crazy, Bill?" he says. The two of them are
standing now in the office doorway, there is no one in the hall.
"Doesn't it seem contradictory?" Swain says. Bill is watching him carefully. "It's okay to believe in God, but only if God is distant. A presence
in history. Is that the idea?"

"I'm sure I don't want to debate this with you," Bill says. "It's only
the will of the committee — "

"I understand your position," Swain says. He does not seek counseling.

When news of the committee's action leaks, a petition circulates
and the members take sides. This time the vote is with Swain. The
letter, signed by the majority of the members, affirms that Dr. Swain
Hammond is in his right mind and will continue to be welcome as
minister. These are not the exact words, but this is the meaning.

Swain mentions this decision from the pulpit, but only as a brief
comment among the day's other announcements. "Thank you for
your love and support," he says. Unexpectedly, as he says it, he feels a
tightness in his throat. He looks from face to face. He won't be leaving. If he thinks about it, he'll lose his composure. He summons a bit
of the anger that has sustained him through the last few weeks. It
works, he manages to keep the wave of love at bay.

"Besides," he tells Julie later that day, "I don't completely trust
it." They are taking a late afternoon walk through the neighborhood
around their house. "I feel like all this could change, if the balance
shifted just a little. I'm reasonably secure for the moment," he says. "I
suppose that will have to do."

She doesn't say anything. She has said her part several times already:
that she is proud of him, that she is proud of what he did.

"I'm also disappointed," he says. They stop for a moment to avoid the arc of spray from a sprinkler cutting across the sidewalk. "I thought maybe a few people would be curious about what actually happened. Would want to hear more." He shakes his head. "They don't." It makes him mad to think about it. They've decided to put up with him — that's what they've made of all this. They're being broad-minded and tolerant, that's all.

Swain does hear the voice of God again. This time — last Tuesday morning — it is as a note of music, as he is just waking up. Julie lies beside him asleep. It is early, still twenty minutes before the alarm is set to go off. He knows before it happens that it's coming. He does not move. He waits, while the note emerges from a sound too deep to be heard. Then it is audible, filling the room, humming against his bare stomach, like the live warm touch of a hand. In the same moment, it begins to diminish, a dwindling vibration on piano strings.

Swain lies still. He does not cry this time, or soak the sheets with his sweat. He does not wake Julie, whose breath he can feel on the curve of his shoulder. He looks at the morning light on the far wall, shifting with the shadows of tree branches. He watches the triangles and splinters of light, forming and re-forming, and feels the slow rise and fall of his own chest. Everything is quiet: the room, the yard beneath the window, the street out front. He can see it all in his mind now, one surface, connected, breathing with his same slow breath. What he feels then, flooding the whole space of his being, is joy, undeniably joy, though it has not come as he would have expected. It is not what he looked for at all.

Eileen Pollack

....

The Rabbi in the Attic

I

THE RABBI WOULDN'T MOVE OUT. The house he wouldn't leave was for the use only of the spiritual leader of Emess Yisroel, which he was no longer. But how could we ask the burly police to break in with axes, to browbeat and handcuff a tiny old man, to cart off our rabbi to a black paddy wagon under the gaze of the town's gentle Christians?

Crushed in dilemma, our synagogue's leaders couldn't help but think what a delight the coming Holidays would be if only the rabbi had retained all his marbles. Such a throat — made of gold! And the cords in that throat — as sweet as the strings of King David's harp. His voice carried forward all for which we Jews were most nostalgic. To hear it, our hearts leapt. This was a voice that usually would bless only the wealthiest Reform congregations, not Jews in the Borscht Belt who kept alive serving the few old-age resorts that hadn't yet died.

And, at first, Rabbi Heckler had seemed sane, though intense. He scuttled through the synagogue and the streets of our town with his bloodshot eyes blinking, a fossil crustacean whose invisible feelers were taking in details, which he wrote in a book, licking the pen. Everyone assumed he was getting acquainted, keeping straight the names of important people. His sermons were harsh, but the tottering deaf men and chattering widows who made up attendance on most Sabbaths didn't hear what he said. Even when he addressed the younger members at the *bar mitsve* of Natty Cook's eldest, his voice was so soothing, so resonant, so moving — especially after the *boytshik* screeching of Natty Cook's eldest — that few of us realized he had issued a warning that if we kept sinning, he would "whip us in ship-shape."

He began with the children. In their after-school classes he drilled them in prayers, grammar, laws, these children who had only been asked until then to color with crayons or gamble with *dreydels*. Now, he clicked in his black shoes up and down the aisles. Holding a pen cocked in his hand, he would stop by a desk. "Okay, you will please to recite the *Alenu*. No looking, no stopping, and please, no mistaking."

The unlucky student gripped the sides of his desk and tried to remember even the first word of the *Alenu*. Though this was *"alenu,"* the student couldn't think with the rabbi's black shoe rat-tat-tatting the floor.

"So? You have finished?"

When the student said nothing, the pen thwacked his head so loudly that his classmates jerked in their seats. Then the rabbi stepped forward to stand by the next chair.

"Rabbi, I'm sorry, I didn't have the time. My basketball team — "

"So! Time for bouncing, but not for study? How! Are we Greeks? You memorize — or else!"

All of them wriggled, anxious to escape, but the rabbi pulled out his notebook and barked: "Schwartz, tell your father he must come to *shul* on *shabbes,* he does this — or else!" And: "Rosen, your mother buys *treyf* meat from A & P when Rachlis, who is kosher, is next door. Tell her she must buy kosher — or else!"

This went on until the children lived in such terror of "Rabbi Or Else," his drills and his pen, his recruitment of spies, that they pleaded with their parents to let them stay home, feigned stomachache or headache, and if this failed, played hooky.

He turned next on their mothers. Interrupting a session of the Board of Trustees, he told the twelve men: "I must speak of your wives."

The Board heard his shoes click on the floor as he circled their backs.

"Our wives?" The men twisted, trying to see.

"Too visible," he said.

"I don't understand," said Herman Zlotkin, the Board's longtime Treasurer and the largest man on it, though smaller than his wife, a woman who was prone to wearing bright colors. "Too visible, Rabbi? You don't mean to say — "

"Hidden. They must not be seen."

"Are you insinuating we must lock up our wives?"

"No, no, not locking. A balcony will do. With a tall screen around."

"A balcony? Tall screen? It isn't enough the women sit apart, they must also be hidden? Even if we thought our wives were so beautiful that they might distract us, are you suggesting we completely rebuild the sanctuary, spend thousands of dollars, money we don't have . . ." Zlotkin waved his enormous ledger, then started to push himself up from his chair.

The rabbi, half his size, put a hand on his shoulder and kept him from rising. "Rebuilding is ideal, but no one will say I am not reasonable person. For cheaper money, we build a wall down the aisle between us."

The meeting, which had been intended to last only a short time so the Trustees could finalize plans for a Monte Carlo fundraiser, kept the men from their wives until early that morning. The rabbi kept circling, didn't weaken or sweat, shot Scripture at their backs while they drew together like settlers in a wagon train with no ammunition. They suffered besiegement until they were able to convince Rabbi Heckler that his motion be tabled to give them a chance to look into the cost of partitions and walls.

At this he decided that the Trustees were worthless. He must try his own method: He would harry the few old ladies who still worshipped at the synagogue in the hope they would eventually stay home altogether. In the midst of a service he would say from the pulpit: "Mrs. So-and-so, quiet, no gossip or leave." And Mrs. So-and-so left, as fast as she could on legs that were feathers. Even Miss Abel, who prepared the *kiddush* that followed the service, was reprimanded for rattling her trays in the next room while prayers were in progress.

At the beginning, since the rabbi lived alone, his wife having passed on from lumps in the breast, the women took pity and asked him to supper. Miss Abel, who had waited fifty years for a man of rigorous principle — iron in his bones, a Jewish crusader — to come to her town, invited the rabbi to dinner in her tiny apartment, then spent the weekend soaking a brisket in brine and squinting at labels in frozen-food cases in search of "Ⓤ's" and "*Pareve's*" that would have been too small for eyes that were younger and aided by much cleaner spectacles. When she finally set the table, the linen was new, the silver just-boiled and the sweet wine and soda sealed with the approval of convocations of rabbis.

Promptly at seven Rabbi Heckler buzzed and entered, by-passed the table without even glancing, made straight for the kitchen and cited infractions she never had heard of — the wrong brand marshmallow, wrong washing arrangement. He nibbled a few grapes, swallowed a mouthful of raspberry soda, then excused himself early, at which Miss Abel declared to her empty apartment: "Let him eat his so-very-kosher meals alone!"

Even at weddings he often would not eat. Many times he refused even to perform the service. He would tie up an engagement in such knots of Talmudic objection that no one was able to untangle his logic. Not only wouldn't he marry a couple if each child and parent were not one-hundred-percent Jewish by his specifications, he would visit those couples united by previous rabbis or judges and harangue and harass them until they were crying.

One afternoon he confronted the McCoys (Adele née Rabinowitz and Frank Patrick Randall) in front of Woolworth's and accused them of completing the project that had been started by Hitler.

"And this? What is this?" He grabbed Frank Junior's arm. "Is fowl? Is fish? Is circumcised? Is not?"

While Frank Junior wailed and tried to get free, Adele's mother, Eva, happened by in her car. She parked, gaped, got out, and grew so incensed that although she had not spoken to her mix-married daughter in five years, she reconciled herself to a situation that seemed less sinful the longer the rabbi ranted. By the end of his tirade Eva was shouting: "Frank McCoy is a good and kind man who cares for my daughter. He does not scream on Main Street or make innocent boys cry. And if you, Rabbi Heckler, continue to represent the Jewish religion in my town, I just might convert to Catholicism." At which Eva embraced her son-in-law Frank with a passion that made all three McCoys gasp.

A separatist rabbi: No mixing! No *goyim*! He shamed us in front of our liberal neighbors — a Jew had to look down in front of liberals! He would not even take part in the yearly meeting of the town's clergy, a discussion of projects of mutual concern, merely because he wouldn't enter a church — as if a Unitarian Social Hall could be mistaken for a church!

Our embarrassment mounted as he began to wage holy war on us men. If an office or store remained open on the Sabbath, he would burst through the door, disregard patrons, lecture and threaten. So incensed was he when he discovered that Isidore Pipchuck, the town chiropractor and synagogue *shammes,* the man who on weekdays manipulated the affairs of the congregation with such dexterity that the very building might have crumbled without his efforts to hold it together, on Saturday afternoons, not more than an hour after the service, this same Izzy Pipchuck was back in his office manipulating the strained muscles of patients, writing bills for them, handling their money.

The rabbi steamed across Pipchuck's waiting room with such speed that three *Reader's Digests* were sucked in his wake. From the threshold of Pipchuck's inner office the rabbi issued this ultimatum, right across the shirtless back of a patient: "You must abide by the *shabbes* rule of no labor — or else you must step down as *shammes.*"

"These hands heal suffering!" hissed Pipchuck, a man made of wires with a fine skin stretched over them, his entire being an organ of such refined sensitivity to slight that he registered every mis-said word as an insult to his name, faith, profession. This triggered revenge, whether real or imagined. He would grab in his hands the flesh of the slighter and pull it and twist it until he heard moaning: "Thank you, oh, thanks Doc, I owe you my life."

Pipchuck faced the rabbi. "This man was in pain! Could God object to the art of healing? And who else would perform the duties of the *shammes* for no pay? Just try to manage without Izzy Pipchuck!"

"We manage," he said. "We manage without a pagan who spends *shabbes* rubbing naked bodies."

The patient who had been stretched on the table in Pipchuck's office struggled to sit up, uncertain whether he had been insulted, or only Pipchuck. Since this patient also happened to be Hyman Abromovitz, the synagogue president, Pipchuck availed himself of the chance to express his anger by taking leave from the sexton's duties — let the building crumble! — and to declare that he would not attend another service if the rabbi ran it.

Attendance fell further when the rabbi nosed out the secret parking lot where the old men who judged themselves too feeble to walk to *shul* on the Sabbath parked their cars. He crouched by the dumpsters of Sy's Hotel Plumbing. When a car would sneak in, the rabbi pounced. *Ambush!* His sharp shoes kicked tires, his small fists beat windshields. Even Herman Zlotkin he kept imprisoned inside his black Buick, though Zlotkin howled: "I must ride! A heavyset man with emphysema cannot be expected to walk up a steep hill. How would it look if the Treasurer, who is an elected official, was found dead in the weeds!" Because this Herman Zlotkin did indeed live in terror that he would drop dead the next instant. He frequently pictured his collapse among the corroded remains of hotels in his junkyard, and, as bulky as he was, he feared he might lie unnoticed and rusting among the old stoves and bedsprings for weeks.

"So lose weight!" the rabbi shouted at Zlotkin, who even now was sitting in tears at the image of his own oxidation. "Lose weight, but don't drive!"

The ten of us men who walked to the *shul* he covered with shame. "How dare arrive late! Come at beginning or don't come at all." He saw into our pockets: "How dare carry money on God's holy day!" And: "Abromovitz, get up!" (Yes, he called even the curve-backed president to account.) "If you can't stand up quicker don't sit on the stage, a bad example to all." (Or maybe, we murmured, this rabbi thinks that he is the only person who belongs on the stage.)

Finally, he expelled Lazarus Schmuckler, the retired *shoychet*, little old mushroom Lazarus Schmuckler, because he made noise. This wispy nothing who *davened* so only the white hairs in his nose got the pleasure of hearing, he made too much noise? No, he prayed softly. But after each *aw-mayn* he added a coda, put all his tiny soul of a mushroom into chanting: da-DAI-dai-dai-ai-ai-DAI-ai-ai. And the rabbi couldn't stand this donkey tail being pinned on his voice, so out Schmuckler went.

The very next night Rabbi Heckler revealed just how badly he was infatuated with his own voice, so we realized that he was not just a stickler, but a lunatic also. He commanded a taxi to drive to the fanciest hotel in the Mountains, and when the gatekeeper inquired whether the man in the back seat was a paying guest or not — the hotel, after all, was not for town riffraff who sought free amusement — the rabbi informed him: "I play the piano!" and the gatekeeper nodded and let him pass through, thinking this must be tonight's entertainment.

When Rabbi Heckler appeared in the dining room he was noticed with amazement and alarm by Pipchuck and Schmuckler, neither man riffraff, each had a purpose: Pipchuck rubbed the limbs of guests who had contorted themselves in Simon Sez and shuffleboard, while Schmuckler, who had once been the chief inspector of the hotel's kitchens — an inspector who kindly averted his eyes when a beef cut or saucepan wasn't quite kosher — had been given permission to eat here for free whenever he pleased, which was often, it seemed.

Pipchuck and Schmuckler watched as the rabbi wiped off the keys of the piano in front of the room and began serenading the guests as they dined. And did Rabbi Heckler enlighten this crowd with melodies or folk songs from Hebrew culture? No. Broadway show tunes. *South Pacific. Oklahoma!* A medley of love songs from Gershwin and Berlin.

Between soup and fish, the guests clapped their hands.

"Such a wonderful voice! What timbre! What range!"

"But there's something peculiar . . ."

"So cute, though. Old-fashioned."

"Once, he was someone. Now he's a has-been. A *shikker,* may be."

Pipchuck jumped up. Already he was tying the straitjacket behind Rabbi Heckler. Schmuckler, in whom the flavor of revenge would have revolted as strongly as oysters, tugged at Pipchuck's sleeve. "Perhaps if we ask very nicely he'll go."

"And perhaps the owners will call the asylum and have him hauled off!" At this Pipchuck skipped to the manager's office. He returned with two bellhops, who casually approached the mystery pianist and asked him to stop. Once more. A third time. They lifted him by an armpit, an arm.

He started to rave: "A rabbi! How dare!"

The young bellhops paused, but what could they do? Holy man or not, he was still a disruption. Egged on by Pipchuck ("Don't trust him! He's crazy! Look at his eyes!"), they dragged him outside.

But the rabbi kept screaming from beyond the locked door. Everyone heard him over dessert: "Philistines! Cossacks! Let me in — or else!"

This straw was the last. The Trustees appointed their most tactful threesome to visit, advise. Over tea Zlotkin scolded: The time was approaching to vote on his contract (two sugars, stirring), and if Rabbi Heckler didn't change his behavior . . . a reprimand only, and thanks for the tea.

For a week Rabbi Heckler lessened his fervor . . . until the next Sabbath, when he delivered a sermon whose theme was forgiveness. Those few of us who heard it assumed he was asking a second chance, mercy, and we thanked the Almighty that his madness had gone. Several eyes were moist, and Miss Abel's arms lifted as if to welcome her errant crusader back to the bosom of his congregation. Then came the end of the sermon, its moral: "And so you must find in your hearts to forgive, show your enemy kindness, give him a contract — or else he will sue!"

The Board of Trustees gathered around their table, as grim as twelve hangmen. They would let Rabbi Heckler present his defense. He still had supporters, for what was his crime except for devotion, and wasn't his voice as rare as a lark's?

But when he was summoned, he taunted the men: "You'll regret! I won't go!"

"Is that a threat, Rabbi?"

"Yes," he said simply, and lost his supporters.

His contract expired. The Board didn't renew it. But the rabbi wouldn't leave the house to which his right also had expired. Pipchuck (self-banished no longer, his value now proved) shared surveillance of the house with Abromovitz and Zlotkin. As far as they knew, the rabbi never went out, and when the three men peered through the shutters, they saw bare floors and walls. The rabbi had lived there with only a suitcase, a few books, a cot, all of which he must have moved to the attic to gain a better perspective, one room to defend. The only light shimmered from the third-story window.

To pass the dark evenings they imagined him spooning cold food from tin cans, pissing in the empties and pouring the contents from his window at dawn. Secretly, each of the sentinels was glad the rabbi didn't come down to breathe the night air. Who knew but they might appear in the next morning's paper, rolling across a lawn while choking a rabbi?

"Time is on our side," said Pipchuck one night as the three men kept watch. "Also, the law."

"The law, eh? The law — *feh!*" Thus spoke Herman Zlotkin, with the contempt of a man who has just been told by the Town Council to put up a high fence to conceal his big house and the scrap yard around it. ("To him all that rusty metal looks green," the synagogue wags said, though not to his face.) "Not only won't the law solve our problem," Zlotkin went on, "if no law existed, our problem wouldn't either." He hacked and growled harshly, as if he had installed in his throat a crane such as he employed to hoist scrap in his yard, and when the phlegm came up, he wrapped it in cotton and made a deposit in his trouser pockets. His companions ignored this. They told themselves mucus was not mucus in the pockets of Herman Zlotkin, it congealed to silver and fell from the cloth in thick coins, which he donated to the synagogue and the public library with such generosity that even the Town Council had taken four decades to politely request that he put up the fence.

"No Christian could comprehend how a congregation could dismiss a reverend for too-strict observance," said Hyman Abromovitz, who not only presided over our synagogue, but also taught science at the junior high school in town. He was missing one eye, but, even so, his discernment was keen; he dissected the world into microscopic divisions. "The Catholics," he went on, "have many laws also, but a church cannot dismiss. The Pope has that power, but he too is zealous. Complaints of this nature would only be taken in the priest's favor. And Protestants? Their idea of a zealot is a minister who asks them politely on Sunday to help with the bake sale that's coming on Wednesday. No Christian could conceive that our laws number six-hundred-thirty."

"Excuse me, Hyman, but the laws number only six hundred," said Pipchuck.

Abromovitz pawed his cane through the dirt, one stroke, another, tallying the laws as they came to his head. As a man of science he placed chiropractors in the same category as faith healers and dispensers of hoodoo, but his bent back responded better to Pipchuck's hoodoo than science, a dependence so irksome that Abromovitz always looked out through his good eye for any chance to catch Pipchuck in error. "It is six-hundred-thirty, not one more or less!"

"Please, please," said Zlotkin. "You'll both agree, I'm sure, that all but a few of these laws are worthless — rusty bits, spare parts that should have been scrapped in the days of King Solomon. I suggest that we tackle our immediate trouble. In four days, Rosh Hashanah, and we have no rabbi."

Each of the wise men now stood in silence, entertaining this notion: They would lure Rabbi Heckler from the house with flattery, and, after the last prayer on Yom Kippur, they would nab him and drive him to New York, where they would leave him with a few dollars to tide him over. But sadly they each reached this conclusion: The madman was too smart. He would never come out of the house unless the congregation promised to renew his contract, binding for one year, perhaps forever. This was his design. He knew we would get frantic as the New Year approached and we had no rabbi to sing on our behalf, apologize for us in tones that were pleasing, deliver a honeyed petition to insure our inclusion in the Book of Life, which now lay open on the Almighty's lap. So many people always attended the service on Rosh Hashanah that the secretary had to sell reservations. Such a mob and no rabbi . . . there might be a riot. And who could be hired on such a short notice? What rabbi would come to this impoverished nowhere for the *pishochs* we offered, especially if he had to rent his own lodgings — the congregation had no money for an apartment when a perfectly good house (with expensive upkeep) adjoined it already.

"Gentlemen," said Zlotkin, who had been meditating in just this manner, "the answer has come to me at last." While he hacked they waited, as if his insides were fertile not only for mucus and money, but also ideas. "We obviously must seek out a rabbi who is desperate for a post. Perhaps he is — you'll excuse me, Hyman — a cripple in some way that makes him undesirable for a less tolerant congregation than ourselves. Perhaps he has a new wife, who is pregnant, he's fresh from the Yeshiva, he's in debt, whatever. Now, when he gets here, we tell him: 'This house is your house, but you must get out the current occupant. He will listen to you. A rabbi knows what arguments to use on a rabbi. If you do not succeed, we're very sorry, but you must find your own lodgings.' And, if he's desperate, he will make the attempt."

No need to relate in Talmudic detail the objections of Pipchuck, Abromovitz's rejoinders. These were for show. In their hearts all three men acknowledged that such an understanding of human behavior lay at the base of Zlotkin's riches. And the next day, when they were driving in Zlotkin's Buick to New York to ask the Director of the Yeshiva if he could assign an Orthodox rabbi who was desperate for a post, the only dissension among them was as to the best way to phrase the request.

Now, you might well ask: Why should a congregation that prefers free living to rigid obedience look for a rabbi of the Orthodox persuasion instead of the newer, more liberal traditions — Conservative, Reform? The answer is simple: Orthodox comes cheapest.

But the dispenser of Orthodox rabbis was tired of seeing his graduates abused. "Ten rabbis in twelve years! You treat them like sawdust. And now you want my help in order so you can treat *two* rabbis bad at the same time."

"Begging your pardon, Honored Rabbi Doctor," said Pipchuck, "but we have none at all. If you will remember, our previous rabbi now has no contract."

"And you have no compassion! I can guess your plan. You would subject a fresh-new rabbi to kicking his elder into the street. You would treat an old man who is unwell in the head to this disgrace."

"Begging your pardon, Honored Rabbi Doctor," said Pipchuck, "but if you knew he was unwell in the head, you might have warned us before we hired — "

The rabbi lifted a fist. "You say this to me? When you needed a rabbi, did you dare come and say: 'Assign us a rabbi, this is your job'? No! And why not? Because you are ashamed. Because you pay less and treat worse than any congregation in New York — in United States, perhaps! No, you cannot face me, so what do you do? You get a rabbi from a newspaper. Does it never occur to you that a rabbi who is trying to sell himself in an advertisement under the notice for old refrigerators, is something wrong with him? That if something is not fishy, he would get his job through me? No, you are perfect matches for each other. You have him, you keep him. You will not drive crazy a young man who has a future before him. And God help the poor old rabbi you have driven to seek refuge in that house."

"Perhaps true," said Abromovitz, "but if you will not help us, we must seek a rabbi from one of the other seminaries. This will mean one less Orthodox congregation in the world, and it will be your fault."

"My fault? Is my fault? One less of your kind, good rubbish! Go hire a bishop, a Buddhist for all I care!"

Subdued, the three left, conferred among themselves, descended by car from the Bronx to Manhattan, parked the Buick in what they hoped was a safe spot not far from the Conservative college and stepped onto the sidewalk, where all three, even Zlotkin, were jostled by strangers with faces as indifferent and battered as the bottoms of old kettles and taunted by hoodlums who carried on their shoulders demon-filled boxes. Pipchuck healed cripples, but here were so many deformed human beings, people in pain that lay beyond even his knowledge of vertebrae to cure, that his own legs grew heavy from despair. Abromovitz, whose single joy in life was the bringing of order, especially to youngsters, saw that the larger world was so powerful and ruthless that it would never let itself be stuffed into the compartments he so cherished. In the minds of all three men was one thought: Abandon this mission, get back to the Catskills. But how could they do this if they didn't bring a rabbi?

"Gentlemen," said Zlotkin, "let us gird up our courage. Because we have no choice. We must ask directions." Which Zlotkin himself did, thinking he would rather die from a knife wound, a martyr for his friends, than collapse to no use among toilets and tubs.

With Zlotkin in front, the three men at last scaled Morningside Heights. They found the right office, gained an appointment, waited and waited, and ten minutes later were back on the sidewalk, daunted not only by the price they had heard quoted, but also by the black name our town had acquired even among the Conservative rabbis.

"Unfairly! Unfairly!" said Pipchuck.

"If the price is so much for Conservative, should we even bother with Reform, for whom the richest congregations must compete for the few that exist?" Abromovitz forgot his hopelessness of a minute before to revel in this analysis according to the laws of supply and demand. "And what will the Board say if we should return with a young Reform rabbi who wears blue jeans, strums a guitar and eats roast pork in public, a man who goes farther than even we are willing to go?"

"Gentlemen," said Zlotkin, "we must recall," and he hitched up his trousers, "that we have no choice."

But even the well-insulated stomach deep in Zlotkin's belly grew cold when the Director of Placements at the Reform seminary mentioned the salary that would purchase the least-outstanding rabbi among his recent graduates.

Pipchuck was the first to recover, reassured slightly because the Director had not heard of the town's reputation or the rabbi who wouldn't leave the attic. "But isn't there one new graduate who is, how might I put this, so unfortunate in some respect, so eager for employment, that he would be glad to receive any position, even at the meager salary which is, regrettably, all we can afford?"

The Director pursed his lips. He shook his head no. Then he said: Well, he did have one rabbi . . . a good heart, not brainless, but, well, this one graduate had been lacking in . . . discipline. No, not immoral, but no head for study. Not ignorant, just . . . fuzzy. And yes, to be frank, the singing was atrocious. But then again, she . . .

In chorus, with no disharmony from the grudges among them, there issued a wailing that sounded as if it had reached the present after a long and tear-stained journey from the Middle Ages, a prolonged lamentation of a three-letter pronoun.

But when the lament had died from their lips, they nodded, accepted, for as Zlotkin put it on the drive home: "Gentlemen, we must face up, this world is changing." He hacked, then smiled slightly. "And let us consider . . . When opposing parties are set in conflict, when the struggle is over and the dust has settled, there may be no victor, only two vanquished, and the field is left open for the appearance of a new leader, a man whom the Lord sends from only-He-knows-where to care for His people."

And with this faint comfort the men took advantage of the ten exits left them to think of the words to explain to the Board why they had hired a Reform woman rabbi with no mind or voice, even for two weeks, on a trial basis.

II

Marion Bloomgarten had achieved ordination through the force of a good heart, then watched as her classmates were one by one chosen, even the other women, who, because they had been doubted, worked twice as hard and earned highest honors. Left on the sidelines, alone in New York, she waited for winter with no hope for work. So when Marion was summoned by the Director of Placements and told she had been given a trial position, no application or interview needed, then handed a ticket for a bus to the Catskills, she was ecstatic. True, the congregation to which she was going had been led until now by Orthodox rabbis. But this gave her visions of blowing the shofar and causing the wall between the sexes to crumble. She saw Jew and gentile sharing grapes beneath the viney roof of the *succah;* began to plan outings on which the children would open themselves to I-Thou encounters with deer, sparrows, bushes; saw a temple where the blessed could gather, a center from which a renewal could ripple outward until it encompassed a town so small that one congregation of good Jews could effect decency, clean streets, parks, playgrounds and visits to elderly shut-ins. Under her guidance, Emess Yisroel would become a synonym in the minds of people of all faiths for justice, peace, caring.

The bus terminal was a flimsy gray shack at the more decayed end of Main Street. Three men were waiting. One was so sloppy, always spitting in a rag, that she barely could look at him. The second man was nervous, with the hands of a strangler clawing the air. Behind these two creatures skulked a humpback old pirate with a patch on one eye.

She stepped from the bus.

"Miss . . . Madam . . . Rabbi . . ."

The ride in the Buick to the three-story house that stood by the synagogue was mercifully short. The house was as crooked and unkempt as the members of the greeting committee. But, to a woman who had grown up in a borough where half a duplex was considered spacious, it presented a prospect so expansive that her heart swelled to fill it. She imagined the orphans and unwed mothers, the emigrées from Russia and boat people from Asia who soon would share it with her.

She jumped from the car. A storm of tin cans ricocheted from the sidewalk. Marion ducked.

"Please, Rabbi Heckler," the strangler shouted toward the roof, "this is also a rabbi. Don't you think you should give her the same treatment as you yourself would want? Take pity on a poor struggling scholar. Take pity on . . . a woman of Torah."

This brought a bald ghost to the third-story dormer. "A woman rabbi is an a-bom-in-a-tion!" Another can flew. It bounced on the slate and rolled to her feet. She had just read the label — Rokeach Stuffed Cabbage — when the strangler pulled her back into the car.

"You will understand, I'm sure" — Zlotkin sounded offhand — "that we can neither afford to pay for a second rabbinical lodging, nor go to the courts." Cans struck the roof and windows like hail. "For two weeks, until Yom Kippur is finished, we will pay for a room at a motel. If you haven't persuaded your predecessor to vacate by then, you will have to make do as best as you're able."

When Marion heard this, comprehended their intrigue, she felt as if each word from Zlotkin had been a worm she had been forced to swallow. Angry and fearful, she started to demand that he drive her back to the station, but was stopped by the realization that she had no money for a return ticket, and that even if she did get back to New York, nothing was there — no apartment, no job. Before she knew it, she had let them drive her to the Motel on the Cliff, the only lodging within walking distance of the synagogue.

The Cliff was not a cliff at all, just a few feet of rock overlooking the town. The door of each unit once had been painted a different bright color, but these had now faded, so the motel stretched across the hill like a lurid slattern who reclined on one arm and mocked the town below.

Marion refused to let the committee carry her suitcase, less from conviction than distrust. They would meet her at the synagogue the next day, they said. Then they drove off. Marion looked up. A few of the letters of the neon were dark. MOTEL ON THE IF. "I don't mind if you test me," she muttered to God. "But cut out the wise-cracks!" Suitcase in hand, she limped to her room and threw her-self down on the worn chenille bedspread, where she lay the whole night searching for solace in the trials of Queen Esther, Deborah and Ruth.

III

Prophet of the Bronx. Redeemer of New York. Marion Bloomgarten always had known that she would lead the Jews of her borough, state, country to liberation. No longer would they be slaves to their small stores, drones with no spirit, no culture except for a paper menorah taped to the window in December and a few words of Yiddish that even black actors on TV now used. But Marion would not bring the Law to redeem them, injunctions as weightless as the dandruff that sifted from the round shoulders of her Hebrew school teacher, Pa-thetic Pearlie, who, like Rabbi Heckler, also belonged to the cheapest of orders. Because this congregation was also not well off, and even less faithful than we Jews in the Catskills. Marion's parents and their neighbors were concerned only that they and their children not be taken for Christians, whose beliefs in religion they considered even sillier than their own. For this purpose they hired an obsolete rabbi who whispered his lessons and scratched at his crotch while his stu-dents pitched pennies into a *yarmulke* at the back of the room.

In the midst of this chaos, Marion would try composing a speech. Across a clean sheet of paper she would laboriously inscribe: THE PROPHESY OF MARION BLOOMGARTEN. Then she'd wait for God, who often spoke to her, to confide the right words. But the right words wouldn't come, no stirring phrases, and with the excuse of an asthmatic's need for water she escaped from the uproar and sat in the ladies' room until she could go home.

When Marion was twelve, Rabbi Pearl was found in the supply closet slumped over a box of paper towels, his face as blue as the numbers on his wrist. The man who replaced him was Orthodox also, but slightly progressive. To show this, he announced that he would allow the confirmation not only of males, but females as well. Though Orthodox law didn't permit a young woman to read from the Torah, she might lead a special Friday night songfest to welcome the Sabbath. Hearing this, Marion jumped from her seat and begged to be first.

As the new rabbi tutored her in the tunes and inflections of the psalms she would sing, Marion told herself that leading her people in song was preferable to reading them a portion of Torah. Songs wouldn't enchain them the way the Law would, might even pipe the way to a new life. She would not give a speech. Instead, she would make up a song on the spot and lead all of them, singing, up and down the Bronx.

Except she couldn't sing.

"Your voice sounds like fishbones," her mother had told her. "When you sing, it's like your throat is full of fish, and the notes that you spit out, like fishbones."

This certainly was true. Between the note that she wanted and the note she could reach, whole cities might slip through, whole cultures, the entire system of Western music. Even the rabbi shrank from her singing, as if her voice were as onion-and-garlic as his breath. Marion's mother, not wanting to witness her daughter's shame, threatened to boycott the service. (Her father, she knew, would beam with approval even if she squealed like the vermin that were his business to rid from houses.)

"Mother," she said, "you're forgetting one thing: I'll be inspired."

"Never mind inspiration, you'll still spit out fishbones."

But Marion was sure that God would tune her voice, enrich it with feeling. She would wear a white dress, and with her cascades of rippling black hair she would look like a prophet. The vibrations from her throat would tickle the thin brass flames of the Pillar of Fire above the pulpit until the sculpture hummed. The mouths of the goblets inside the display case of the Hadassah gift shop would trill hymns of praise. In the room where the *kiddush* would eventually take place, the Dixie cups full of heavy dark wine and the bowls of red gelatin would oscillate, tremble, and the dainty egg *kichel* would rise in the air, sweetness borne on sweetness.

None of this happened. But hours of practice, intense concentration, and yes, inspiration, softened the fishbones, exalted the pitch so that only a few times did the abyss gape between the real and ideal. Marion saw her mother lift her head, look timidly, proudly, sit straight

by her husband — who had been beaming for hours — and arrange
the folds of her new dress, preparing for the admiring glances of her
friends, which did indeed follow.

"The voice of the Lord is mighty; the voice of the Lord is majestic,"
Marion bellowed, trying to match Him.

"The voice of the Lord breaks the cedars; the Lord shatters the
cedars of Lebanon," her listeners mumbled in response, so she knew
they were feeling His power, and hers.

When Marion at last threw back her hair and sang out a greeting to
the Bride of the Sabbath, she thought she saw the Bride enter the
room, though this turned out to be a dirty white curtain tossed this
way and that by the wind from a truck.

The rabbi came toward her, holding out gifts — a prayerbook with
her name in gold on the cover, and collapsible candlesticks designed for
a girl who would one day leave home. As her parents' friends clapped,
she heard the Lord's voice sing a psalm in her ear. She waited for her
chance to sing it out loud.

The rabbi was saying: "I think it is obvious to us all that Marion has
performed a magnificent service this evening, and that she certainly
would make a wonderful rabbi."

A rabbi, she thought, and suddenly was filled with heaven's contentment. Rabbi Bloomgarten! A life's work, a mission.

The whole room was chuckling. What was the joke? A rabbi —
why not? Hadn't her voice been inspired tonight? Yes, she thought,
yes, but the voice of a woman, no matter how inspired, was good for
one thing: lulling babies to sleep. And the woman herself — a woman
rabbi, at least — was good for a laugh.

Blindly, she felt the weight of the prayer book, the cold metal of the
candlesticks, and wanted to hurl them. She walked in a daze through
the *kiddush*, the handshakes. As she and her parents were saying goodbye, the rabbi told her that since she couldn't carry her gifts on the
Sabbath, he would lock them in his office. Marion nodded, but she
knew she would never come back to retrieve them.

And so, when she finally did leave home for college, Marion packed
no candlesticks, collapsible or otherwise. Though she still thought of
herself as a potential prophet, she lacked a focus of inspiration. No
sooner would a philosophy or exotic religion engage her attention than
she would rebel against its outlines, the very bones that held up its
skin. She raised her banner against the tyranny of footnotes, the de-

tachment of scholarship. All but the most radical instructor on campus scrawled disapproval across her essays, and when this one instructor went mad and left town, Marion felt abandoned.

She turned to causes — these required no essays — but nothing in her demeanor incited the enthusiasm of converts. Her eyes seemed a bit crossed, as though she were looking in two directions at once. And she spoke through her nose, which she frequently rubbed to help clear her asthma. Her fellow reformers mistook this as a sign of her wish to rub her nose from her face and therefore doubted her ethnic self-respect — her seriousness also, for she rarely took part in dangerous protests, because if she were to suffer an asthma attack locked in a cell, she could suffocate to death.

One Friday night in her last term at school, Marion wandered the campus alone. From the open window of the student union, over the ringing of pinball machines, old melodies reached her — an octave too high. Even God's voice was high above middle C as it urged her to enter and turn, turn full circle. . . .

Marion obeyed, and discovered that women at last had been embraced, if not in the folded-tight arms of Orthodox Judaism, then in the reluctant arms of Reform.

Judaism had changed, yes, but Marion had not. In seminary her teachers charged that her concern for the freedom of homosexuals and the full expression of the artistic potential of people on Welfare sapped her attention from Liturgy, Midrash and Homiletics. They cringed at her singing and practice sermons. When she spoke up in class to question even the weak rituals and watered traditions the Reform had not shed, her classmates demanded: Why did she stay at the seminary if she despised its teachings? Although she didn't answer, she did know the reason: She had been called twice by God, called as a rabbi to re-instill ideals in the Jews of America. Being a rabbi satisfied something deep and inherent in Marion, and this was a good thing, because she was nearing age twenty-seven, having rejected all other paths and choices in life.

For this same reason Marion kept her appointment with the greeting committee of our congregation, allowed Zlotkin, Abromovitz and Pipchuck to guide her through the synagogue, a cinderblock bunker painted sharp green. The sanctuary had a dirty gray carpet and a holy ark that seemed more fit for a dustpan and broom than a Torah. In the entire building Marion saw no niche where a thirsty soul might find refreshment (even the fountain by the bathrooms emitted a trickle of rust).

The classroom had no windows, and when the walls started to close in on Marion, she imagined the cinderblocks covered with fronds, buds and lilies gathered by Jewish children who were at home in nature and photos of the African foster child her class would adopt by mailing a check for $15 each month. This helped her restrain herself from denouncing the treachery of her three guides or correcting them when they spoke to her as if she were block-deaf and hadn't a clue what a Jew was ("These are *siddurim,* the PRAYER BOOKS, which, you know, we PRAY FROM"), as if she were ignorant even of English ("This is where the children play PING PONG," they told her. "PADDLE, NET, BALL"). Just when she thought she could bear it no longer, her guides halted in front of a closet and told her, "This is your office," then hurried away, relief sighing from the soles of their shoes.

Marion entered the closet and sagged into the only piece of furniture inside. She had rested just long enough to discover that two of the chair's legs were broken when the door of the closet swung open again and admitted a sour woman with neck growths like grapes, which she kept squeezing with purple fingers. She thrust a purple palm forward and introduced herself as Masha Stonehammer. For two hours daily she typed, took dictation, answered the phone, and once a month dittoed the synagogue news on the mimeograph machine, which, she told Marion, had just sprung a leak.

"I am also the Sabbath *goy,*" she announced in a husky Slav accent.

Marion shook her head. What was that?

Scornful, Stonehammer informed the new rabbi: "I do for the Jews what the Jews will not do for themselves. On the Sabbath I light lights. If the furnace breaks on a day when the use of a phone is not permitted, I call the oil man. I check reservations at the door on Yom Kippur, and I write the amount each person contributes in memory of the dead."

Marion wanted to tell her that in a Reform temple these tasks would no longer be prohibited to Jews, so a non-Jew wouldn't be needed to act as a servant. But she sensed that the secretary was proud of her duties and would be disappointed to have them stripped from her, as if flicking switches when others feared God proved her courage.

"Sometimes I think I am the only person in town who celebrates every Jewish holiday," the secretary went on. "Except that I follow my own ritual for each. For me, the Sabbath is a festival of lights, Passover is a time to buy breadstuffs. I know the laws because I am called on to break them. I know the Jews better than the Jews know themselves."

Not only did she know the Jews in general, she knew them in particular, every tic and betrayal and charitable gesture of Emess Yisroel as it had passed through the previous twelve years and ten rabbis. Much of this knowledge she now imparted to Rabbi Eleven, especially the history of the lately deposed Tenth. Marion until then had been so repulsed by the greeting committee that she had felt sorry for Rabbi Heckler. Yes, he had thrown cans at her, but she had, after all, been in the company of three horrible persons. Now she was disillusioned to learn that he represented the most fanatic blindness of the Orthodoxy she hated. She also realized that Masha Stonehammer was still loyal to his regime.

"What would America be if its citizens thought all its laws were jokes?" the secretary demanded.

Marion would have tried to explain that the Reform movement was based on the principle that many Jewish laws no longer had meaning. Revelation was ongoing. Jews could decide which laws to preserve according to which strengthened their spirits, could design new forms of worship that held beauty for them, abide by a faith whose practices did not separate them from their fellow human beings but drew them closer to all creatures on Earth and to the God who still lived, not in a law book or a cloud on Mt. Sinai, but in all hearts and heads, Lord God of Ideals. But Masha Stonehammer already had left. Marion could hear the regular whumping of the mimeograph drum, the whipping of paper, as if a prisoner in some secret chamber were being flayed, his skin sifting to the floor in great sheets.

She sat in her closet and tried not to listen. She desperately needed a sermon for Rosh Hashanah. The title came easily: "New Ways for a New Year: The Essence of Reform." Then, rocking in her chair, she waited for God to write the rest of the speech. Two little boys peeked in, shot giggles at her and ran away shrieking. Then, shuffle, shuffle, a small man with white hairs that curled like frost from his nose asked permission to enter. "Missus, have you maybe seen the new rabbi?"

She stood, introduced herself and stretched out her hand. She expected rejection, but held her smile bravely.

He examined her palm as if it might conceal a buzzer, then touched two damp fingers to it. A fleeting smile, shyly: "I am Schmuckler, the exile, a leper for singing." He had come to inquire if he would be welcome on Rosh Hashanah. He would try to refrain from his dai-dai-ing, but this was a habit and he could not be sure. . . .

"Mr. Schmuckler," she told him, "sing as loud as you want. Because, to be honest, I'll need all the backup on vocals I can get."

His mushroom eyes brightened. "Really? Your singing, it's not so . . . impressive?" He bobbed on worn heels. "Oh, I must tell you, so happy to meet you!"

He began bobbing backwards. She plunged with a question. "You don't mind, Mr. Schmuckler? That I'm a woman, I mean?"

"Mind? Mind? Of course not!" Humming and smiling. "Of course, all the others . . . but good luck, Rabbi Missus, I see you tomorrow."

A spark, optimism — too soon extinguished by the appearance of a stiff, startled woman who muttered that she had come to ask the new rabbi if the menu for the *kiddush* — lime gelatin, Mogen David, egg *kichel* and fish bits — was to his liking. But Miss Abel didn't bother to wait for an answer. What good was the opinion of a woman, a girl, how better than her own?

When Marion at last gave up on her sermon, a wine-colored sun was dripping its light through heavy gray clouds. Reluctant to confront the Slattern On the Cliff, she wandered toward the house that should have been hers. The lawn looked alluring. She thrust out a sandal and brushed her toes on the grass. Why had she conceded this house to the rabbi after only one skirmish? But then, what methods would have prevailed against such a fanatic? Oh, why had she come here? Where would she go next? Where was God's voice, giving direction?

Marion looked up. The tall tree was red. Its leaves were like flame licks in the last slant of sunlight.

A voice told her: Climb it. Perhaps the rabbi lay half-dead on the floor. She would carry him down, as one carried a child.

Again the voice: Climb it.

She put a sandal on each rung, climbed higher through the flames. Dark windows on the first floor. Dark on the second. But there, in the attic, a white shirt, a man bending over a trunk. Then, two white candles. At first she assumed he was lighting the candles because he had no lamps in the attic, but all his preparations made her suspicious that, although this was Wednesday, he was lighting a welcome for the Sabbath. Why give a welcome two evenings early? Or had he decreed that each day was a Sabbath, each eve a welcome? Marion felt chilled.

Such devout overdoing was the stuff only of Talmudic folklore, tales of *tsadikim*.

Suddenly he was singing, blessing the candles. His voice was so mighty that she had to hold tight so she wouldn't lose her perch. He kept his eyes shut. His palms cupped the gold light he had kindled and splashed it upward, bathing his neck, face and eyelids, painting the ceiling with gold while he sang a prayer so richly drawn out it might have lasted forever, and Marion had to whisper the same prayer in English, over and over, "Blessed art thou, O Lord our God, King of the universe, who hast sanctified us with thy commandments . . . ," ten prayers to his one, so as not to lose sense of the common world's time.

By the end of his blessings dark clouds were shoving each other across the shadowy sky. A wind had blown up. Then, in the distance, a great yellow slash. The rabbi lifted his head and walked to the window, pushed it up, open. Marion crouched in a crook of the tree not two yards before him, but the rabbi was looking beyond to the lightning, singing the blessing, not drawn out this time, but searing and sharp: Blessed art thou, Lord our God, King of the universe, whose might and power fill the world.

He saw her. She didn't move. His nose twitched. She thought: There's no screen between us, I could surprise him. But to grapple with a saint . . . Yes, Jacob had tried it, but even he was left wounded.

The rabbi stepped closer and lifted one hand. To reach out and strike her? Or to pull down the window? She had to forestall him.

"Isn't there also a benediction that's supposed to be said upon seeing a beautiful woman?" She smiled weakly.

His voice was even. "A fish who lives on land is not a fish. A woman who lives in a tree is not a woman. And a woman who acts like a man is not beautiful. She is an a-bom-in-a-tion." He clawed at the window, but the humidity kept it from closing.

In an instant she thought this: Since he loves the Talmud, he must love a good debate. "God hates a hermit," Marion proclaimed. "And you, Rabbi Heckler, have become a hermit. Doesn't Genesis itself declare that life is good? And haven't the rabbis decreed that a person should live to the fullest, enjoy God's creation, go down in the world among men, among women?"

"Maybe, to enjoy myself, I should sit in a tree? When I am in Sodom, I should do as in Sodom?"

"If you think this is Sodom, maybe you should leave here and save yourself before God destroys the town."

"*Adoshem,* blessed be He, always gives the people of Sodom a last chance, sends one to warn them. If they listen He saves them."

"So you think you're a prophet, Rabbi Heckler?" She had meant to imply this was *chutzpah.* But when she heard her words, Marion realized she had asked a plain question.

"I am a Jew, and these days that is enough. These candles — you see them? For thousands of years a light has been carried, preserved from any who would spit on the flame or drown it in the mud. And what would you do? Scoff at this candle, it must be useless because it is not modern. So blow it out, *pfft,* replace with electric, a flashlight, or nothing. Come, contradict me. Swear that each *shabbes* you light the candles, so the torch doesn't go out that has been burning since Year One." Brow raised, shoe tapping. "So, Mrs. 'Rabbi,' I am waiting."

It was futile to explain that each time she tried to light the candles, each time she saw a candlestick even, she was stabbed by cruel laughter.

"Aha, I am right then. You would let the torch fall. Yet you call yourself a Jew? Tomorrow I show Sodom a real Jew, real rabbi, against a monkey, chimpanzee in a tree. And they will decide among us, and be saved."

"Haven't they decided already, Rabbi Heckler?"

"For a monkey in a tree? Shoo, monkey. Shoo, chimpanzee. Shoo, shoo, go away." He flicked his hands at her, then struggled with the sash until the window slammed shut.

The wind lifted her skirt. The rain would come soon. She would lose her footing, dangle from a branch by her hair. "O Absalom," she whispered, and started down the tree. A silver flash lit up the clouds that raced overhead. "Blessed art thou, Lord our God, King of the universe. . . ." She recited the prayer to fend off her fear of the infinite night. Then she dropped from the tree and trudged to her room to finish the sermon she would give the next day.

IV

At the bomb shelter's entrance the ogre Stonehammer was checking names against a list of the members who had made reservations. "The biggest crowd in years," she informed the new rabbi. "Curiosity, no doubt."

Marion sneaked downstairs to wait in her office and inhale a few last times before the service. The weather was muggy and her asthma had returned. How could she hope to lead the day's prayers, off-key or on, if she couldn't breathe?

At last she went upstairs to the sanctuary and stood at the back of the aisle that divided the women and men. In the chairs to her left sat the young mothers with their squirming little girls in stretchy white tights and colorful dresses that barely covered their bottoms. To her right, the young husbands, on their laps their small sons, who wore white short-sleeve shirts, tiny bow-ties and hand-crocheted *yarmulkes* bobby-pinned to their fine curly hair. In the middle of each aisle sat the middle-aged parents: short grocers who slouched humbly beside the handsome young men who soon would be doctors; dumpy mothers who envied the thin girls they had nursed, now teachers and lawyers in elegant suits. And, in the front pews, nodding already, the elderly ladies in ragged black veils and the gray-stubbled men in misbuttoned jackets and age-yellowed prayer shawls.

She started down the aisle. No one turned or stopped talking. How could this girl in a flowing white garment that appeared to be a nightgown, her wild hair tied back like a beast on a leash, be the new rabbi?

Walking between the women and men, Marion felt an accomplice to the caste system, segregation of sexes because a woman might distract a man from prayer or contaminate him. "For three transgressions do women die in childbirth," she recited to herself in memorized contempt of the Orthodox prayerbook, "for being careless in the observance of the laws of menstruation, for not performing the ritual of *hallah,* and for not lighting the Sabbath lamp." Soon she would free the women from this degradation, free the men also from empty proscription. But slowly, don't rush. . . .

She mounted the dais. Behind her, by the ark, Abromovitz sat hunched on the president's cushions. By the men's door at the rear of the sanctuary stood Zlotkin; by the women's door, Pipchuck. As ushers? Or had the rabbi made known his threat? Other than these three no face was familiar, except for the mushroom, Lazarus Schmuckler, who bobbed in his seat and winked his encouragement.

She rasped twice and started, not singing fully, but using the technique of dramatic actors who find themselves cast in musical movies. She sensed all eyes on her, then heard the room buzz: "A woman, a woman, look at that, a woman." Air-starved, she barely could project above it. No one sang with her, but Marion persisted, fearing the moment when the order of service would require that she blow the ram's horn. At best she would be able to sputter a poor imitation of God's call on Sinai. She felt so dizzy merely from chanting that when a white cloak floated into the sanctuary, she nearly cried out: The Bride of the Sabbath! But from the moment the white cloak opened its mouth, she knew who it was.

With a rustling of shawls, dresses, prayer books, the whole congregation turned to watch the renegade lead his own service. He swayed in the aisle beneath his white cloak as he sang a passionate aria of repentance, his voice an exquisite weapon with which he was able to puncture Marion's puny defenses. And though she continued chanting in English, everyone else began singing with Rabbi Heckler in Hebrew.

She walked to the pulpit, her heart like thunder, a sandstorm in her mouth. Then she saw him sit down in a pew at the back. He intended to let her deliver her speech! The thunder diminished to a low rumble and the words of the sermon she had written the night before came back to her, words that brought news of religion with meaning, justice and beauty, no laws except as they revealed themselves worthy.

Restless disapproval. Bewildered stirring. She had read out a declaration of independence and the ex-slaves were worried about the decisions they might have to make.

"No! This is not true!" Rabbi Heckler jumped up. All turned to face him. "One Revelation! It happened at Sinai!"

Marion wheezed, "Of course it happened. A great trumpet sounded and a deep voice boomed from the whirlwind of clouds at the summit. . . ." She had no more breath.

He took his advantage. "If nobody spoke, why did so many people at Mt. Sinai that day agree they heard God?"

"Oh, yes." All necks twisted (like Ping Pong, she thought). "It must have been God and not men who told us: 'You may keep servants, may even beat them, as long as they don't die, for they are your money.' And: 'Wipe out those nations who live in the lands you would like to inhabit. Disembowel and light fire to innocent lambs and goats to satisfy Me.' Isn't it just possible, Rabbi Heckler, that God spoke more clearly to some prophets than others? Isn't it possible that each generation must listen to God with its own ears?"

"And who are you that God should speak to you? Your ears are as holy as the ears of Moses?"

"It doesn't take Moses to realize that the commandment to give charity is still worth obeying, while the commandment not to mix wool and linen in one cloth is trivial, silly, it means nothing to me."

"This is because nothing means anything to you! God gives commandments to sanctify our lives. No commandment is silly if it comes from Him. This is the entire faith of our people: We heard at Sinai, therefore we obey. God's laws bring freedom. But man as his own judge, revelation in each ear — your way lies danger, self-righteous people, or people who can't move." He gave her a chance to make her reply, but her throat had now closed. "Look, look," he shouted, "I have got her god stumped!"

Swallowing gravel, as angry at herself as if she had been drawn into arguing with a spoiled child, she stood tall and croaked: "Everyone rise!" She wheeled around to the ark, pulled open the doors and lifted out the Torah, the heavy calfskin on its massive wood spindles, all of it wrapped in satin embroidered with scepters and crowns. She hugged it to her chest and prepared to march down from the dais. The people would respond to the Torah from habit. The women would reach out, touch two fingers to the scroll, then kiss these fingers. The men would do likewise with the fringes of their shawls. All of them would sing as she marched among them holding the Torah. Then she would return the scroll to the dais, unroll it and read the Torah selection for Rosh Hashanah. Not even Rabbi Heckler would dare interrupt the reading of the Torah.

She took her first steps, her vision obscured by the wood handles of the scrolls, though she caught a flash of white just a second before she felt someone tug at the scroll in her arms. "The Torah might rip," she whispered. "It might drop to the floor." And so she let go.

Rabbi Heckler ran down the aisle with the Torah, a crab with a bundle as big as itself. We in the audience were too stunned to give chase. Abromovitz still was getting to his feet in honor of the ark's opening five minutes before. But just as the rabbi reached the door, Zlotkin stepped in his path, his arms stretched out wide. Then Pipchuck caught up. With wiry hands he lifted the Torah above the kidnapper's head. Zlotkin spun him around, clamped his arms behind him and started to drag him out through the door, though the rabbi was screaming: "A rabbi! How dare! Cossack! Anti-Semite!"

"Stop! Let him go!"

Not a head turned. Zlotkin kept dragging. Marion went for the shofar, lifted the heavy pearled horn to her lips. With a harsh breath she blasted, or rather, let out a Bronx cheer, but even this startled, brought order, stopped Zlotkin.

"Release him!" she commanded.

The rabbi crumpled, shrank into himself, a little crab creature who skittered past Zlotkin. But before he slipped out, he massed his strength once more and in a prophet's voice shouted: "Ashes and salt! That is what I leave you, ashes and salt!"

Marion shook. She was weak at the knees. She studied first Zlotkin, then each of the other three hundred faces raised toward her own. This was her congregation. Not evil people. Among them were surely good women and men. But which of them knew God? Which loved God, loved the world? For whom was existence more than ashes and salt? What in her power was vital enough to bring light and breathe life into ashes and salt? If Herman Zlotkin could somehow be forced to bless bolts of lightning, first sights of beauty and each bite he chewed, could he possibly remain the same Herman Zlotkin?

The murmuring returned. Still frightened, she retrieved the big scroll from Pipchuck, carried the Torah back to the dais, continued the service, and each word she sang from then on was a cry, a question to God.

The congregation was silent for the rest of the prayers, but few of us stayed to partake of the *kiddush*. Miss Abel, who had been in the kitchen and so missed the showdown, was visibly upset about the leftovers. The handful of people who did stay to eat carefully kept the table between themselves and the new rabbi. Marion hadn't the heart to pursue them. Inside she was crying over the images of the crumpled rabbi, Herman Zlotkin as a mound of ashes, and Isidore Pipchuck as a pillar of salt. How to revive them? How breathe life and shine light?

Only Lazarus Schmuckler came to shake her hand and praise her singing, as if all were normal. Surely, he said, she would lead them in *tashlikh,* bring them to a stream so they could cast their bread on the water and allow it to carry their sins to the sea.

Marion worried that if she consented to this tradition, Schmuckler would have her waving a chicken over her head three times on Yom Kippur. She gave in, however, solely for his sake, and as it turned out he was the only member to take part. Joyfully he led her to the town's outskirts, where the creek that flowed in a tube beneath Main Street escaped from its prison and wandered across a field in the vague direction of the Hudson River, and therefore the sea.

Despite her skepticism that tossing bread crumbs could make her soul clean, Marion gained pleasure from her companion and their ceremony. When Schmuckler had finished sprinkling his fragments of Miss Abel's *hallah* into the stream, he and Marion returned to the synagogue for the evening service. Her mind was elsewhere and she made several errors, but only a few of us were there to hear anyway. The rabbi was exhausted, desiring only to return to the motel, but Pipchuck detained her next to the cloakroom.

"*Gut yontef, gut yontef,*" hands twisting, grin tense. "Not a bad service, Miss Rabbi Bloomgarten. A regrettable disturbance earlier today, but you handled it . . . not badly. And you were quite right that we should release poor Rabbi Heckler. He was already a beaten man, no longer a threat. We had suspected, and therefore were ready, with the result that, I am happy to announce, tonight you will sleep in the house that will be *your* house — for as long as you're with us."

Too weary to question, she scuffed across the street. The ogre was waiting; in her purple hand, a key. Stonehammer related how she had been instructed to keep watch in case the rabbi left the house to attend the service, and, if this happened, to summon a locksmith and have the bolts changed.

Marion said softly: "I thought you were on his side."

Stonehammer's head was high. "For a Jew, calling a locksmith on Rosh Hashanah is not permitted. I am the Sabbath *goy.* It was my duty."

Marion took the key and locked out Stonehammer. Wandering through the house she saw splintered floors, flaked paint and yellow wallpaper with fingernail scratch marks as high as a man's arms. No chair to sit on, no curtain or dish. She climbed to the attic, half-expecting to see him. She found only an old trunk, its lid spattered with white wax, a pyramid of canned kosher meatballs, three black-bound volumes of religious writings, a raincoat, a cot. She lay down in her clothes and soon was asleep.

A nasty buzzing. No clue where she was. The doorbell insisted. Yes, she remembered, this attic, this cot . . . Who was buzzing the bell? A congregant in need?

She found Rabbi Heckler shivering in his shirtsleeves. Rain was falling. His complexion was white and his features compliant. "The hour, I am sorry, but I have been walking. I have not been right. I could go nowhere, and now it is raining. I must have left my coat here. Please, I will get it. Then I will leave."

"Rabbi Heckler, you'll understand if I ask you to wait here while I get the raincoat."

"You do not trust me even to wait in your hallway, inside from the rain, to get warm? An old man, half your strength? If I won't get out, you throw me."

"I don't want to have to wrestle with you, Rabbi. Stand under the eaves until I get back. You'll excuse me if I don't trust a person who would steal a Torah."

"Wait. This reminds me. I have come also to say I have been wrong. This is Rosh Hashanah. I must ask forgiveness of the people I have wronged before I can ask God. Please, let me inside."

It had cost her a great deal to deny him before. Now he looked so shriveled and contrite that she let him enter, though she did block the hall.

"This morning," he said, "when I find myself running away with the Torah, I realize I am not well. Later, in the street, I think of how, when I am trying to pry it from your arms, you whisper, 'It will rip' and let go. From this I realize that you have earned the right to keep it. Little by little from then on, I understand my sins of these past months." Water dripped from his trouser legs onto the floor. "You say that I am now a hermit, but until my wife died I truly lived apart. She was my shelter, God rest her soul, so I could study in peace. Always happy, she is singing, but I say *shaa, shaa,* these songs disturb me, these songs are not meant for God's ears. So my Hattie goes to sing in the bathroom, to sing with the door closed so I can study. Anyone who sought counsel asked my wife. She was wise in the problems of this world, and I could not be bothered, I had to study. The only reason anyone kept me was the voice I have.

"Then she passed on. Then, *then* I no longer can live without knowing how food is purchased, how people act. I go out, I see. The people with 'problems' come now to ask *me*. Adulterers! Idolaters! Sodomites! I abhor! It is no wonder, I think, my wife died. I become angry. I lecture. I visit. I overdo perhaps, and despite my singing, they say I am fired, again and again, until I come here. And the rest you know."

"Rabbi Heckler." She was thoughtful. "The songs that your wife sang . . . were they Broadway show tunes?"

"Yes, yes. How did you know?"

She smiled a small smile.

"Please, I will just go for my coat."

Still smiling, she stepped aside, though she knew what would happen. Perhaps a small part of his story was true, but what part she didn't know.

She heard a devilish screech, a satisfied laugh, though the screech might have been the hinge of the door that led to the attic, and the laughter her own.

V

That first night Rabbi Bloomgarten slept on the floor downstairs. After Yom Kippur, she bought a mattress on credit from Sears. She didn't see Rabbi Heckler, but she constantly heard him praying and singing; the ceiling creaked loudly as he swayed overhead. At dawn he thanked God for having been spared the life of a woman. He prayed at mid-day, and a third time at dusk. In between, she guessed, he studied or napped. At six every night she heated a kosher TV dinner and set it outside the door to the attic, with plastic utensils. For his other two meals she left food that even the most observant Jew wouldn't refuse. In this she was aided by Miss Sarah Abel, who was just as happy to feed her crusader from this safe distance as to have him crusading in her apartment.

Though Miss Abel harbored suspicions about the two rabbis' living arrangement and so treated Marion as a rival always, the rest of us were tacitly grateful for what she had done. As a result of her good deed, Rabbi Bloomgarten soon was accepted by our congregation as thoroughly as had been her predecessors, which meant she was ignored almost completely. To help pass the hours when no one called on her, the rabbi took singing lessons — eventually she could reach seven or eight notes of every ten she sang — and sent for the books she once had studied at seminary, or rather, the books she had been ordered to study, but had deemed too confining and out-of-date to open. Having despaired that her own knowledge would allow her to convert ashes and salt to roses and sunlight, she thought she could do worse than consult the writings of scholars and prophets who had spent their lives in the deepest searching for a way to God.

Neither singing nor study on the part of the rabbi brought much change in Pipchuck. But a few members of our congregation did visit some evenings — Schmuckler, Abromovitz, and often myself. Even Herman Zlotkin, on the nights when his premonitions of rust and decay were so frightening that he could not bear them alone, appeared at the door. All of us feared death — our own, our religion's — and we felt safer in the presence of this rabbi whose very sex and youth seemed an indication that our hopes were still fertile and might yet give birth to a new generation. On these evenings our rabbi, from loneliness, no doubt, talked more than was proper. She talked of her childhood, her dreams, thoughts, frustrations — among which her visitors most likely were numbered.

Because even though we listened, drank herb tea and nodded, we refused to relinquish our weak devotion to Orthodoxy. We were like students who had discovered an art book that was filled with beautiful paintings of nude men and women, and though we desired to study each picture, perhaps even try to sketch these ourselves, we were too frightened of the puritanical tyrant who still ruled our class. Because when Rabbi Bloomgarten was her most ardent and tried to convince her visitors too loudly, Rabbi Heckler would bellow his protests from his home on high, and Rabbi Bloomgarten would shout her shrill rejoinders up the stairs, all with such fervor that none of us wanted to enter the battle and risk a drubbing in front of his fellows.

Rabbi Bloomgarten did enjoy several triumphs. Instead of lime gelatin and stale *kichel* for *kiddush*, worshippers could now enjoy *hallah* baked by the children of the after-school classes under the tutelage of Miss Sarah Abel. Several communions of an I-and-Thou nature were also reported between these same students and various objects. And a boy of sixteen, because of her counseling, decided that his admiration for his lithe teammates in basketball was not sufficient cause to swallow the poison he had bought for the purpose of closing his eyes to their beauty forever.

Still, she wasn't able to relax the laws of the temple as much as she once had hoped. And though she herself was no more Orthodox than before, she found herself feeling guiltier and guiltier with each meal she didn't bless, each candle she didn't light, each bite of *treyfe* she ate, until one morning she caught herself checking the label of a shirt to see if the fabric combined linen and wool. Because wherever she was — in the house, *shul*, out walking — she thought she heard floorboards creaking above her, complaining each time that she failed to observe one of the 613 commandments so carefully inscribed on the scroll she had saved.

Joe Ashby Porter

....

Roof Work

I'M PATRICK CLUSEL and this is a story about two things that happened to me within a week of each other some eight years ago. The things happened to me but the story is really about other people and not so much about me.

I was twenty, making my living then as now driving tourists in a horse-drawn barouche about the old Québec upper town spring, summer, and fall, plowing snow through the winter, and doing odd jobs year round. At the time I was staying rent-free in an efficiency at the back of the house in the lower town my older sister, Laure, and her husband owned (and still own), putting aside nearly everything I earned. A retired couple down the street, the Van Franks, needed me to replace some broken slate on their back roof that fall. I did it one Saturday while the barouche was in the shop. Mr. Van Frank was alive at the time but only Mrs. Van Frank — Anne, though I didn't call her that then — was home. We went upstairs to their bedroom, whose dormer gave onto the damaged roof. I tied one end of a long rope to their heavy bed and the other end first around my waist and then to my tray of slates and tools. Anne held the tray while I stepped out and then she handed it through to me. The three or four broken slates were only a couple of yards from the window but the pitch was steep enough to make the going slow. I hooked the tray and adjusted it so it was level.

The whole time I was working, Anne stood at the window talking with me. She did most of the talking. She had once taught school and it was easy to see her in front of a class of kids. She talked mainly about herself that afternoon, but I could tell she was doing it for its educational value, not because it was her favorite subject. Some pigeons hoping for a handout settled along the peak of the roof and talked pigeon-talk, and kept their eyes peeled, and didn't clatter away till I stood and walked back to the window. Anne Van Frank herself is small and birdlike, and the dormer she stood in reminded me of a cuckoo clock.

She and her husband supported the separatist Free Québec movement more than anyone else in the neighborhood. They were both feminists too, I think, and Alex, who must have been around eighty, twenty years or so older than Anne, had lately started buttonholing people to air his views about the church. As I told Anne, the week before he'd told me he thought the pope was a living joke.

Anne frowned slightly, with a hint of a blush. She asked if I was a practicing believer. Not at all, I said, although I wouldn't have spoken that way of the pope myself.

Anne said, "No. Well, I hope Alex knew your attitude before he said that. He sometimes can be tactless on the subject. All religion is offensive to him. He scorns it."

She must feel the same way, I supposed.

"Not exactly. I tell Alex he shouldn't get his back up so about it, though I understand. You and your contemporaries would hardly imagine how serious a matter it was for him in his youth."

Not for her?

"Less, I think, and it was different. Alex grew up a Roman Catholic in Belgium but I was born here, up in Jonquière, and my family were Calvinist schismatics, fairly embattled and pious ones. I began to feel uncomfortable about it all at an early age. With my family's congregation the main thing was faith, and they expected various testimonials — loyalty oaths. I'd done it as a matter of course but when I was about twelve I started to dislike saying things about myself I knew to be false, and then in another year or two I stopped saying them."

That must have pleased her family, I guessed.

"They were good people but I'm sure they would have given me a hard time about it. Except that when I finally stopped testifying it happened in a way that didn't leave them much room to object."

How did it happen? Anne didn't pause to go misty-eyed, she was just answering my question as she told about her youth. Replacing broken slates is slow, easy work, and I'd done it before, for other neighbors and for my sister and brother-in-law, so I could listen without difficulty.

"Itinerant clerics refueled us from time to time and it happened when one of them was in Jonquière, the last night. For a week my family and I had gone to our church every evening to hear him preach. He was a nice-looking young man with a magnetic manner, and at my age I was susceptible to that, of course. A part of his format — it was the same each night — was a novelty, at least to me. At the end he asked everyone with a troubled heart, a question or a problem, to kneel at the altar and pray silently for an answer. That much I'd seen before. The novelty was, he insisted that no one come to kneel there without a sincere desire for an answer and, what was more remarkable, that no one leave the altar without having received it.

"The problem could be anything, but the one he talked about most was lack of faith, or doubt. Night after night his line was the same: if you honestly requested assurance or belief you'd get it. Even if you were convinced it wouldn't happen, that didn't matter — it would happen if you wanted it to.

"The first night I was astonished by this. It took about twenty minutes, during which three-quarters of the congregation each walked down to the front, knelt for a few minutes, and then returned to the pews. Not a word was spoken, there were only muffled sustained chords except when the organist did his kneeling, and the creaking of floorboards, and coughs. But the hush over everything was impressive. Because, you see, it was very dramatic. There was no way of knowing when the person beside you might stand and walk away to get the guaranteed answer. I found it electrifying, particularly the first time.

"Through the week I thought about this thing that was happening at the service every night. I've thought about it since. He was a shrewd young fellow, that preacher, if he devised it himself."

"What I was trying to work out that week was, should I accept his proposal. It was such a dilemma that I never knew whether or not I was going to, and at the end of the twenty minutes I couldn't tell whether I was relieved or disappointed that I hadn't.

"By then I was feeling pretty sure it was all baloney, and yet the young man seemed to have some kind of authenticity, some charisma. It wasn't supposed to work unless you really wanted it to, so I had to decide if I did. I couldn't imagine what it would be like to receive a direct message from a deity, but I decided that if such knowledge could be had I did indeed want it and I would be a fool not to. But what if my prediction and not the young preacher's should come true? I could imagine what that would be like — it would be demoralizing. I could imagine returning to my pew knowing I had just played a part in a charade. And although I was beginning to think that my very presence in the pew amounted to support for a charade, still this would have been much more degrading. It would have been like actually casting your vote in a rigged election instead of just watching the victor on television with the rest of your family. It was a bind, as it was intended to be. What would you have done, Patrick?"

I smiled and shook my head. No idea.

"I didn't know what to do either but the more I thought about it the more important it seemed. The last evening I was pretty worried, and when the final twenty-minute period started I was trembling. I must have glanced at my wrist watch thirty times as the first ten minutes ticked past. I've never been able to recall what the thoughts were that flashed through my head before I stood and walked to the altar, but it was like an inspiration. All of a sudden I knew with perfect clarity what I was to do.

"I walked forward to the altar, I knelt and bowed my head and shut my eyes and it was as if all my faculties, all my soul and mind were marshaled into one big plea for a divine response, and one big listening for that response. It was as real and honest as could be — it had to be, you see. I didn't move or open my eyes. I've probably never before or since been so absorbed and concentrated. But at the same time, after a while I was aware that no one but me was left at the altar.

"I don't know exactly how long I stayed there. I think it was only fifteen minutes or so beyond the twenty allotted to that part of the service. There were signs of increasing restlessness. I could hear people clear their throats to remind me that I was inconveniencing them. I noticed that the organist had stopped playing after a while, too. I noticed these things as if in passing and they didn't bother me because there was nothing I could do about them. Because the young preacher had insisted that no one leave the altar without having been answered. And I was carrying out his instructions in the best of faith. I was taking him at his word as they pretended to have done, and I was certainly prepared to stay there much longer than fifteen or twenty extra minutes."

You'd think the congregation would have just gone home, some of them anyway.

"It would have been sensible, wouldn't it? I don't think any of them did though. The ceremony was to close with a benediction and it would have seemed almost an act of insubordination to leave without having been dismissed. Also, despite their impatience I think they were curious about what I was up to. Already it was odd enough and I think they thought something still odder might happen that they wouldn't want to miss. And naturally they must have been thinking, we've put up with her preposterous behavior for ten minutes, it won't hurt to give her another minute or two.

"Our own permanent preacher, who was assisting at the service and who, incidentally, was a good man, must have had some inkling of what was happening and realized that no end was in sight as things stood, because he tiptoed over to me and whispered in my ear. He suggested that I go back and sit down, and he said that he and the young preacher would talk with me after the benediction.

"Now I could simply have ignored him or given him an explanation in case he needed one. Because in a sense I was breaking faith by complying. But the same sort of inspiration I had followed to that point now told me to obey him, and I did. I slipped back to the nearest empty space in the pews, our preacher gave a chastened benediction, and the service was over, and with it the special week."

Up in Jonquière half a century ago, the middle of the Depression, those Calvinist lumbermen and farmers and tradespeople and their families all watching the girl leave the altar. I slid another slate into place. If she hadn't gone back to the pews, maybe the message would have come through. Maybe it was on its way and needed only two minutes more to reach her.

Anne stood in the window with her arms folded, no more smiling than a wren would. "Do you think?"

Maybe there was interference.

"Did you ever pick up such a message, Patrick?"

Never, but then I never really tried.

"Good for you. I never did either afterwards. Twenty-five minutes is enough of a life to waste on it. I knew that, by the end of the benediction. When our preacher and the young itinerant took me to the organ loft and the young one wanted me to try again I declined. I explained it all to them and apologized for having held up the service.

Our preacher was thoughtful and subdued but the young fellow let out all the stops. The week had gratified him right up to when I went to the altar, and then at the eleventh hour this bony mite of a girl had rocked the boat. If he'd had a chance to explain me away it wouldn't have rankled so, but the format had precluded that. The format and perhaps also our preacher, who blessed and dismissed the assembly before the young one had a chance to get a last word in edgewise. The young one probably felt like wringing my neck, wouldn't you guess? But the format precluded that too."

"But he was resourceful. People had left the church building and gone home with their impression of the whole week colored by what had just happened. There was no immediate remedy — it wouldn't do for him to follow them and try to put me in my place house by house, and anyway there wasn't time, since he had to be elsewhere on the morrow. But if he could manage to bring me round, if he could sway me there in the organ loft the week might be salvaged because word would seep out that I had seen the light. The week would become a triumph and the very recalcitrance of my case would then count towards his glory. So he let out all the stops he could, given who he was and who I was and the presence and mood of the other cleric, which constrained him.

"He suggested that we kneel together and pray side by side. The seduction probably wouldn't have gone further than that — I don't imagine he'd as much as have laid his hand over my shoulder. But just kneeling side by side with him in the semidarkness there in silence would have been exciting to me, as he well knew. It was tempting but I declined. I said I couldn't see any point in it. So then he switched his tack and tried to intimidate me. He warned me with a simile so peculiar I've remembered it ever since.

"He said that the kingdom of righteousness was like a pendulum. I was supposed to reach out and catch hold when it was near because if I didn't it would swing away without me, out of my reach. He said it would swing back toward me again and I'd have another chance of hopping aboard, and so on for the rest of my life. But he warned me that the pendulum naturally swept out a smaller arc each swing, and therefore I ought to grab it then when it was closer than it ever would be again.

"Well, it was the most ordinary sort of scare tactic — buy now before the prices go up. But the picture his simile presented was peculiar in so many ways I couldn't help wondering about it. He didn't mention devils but I think he must have intended them to be somewhere in the picture."

Somewhere below the pendulum, no? Far enough below so they wouldn't be able to scorch it or jump up onto it.

"Yes, but that would mean I was out of their reach already, as high as the highest point of the pendulum's arc, maybe a little higher. You see how strange it is. But I don't think the young fellow had much considered the implications of his simile.

"Blandishments had rolled off me and now so did intimidations. I had done all I could at the altar before, and the message hadn't reached me — I hadn't been able to reach the pendulum, according to him. However regrettable, it had happened and there was not a thing anyone could do about that."

No sense crying over spilt milk.

"You're a man after my own heart, Patrick. Though the young preacher didn't so much want me to cry as to pretend it hadn't been spilt. I wouldn't and he must have seen he just wasn't going to succeed with me. It made him very angry but he controlled himself and it only came through in a bit of rudeness. He said he suspected I hadn't really wanted an answer when I knelt at the altar. But I absolutely had. I don't know whether he understood that or not, but he could see I was proof against the accusation and so he left in a huff without saying anything more to me.

"Our permanent preacher had said almost nothing in the loft but before the young fellow left he poured oil on the waters. He was looking at the floor, it was as if he was musing aloud. He said, 'Anne has a profound spirit, I know. I trust that in time she will accept our faith profoundly.' I think he knew I wouldn't — I knew it. But I didn't feel like correcting him then or as he saw me home from the church building or ever after. He was a good man regardless of his profession. Alex of course scoffs when I say that. All the same it's true."

I slid another slate up over its nails and then eased out the wedges I had lifted its two overlappers with. I wondered what became of the young preacher.

"I've no idea. He may well be dead now."

But did Anne mean she knew right then and there that it was all over for religion?

"Yes, I did."

It sounded to me like a load off her mind.

"It put a load on my mind for a while."

On?

"My family and some others in the congregation would have guessed the sort of answer I'd been kneeling at the altar so long for. The congregation and the town — Jonquière was much smaller then — thought of me as a bookish child destined for spinsterhood and schoolteaching — I did teach school for a while, but then I married Alex and stopped. They thought of me as overearnest and a bit wilful, which I was. Mainly though they hadn't thought about me at all. But now they would think about me some because of the altar business. I wondered how they would treat me after it. Would they quiz me? Would they be angry?

"No one in the town, none of my family mentioned it to me. Among themselves though there had been some mention. I knew because with people who hadn't been at the service that night I noticed the same change in attitude toward me as with those who had been: they were polite. No instance of it was at all remarkable but I could feel it a hundred times a day. Everyone had become ever-so-slightly reserved and cautious about me. They were watching me out of the corners of their eyes.

"That guardedness didn't so much bother me. In its way it was flattering, you know. The real trouble was in me, in how I thought about them.

"It was a little like the emperor's new clothes. By my obstinacy at the altar I'd as much as said the emperor was naked whereas they, even though they'd certainly heard me, they wouldn't acknowledge it and they were persisting in the pretense. I couldn't imagine their frame of mind. Not at all. My people, the only people I had known, had always seemed more or less like me, more or less understandable and more or less admirable. Now they seemed none of those and I felt a kind of despair for them. And for myself, lodged among them. It was a hard time to get through."

I asked whether her parents wanted her to continue attending church.

"They asked if I would like to. There'd never been any question before but now they invited me. No, I said at first. I was surprised that they'd suppose I might. But after I'd seen more of how things were I didn't see how it could matter a whit whether I went along with them or not. Because the silence and the distance I felt around me seemed to dwarf considerations of my own integrity. And so sometimes I went along, sometimes not, and for the most whimsical reasons as the mood struck me.

"At first when I went they would grow especially polite and wary, some of them. But as they realized I wasn't going to make any more scenes they relaxed. Eventually the slight guardedness ebbed away from all their dealings with me. They seemed to forget how I had once held them captive from their dinners for fifteen minutes, and they accommodated the one anomalous residue of that evening very well. It was as if since childhood I had been not only a humorless spinster-to-be and so forth but also one who missed religious services often as not. Who knows, in time I myself might have come to believe it if I'd stayed there.

"But I wasn't forgetting anywhere near as fast as they seemed to be doing. I found them strange and a little contemptible even when they seemed to have reincorporated me entirely and for some time after. It wasn't very pleasant, Patrick. It was a weight on my mind."

"But I got past it. I came away, for one thing. I met people who didn't seem so fraudulent — some, including Alex, who seemed no more fraudulent than I did. That was liberating. I had fun and work, good medicine the both. Then a member of my family died and I went back for the funeral. It was someone I and most of the town loved. I think the experience sobered me. I think I saw that I had been naïve to take preachers at their word. In and of itself, the apparatus of the religion — what the townspeople believed or pretended to believe about messages from a deity, for instance — was a patent fraud. Yet with them at least it seemed a harmless, even good, fraud. It didn't even quite seem a fraud any more. It seemed as if it might be a figure for some truth. Because somehow it was consoling some of the people in a way no such flimsy lie as I had taken it to be could have done. It seemed to me that many of them saw the flimsiness and the falsehood quite as clearly as I did.

"I thought more about it after I left. I began to be surprised at how patient they had been with me before. If the emperor weren't naked, talk of his clothes would be merely that, and there wouldn't be much reason for it. But since he was naked as a jaybird for all to see, when you talked of his new clothes you couldn't fool anybody and you weren't trying to. You were trying to talk about something altogether different and you were probably trying to tell the truth about it. It must not be easy. When a pubescent child in the crowd squeaks out, 'I don't see any clothes on him,' she must seem either perverse or awfully simple-minded. I suppose the best you can do is tell her, 'Ssh.' Because you'll adhere to the fiction if its real subject is important enough and if you seem to be telling the truth about it. You say, 'Ssh' or just ignore her. You hope she won't distract you again. If she keeps quiet and watches what's going on, she may even come to understand what it is you're up to. You hope for that too.

"Alex disagrees. He thinks no dealing in falsehood should be countenanced. He objects not to the shame or dishonor that made me pipe up but to the danger. It certainly can be dangerous. Do you know what I'm thinking of?"

It could be dangerous if you forget that it's not true, that it's a code for something else.

"Why is that dangerous?"

Well, in Anne's case in the church, she might have crippled herself kneeling.

"And crippled anybody else who was making the same mistake and waiting for me to move. You're right, Patrick. And it's dangerous in other ways. It can be dangerous even if you don't make that mistake."

How so, I asked, as I made room for the last slate to slip into place.

"At my relative's funeral the fiction was working properly, I think. I knew that and yet I knew full well that that particular fiction — Christianity, I mean — had a long history of working very badly indeed. Some of its evil did come from people's having made the mistake of taking it for the truth it was only a code or figure for. But I think such literal-mindedness accounts more for the folly than for the evil. Because so far as I remember, the religion itself doesn't contain too many counsels to wrongdoing. And yet its professors have done enormous amounts of many kinds of wrong and harm, and they've sanctioned those wrongs and harms with the religion, even though it itself contains explicit counsels against some of them. It says that its god says not to kill people, for instance. So I don't think many of its professors have ever taken it very literally.

"But if it's possible to tell each other real truths by talking about the emperor's clothes, it must also be possible to tell each other real falsehoods that way too. That's the danger I was thinking of. And knowing which is which may not be easy. With the Christian fiction, it seems to have been close to impossible."

"So I agree with Alex that dealing in patent falsehoods is dangerous. But I don't think it's as pernicious as he does. I'm more inclined now to see it as like some powerful machine, say an electric lawnmower. It's more hazardous than an ordinary lawnmower, if it's working badly. But if it's working well you may be able to do a job faster with it. It may even enable you to cut grass you simply couldn't with an ordinary mower. Something like that. I wish Alex could see it that way.

"Where did you learn slate roofing, by the way, Patrick? You seem expert."

Hardly, but this should stop the leaks. It's the kind of thing you just pick up, really. The first time I did it must have been back in Trois Rivières with my father.

"Is he still there?"

I laid the tools and the last broken slate in the tray. Yes, my father is still in Trois Rivières. He's in the cemetery. My mother too — she died when I was a baby. My father was killed in an automobile accident three years back. Nobody at fault. It was raining and there was a blowout, skidding. The driver of the other car got off with a broken arm. Some machines are more hazardous than others.

I stood and the pigeons flapped away. Anne blinked.

"Times like that, Patrick, as a rule the emperor's new clothes come out of the wardrobe."

I stepped gingerly up to the window. There was a requiem mass for Poppa, the only one I remember ever going to. His sisters and brother took care of everything. I think they and their families have stayed with the church, but Poppa, as far back as I can remember, was pretty well lapsed. The accident's why I came here for my last year of school — Laure and her husband had the vacant efficiency. I handed the tray through the window and stepped over the sill. As I unhitched myself and the tray from the bedstead, Anne walked to the dresser for her purse. No, I said, it's on the house. She had provided the slates and, as for the little labor, her story had more than reimbursed me. She shook her head and started to protest, but she was studying my face and she changed her mind. Downstairs on her doorstep, she held out her small hand to me.

11

Four days later the carriage was ready to roll, and my piebald gelding and I had a profitable Wednesday showing Old Québec to tourists. I stabled him around six and took a bus out to a cut-rate electronics outlet in the new town to pick up a tuner and amplifier kit. After dinner my friend Hammed came over and we assembled it.

Hammed wasn't a real friend but he was the closest thing to it I had. Even back in Trois Rivières before Poppa died, I'd been a bit of a loner. I was always cheerful and outgoing — you had to be to make anything driving the barouche — and I liked talking with most anybody for a while, but I just didn't seem cut out for close friendships. People who knew me didn't mind.

Hammed was a naturalized Tunisian. His family had come to Québec the year before I moved here. He brought some kif along and we smoked it as we assembled the equipment and then listened to its performance. Between us we had more than adequate knowledge of the basic electronics. The sound was good even discounting the enhancement of the kif, and most of the old background noise had dropped away. Hammed left around eleven-thirty to catch a bus back to his family's high rise in the new town. Residual effects of his African dope, together with a kind of echo of my rooftop talk with Mrs. Van Frank, and the fatigue of an unusually full day, must have contributed to something that happened an hour or so later.

Hammed and I had listened to Claude Léveillée and Gilles Vigneault sing Québec songs, and then I'd heard a Tschaikovsky piano concerto and then one side of a record of whale songs as I drank a cup of instant hot chocolate. Then I kicked off my shoes and lay on my day bed for an indeterminate period. I was doing that kind of thoughtless thought near sleep you never remember — little pictures, little thoughts coming and going, with a heightened sense of touch along the rims of my eyelids.

Then out of nowhere like a shock came an image of my father's rotted face, close and physical. Immediately the image changed into its memory, variable and fading and vivid. All this was quick, and the memory had become its own memory before the shock registered in my heart and pulse. When that came it was like a reembodiment for me out of a presence diffused around the patient face. My eyelids retracted to the maximum and I raised myself to a half-crouch on the day bed, not to fight or flee, but because I was in a pure free state of extreme alertness. By then the compounding memory was changing into knowledge.

The night in Trois Rivières at the house when the highway patrolman woke me to inform me of Poppa's death I had gone kind of gruff, wiping away the tears like sweat during a hard day's work in the sun. Coming to terms with it was hard for Laure even though she was already married and living in Québec, and it was sure hard for me. We had drawn together, and got through it. Poppa's death had been on my mind like a big fact to be coped with during the move to Québec and all. It meant, for instance, that I reviewed what I knew of his goodness and tried to keep it from going to waste by fostering what I could of it in myself — though that was tricky because people would then want to give me the credit. Anyway, by now Poppa didn't seem so much on my mind. The fact that he wasn't alive had come to be just a fact, no more to be coped with than the fact that my mother wasn't either.

I fell out of the crouch into a rag-doll collapse, my back against the wall, to think over what I had just seen. Three phrases I still remember passed through my mind: "The most important thing. Him not me. All this time."

The mental shorthand meant that the sight of Poppa's face, his rotted face, made a mockery of all my coping, because not once since the accident had I been sensible of what the vision now forced me to reckon with. When the officer had first told me about it I had shed tears but even those first tears were from grief at losing Poppa. Similarly, what I had come to terms with wasn't really the fact that he was dead but rather the fact that he wasn't living, which soon became the fact that I was without a living parent. But all this time Poppa himself had been dead, his body had been decomposing all the while I had been trying to deal with the loss, Laure's and my loss. From the start, and increasingly, I had taken the death as a fact about me (which it was) and strangely not taken it as what it was above all, a fact about Poppa, his face half-gone by now. None of which had a thing to do with me or me with it — there my grief or coping counted for nothing.

I felt ashamed of having occupied myself with something so remote from the main truth as how the death bore on me. Not exactly because I had dishonored my father or been remiss. Maybe I had, but in his being dead nothing I might do mattered. It was rather that my mind seemed to have been small. I undressed, brushed my teeth, peed, and turned the lights out.

It was raining the next morning when I awoke, a cold steady autumn rain the Van Franks would be glad to have their roof repaired against. The barouche has an accordion roof I can pull up in a shower, but I knew no visitors would be looking for a horse-drawn tour in that weather, so I spent the morning doing some more testing and adjusting of the new sound system, and thinking over what had happened to me the night before.

My assessment of it was more or less the same except that it didn't seem at all strange now. It had happened last night but it could as well have happened months before, it seemed so settled in my mind. It had become something to think about and generalize from. For instance, mightn't it be that somehow with living people I made the same kind of mistake I'd been making with Poppa the past three years? What would that mean? Well, I supposed it would mean coping and coming to terms with them from my standpoint until a corresponding vision of a living face finally alerted me. I tried to imagine what that would be like, with Laure, or with Hammed, say, or with Mrs. Van Frank, a vision out of the blue or even actually seeing the person in a way that disembodied me. I couldn't quite imagine it, though I felt (and still do) that something like that could happen one day. I decided to compliment Hammed on his kif the next time I saw him, even though I knew the real catalyst had been Anne Van Frank's story.

J. F. Powers

....

Zeal

SOUTH OF ST. PAUL the conductor appeared at the head of the coach, held up his ticket punch, and clicked it.

The Bishop felt for his ticket. It was there.

"I know it's not a pass," said Father Early. He had been talking across the aisle to one of the pilgrims he was leading to Rome, but now he was back on the subject of the so-called clergy pass. "But it is a privilege."

The Bishop said nothing. He'd meant to imply by his silence before, when Father Early brought up the matter, that there was nothing wrong with an arrangement which permitted the clergy to travel in parlor cars at coach rates. The Bishop wished the arrangement were in effect in all parts of the country, and on all trains.

"But on a run like this, Bishop, with these fine coaches, I daresay there aren't many snobs who'll go to the trouble of filling out the form."

The Bishop looked away. Father Early had a nose like a parrot's and something on it like psoriasis that held the Bishop's attention — unfortunately, for Father Early seemed to think it was his talk. The Bishop had a priest or two in his diocese like Father Early.

"Oh, the railroads, I daresay, mean well."

"Yes," said the Bishop distantly. The voice at his right ear went on without him. He gazed out the window, up at the limestone scarred by its primeval intercourse with the Mississippi, now shrunk down into itself, and there he saw a cave, another cave, and another. Criminals had been discovered in them, he understood, and ammunition from the Civil War, and farther down the river, in the high bluffs, rattlesnakes were said to be numerous still.

"Bishop, I don't think I'm one to strain at a gnat." (The Bishop glanced at Father Early's nose with interest.) "But I must say I fear privilege more than persecution. Of course the one follows the other, as the night the day."

"Is it true, Father, that there are rattlesnakes along here?"

"Very likely," said Father Early, hardly bothering to look out the window. "Bishop, I was dining in New York, in a crowded place, observed by all and sundry, when the management tried to present me with a bottle of wine. Well!"

The Bishop, spying a whole row of caves, thought of the ancient Nile. Here, though, the country was too fresh and frigid. Here the desert fathers would've married early and gone fishing. The aborigines, by their fruits, pretty much proved that. He tried again to interrupt Father Early. "There must be a cave for you up there, somewhere, Father."

Father Early responded with a laugh that sounded exactly like ha-ha, no more or less. "I'll tell you a secret, Bishop. When I was in seminary, they called me Crazy Early. I understand they still do. Perhaps you knew."

"No," said the Bishop. Father Early flattered himself. The Bishop had never heard of him until that day.

"I thought perhaps Monsignor Reed had told you."

"I seldom see him." He saw Reed only by accident, at somebody's funeral or jubilee celebration or, it seemed, in railroad stations, which had happened again in Minneapolis that morning. It was Reed who had introduced Father Early to him then. Had Reed known what he was doing? It was six hours to Chicago, hours of this . . .

"I suppose you know Macaulay's *England,* Bishop."

"No." There was something to be gained by a frank admission of ignorance when it was assumed anyway.

"Read the section dealing with the status of the common clergy in the eighteenth century. I'm talking about the Anglican clergy. Hardly the equal of servants, knaves, figures of fun! The fault of the Reformation, you say? Yes, of course" — the Bishop had in no way signified assent — "but I say it could happen anywhere, everywhere, any time! Take what's going on in parts of Europe today. When you consider the status of the Church there in the past, and the overwhelmingly Catholic population even now. I wonder, though, if it doesn't take something to bring us to our senses from time to time — *now* what do you say, Bishop?"

If the conductor hadn't been upon them, the Bishop would've said there was probably less danger of the clergy getting above themselves than there was of their being accepted for less than they were; or at least for less than they were supposed to be; or was that what Father Early was saying?

The conductor took up their tickets, placed two receipts overhead, one white and one blue. Before he moved on, he advised the Bishop to bring his receipt with him, the blue one, when he moved into the parlor car.

The Bishop nodded serenely.

Beside him, Father Early was full of silence, and opening his breviary.

The Bishop, who had expected to be told apologetically that it was a matter of no importance if he'd used his clergy pass, had an uncomfortable feeling that Father Early was praying for him.

At Winona, the train stopped for a minute. The Bishop from his window saw Father Early on the platform below talking to an elderly woman. In parting, they pecked at each other, and she handed him a box. Returning to his seat, he said he'd had a nice visit with his sister. He went to the head of the coach with the box, and came slowly back down the aisle, offering the contents to the pilgrims. "Divinity? Divinity?" The Bishop, when his turn came, took a piece, and consumed it. Then he felt committed to stay with Father Early until Chicago.

It was some time before Father Early returned to his seat — from making the acquaintance of Monsignor Reed's parishioners. "What we did was split the responsibility. Miss Culhane's in charge of Monsignor's people. Of course, the ultimate responsibility is mine." Peering up the aisle at two middle-aged women drawing water from the cooler, Father Early said, "The one coming this way now," and gazed out the window.

Miss Culhane, a paper cup in each hand, smiled at the Bishop. He smiled back.

When Miss Culhane had passed, Father Early said, "She's been abroad once, and that's more than most of 'em can say. She's a secretary in private life, and it's hard to find a man with much sense of detail. But I don't know . . . From what I've heard already I'd say the good people don't like the idea. I'm afraid they think she stands between them and me."

The other woman, also carrying paper cups, came down the aisle, and again Father Early gazed out the window. So did the Bishop. When the woman had gone by, Father Early commented dryly, "Her friend, whose name escapes me. Between the two of 'em, Bishop . . . Oh, it'll be better for all concerned when Monsignor joins us."

The Bishop knew nothing about this. Reed had told him nothing. *"Monsignor?"*

"Claims he's allergic to trains."

"Reed?"

Again Father Early treated the question as rhetorical. "His plane doesn't arrive until noon tomorrow. We sail at four. That doesn't give us much time in New York."

The Bishop was putting it all together. Evidently Reed was planning to have as much privacy as he could on the trip. Seeing his little flock running around loose in the station, though, he must have felt guilty — and then the Bishop had happened along. Would Reed do this to him? Reed had done this to him. Reed had once called the Bishop's diocese the next thing to a titular see.

"I'm sorry he isn't sailing with us," said Father Early.

"Isn't he?"

"He's got business of some kind — stained glass, I believe — that'll keep him in New York for a few days. He may have to go to Boston. So he's flying over. I wonder, Bishop, if he isn't allergic to boats too." Father Early smiled at the Bishop as one good sailor to another.

The Bishop wasn't able to smile back. He was thinking how much he preferred to travel alone. When he was being hustled into the coach by Reed and Father Early, he hadn't considered the embarrassment there might be in the end; together on the train to Chicago and again on the one to New York and then crossing on the same liner, apart, getting an occasional glimpse of each other across the barriers. The perfidious Reed had united them, knowing full well that the Bishop was traveling first class and that Father Early and the group were going tourist. The Bishop hoped there would be time for him to see Reed in New York. According to Father Early, though, Reed didn't want them to look for him until they saw him. The Bishop wouldn't.

Miss Culhane, in the aisle again, returned with more water. When she passed, the Bishop and Father Early were both looking out the window. "You can't blame 'em," Father Early said. "I wish he'd picked a man for the job. No, they want more than a man, Bishop. They want a priest."

"They've got you," said the Bishop. "And Monsignor will soon be with you."

"Not until we reach Rome."

"*No?*" The Bishop was rocked by this new evidence of Reed's ruthlessness. Father Early and the group were going to Ireland and England first, as the Bishop was, but they'd be spending more time in those countries, about two weeks.

"No," said Father Early. "He won't."

The Bishop got out his breviary. He feared that Father Early would not be easily discouraged. The Bishop, if he could be persuaded to join the group, would more than make up for the loss of Reed. To share the command with such a man as Father Early, however, would be impossible. It would be to serve under him — as Reed may have realized. The Bishop would have to watch out. It would be dangerous for him to offer Father Early plausible excuses, to point out, for instance, that they'd be isolated from each other once they sailed from New York. Such an excuse, regretfully tendered now, could easily commit him to service on this train, and on the next one, and in New York — and the Bishop wasn't at all sure that Father Early wouldn't find a way for him to be with the group aboard ship. The Bishop turned a page.

When Father Early rose and led the pilgrims in the recitation of the rosary, the Bishop put aside his breviary, took out his beads and prayed along with them. After that, Father Early directed the pilgrims in the singing of "Onward, Christian Soldiers" — which was *not* a Protestant hymn, not originally, he said. Monsignor Reed's parishioners didn't know the words, but Father Early got around that difficulty by having everyone sing the notes of the scale, the ladies *la,* the men *do.* The Bishop cursed his luck and wouldn't even pretend to sing. Father Early was in the aisle, beating time with his fist, exhorting some by name to contribute more to the din, clutching others (males) by the shoulders until they did. The Bishop grew afraid that even he might not be exempt, and again sought the protection of his breviary.

He had an early lunch. When he returned to his seat, it was just past noon, and Father Early was waiting in the aisle for him.

"How about a bite to eat, Bishop?"

"I've eaten, Father."

"You eat early, Bishop."

"I couldn't wait."

Father Early did his little ha-ha laugh. "By the way, Bishop, are you planning anything for the time we'll have in Chicago between trains?" Before the Bishop, who was weighing the significance of the question, could reply, Father Early told him that the group was planning a visit to the Art Institute. "The Art Treasures of Vienna are there now."

"I believe I've seen them, Father."

"In Vienna, Bishop?"

"Yes."

"Well, they should be well worth seeing again."

"Yes. But I don't think I'll be seeing them." Not expecting the perfect silence that followed — this from Father Early was more punishing than his talk — the Bishop added, "Not today." Then, after more of that silence, "I've nothing planned, Father." Quickly, not liking the sound of that, "I do have a few things I might do."

Father Early nodded curtly and went away.

The Bishop heard him inviting some of the group to have lunch with him.

During the rest of the afternoon, the indefatigable voice of Father Early came to the Bishop from all over the coach, but the man himself didn't return to his seat. And when the train pulled into the station, Father Early wasn't in the coach. The Bishop guessed he was with the conductor, to whom he had a lot to say, or with the other employees of the railroad, who never seem to be around at the end of a journey. Stepping out of the coach, the Bishop felt like a free man.

Miss Culhane, however, was waiting for him. She introduced him to an elderly couple, the Doyles, who were the only ones in the group not planning to visit the Art Institute. Father Early, she said, understood that the Bishop wasn't planning to do anything in Chicago and would be grateful if the Bishop would keep an eye on the Doyles there. They hadn't been there before.

The Bishop showed them Grant Park from a taxicab, and pointed out the Planetarium, the Aquarium, the Field Museum. "Thought it was the stockyards," Mr. Doyle commented on Soldier Field, giving Mrs. Doyle a laugh. "I'm afraid there isn't time to go there," the Bishop said. He was puzzled by the Doyles. They didn't seem to realize the sight-seeing was for them. He tried them on foot in department stores until he discovered from something Mrs. Doyle said that they were bearing with him. Soon after that they were standing across the street from the Art Institute, with the Bishop asking if they didn't want to cross over and join the group inside. Mr. Doyle said he didn't think they could make it over there alive — a reference to the heavy traffic, serious or not, the Bishop couldn't tell, but offered to take them across. The Doyles could not be tempted. So the three of them wandered around some more, the Doyles usually a step or two behind the Bishop. At last, in the lobby of the Congress Hotel, Mrs. Doyle expressed a desire to sit down. And there they sat, three in a row, in silence, until it was time to take a cab to the station. On the way over, Mr. Doyle, watching the meter, said, "These things could sure cost you."

In the station the Bishop gave the Doyles a gentle shove in the direction of the gate through which some members of the group were passing. A few minutes later, after a visit to the newsstand, he went through the gate unaccompanied. As soon as he entered his Pullman his ears informed him that he'd reckoned without Mr. Hope, the travel agent in Minneapolis. Old pastors wise in the ways of the world and to the escapist urge to which so many of the men, sooner or later, succumbed, thinking it only a love of travel, approved of Mr. Hope's system. If Mr. Hope had a priest going somewhere, he tried to make it a pair; dealt two, he worked for three of a kind; and so on — and nuns, of course, were wild, their presence eminently sobering. All day the Bishop had thought the odds safely against their having accommodations in the same Pullman car, but he found himself next door to Father Early.

They had dinner together. In the Bishop's view, it was fortunate that the young couple seated across the table was resilient from drink. Father Early opened up on the subject of tipping.

"These men," he said, his glance taking in several waiters, and his mouth almost in the ear of the one who was serving them, a cross-looking colored man, "are in a wonderful position to assert their dignity as human beings — which dignity, being from God, may not be sold with impunity. And for a mere pittance at that! Or, what's worse, bought!"

The Bishop, laying down his soup spoon, sat gazing out the window, for which he was again grateful. It was getting dark. The world seen from a train always looked sadder then. Indiana. Ohio next, but he wouldn't see it. Pennsylvania, perhaps, in the early morning, if he didn't sleep well.

"I see what you mean," he heard the young woman saying, "but I just charge it up to expenses."

"Ah, ha," said Father Early. "Then you don't see what I mean."

"Oh, don't I? Well, it's not important. And *please* — don't explain."

The Bishop, coloring, heard nothing from Father Early and thanked God for that. They had been coming to this, or something like it, inevitably they had. And again the Bishop suffered the thought that the couple was associating him with Father Early.

When he had served dessert across the table, the waiter addressed himself to Father Early. "As far as I'm concerned, sir, you're right," he said, and moved off.

The young woman, watching the waiter go, said, "He can't do that to me."

Airily, Father Early was saying, "And this time tomorrow we'll be on our way to Europe."

The Bishop was afraid the conversation would lapse entirely — which might have been the best thing for it in the long run — but the young man was nodding.

"Will this be your first trip?" asked the young woman. She sounded as though she thought it would be.

"My fifth, God willing," Father Early said. "I don't mean that as a commentary on the boat we're taking. Only as a little reminder to myself that we're all of us hanging by a thread here, only a heart's beat from eternity. Which doesn't mean we shouldn't do our best while here. On the contrary. Some people think Catholics oppose progress here below. Look on your garbage can and what do you see? Galvanized. Galvan was a Catholic. Look on your light bulb. Watts. Watt was a Catholic. The Church never harmed Galileo."

Father Early, as if to see how he was doing, turned to the Bishop. The Bishop, however, was dining with his reflection in the window. He had displayed a spark of interest when Father Early began to talk of the trip, believing there was to be a change of subject matter, but Father Early had tricked him.

"And how long in Rome?" asked the young woman.

"Only two days. Some members of the group intend to stay longer, but they won't return with me. Two days doesn't seem long enough, does it? Well, I can't say that I care for Rome. I didn't feel at home there, or anywhere on the Continent. We'll have two good weeks in the British Isles."

"Some people don't travel to feel at home," said the young woman.

To this Father Early replied, "Ireland first and then England. It may interest you to know that about half of the people in the group are carrying the complete works of Shakespeare. I'm hoping the rest of the group will manage to secure copies of the plays and read them before we visit Stratford."

"It sounds like a large order," said the young woman.

"Paperback editions are to be had everywhere," Father Early said with enthusiasm. "By the way, what book would you want if you were shipwrecked on a desert island?"

Apparently the question had novelty for the young man. "That's a hard one," he said.

"Indeed it is. Chesterton, one of the great Catholic writers, said he'd like a manual of shipbuilding, but I don't consider that a serious answer to the question. I'll make it two books because, of course, you'd want the Bible. Some people think Catholics don't read the Bible. But who preserved Scripture in the Dark Ages? Holy monks. Now what do you say? No. Ladies first."

"I think I'd like that book on shipbuilding," said the young woman.

Father Early smiled. "And you, sir?"

"Shakespeare, I guess."

"I was hoping you'd say that."

Then the Bishop heard the young woman inquiring:

"Shakespeare wasn't a Catholic, was he?"

The Bishop reached for his glass of water, and saw Father Early observing a moment of down-staring silence. When he spoke his voice was deficient. "As a matter of fact, we don't know. Arguments both ways. But we just don't know. Perhaps it's better that way," he said, and that was all he said. At last he was eating his dinner.

When the young couple rose to leave, the Bishop, who had been waiting for this moment, turned in time to see the young man almost carry out Father Early's strict counsel against tipping. With one look, however, the young woman prevailed over him. The waiter came at once and removed the tip. With difficulty, the Bishop put down the urge to comment. He wanted to say that he believed people should do what they could do, little though it might be, and shouldn't be asked to attempt what was obviously beyond them. The young woman, who probably thought Father Early was just tight, was better off than the young man.

After the waiter came and went again, Father Early sat back and said, "I'm always being surprised by the capacity ordinary people have for sacrifice."

The Bishop swallowed what — again — would have been his comment. Evidently Father Early was forgetting about the young man.

"Thanks for looking after the Doyles. I would've asked you myself but I was in the baggage car. Someone wanted me to say hello to a dog that's going to South Bend. No trouble, were they? What'd you see?"

The Bishop couldn't bring himself to answer either question. "It's hard to know what other people want to do," he said. "They might've had a better guide."

"I can tell you they enjoyed your company, Bishop."

"Oh?" The Bishop, though touched, had a terrible vision of himself doing the capitals of the world with the Doyles.

Father Early handed the Bishop a cigar. "Joe Quirke keeps me well supplied with these," he said, nodding to a beefy middle-aged man two tables away who looked pleased at having caught Father Early's eye. "I believe you know him."

"I met him," the Bishop said, making a distinction. Mr. Quirke had sat down next to him in the club car before dinner, taken up a magazine, put it down after a minute, and offered to buy the Bishop a drink. When the Bishop (who'd been about to order one) refused, Mr. Quirke had apparently taken him for a teetotaler with a past. He said he'd had a little problem until Father Early got hold of him.

Father Early was discussing the youth eating with Mr. Quirke. "Glenn's been in a little trouble at home — and at school. Three schools, I believe. Good family. I have his father's permission to leave him with the Christian Brothers in Ireland, if they'll have him."

When Glenn got up from the table, the Bishop decided he didn't like the look of him. Glenn was short-haired, long-legged, a Doberman pinscher of a boy. He loped out of the diner, followed by Mr. Quirke.

Two problems, thought the Bishop, getting ready to happen — and doubtless there were more of them in the group. Miss Culhane, in her fashion, could make trouble.

"There's something I'd like to discuss with you, Bishop."

The Bishop stiffened. Now it was coming, he feared, the all-out attempt to recruit him.

Father Early was looking across the table, at the empty places there. "You realize they'd been drinking?"

The Bishop refused to comment. *Now what?*

"It wouldn't surprise me if they met on this train."

"Yes, well . . ."

"Bishop, in my opinion, the boy is or has been a practicing Catholic."

In the Bishop's opinion, it was none of Father Early's business. He knew what Father Early was getting at, and he didn't like it. Father Early was thinking of taking on more trouble.

"I believe the boy's in danger," Father Early said. "Real danger."

The Bishop opened his mouth to tell Father Early off, but not much came out. "I wouldn't call him a boy." The Bishop felt that Father Early had expected something of the sort from him, nothing, and no support. Father Early had definitely gone into one of his silences. The Bishop, fussing with his cuffs, suddenly reached, but Father Early beat him to the checks.

Father Early complimented the waiter on the service and food, rewarding him with golden words.

The Bishop was going to leave a tip, to be on the safe side, but apparently the waiter was as good as his word. They left the diner in the blaze of his hospitality.

The Bishop had expected to be asked where in New York he'd be saying Mass in the morning, but when they arrived at their doors, Father Early smiled and put out his hand. It certainly looked like good-by.

They shook hands.

And then, suddenly, Father Early was on his knees, his head bowed and waiting for the Bishop's blessing.

His mind was full of the day and he was afraid he was in for one of those nights he'd had on trains before. He kept looking at his watch in the dark, listening for sounds of activity next door, and finally he admitted to himself that he was waiting for Father Early to come in. So he gave Father Early until midnight — and then he got dressed and went out to look for him.

Up ahead he saw Glenn step into the corridor from an end room and go around the corner. The Bishop prepared to say hello. But when he was about to pass, the atmosphere filled up with cigarette smoke. The Bishop hurried through it, unrecognized, he hoped, considering the lateness of the hour and the significance of another visit to the club car, as it might appear to Glenn, who could have observed him there earlier in the evening.

The club car was empty except for a man with a magazine in the middle of the car, the waiter serving him a drink, and the young man and Father Early at the tail end of the train, seated on a sofa facing upon the tracks. The Bishop advanced with difficulty to the rear. The train was traveling too fast.

Father Early glanced around. He moved over on the sofa to make room for the Bishop, and had the young man move. The Bishop sat down beside the young man, who was now in the middle.

"One I went to — we're talking about fairs, Bishop — had an educated donkey, as the fellow called it. This donkey could tell one color from another — knew them all by name. The fellow had these paddles, you've seen them, painted different colors. Red, green, blue, brown, black, orange, yellow, white — oh, all colors . . ."

The Bishop, from the tone of this, sensed that nothing had been resolved and that Father Early's objective was to keep the young man up all night with him. It was a siege.

"The fellow would say, 'Now, Trixie' — I remember the little donkey's name. You might've seen her at some time."

The young man shook his head.

"'Now, Trixie,' the fellow would say, 'bring me the yellow paddle,' and that's what she'd do. She'd go to the rack, where all the paddles were hanging, pick out the yellow one, and carry it to the fellow. Did it with her teeth, of course. Then the fellow would say, 'Trixie, bring me the green paddle.'"

"And she brought the green one," said the young man patiently.

"That's right. The fellow would say, 'Now, Trixie, bring me the paddles that are the colors of the flag.'" Father Early addressed the Bishop: "Red, white, and blue."

"Yes," said the Bishop. What an intricate instrument for good a simple man could be! Perhaps Father Early was only a fool, a ward of heaven, not subject to the usual penalties for meddling. No, it was zeal, and people, however far gone, still expected it from a man of God. But, even so, Father Early ought to be more careful, humbler before the mystery of iniquity. And still . . .

"My, that was a nice little animal, that Trixie." Father Early paused, giving his attention to the signal lights blinking down the tracks, and continued. "Red, green, all colors. Most fairs have little to recommend them. Some fairs, however, are worth while." Father Early stood up. "I'll be right back," he said, and went to the lavatory.

The Bishop was about to say something — to keep the ball rolling — when the young man got up and left, without a word.

The Bishop sat where he was until he heard the lavatory door open and shut. Then he got up to meet Father Early. Father Early looked beyond the Bishop, toward the place where the young man had been, and then at the Bishop. He didn't appear to blame the Bishop at all. Nothing was said.

They walked in the direction from which Father Early had just come. The Bishop thought they were calling it a day, but Father Early was onto something else, trying the waiter on baseball.

"Good night, Father."

"Oh?" said Father Early, as if he'd expected the Bishop to stick around for it.

"Good night, Father." The Bishop had a feeling that baseball wouldn't last, that the sermon on tipping was due again.

"Good night, Bishop."

The Bishop moved off comically, as the train made up for lost time. Entering his Pullman car, he saw the young man, who must have been kept waiting, disappear into the room Glenn had come out of earlier.

The Bishop slept well that night, after all, but not before he thought of Father Early still out there, on his feet and trying, which was what counted in the sight of God, not success. *Thinkest thou that I cannot ask my Father, and he will give me presently more than twelve legions of angels?*

"Would you like me to run through these names with you, Bishop, or do you want to familiarize yourself with the people as we go along?"

"I'd prefer that, I think. And I wish you'd keep the list, Miss Culhane."

"I don't think Father Early would want you to be without it, Bishop."

"No? Very well, I'll keep it then."

Philip Roth

....

Defender of the Faith

IN MAY OF 1945, only a few weeks after the fighting had ended
in Europe, I was rotated back to the States, where I spent the
remainder of the war with a training company at Camp Crowder,
Missouri. Along with the rest of the Ninth Army, I had been racing
across Germany so swiftly during the late winter and spring that when
I boarded the plane, I couldn't believe its destination lay to the west.
My mind might inform me otherwise, but there was an inertia of the
spirit that told me we were flying to a new front, where we would dis-
embark and continue our push eastward — eastward until we'd circled
the globe, marching through villages along whose twisting, cobbled
streets crowds of the enemy would watch us take possession of what,
up till then, they'd considered their own. I had changed enough in two
years not to mind the trembling of the old people, the crying of the
very young, the uncertainty and fear in the eyes of the once arrogant. I
had been fortunate enough to develop an infantryman's heart, which,
like his feet, at first aches and swells but finally grows horny enough for
him to travel the weirdest paths without feeling a thing.

Captain Paul Barrett was my C.O. in Camp Crowder. The day I
reported for duty, he came out of his office to shake my hand. He was
short, gruff, and fiery, and — indoors or out — he wore his polished
helmet liner pulled down to his little eyes. In Europe, he had received a
battlefield commission and a serious chest wound, and he'd been returned to the States only a few months before. He spoke easily to me,
and at the evening formation he introduced me to the troops. "Gentlemen," he said, "Sergeant Thurston, as you know, is no longer with this
company. Your new first sergeant is Sergeant Nathan Marx, here. He is

a veteran of the European theater, and consequently will expect to find a company of soldiers here, and not a company of *boys*."

I sat up late in the orderly room that evening, trying half-heartedly to solve the riddle of duty rosters, personnel forms, and morning reports. The Charge of Quarters slept with his mouth open on a mattress on the floor. A trainee stood reading the next day's duty roster, which was posted on the bulletin board just inside the screen door. It was a warm evening, and I could hear radios playing dance music over in the barracks. The trainee, who had been staring at me whenever he thought I wouldn't notice, finally took a step in my direction.

"Hey, Sarge — we having a G.I. party tomorrow night?" he asked. A G.I. party is a barracks cleaning.

"You usually have them on Friday nights?" I asked him.

"Yes," he said, and then he added, mysteriously, "that's the whole thing."

"Then you'll have a G.I. party."

He turned away, and I heard him mumbling. His shoulders were moving, and I wondered if he was crying.

"What's your name, soldier?" I asked.

He turned, not crying at all. Instead, his green-speckled eyes, long and narrow, flashed like fish in the sun. He walked over to me and sat on the edge of my desk. He reached out a hand. "Sheldon," he said.

"Stand on your feet, Sheldon."

Getting off the desk, he said, "Sheldon Grossbart." He smiled at the familiarity into which he'd led me.

"You against cleaning the barracks Friday night, Grossbart?" I said. "Maybe we shouldn't have G.I. parties. Maybe we should get a maid." My tone startled me. I felt I sounded like every top sergeant I had ever known.

"No, Sergeant." He grew serious, but with a seriousness that seemed to be only the stifling of a smile. "It's just — G.I. parties on Friday night, of all nights."

He slipped up onto the corner of the desk again — not quite sitting, but not quite standing, either. He looked at me with those speckled eyes flashing, and then made a gesture with his hand. It was very slight — no more than a movement back and forth of the wrist — and yet it managed to exclude from our affairs everything else in the orderly room, to make the two of us the center of the world. It seemed, in fact, to exclude everything even about the two of us except our hearts.

"Sergeant Thurston was one thing," he whispered, glancing at the sleeping C.Q., "but we thought that with you here things might be a little different."

"We?"

"The Jewish personnel."

"Why?" I asked, harshly. "What's on your mind?" Whether I was still angry at the "Sheldon" business, or now at something else, I hadn't time to tell, but clearly I was angry.

"We thought you — Marx, you know, like Karl Marx. The Marx Brothers. Those guys are all — M-a-r-x. Isn't that how *you* spell it, Sergeant?"

"M-a-r-x."

"Fishbein said — " He stopped. "What I mean to say, Sergeant — " His face and neck were red, and his mouth moved but no words came out. In a moment, he raised himself to attention, gazing down at me. It was as though he had suddenly decided he could expect no more sympathy from me than from Thurston, the reason being that I was of Thurston's faith, and not his. The young man had managed to confuse himself as to what my faith really was, but I felt no desire to straighten him out. Very simply, I didn't like him.

When I did nothing but return his gaze, he spoke, in an altered tone. "You see, Sergeant," he explained to me, "Friday nights, Jews are supposed to go to services."

"Did Sergeant Thurston tell you you couldn't go to them when there was a G.I. party?"

"No."

"Did he say you had to stay and scrub the floors?"

"No, Sergeant."

"Did the Captain say you had to stay and scrub the floors?"

"That isn't it, Sergeant. It's the other guys in the barracks." He leaned toward me. "They think we're goofing off. But we're not. That's when Jews go to services, Friday night. We have to."

"Then go."

"But the other guys make accusations. They have no right."

"That's not the Army's problem, Grossbart. It's a personal problem you'll have to work out yourself."

"But it's un*fair*."

I got up to leave. "There's nothing I can do about it," I said.

Grossbart stiffened and stood in front of me. "But this is a matter of *religion,* sir."

"Sergeant," I said.

"I mean 'Sergeant,'" he said, almost snarling.

"Look, go see the chaplain. You want to see Captain Barrett, I'll arrange an appointment."

"No, no. I don't want to make trouble, Sergeant. That's the first thing they throw up to you. I just want my rights!"

"Damn it, Grossbart, stop whining. You have your rights. You can stay and scrub floors or you can go to shul — "

The smile swam in again. Spittle gleamed at the corners of his mouth. "You mean church, Sergeant."

"I mean shul, Grossbart!"

I walked past him and went outside. Near me, I heard the scrunching of a guard's boots on gravel. Beyond the lighted windows of the barracks, young men in T-shirts and fatigue pants were sitting on their bunks, polishing their rifles. Suddenly there was a light rustling behind me. I turned and saw Grossbart's dark frame fleeing back to the barracks, racing to tell his Jewish friends that they were right — that, like Karl and Harpo, I was one of them.

The next morning, while chatting with Captain Barrett, I recounted the incident of the previous evening. Somehow, in the telling, it must have seemed to the Captain that I was not so much explaining Grossbart's position as defending it. "Marx, I'd fight side by side with a nigger if the fella proved to me he was a man. I pride myself," he said, looking out the window, "that I've got an open mind. Consequently, Sergeant, nobody gets special treatment here, for the good *or* the bad. All a man's got to do is prove himself. A man fires well on the range, I give him a weekend pass. He scores high in P.T., he gets a weekend pass. He *earns* it." He turned from the window and pointed a finger at me. "You're a Jewish fella, am I right, Marx?"

"Yes, sir."

"And I admire you. I admire you because of the ribbons on your chest. I judge a man by what he shows me on the field of battle, Sergeant. It's what he's got *here,*" he said, and then, though I expected he would point to his chest, he jerked a thumb toward the buttons straining to hold his blouse across his belly. "Guts," he said.

"O.K., sir. I only wanted to pass on to you how the men felt."

"Mr. Marx, you're going to be old before your time if you worry about how the men feel. Leave that stuff to the chaplain — that's his business, not yours. Let's us train these fellas to shoot straight. If the Jewish personnel feels the other men are accusing them of goldbricking — well, I just don't know. Seems awful funny that suddenly the Lord is calling so loud in Private Grossman's ear he's just got to run to church."

"Synagogue," I said.

"Synagogue is right, Sergeant. I'll write that down for handy reference. Thank you for stopping by."

That evening, a few minutes before the company gathered outside the orderly room for the chow formation, I called the C.Q., Corporal Robert LaHill, in to see me. LaHill was a dark, burly fellow whose hair curled out of his clothes wherever it could. He had a glaze in his eyes that made one think of caves and dinosaurs. "LaHill," I said, "when you take the formation, remind the men that they're free to attend church services *whenever* they are held, provided they report to the orderly room before they leave the area."

LaHill scratched his wrist, but gave no indication that he'd heard or understood.

"LaHill," I said, "*church.* You remember? Church, priest, Mass, confession."

He curled one lip into a kind of smile; I took it for a signal that for a second he had flickered back up into the human race.

"Jewish personnel who want to attend services this evening are to fall out in front of the orderly room at 1900," I said. Then, as an afterthought, I added, "By order of Captain Barrett."

A little while later, as the day's last light — softer than any I had seen that year — began to drop over Camp Crowder, I heard LaHill's thick, inflectionless voice outside my window: "Give me your ears, troopers. Toppie says for me to tell you that at 1900 hours all Jewish personnel is to fall out in front, here, if they want to attend the Jewish Mass."

At seven o'clock, I looked out the orderly-room window and saw three soldiers in starched khakis standing on the dusty quadrangle. They looked at their watches and fidgeted while they whispered back and forth. It was getting dimmer, and, alone on the otherwise deserted field, they looked tiny. When I opened the door, I heard the noises of the G.I. party coming from the surrounding barracks — bunks being pushed to the walls, faucets pounding water into buckets, brooms whisking at the wooden floors, cleaning the dirt away for Saturday's inspection. Big puffs of cloth moved round and round on the window-panes. I walked outside, and the moment my foot hit the ground I thought I heard Grossbart call to the others, "'Ten-*hut!*" Or maybe, when they all three jumped to attention, I imagined I heard the command.

Grossbart stepped forward. "Thank you, sir," he said.

"'Sergeant,' Grossbart," I reminded him. "You call officers 'sir.' I'm not an officer. You've been in the Army three weeks — you know that."

He turned his palms out at his sides to indicate that, in truth, he and I lived beyond convention. "Thank you, anyway," he said.

"Yes," a tall boy behind him said. "Thanks a lot."

And the third boy whispered, "Thank you," but his mouth barely fluttered, so that he did not alter by more than a lip's movement his posture of attention.

"For what?" I asked.

Grossbart snorted happily. "For the announcement. The Corporal's announcement. It helped. It made it — "

"Fancier." The tall boy finished Grossbart's sentence.

Grossbart smiled. "He means formal, sir. Public," he said to me. "Now it won't seem as though we're just taking off — goldbricking because the work has begun."

"It was by order of Captain Barrett," I said.

"Aaah, but you pull a little weight," Grossbart said. "So we thank you." Then he turned to his companions. "Sergeant Marx, I want you to meet Larry Fishbein."

The tall boy stepped forward and extended his hand. I shook it. "You from New York?" he asked.

"Yes."

"Me, too." He had a cadaverous face that collapsed inward from his cheekbone to his jaw, and when he smiled — as he did at the news of our communal attachment — revealed a mouthful of bad teeth. He was blinking his eyes a good deal, as though he were fighting back tears. "What borough?" he asked.

I turned to Grossbart. "It's five after seven. What time are services?"

"Shul," he said, smiling, "is in ten minutes. I want you to meet Mickey Halpern. This is Nathan Marx, our sergeant."

The third boy hopped forward. "Private Michael Halpern." He saluted.

"Salute officers, Halpern," I said. The boy dropped his hand, and, on its way down, in his nervousness, checked to see if his shirt pockets were buttoned.

"Shall I march them over, sir?" Grossbart asked. "Or are you coming along?"

From behind Grossbart, Fishbein piped up. "Afterward, they're having refreshments. A ladies' auxiliary from St. Louis, the rabbi told us last week."

"The chaplain," Halpern whispered.

"You're welcome to come along," Grossbart said.

To avoid his plea, I looked away, and saw, in the windows of the barracks, a cloud of faces staring out at the four of us. "Hurry along, Grossbart," I said.

"O.K., then," he said. He turned to the others. "Double time, *march!*"

They started off, but ten feet away Grossbart spun around and, running backward, called to me, "Good *shabbus,* sir!" And then the three of them were swallowed into the alien Missouri dusk.

Even after they had disappeared over the parade ground, whose green was now a deep blue, I could hear Grossbart singing the double-time cadence, and as it grew dimmer and dimmer, it suddenly touched a deep memory — as did the slant of the light — and I was remembering the shrill sounds of a Bronx playground where, years ago, beside the Grand Concourse, I had played on long spring evenings such as this. It was a pleasant memory for a young man so far from peace and home, and it brought so many recollections with it that I began to grow exceedingly tender about myself. In fact, I indulged myself in a reverie so strong that I felt as though a hand were reaching down inside me. It had to reach so very far to touch me! It had to reach past those days in the forests of Belgium, and past the dying I'd refused to weep over; past the nights in German farmhouses whose books we'd burned to warm us; past endless stretches when I had shut off all softness I might feel for my fellows, and had managed even to deny myself the posture of a conqueror — the swagger that I, as a Jew, might well have worn as my boots whacked against the rubble of Wesel, Münster, and Braunschweig.

But now one night noise, one rumor of home and time past, and memory plunged down through all I had anesthetized, and came to what I suddenly remembered was myself. So it was not altogether curious that, in search of more of me, I found myself following Grossbart's tracks to Chapel No. 3, where the Jewish services were being held.

I took a seat in the last row, which was empty. Two rows in front of me sat Grossbart, Fishbein, and Halpern, holding little white Dixie cups. Each row of seats was raised higher than the one in front of it, and I could see clearly what was going on. Fishbein was pouring the contents of his cup into Grossbart's, and Grossbart looked mirthful as the liquid made a purple arc between Fishbein's hand and his. In the glaring yellow light, I saw the chaplain standing on the platform at the front; he was chanting the first line of the responsive reading. Grossbart's prayer book remained closed on his lap; he was swishing the cup around. Only Halpern responded to the chant by praying. The fingers of his right hand were spread wide across the cover of his open book. His cap was pulled down low onto his brow, which made it round, like a yarmulke. From time to time, Grossbart wet his lips at the cup's edge; Fishbein, his long yellow face a dying light bulb, looked from here to there, craning forward to catch sight of the faces down the row, then of those in front of him, then behind. He saw me, and his eyelids beat a tattoo. His elbow slid into Grossbart's side, his neck inclined toward his friend, he whispered something, and then, when the congregation next responded to the chant, Grossbart's voice was among the others. Fishbein looked into his book now, too; his lips, however, didn't move.

Finally, it was time to drink the wine. The chaplain smiled down at them as Grossbart swigged his in one long gulp, Halpern sipped, meditating, and Fishbein faked devotion with an empty cup. "As I look down amongst the congregation" — the chaplain grinned at the word — "this night, I see many new faces, and I want to welcome you to Friday-night services here at Camp Crowder. I am Major Leo Ben Ezra, your chaplain." Though an American, the chaplain spoke deliberately — syllable by syllable, almost — as though to communicate, above all, with the lip readers in his audience. "I have only a few words to say before we adjourn to the refreshment room, where the kind ladies of the Temple Sinai, St. Louis, Missouri, have a nice setting for you."

Applause and whistling broke out. After another momentary grin, the chaplain raised his hands, palms out, his eyes flicking upward a moment, as if to remind the troops where they were and Who Else might be in attendance. In the sudden silence that followed, I thought I heard Grossbart cackle, "Let the goyim clean the floors!" Were those the words? I wasn't sure, but Fishbein, grinning, nudged Halpern. Halpern looked dumbly at him, then went back to his prayer book, which had been occupying him all through the rabbi's talk. One hand tugged at the black kinky hair that stuck out under his cap. His lips moved.

The rabbi continued. "It is about the food that I want to speak to you for a moment. I know, I know, I know," he intoned, wearily, "how in the mouths of most of you the *trafe* food tastes like ashes. I know how you gag, some of you, and how your parents suffer to think of their children eating foods unclean and offensive to the palate. What can I tell you? I can only say, close your eyes and swallow as best you can. Eat what you must to live, and throw away the rest. I wish I could help more. For those of you who find this impossible, may I ask that you try and try, but then come to see me in private. If your revulsion is so great, we will have to seek aid from those higher up."

A round of chatter rose and subsided. Then everyone sang "Ain Kelohainu"; after all those years, I discovered I still knew the words. Then, suddenly, the service over, Grossbart was upon me. "Higher up? He means the General?"

"Hey, Shelly," Fishbein said, "he means God." He smacked his face and looked at Halpern. "How high can you go!"

"Sh-h-h!" Grossbart said. "What do you think, Sergeant?"

"I don't know," I said. "You better ask the chaplain."

"I'm going to. I'm making an appointment to see him in private. So is Mickey."

Halpern shook his head. "No, no, Sheldon — "

"You have rights, Mickey," Grossbart said. "They can't push us around."

"It's O.K.," said Halpern. "It bothers my mother, not me."

Grossbart looked at me. "Yesterday he threw up. From the hash. It was all ham and God knows what else."

"I have a cold — that was why," Halpern said. He pushed his yarmulke back into a cap.

"What about you, Fishbein?" I asked. "You kosher, too?"

He flushed. "A little. But I'll let it ride. I have a very strong stomach, and I don't eat a lot anyway." I continued to look at him, and he held up his wrist to reinforce what he'd just said; his watch strap was tightened to the last hole, and he pointed that out to me.

"But services are important to you?" I asked him.

He looked at Grossbart. "Sure, sir."

"'Sergeant.'"

"Not so much at home," said Grossbart, stepping between us, "but away from home it gives one a sense of his Jewishness."

"We have to stick together," Fishbein said.

I started to walk toward the door; Halpern stepped back to make way for me.

"That's what happened in Germany," Grossbart was saying, loud enough for me to hear. "They didn't stick together. They let themselves get pushed around."

I turned. "Look, Grossbart. This is the Army, not summer camp."

He smiled. "So?"

Halpern tried to sneak off, but Grossbart held his arm.

"Grossbart, how old are you?" I asked.

"Nineteen."

"And you?" I said to Fishbein.

"The same. The same month, even."

"And what about him?" I pointed to Halpern, who had by now made it safely to the door.

"Eighteen," Grossbart whispered. "But like he can't tie his shoes or brush his teeth himself. I feel sorry for him."

"I feel sorry for all of us, Grossbart," I said, "but just act like a man. Just don't overdo it."

"Overdo what, sir?"

"The 'sir' business, for one thing. Don't overdo that," I said.

I left him standing there. I passed by Halpern, but he did not look at me. Then I was outside, but, behind, I heard Grossbart call, "Hey, Mickey, my *leben,* come on back. Refreshments!"

"*Leben!*" My grandmother's word for me!

One morning a week later, while I was working at my desk, Captain Barrett shouted for me to come into his office. When I entered, he had his helmet liner squashed down so far on his head that I couldn't even see his eyes. He was on the phone, and when he spoke to me, he cupped one hand over the mouthpiece. "Who the hell is Grossbart?"

"Third platoon, Captain," I said. "A trainee."

"What's all this stink about food? His mother called a goddam congressman about the food." He uncovered the mouthpiece and slid his helmet up until I could see his bottom eyelashes. "Yes, sir," he said into the phone. "Yes, sir. I'm still here, sir. I'm asking Marx, here, right now — "

He covered the mouthpiece again and turned his head back toward me. "Lightfoot Harry's on the phone," he said, between his teeth. "This congressman calls General Lyman, who calls Colonel Sousa, who calls the Major, who calls me. They're just dying to stick this thing on me. Whatsa matter?" He shook the phone at me. "I don't feed the troops? What is this?"

"Sir, Grossbart is strange — " Barrett greeted that with a mockingly indulgent smile. I altered my approach. "Captain, he's a very orthodox Jew, and so he's only allowed to eat certain foods."

"He throws up, the congressman said. Every time he eats something, his mother says, he throws up!"

"He's accustomed to observing the dietary laws, Captain."

"So why's his old lady have to call the White House?"

"Jewish parents, sir — they're apt to be more protective than you expect. I mean, Jews have a very close family life. A boy goes away from home, sometimes the mother is liable to get very upset. Probably the boy mentioned something in a letter, and his mother misinterpreted."

"I'd like to punch him one right in the mouth," the Captain said. "There's a war on, and he wants a silver platter!"

"I don't think the boy's to blame, sir. I'm sure we can straighten it out by just asking him. Jewish parents worry — "

"*All* parents worry, for Christ's sake. But they don't get on their high horse and start pulling strings — "

I interrupted, my voice higher, tighter than before. "The home life, Captain, is very important — but you're right, it may sometimes get out of hand. It's a very wonderful thing, Captain, but because it's so close, this kind of thing . . ."

He didn't listen any longer to my attempt to present both myself and Lightfoot Harry with an explanation for the letter. He turned back to the phone. "Sir?" he said. "Sir — Marx, here, tells me Jews have a tendency to be pushy. He says he thinks we can settle it right here in the company. . . . Yes, sir. . . . I *will* call back, sir, soon as I can." He hung up. "Where are the men, Sergeant?"

"On the range."

With a whack on the top of his helmet, he crushed it down over his eyes again, and charged out of his chair. "We're going for a ride," he said.

The Captain drove, and I sat beside him. It was a hot spring day, and under my newly starched fatigues I felt as though my armpits were melting down onto my sides and chest. The roads were dry, and by the time we reached the firing range, my teeth felt gritty with dust, though my mouth had been shut the whole trip. The Captain slammed the brakes on and told me to get the hell out and find Grossbart.

I found him on his belly, firing wildly at the five-hundred-feet target. Waiting their turns behind him were Halpern and Fishbein. Fishbein, wearing a pair of steel-rimmed G.I. glasses I hadn't seen on him before, had the appearance of an old peddler who would gladly have sold you his rifle and the cartridges that were slung all over him. I stood back by the ammo boxes, waiting for Grossbart to finish spraying the distant targets. Fishbein straggled back to stand near me.

"Hello, Sergeant Marx," he said.

"How are you?" I mumbled.

"Fine, thank you. Sheldon's really a good shot."

"I didn't notice."

"I'm not so good, but I think I'm getting the hang of it now. Sergeant, I don't mean to, you know, ask what I shouldn't — " The boy stopped. He was trying to speak intimately, but the noise of the shooting forced him to shout at me.

"What is it?" I asked. Down the range, I saw Captain Barrett standing up in the jeep, scanning the line for me and Grossbart.

"My parents keep asking and asking where we're going," Fishbein said. "Everybody says the Pacific. I don't care, but my parents — If I could relieve their minds, I think I could concentrate more on my shooting."

"I don't know where, Fishbein. Try to concentrate anyway."

"Sheldon says you might be able to find out."

"I don't know a thing, Fishbein. You just take it easy, and don't let Sheldon — "

"*I'm* taking it easy, Sergeant. It's at home — "

Grossbart had finished on the line, and was dusting his fatigues with one hand. I called to him. "Grossbart, the Captain wants to see you."

He came toward us. His eyes blazed and twinkled. "Hi!"

"Don't point that rifle!" I said.

"I wouldn't shoot you, Sarge." He gave me a smile as wide as a pumpkin, and turned the barrel aside.

"Damn you, Grossbart, this is no joke! Follow me."

I walked ahead of him, and had the awful suspicion that, behind me, Grossbart was *marching,* his rifle on his shoulder, as though he were a one-man detachment. At the jeep, he gave the Captain a rifle salute. "Private Sheldon Grossbart, sir."

"At ease, Grossman." The Captain sat down, slid over into the empty seat, and, crooking a finger, invited Grossbart closer.

"Bart, sir. Sheldon Gross*bart*. It's a common error." Grossbart nodded at me; I understood, he indicated. I looked away just as the mess truck pulled up to the range, disgorging a half-dozen K.P.s with rolled-up sleeves. The mess sergeant screamed at them while they set up the chow-line equipment.

"Grossbart, your mama wrote some congressman that we don't feed you right. Do you know that?" the Captain said.

"It was my father, sir. He wrote to Representative Franconi that my religion forbids me to eat certain foods."

"What religion is that, Grossbart?"

"Jewish."

"'Jewish, *sir,*'" I said to Grossbart.

"Excuse me, sir. Jewish, sir."

"What have you been living on?" the Captain asked. "You've been in the Army a month already. You don't look to me like you're falling to pieces."

"I eat because I have to, sir. But Sergeant Marx will testify to the fact that I don't eat one mouthful more than I need to in order to survive."

"Is that so, Marx?" Barrett asked.

"I've never seen Grossbart eat, sir," I said.

"But you heard the rabbi," Grossbart said. "He told us what to do, and I listened."

The Captain looked at me. "Well, Marx?"

"I still don't know what he eats and doesn't eat, sir."

Grossbart raised his arms to plead with me, and it looked for a moment as though he were going to hand me his weapon to hold. "But, Sergeant —"

"Look, Grossbart, just answer the Captain's questions," I said sharply.

Barrett smiled at me, and I resented it. "All right, Grossbart," he said. "What is it you want? The little piece of paper? You want out?"

"No, sir. Only to be allowed to live as a Jew. And for the others, too."

"What others?"

"Fishbein, sir, and Halpern."

"They don't like the way we serve, either?"

"Halpern throws up, sir. I've seen it."

"I thought *you* throw up."

"Just once, sir. I didn't know the sausage was sausage."

"We'll give menus, Grossbart. We'll show training films about the food, so you can identify when we're trying to poison you."

Grossbart did not answer. The men had been organized into two long chow lines. At the tail end of one, I spotted Fishbein — or, rather, his glasses spotted me. They winked sunlight back at me. Halpern stood next to him, patting the inside of his collar with a khaki handkerchief. They moved with the line as it began to edge up toward the food. The mess sergeant was still screaming at the K.P.s. For a moment, I was actually terrified by the thought that somehow the mess sergeant was going to become involved in Grossbart's problem.

"Marx," the Captain said, "you're a Jewish fella — am I right?"

I played straight man. "Yes, sir."

"How long you been in the Army? Tell this boy."

"Three years and two months."

"A year in combat, Grossbart. Twelve goddam months in combat all through Europe. I admire this man." The Captain snapped a wrist against my chest. "Do you hear him peeping about the food? Do you? I want an answer, Grossbart. Yes or no."

"No, sir."

"And why not? He's a Jewish fella."

"Some things are more important to some Jews than other things to other Jews."

Barrett blew up. "Look, Grossbart. Marx, here, is a good man — a goddam hero. When you were in high school, Sergeant Marx was killing Germans. Who does more for the Jews — you, by throwing up over a lousy piece of sausage, a piece of first-cut meat, or Marx, by killing those Nazi bastards? If I was a Jew, Grossbart, I'd kiss this man's feet. He's a goddam hero, and *he* eats what we give him. Why do you

have to cause trouble is what I want to know! What is it you're buckin'
for — a discharge?"

"No, sir."

"I'm talking to a wall! Sergeant, get him out of my way." Barrett
swung himself back into the driver's seat. "I'm going to see the chaplain." The engine roared, the jeep spun around in a whirl of dust, and
the Captain was headed back to camp.

For a moment, Grossbart and I stood side by side, watching the jeep.
Then he looked at me and said, "I don't want to start trouble. That's
the first thing they toss up to us."

When he spoke, I saw that his teeth were white and straight, and the
sight of them suddenly made me understand that Grossbart actually
did have parents — that once upon a time someone had taken little
Sheldon to the dentist. He was their son. Despite all the talk about his
parents, it was hard to believe in Grossbart as a child, an heir — as
related by blood to anyone, mother, father, or, above all, to me. This
realization led me to another.

"What does your father do, Grossbart?" I asked as we started to walk
back toward the chow line.

"He's a tailor."

"An American?"

"Now, yes. A son in the Army," he said, jokingly.

"And your mother?" I asked.

He winked. "A *ballabusta*. She practically sleeps with a dustcloth in
her hand."

"She's also an immigrant?"

"All she talks is Yiddish, still."

"And your father, too?"

"A little English. 'Clean,' 'Press,' 'Take the pants in.' That's the extent of it. But they're good to me."

"Then, Grossbart — " I reached out and stopped him. He turned
toward me, and when our eyes met, his seemed to jump back, to shiver
in their sockets. "Grossbart — you were the one who wrote that letter,
weren't you?"

It took only a second or two for his eyes to flash happy again. "Yes."
He walked on, and I kept pace. "It's what my father *would* have written
if he had known how. It was his name, though. *He* signed it. He even
mailed it. I sent it home. For the New York postmark."

I was astonished, and he saw it. With complete seriousness, he thrust his right arm in front of me. "Blood is blood, Sergeant," he said, pinching the blue vein in his wrist.

"What the hell *are* you trying to do, Grossbart?" I asked. "I've seen you eat. Do you know that? I told the Captain I don't know what you eat, but I've seen you eat like a hound at chow."

"We work hard, Sergeant. We're in training. For a furnace to work, you've got to feed it coal."

"Why did you say in the letter that you threw up all the time?"

"I was really talking about Mickey there. I was talking *for* him. He would never write, Sergeant, though I pleaded with him. He'll waste away to nothing if I don't help. Sergeant, I used my name — my father's name — but it's Mickey, and Fishbein, too, I'm watching out for."

"You're a regular Messiah, aren't you?"

We were at the chow line now.

"That's a good one, Sergeant," he said, smiling. "But who knows? Who can tell? Maybe you're the Messiah — a little bit. What Mickey says is the Messiah is a collective idea. He went to Yeshiva, Mickey, for a while. He says *together* we're the Messiah. Me a little bit, you a little bit. You should hear that kid talk, Sergeant, when he gets going."

"Me a little bit, you a little bit," I said. "You'd like to believe that, wouldn't you, Grossbart? That would make everything so clean for you."

"It doesn't seem too bad a thing to believe, Sergeant. It only means we should all *give* a little, is all."

I walked off to eat my rations with the other noncoms.

Two days later, a letter addressed to Captain Barrett passed over my desk. It had come through the chain of command — from the office of Congressman Franconi, where it had been received, to General Lyman, to Colonel Sousa, to Major Lamont, now to Captain Barrett. I read it over twice. It was dated May 14, the day Barrett had spoken with Grossbart on the rifle range.

Dear Congressman:

First let me thank you for your interest in behalf of my son, Private Sheldon Grossbart. Fortunately, I was able to speak with Sheldon on the phone the other night, and I think I've been able to solve our problem. He is, as I mentioned in my last letter, a very religious boy, and it was only with the greatest difficulty that I could persuade him that the religious thing to do — what God Himself would want Sheldon to do — would be to suffer the pangs of religious remorse for the good of his country and all mankind. It took some doing, Congressman, but finally he saw the light. In fact, what he said (and I wrote down the words on a scratch pad so as never to forget), what he said was "I guess you're right, Dad. So many millions of my fellow-Jews gave up their lives to the enemy, the least I can do is live for a while minus a bit of my heritage so as to help end this struggle and regain for all the children of God dignity and humanity." That, Congressman, would make any father proud.

By the way, Sheldon wanted me to know — and to pass on to you — the name of a soldier who helped him reach this decision: SERGEANT NATHAN MARX. Sergeant Marx is a combat veteran who is Sheldon's first sergeant. This man has helped Sheldon over some of the first hurdles he's had to face in the Army, and is in part responsible for Sheldon's changing his mind about the dietary laws. I know Sheldon would appreciate any recognition Marx could receive.

Thank you and good luck. I look forward to seeing your name on the next election ballot.

Respectfully,
Samuel E. Grossbart

Attached to the Grossbart communiqué was another, addressed to General Marshall Lyman, the post commander, and signed by Representative Charles E. Franconi, of the House of Representatives. The communiqué informed General Lyman that Sergeant Nathan Marx was a credit to the U.S. Army and the Jewish people.

What was Grossbart's motive in recanting? Did he feel he'd gone too far? Was the letter a strategic retreat — a crafty attempt to strengthen what he considered our alliance? Or had he actually changed his mind, via an imaginary dialogue between Grossbart *père* and Grossbart *fils*? I was puzzled, but only for a few days — that is, only until I realized that, whatever his reasons, he had actually decided to disappear from my life; he was going to allow himself to become just another trainee. I saw him at inspection, but he never winked; at chow formations, but he never flashed me a sign. On Sundays, with the other trainees, he would sit around watching the noncoms' softball team, for which I pitched, but not once did he speak an unnecessary word to me. Fishbein and Halpern retreated, too — at Grossbart's command, I was sure. Apparently he had seen that wisdom lay in turning back before he plunged over into the ugliness of privilege undeserved. Our separation allowed me to forgive him our past encounters, and, finally, to admire him for his good sense.

Meanwhile, free of Grossbart, I grew used to my job and my administrative tasks. I stepped on a scale one day, and discovered I had truly become a noncombatant; I had gained seven pounds. I found patience to get past the first three pages of a book. I thought about the future more and more, and wrote letters to girls I'd known before the war. I even got a few answers. I sent away to Columbia for a Law School catalogue. I continued to follow the war in the Pacific, but it was not my war. I thought I could see the end, and sometimes, at night, I dreamed that I was walking on the streets of Manhattan — Broadway, Third Avenue, 116th Street, where I had lived the three years I attended Columbia. I curled myself around these dreams and I began to be happy.

And then, one Sunday, when everybody was away and I was alone in the orderly room reading a month-old copy of the *Sporting News*, Grossbart reappeared.

"You a baseball fan, Sergeant?"

I looked up. "How are you?"

"Fine," Grossbart said. "They're making a soldier out of me."

"How are Fishbein and Halpern?"

"Coming along," he said. "We've got no training this afternoon. They're at the movies."

"How come you're not with them?"

"I wanted to come over and say hello."

He smiled — a shy, regular-guy smile, as though he and I well knew that our friendship drew its sustenance from unexpected visits, remembered birthdays, and borrowed lawnmowers. At first it offended me, and then the feeling was swallowed by the general uneasiness I felt at the thought that everyone on the post was locked away in a dark movie theater and I was here alone with Grossbart. I folded up my paper.

"Sergeant," he said, "I'd like to ask a favor. It is a favor, and I'm making no bones about it."

He stopped, allowing me to refuse him a hearing — which, of course, forced me into a courtesy I did not intend. "Go ahead."

"Well, actually it's two favors."

I said nothing.

"The first one's about these rumors. Everybody says we're going to the Pacific."

"As I told your friend Fishbein, I don't know," I said. "You'll just have to wait to find out. Like everybody else."

"You think there's a chance of any of us going East?"

"Germany?" I said. "Maybe."

"I meant New York."

"I don't think so, Grossbart. Offhand."

"Thanks for the information, Sergeant," he said.

"It's not information, Grossbart. Just what I surmise."

"It certainly would be good to be near home. My parents — you know." He took a step toward the door and then turned back. "Oh, the other thing. May I ask the other?"

"What is it?"

"The other thing is — I've got relatives in St. Louis, and they say they'll give me a whole Passover dinner if I can get down there. God, Sergeant, that'd mean an awful lot to me."

I stood up. "No passes during basic, Grossbart."

"But we're off from now till Monday morning, Sergeant. I could leave the post and no one would even know."

"I'd know. You'd know."

"But that's all. Just the two of us. Last night, I called my aunt, and you should have heard her. 'Come — come,' she said. 'I got gefilte fish, *chrain* — the works!' Just a day, Sergeant. I'd take the blame if anything happened."

"The Captain isn't here to sign a pass."

"You could sign."

"Look, Grossbart — "

"Sergeant, for two months, practically, I've been eating *trafe* till I want to die."

"I thought you'd made up your mind to live with it. To be minus a little bit of heritage."

He pointed a finger at me. "You!" he said. "That wasn't for you to read."

"I read it. So what?"

"That letter was addressed to a congressman."

"Grossbart, don't feed me any baloney. You *wanted* me to read it."

"Why are you persecuting me, Sergeant?"

"Are you kidding!"

"I've run into this before," he said, "but never from my own!"

"Get out of here, Grossbart! Get the hell out of my sight!"

He did not move. "Ashamed, that's what you are," he said. "So you take it out on the rest of us. They say Hitler himself was half a Jew. Hearing you, I wouldn't doubt it."

"What are you trying to do with me, Grossbart?" I asked him. "What are you after? You want me to give you special privileges, to change the food, to find out about your orders, to give you weekend passes."

"You even talk like a goy!" Grossbart shook his fist. "Is this just a weekend pass I'm asking for? Is a Seder sacred, or not?"

Seder! It suddenly occurred to me that Passover had been celebrated weeks before. I said so.

"That's right," he replied. "Who says no? A month ago — and I was in the field eating hash! And now all I ask is a simple favor. A Jewish boy I thought would understand. My aunt's willing to go out of her way — to make a Seder a month later. . . ." He turned to go, mumbling.

"Come back here!" I called. He stopped and looked at me. "Grossbart, why can't you be like the rest? Why do you have to stick out like a sore thumb?"

"Because I'm a Jew, Sergeant. I *am* different. Better, maybe not. But different."

"This is a war, Grossbart. For the time being *be* the same."

"I refuse."

"What?"

"I refuse. I can't stop being me, that's all there is to it." Tears came to his eyes. "It's a hard thing to be a Jew. But now I understand what Mickey says — it's a harder thing to stay one." He raised a hand sadly toward me. "Look at *you*."

"Stop crying!"

"Stop this, stop that, stop the other thing! *You* stop, Sergeant. Stop closing your heart to your own!" And, wiping his face with his sleeve, he ran out the door. "The least we can do for one another — the least . . ."

An hour later, looking out the window, I saw Grossbart headed across the field. He wore a pair of starched khakis and carried a little leather ditty bag. I went out into the heat of the day. It was quiet; not a soul was in sight except, over by the mess hall, four K.P.s sitting around a pan, sloped forward from their waists, gabbing and peeling potatoes in the sun.

"Grossbart!" I called.

He looked toward me and continued walking.

"Grossbart, get over here!"

He turned and came across the field. Finally, he stood before me.

"Where are you going?" I asked.

"St. Louis. I don't care."

"You'll get caught without a pass."

"So I'll get caught without a pass."

"You'll go to the stockade."

"I'm *in* the stockade." He made an about-face and headed off.

I let him go only a step or two. "Come back here," I said, and he followed me into the office, where I typed out a pass and signed the Captain's name, and my own initials after it.

He took the pass and then, a moment later, reached out and grabbed my hand. "Sergeant, you don't know how much this means to me."

"O.K.," I said. "Don't get in any trouble."

"I wish I could show you how much this means to me."

"Don't do me any favors. Don't write any more congressmen for citations."

He smiled. "You're right. I won't. But let me do something."

"Bring me a piece of that gefilte fish. Just get out of here."

"I will!" he said. "With a slice of carrot and a little horseradish. I won't forget."

"All right. Just show your pass at the gate. And don't tell *anybody*."

"I won't. It's a month late, but a good Yom Tov to you."

"Good Yom Tov, Grossbart," I said.

"You're a good Jew, Sergeant. You like to think you have a hard heart, but underneath you're a fine, decent man. I mean that."

Those last three words touched me more than any words from Grossbart's mouth had the right to. "All right, Grossbart," I said. "Now call me 'sir,' and get the hell out of here."

He ran out the door and was gone. I felt very pleased with myself; it was a great relief to stop fighting Grossbart, and it had cost me nothing. Barrett would never find out, and if he did, I could manage to invent some excuse. For a while, I sat at my desk, comfortable in my decision. Then the screen door flew back and Grossbart burst in again. "Sergeant!" he said. Behind him I saw Fishbein and Halpern, both in starched khakis, both carrying ditty bags like Grossbart's.

"Sergeant, I caught Mickey and Larry coming out of the movies. I almost missed them."

"Grossbart — did I say tell no one?" I said.

"But my aunt said I could bring friends. That I should, in fact."

"*I'm* the Sergeant, Grossbart — not your aunt!"

Grossbart looked at me in disbelief. He pulled Halpern up by his sleeve. "Mickey, tell the Sergeant what this would mean to you."

Halpern looked at me and, shrugging, said, "A lot."

Fishbein stepped forward without prompting. "This would mean a great deal to me and my parents, Sergeant Marx."

"No!" I shouted.

Grossbart was shaking his head. "Sergeant, I could see you denying me, but how you can deny Mickey, a Yeshiva boy — that's beyond me."

"I'm not denying Mickey anything," I said. "You just pushed a little too hard, Grossbart. *You* denied him."

"I'll give him my pass, then," Grossbart said. "I'll give him my aunt's address and a little note. At least let him go."

In a second, he had crammed the pass into Halpern's pants pocket. Halpern looked at me, and so did Fishbein. Grossbart was at the door, pushing it open. "Mickey, bring me a piece of gefilte fish, at least," he said, and then he was outside again.

The three of us looked at one another, and then I said, "Halpern, hand that pass over."

He took it from his pocket and gave it to me. Fishbein had now moved to the doorway, where he lingered. He stood there for a moment with his mouth slightly open, and then he pointed to himself. "And me?" he asked.

His utter ridiculousness exhausted me. I slumped down in my seat and felt pulses knocking at the back of my eyes. "Fishbein," I said, "you understand I'm not trying to deny you anything, don't you? If it was my Army, I'd serve gefilte fish in the mess hall. I'd sell *kugel* in the PX, honest to God."

Halpern smiled.

"You understand, don't you, Halpern?"

"Yes, Sergeant."

"And you, Fishbein? I don't want enemies. I'm just like you — I want to serve my time and go home. I miss the same things you miss."

"Then, Sergeant," Fishbein said, "why don't you come, too?"

"Where?"

"To St. Louis. To Shelly's aunt. We'll have a regular Seder. Play hide-the-matzoh." He gave me a broad, black-toothed smile.

I saw Grossbart again, on the other side of the screen.

"Pst!" He waved a piece of paper. "Mickey, here's the address. Tell her I couldn't get away."

Halpern did not move. He looked at me, and I saw the shrug moving up his arms into his shoulders again. I took the cover off my typewriter and made out passes for him and Fishbein. "Go," I said. "The three of you."

I thought Halpern was going to kiss my hand.

That afternoon, in a bar in Joplin, I drank beer and listened with half an ear to the Cardinal game. I tried to look squarely at what I'd become involved in, and began to wonder if perhaps the struggle with Grossbart wasn't as much my fault as his. What was I that I had to *muster* generous feelings? Who was I to have been feeling so grudging, so tight-hearted? After all, I wasn't being asked to move the world. Had I a right, then, or a reason, to clamp down on Grossbart, when that meant clamping down on Halpern, too? And Fishbein — that ugly, agreeable soul? Out of the many recollections of my childhood that had tumbled over me these past few days I heard my grandmother's voice: "What are you making a *tsimmes*?" It was what she would ask my mother when, say, I had cut myself while doing something I shouldn't have done, and her daughter was busy bawling me out. I needed a hug and a kiss, and my mother would moralize. But my grandmother knew — mercy overrides justice. I should have known it, too. Who was Nathan Marx to be such a penny pincher with kindness? Surely, I thought, the Messiah himself — if He should ever come — won't niggle over nickels and dimes. God willing, he'll hug and kiss.

The next day, while I was playing softball over on the parade ground, I decided to ask Bob Wright, who was noncom in charge of Classification and Assignment, where he thought our trainees would be sent when their cycle ended, in two weeks. I asked casually, between innings, and he said, "They're pushing them all into the Pacific. Shulman cut the orders on your boys the other day."

The news shocked me, as though I were the father of Halpern, Fishbein, and Grossbart.

That night, I was just sliding into sleep when someone tapped on my door. "Who is it?" I asked.

"Sheldon."

He opened the door and came in. For a moment, I felt his presence without being able to see him. "How was it?" I asked.

He popped into sight in the near-darkness before me. "Great, Sergeant." Then he was sitting on the edge of the bed. I sat up.

"How about you?" he asked. "Have a nice weekend?"

"Yes."

"The others went to sleep." He took a deep, paternal breath. We sat silent for a while, and a homey feeling invaded my ugly little cubicle; the door was locked, the cat was out, the children were safely in bed.

"Sergeant, can I tell you something? Personal?"

I did not answer, and he seemed to know why. "Not about me. About Mickey. Sergeant, I never felt for anybody like I feel for him. Last night I heard Mickey in the bed next to me. He was crying so, it could have broken your heart. Real sobs."

"I'm sorry to hear that."

"I had to talk to him to stop him. He held my hand, Sergeant — he wouldn't let it go. He was almost hysterical. He kept saying if he only knew where we were going. Even if he knew it *was* the Pacific, that would be better than nothing. Just to know."

Long ago, someone had taught Grossbart the sad rule that only lies can get the truth. Not that I couldn't believe in the fact of Halpern's crying; his eyes *always* seemed red-rimmed. But, fact or not, it became a lie when Grossbart uttered it. He was entirely strategic. But then — it came with the force of indictment — so was I! There were strategies of aggression, but there are strategies of retreat as well. And so, recognizing that I myself had not been without craft and guile, I told him what I knew. "It is the Pacific."

He let out a small gasp, which was not a lie. "I'll tell him. I wish it was otherwise."

"So do I."

He jumped on my words. "You mean you think you could do something? A change, maybe?"

"No, I couldn't do a thing."

"Don't you know anybody over at C. and A.?"

"Grossbart, there's nothing I can do," I said. "If your orders are for the Pacific, then it's the Pacific."

"But Mickey — "

"Mickey, you, me — everybody, Grossbart. There's nothing to be done. Maybe the war'll end before you go. Pray for a miracle."

"But — "

"Good night, Grossbart." I settled back, and was relieved to feel the springs unbend as Grossbart rose to leave. I could see him clearly now; his jaw had dropped, and he looked like a dazed prizefighter. I noticed for the first time a little paper bag in his hand.

"Grossbart." I smiled. "My gift?"

"Oh, yes, Sergeant. Here — from all of us." He handed me the bag. "It's egg roll."

"Egg roll?" I accepted the bag and felt a damp grease spot on the bottom. I opened it, sure that Grossbart was joking.

"We thought you'd probably like it. You know — Chinese egg roll. We thought you'd probably have a taste for — "

"Your aunt served egg roll?"

"She wasn't home."

"Grossbart, she invited you. You told me she invited you and your friends."

"I know," he said. "I just reread the letter. *Next* week."

I got out of bed and walked to the window. "Grossbart," I said. But I was not calling to him.

"What?"

"What are you, Grossbart? Honest to God, what are you?"

I think it was the first time I'd asked him a question for which he didn't have an immediate answer.

"How can you do this to people?" I went on.

"Sergeant, the day away did us all a world of good. Fishbein, you should see him, he *loves* Chinese food."

"But the Seder," I said.

"We took second best, Sergeant."

Rage came charging at me. I didn't sidestep. "Grossbart, you're a liar!" I said. "You're a schemer and a crook. You've got no respect for anything. Nothing at all. Not for me, for the truth — not even for poor Halpern! You use us all — "

"Sergeant, Sergeant, I feel for Mickey. Honest to God, I do. I *love* Mickey. I try — "

"You try! You feel!" I lurched toward him and grabbed his shirt front. I shook him furiously. "Grossbart, get out! Get out and stay the hell away from me. Because if I see you, I'll make your life miserable. *You understand that?*"

"Yes."

I let him free, and when he walked from the room, I wanted to spit on the floor where he had stood. I couldn't stop the fury. It engulfed me, owned me, till it seemed I could only rid myself of it with tears or an act of violence. I snatched from the bed the bag Grossbart had given me and, with all my strength, threw it out the window. And the next morning, as the men policed the area around the barracks, I heard a great cry go up from one of the trainees, who had been anticipating only his morning handful of cigarette butts and candy wrappers. "Egg roll!" he shouted. "Holy Christ, Chinese goddam egg roll!"

A week later, when I read the orders that had come down from C. and A., I couldn't believe my eyes. Every single trainee was to be shipped to Camp Stoneman, California, and from there to the Pacific — every trainee but one. Private Sheldon Grossbart. He was to be sent to Fort Monmouth, New Jersey. I read the mimeographed sheet several times. Dee, Farrell, Fishbein, Fuselli, Fylypowycz, Glinicki, Gromke, Gucwa, Halpern, Hardy, Helebrandt, right down to Anton Zygadlo — all were to be headed West before the month was out. All except Grossbart. He had pulled a string, and I wasn't it.

I lifted the phone and called C. and A.

The voice on the other end said smartly, "Corporal Shulman, sir."

"Let me speak to Sergeant Wright."

"Who is this calling, sir?"

"Sergeant Marx."

And, to my surprise, the voice said, "Oh!" Then, "Just a minute, Sergeant."

Shulman's "Oh!" stayed with me while I waited for Wright to come to the phone. Why "Oh!"? Who was Shulman? And then, so simply, I knew I'd discovered the string that Grossbart had pulled. In fact, I could hear Grossbart the day he'd discovered Shulman in the PX, or in the bowling alley, or maybe even at services. "Glad to meet you. Where you from? Bronx? Me, too. Do you know So-and-So? And So-and-So? Me, too! You work at C. and A.? Really? Hey, how's chances of getting East? Could you do something? Change something? Swindle, cheat, lie? We gotta help each other, you know. If the Jews in Germany . . ."

Bob Wright answered the phone. "How are you, Nate? How's the pitching arm?"

"Good. Bob, I wonder if you could do me a favor." I heard clearly my own words, and they so reminded me of Grossbart that I dropped more easily than I could have imagined into what I had planned. "This may sound crazy, Bob, but I got a kid here on orders to Monmouth who wants them changed. He had a brother killed in Europe, and he's hot to go to the Pacific. Says he'd feel like a coward if he wound up Stateside. I don't know, Bob — can anything be done? Put somebody else in the Monmouth slot?"

"Who?" he asked cagily.

"Anybody. First guy in the alphabet. I don't care. The kid just asked if something could be done."

"What's his name?"

"Grossbart, Sheldon."

Wright didn't answer.

"Yeah," I said. "He's a Jewish kid, so he thought I could help him out. You know."

"I guess I can do something," he finally said. "The Major hasn't been around here for weeks. Temporary duty to the golf course. I'll try, Nate, that's all I can say."

"I'd appreciate it, Bob. See you Sunday." And I hung up, perspiring.

The following day, the corrected orders appeared: Fishbein, Fuselli, Fylypowycz, Glinicki, Gromke, Grossbart, Gucwa, Halpern, Hardy . . . Lucky Private Harley Alton was to go to Fort Monmouth, New Jersey, where, for some reason or other, they wanted an enlisted man with infantry training.

After chow that night, I stopped back at the orderly room to straighten out the guard-duty roster. Grossbart was waiting for me. He spoke first.

"You son of a bitch!"

I sat down at my desk, and while he glared at me, I began to make the necessary alterations in the duty roster.

"What do you have against me?" he cried. "Against my family? Would it kill you for me to be near my father, God knows how many months he has left to him?"

"Why so?"

"His heart," Grossbart said. "He hasn't had enough troubles in a lifetime, you've got to add to them. I curse the day I ever met you, Marx! Shulman told me what happened over there. There's no limit to your anti-Semitism, is there? The damage you've done here isn't enough. You have to make a special phone call! You really want me dead!"

I made the last few notations in the duty roster and got up to leave. "Good night, Grossbart."

"You owe me an explanation!" He stood in my path.

"Sheldon, you're the one who owes explanations."

He scowled. "To *you*?"

"To me, I think so — yes. Mostly to Fishbein and Halpern."

"That's right, twist things around. I owe nobody nothing, I've done all I could do for them. Now I think I've got the right to watch out for myself."

"For each other we have to learn to watch out, Sheldon. You told me yourself."

"You call this watching out for me — what you did?"

"No. For all of us."

I pushed him aside and started for the door. I heard his furious breathing behind me, and it sounded like steam rushing from an engine of terrible strength.

"*You'll* be all right," I said from the door. And, I thought, so would Fishbein and Halpern be all right, even in the Pacific, if only Grossbart continued to see — in the obsequiousness of the one, the soft spirituality of the other — some profit for himself.

I stood outside the orderly room, and I heard Grossbart weeping behind me. Over in the barracks, in the lighted windows, I could see the boys in their T-shirts sitting on their bunks talking about their orders, as they'd been doing for the past two days. With a kind of quiet nervousness, they polished shoes, shined belt buckles, squared away underwear, trying as best they could to accept their fate. Behind me, Grossbart swallowed hard, accepting his. And then, resisting with all my will an impulse to turn and seek pardon for my vindictiveness, I accepted my own.

Elizabeth Spencer

....

A Christian Education

I T W A S A S U N D A Y like no other, for we were there alone for the first time. I hadn't started to school yet, and he had finished it so long ago it must have been like a dream of something that was meant to happen but had never really come about, for I can remember no story of school that he ever told me, and to think of him as sitting in a class equal with others is as beyond me now as it was then. I cannot imagine it. He read a lot and might conceivably have had a tutor — that I can imagine, in his plantation world.

But this was a town he'd finally come to, to stay with his daughter in his old age, she being also my mother. I was the only one free to be with him all the time and the same went for his being with me — we baby-sat one another.

But that word wasn't known then.

A great many things were known, however; among them, I always had to go to Sunday School.

It was an absolute that the whole world was meant to be part of the church, and if my grandfather seldom went, it was a puzzle no one tried to solve. Sermons were a fate I had only recently got big enough to be included in, but Sunday School classes had had me enrolled in them since I could be led through the door and placed on a tiny red chair, feet not even at that low height connecting to the floor. It was always cold at the church; even in summer, it was cool inside. We were given pictures to color and Bible verses to memorize, and at the end a colored card with a picture of Moses or Jesus or somebody else from the Bible, exotically bearded and robed.

Today I might not be going to Sunday School, and my regret was only for the card. I wondered what it would be like. There was no one to bring it to me. My mother and father were not even in town. They had got into the car right after breakfast and had driven away to a neighboring town. My aunt by marriage had died and they were going to the funeral. I was too little to go to funerals, my mother said.

After they left I sat on the rug near my grandfather. He was asleep in his chair before the fire, snoring. Presently, his snoring woke him up. He cut himself some tobacco and put it in his mouth. "Are you going to Sunday School?" he asked me. "I can't go there by myself," I said. "Nobody said I had to take you," he remarked, more to himself than to me. It wasn't the first time I knew we were in the same boat, he and I. We had to do what they said, being outside the main scale of life where things really happened, but by the same token we didn't have to do what they didn't say. Somewhere along the line, however, my grandfather had earned rights I didn't have. Not having to attend church was one; also, he had his own money and didn't have to ask for any.

He looked out the window.

"It's going to be a pretty day," he said.

How we found ourselves on the road downtown on Sunday morning, I don't remember. It was as far to get to town as it was to get to church, though in the opposite direction, and we both must have known that, but didn't remark upon it as we went along. My grandfather walked to town every day except Sunday, when it was considered a sin to go there, for the drugstore was open and the barbershop, too, on occasions, if the weather was fair; and the filling station was open. My parents thought that the drugstore had to be open but should sell drugs only, and that filling stations and barbershops shouldn't open at all. There should be a way to telephone the filling station in case you had to have gas for emergency use. This was all worked out between them. I had often heard them talk about it. No one should go to town on Sunday, they said, for it encouraged the error of the ones who kept their places open.

My grandfather was a very tall man; I had to reach up to hold his hand while walking. He wore dark blue and dark gray herringbone worsted suits, and the coat flap was a long way up, the gold watch chain almost out of sight. I could see his walking cane moving opposite me, briskly swung with the rhythm of his stride: it was my companion. Along the way it occurred to me that we were terribly excited, that the familiar way looked new and different, as though a haze which had hung over everything had been whipped away all at once, like a scarf. I was also having more fun than I'd ever had before.

When he came to the barbershop, my grandfather stepped inside and spoke to the barber and to all who happened to be hanging around, brought out by the sunshine. They spoke about politics, the crops, and the weather. The barber who always cut my hair came over and looked to see if I needed another trim and my grandfather said he didn't think so, but I might need a good brushing: they'd left so soon after breakfast it was a wonder I was dressed. Somebody who'd come in after us said, "Funeral in Grenada, ain't it?" which was the first anybody had mentioned it, but I knew they hadn't needed to say anything, that everybody knew about my parents' departure and why and where. Things were always known about, I saw, but not cared about too much either. The barber's strong arms, fleecy with reddish hair, swung me up into his big chair where I loved to be. He brushed my hair, then combed it. The great mirrors sparkled and everything was fine.

We presently moved on to the drugstore. The druggist, a small, crippled man, hobbled toward us, grinning to see us, and he and my grandfather talked for quite some time. Finally my grandfather said, "Give the child a strawberry cone," and so I had it, miraculous, and the world of which it was the center expanded about it with gracious, silent delight. It was a thing too wondrous actually to have eaten, and I do not remember eating it. It was only after we at last reached home and I entered the house, which smelled like my parents' clothes and their things, that I knew what they would think of what we had done and I became filled with anxiety and other dark feelings.

Then the car was coming up the drive and they were alighting in a post-funeral manner, full of heavy feelings and reminiscence and inclined not to speak in an ordinary way. When my mother put dinner in order, we sat around the table not saying very much.

"Did the fire hold out all right?" she asked my grandfather.

"Oh, it was warm," he said. "Didn't need much." He ate quietly and so did I.

In the afternoons on Sunday we all sat around looking at the paper. My mother had doubts about this, but we all indulged the desire anyway. After the ordeal of dressing up, of Sunday School and the long service and dinner, it seemed almost a debauchery to be able to pitch into those large crackling sheets, especially the funny papers, which were garish with color and loud with exclamation points, question marks, shouting, and all sorts of misdeeds. My grandfather had got sleepy before the fire and retired to his room while my mother and father had climbed out of their graveside feelings enough to talk a little and joke with one another.

"What did you all do?" my mother asked me. "How did you pass the time while we were gone?"

"We walked downtown," I said, for I had been laughing at something they had said to one another and wanted to share the morning's happiness with them without telling any more or letting any real trouble in. But my mother was on it, quicker than anything.

"You didn't go in the drugstore, did you?"

I looked up. Why did she have to ask? It wasn't in my scheme of thinking about things that she would ever do so. My father was looking at me now, too.

"Yes, ma'am," I slowly said. "But not for long," I added.

"You didn't get an ice cream cone, did you?"

And they both were looking. My face must have had astonishment on it as well as guilt. Not even I could have imagined them going this far. Why, on the day of a funeral, should they care if anybody bought an ice cream cone?

"Did you?" my father asked.

The thing to know is that my parents really believed everything they said they believed. They believed that awful punishments were meted out to those who did not remember the Sabbath was holy. They believed about a million other things. They were terribly honest about it.

Much later on, my mother went into my grandfather's room. I was silently behind her, and I heard her speak to him.

"She says you took her to town while we were gone and got an ice cream."

He had waked up and was reading by his lamp. At first he seemed not to hear; at last, he put his book face down in his lap and looked up. "I did," he said lightly.

A silence fell between them. Finally she turned and went away.

This, so far as I know, was all.

Because of the incident, that certain immunity of spirit my grandfather possessed was passed on to me. It came, I think, out of the precise way in which he put his book down on his lap to answer. There was a lifetime in the gesture, distilled, and I have been a good part of that long, growing up to all its meaning.

After this, though all went on as before, there was nothing much my parents could finally do about the church and me. They could lock the barn door, but the bright horse of freedom was already loose in my world. Down the hill, across the creek, in the next pasture — where? Somewhere, certainly: that much was proved; and all was different for its being so.

William Trevor

....

Autumn Sunshine

THE RECTORY WAS in County Wexford, eight miles from
Enniscorthy. It was a handsome eighteenth-century house,
with Virginia creeper covering three sides and a tangled garden
full of buddleia and struggling japonica which had always been too
much for its incumbents. It stood alone, seeming lonely even, approxi-
mately at the center of the country parish it served. Its church — St.
Michael's Church of Ireland — was two miles away, in the village of
Boharbawn.

For twenty-six years the Morans had lived there, not wishing to live
anywhere else. Canon Moran had never been an ambitious man; his
wife, Frances, had found contentment easy to attain in her lifetime.
Their four girls had been born in the rectory, and had become a happy
family there. They were grown up now, Frances's death was still recent:
like the rectory itself, its remaining occupant was alone in the countryside. The death had occurred in the spring of the year, and the summer
had somehow been bearable. The clergyman's eldest daughter had
spent May and part of June at the rectory with her children. Another
one had brought her family for most of August, and a third was to
bring her newly married husband in the winter. At Christmas nearly all
of them would gather at the rectory and some would come at Easter.
But that September, as the days drew in, the season was melancholy.

Then, one Tuesday morning, Slattery brought a letter from Canon
Moran's youngest daughter. There were two other letters as well, in
unsealed buff envelopes which meant that they were either bills or
receipts. Frail and gray-haired in his elderliness, Canon Moran had
been wondering if he should give the lawn in front of the house a last

cut when he heard the approach of Slattery's van. The lawn-mower was the kind that had to be pushed, and in the spring the job was always easier if the grass had been cropped close at the end of the previous summer.

"Isn't that a great bit of weather, Canon?" Slattery remarked, winding down the window of the van and passing out the three envelopes. "We're set for a while, would you say?"

"I hope so, certainly."

"Ah, we surely are, sir."

The conversation continued for a few moments longer, as it did whenever Slattery came to the rectory. The postman was young and easy-going, not long the successor to old Mr. O'Brien, who'd been making the round on a bicycle when the Morans first came to the rectory in 1952. Mr. O'Brien used to talk about his garden; Slattery talked about fishing, and often brought a share of his catch to the rectory.

"It's a great time of year for it," he said now, "except for the darkness coming in."

Canon Moran smiled and nodded; the van turned round on the gravel, dust rising behind it as it moved swiftly down the avenue to the road. Everyone said Slattery drove too fast.

He carried the letters to a wooden seat on the edge of the lawn he'd been wondering about cutting. Deirdre's handwriting hadn't changed since she'd been a child; it was round and neat, not at all a reflection of the girl she was. The blue English stamp, the Queen in profile blotched a bit by the London postmark, wasn't on its side or half upside down, as you might possibly expect with Deirdre. Of all the Moran children, she'd grown up to be the only difficult one. She hadn't come to the funeral and hadn't written about her mother's death. She hadn't been to the rectory for three years.

I'm sorry, she wrote now. *I couldn't stop crying actually. I've never known anyone as nice or as generous as she was. For ages I didn't even want to believe she was dead. I went on imagining her in the rectory and doing the flowers in church and shopping in Enniscorthy.*

Deirdre was twenty-one now. He and Frances had hoped she'd go to Trinity and settle down, but although at school she'd seemed to be the cleverest of their children she'd had no desire to become a student. She'd taken the Rosslare boat to Fishguard one night, having said she was going to spend a week with her friend Maeve Coles in Cork. They hadn't known she'd gone to England until they received a picture postcard from London telling them not to worry, saying she'd found work in an egg-packing factory.

Well, I'm coming back for a little while now, she wrote, *if you could put up with me and if you wouldn't find it too much. I'll cross over to Rosslare on the 29th, the morning crossing, and then I'll come on to Enniscorthy on the bus. I don't know what time it will be but there's a pub just by where the bus drops you so could we meet in the small bar there at six o'clock and then I won't have to lug my cases too far? I hope you won't mind going into such a place. If you can't make it, or don't want to see me, it's understandable, so if you don't turn up by half six I'll see if I can get a bus on up to Dublin. Only I need to get back to Ireland for a while.*

It was, as he and Slattery had agreed, a lovely autumn. Gentle sunshine mellowed the old garden, casting an extra sheen of gold on leaves that were gold already. Roses that had been ebullient in June and July bloomed modestly now. Michaelmas daisies were just beginning to bud. Already the crab-apples were falling, hydrangeas had a forgotten look. Canon Moran carried the letter from his daughter into the walled vegetable garden and leaned against the side of the greenhouse, half sitting on a protruding ledge, reading the letter again. Panes of glass were broken in the greenhouse, white paint and putty needed to be renewed, but inside a vine still thrived, and was heavy now with black ripe fruit. Later that morning he would pick some and drive into Enniscorthy, to sell the grapes to Mrs. Neary in Slaney Street.

Love, Deirdre: the letter was marvelous. Beyond the rectory the fields of wheat had been harvested, and the remaining stubble had the same tinge of gold in the autumn light; the beech trees and the chestnuts were triumphantly magnificent. But decay and rotting were only weeks away, and the letter from Deirdre was full of life. *"Love, Deirdre"* were words more beautiful than all the season's glories. He prayed as he leaned against the sunny greenhouse, thanking God for this salvation.

For all the years of their marriage Frances had been a help. As a younger man, Canon Moran hadn't known quite what to do. He'd been at a loss among his parishioners, hesitating in the face of this weakness or that: the pregnancy of Alice Pratt in 1954, the argument about grazing rights between Mr. Willoughby and Eugene Dunlevy in 1960, the theft of an altar cloth from St. Michael's and reports that Mrs.

Tobin had been seen wearing it as a skirt. Alice Pratt had been going out with a Catholic boy, one of Father Gowan's flock, which made the matter more difficult than ever. Eugene Dunlevy was one of Father's Gowan's also, and so was Mrs. Tobin.

"Father Gowan and I had a chat," Frances had said, and she'd had a chat as well with Alice Pratt's mother. A month later Alice Pratt married the Catholic boy, but to this day attended St. Michael's every Sunday, the children going to Father Gowan. Mrs. Tobin was given Hail Marys to say by the priest; Mr. Willoughby agreed that his father had years ago granted Eugene Dunlevy the grazing rights. Everything, in these cases and in many others, had come out all right in the end: order emerged from the confusion that Canon Moran so disliked, and it was Frances who had always begun the process, though no one ever said in the rectory that she understood the mystery of people as well as he understood the teachings of the New Testament. She'd been a freckle-faced girl when he'd married her, pretty in her way. He was the one with the brains.

Frances had seen human frailty everywhere: it was weakness in people, she said, that made them what they were as much as strength did. And she herself had her own share of such frailty, falling short in all sorts of ways of the God's image her husband preached about. With the small amount of housekeeping money she could be allowed she was a spendthrift, and she said she was lazy. She loved clothes and often overreached herself on visits to Dublin; she sat in the sun while the rectory gathered dust and the garden became rank; it was only where people were concerned that she was practical. But for what she was her husband had loved her with unobtrusive passion for fifty years, appreciating her conversation and the help she'd given him because she could so easily sense the truth. When he'd found her dead in the garden one morning he'd felt he had lost some part of himself.

Though many months had passed since then, the trouble was that Frances hadn't yet become a ghost. Her being alive was still too recent, the shock of her death too raw. He couldn't distance himself; the past refused to be the past. Often he thought that her fingerprints were still in the rectory, and when he picked the grapes or cut the grass of the lawn it was impossible not to pause and remember other years. Autumn had been her favorite time.

"Of course I'd come," he said. "Of course, dear. Of course."

"I haven't treated you very well."

"It's over and done with, Deirdre."

She smiled, and it was nice to see her smile again, although it was strange to be sitting in the back bar of a public house in Enniscorthy. He saw her looking at him, her eyes passing over his clerical collar and black clothes, and his quiet face. He could feel her thinking that he had aged, and putting it down to the death of the wife he'd been so fond of.

"I'm sorry I didn't write," she said.

"You explained in your letter, Deirdre."

"It was ages before I knew about it. That was an old address you wrote to."

"I guessed."

In turn he examined her. Years ago she'd had her long hair cut. It was short now, like a black cap on her head. And her face had lost its chubbiness; hollows where her cheeks had been made her eyes more dominant, pools of seaweed green. He remembered her child's stocky body, and the uneasy adolescence that had spoilt the family's serenity. Her voice had lost its Irish intonation.

"I'd have met you off the boat, you know."

"I didn't want to bother you with that."

"Oh, now, it isn't far, Deirdre."

She drank Irish whiskey, and smoked a brand of cigarettes called Three Castles. He'd asked for a mineral himself, and the woman serving them had brought him a bottle of something that looked like water but which fizzed up when she'd poured it. A kind of lemonade he imagined it was, and didn't much care for it.

"I have grapes for Mrs. Neary," he said.

"Who's that?"

"She has a shop in Slaney Street. We always sold her the grapes. You remember?"

She didn't, and he reminded her of the vine in the greenhouse. A shop surely wouldn't be open at this hour of the evening, she said, forgetting that in a country town of course it would be. She asked if the cinema was still the same in Enniscorthy, a cement building halfway up a hill. She said she remembered bicycling home from it at night with her sisters, not being able to keep up with them. She asked after her sisters and he told her about the two marriages that had taken place since she'd left: she had in-laws she'd never met, and nephews and a niece.

They left the bar, and he drove his dusty black Vauxhall straight to the small shop he'd spoken of. She remained in the car while he carried into the shop two large chip-baskets full of grapes. Afterwards Mrs. Neary came to the door with him.

"Well, is that Deirdre?" she said as Deirdre wound down the window of the car. "I'd never know you, Deirdre."

"She's come back for a little while," Canon Moran explained, raising his voice a little because he was walking round the car to the driver's seat as he spoke.

"Well, isn't that grand?" said Mrs. Neary.

Everyone in Enniscorthy knew Deirdre had just gone off, but it didn't matter now. Mrs. Neary's husband, who was a red-cheeked man with a cap, much smaller than his wife, appeared beside her in the shop doorway. He inclined his head in greeting, and Deirdre smiled and waved at both of them. Canon Moran thought it was pleasant when she went on waving while he drove off.

In the rectory he lay wakeful that night, his mind excited by Deirdre's presence. He would have loved Frances to know, and guessed that she probably did. He fell asleep at half past two and dreamed that he and Frances were young again, that Deirdre was still a baby. The freckles on Frances's face were out in profusion, for they were sitting in the sunshine in the garden, tea things spread about them, the children playing some game among the shrubs. It was autumn then also, the last of the September heat. But because he was younger in his dream he didn't feel part of the season himself, or sense its melancholy.

A week went by. The time passed slowly because a lot was happening, or so it seemed. Deirdre insisted on cooking all the meals and on doing the shopping in Boharbawn's single shop or in Enniscorthy. She still smoked her endless cigarettes, but the peakiness there had been in her face when she'd first arrived wasn't quite so pronounced — or perhaps, he thought, he'd become used to it. She told him about the different jobs she'd had in London and the different places she'd lived in, because on the postcards she'd occasionally sent there hadn't been room to go into detail. In the rectory they had always hoped she'd managed to get a training of some sort, though guessing she hadn't. In fact, her jobs had been of the most rudimentary kind: as well as her spell in the egg-packing factory, there'd been a factory that made plastic earphones, a cleaning job in a hotel near Euston, and a year working for the Use-Us Office Cleansing Service. "But you can't have liked any of that work, Deirdre?" he suggested, and she agreed she hadn't.

From the way she spoke he felt that that period of her life was over: adolescence was done with, she had steadied and taken stock. He didn't suggest to her that any of this might be so, not wishing to seem either too anxious or too pleased, but he felt she had returned to the rectory in a very different frame of mind from the one in which she'd left it. He imagined she would remain for quite a while, still taking stock, and in a sense occupying her mother's place. He thought he recognized in her a loneliness that matched his own, and he wondered if it was a feeling that their loneliness might be shared which had brought her back at this particular time. Sitting in the drawing-room while she cooked or washed up, or gathering grapes in the greenhouse while she did the shopping, he warmed delightedly to this theme. It seemed like an act of God that their circumstances should interlace this autumn. By Christmas she would know what she wanted to do with her life, and in the spring that followed she would perhaps be ready to set forth again. A year would have passed since the death of Frances.

"I have a friend," Deirdre said when they were having a cup of coffee together in the middle of one morning. "Someone who's been good to me."

She had carried a tray to where he was composing next week's sermon, sitting on the wooden seat by the lawn at the front of the house. He laid aside his exercise book, and a pencil and a rubber. "Who's that?" he inquired.

"Someone called Harold."

He nodded, stirring sugar into his coffee.

"I want to tell you about Harold, Father. I want you to meet him."

"Yes, of course."

She lit a cigarette. She said, "We have a lot in common. I mean, he's the only person . . ."

She faltered and then hesitated. She lifted her cigarette to her lips and drew on it.

He said, "Are you fond of him, Deirdre?"

"Yes, I am."

Another silence gathered. She smoked and drank her coffee. He added more sugar to his.

"Of course I'd like to meet him," he said.

"Could he come to stay with us, Father? Would you mind? Would it be all right?"

"Of course I wouldn't mind. I'd be delighted."

*   *   *

Harold was summoned, and arrived at Rosslare a few days later. In the meantime Deirdre had explained to her father that her friend was an electrician by trade and had let it fall that he was an intellectual kind of person. She borrowed the old Vauxhall and drove it to Rosslare to meet him, returning to the rectory in the early evening.

"How d'you do?" Canon Moran said, stretching out a hand in the direction of an angular youth with a birthmark on his face. His dark hair was cut very short, cropped almost. He was wearing a black leather jacket.

"I'm fine," Harold said.

"You've had a good journey?"

"Lousy, 'smatter of fact, Mr. Moran."

Harold's voice was strongly Cockney, and Canon Moran wondered if Deirdre had perhaps picked up some of her English vowel sounds from it. But then he realized that most people in London would speak like that, as people did on the television and the wireless. It was just a little surprising that Harold and Deirdre should have so much in common, as they clearly had from the affectionate way they held one another's hand. None of the other Moran girls had gone in so much for holding hands in front of the family.

He was to sit in the drawing-room, they insisted, while they made supper in the kitchen, so he picked up the *Irish Times* and did as he was bidden. Half an hour later Harold appeared and said that the meal was ready: fried eggs and sausages and bacon, and some tinned beans. Canon Moran said grace.

Having stated that County Wexford looked great, Harold didn't say much else. He didn't smile much, either. His afflicted face bore an edgy look, as if he'd never become wholly reconciled to his birthmark. It was like a scarlet map on his left cheek, a shape that reminded Canon Moran of the toe of Italy. Poor fellow, he thought. And yet a birthmark was so much less to bear than other afflictions there could be.

"Harold's fascinated actually," Deirdre said, "by Ireland."

Her friend didn't add anything to that remark for a moment, even though Canon Moran smiled and nodded interestedly. Eventually Harold said, "The struggle of the Irish people."

"I didn't know a thing about Irish history," Deirdre said. "I mean, not anything that made sense."

The conversation lapsed at this point, leaving Canon Moran greatly puzzled. He began to say that Irish history had always been of considerable interest to him also, that it had a good story to it, its tragedy uncomplicated. But the other two didn't appear to understand what he was talking about and so he changed the subject. It was a particularly splendid autumn, he pointed out.

"Harold doesn't go in for anything like that," Deirdre replied.

During the days that followed Harold began to talk more, surprising Canon Moran with almost everything he said. Deirdre had been right to say he was fascinated by Ireland, and it wasn't just a tourist's fascination. Harold had read widely: he spoke of ancient battles, and of the plantations of James I and Elizabeth, of Robert Emmet and the Mitchelstown martyrs, of Pearse and de Valera. "The struggle of the Irish people" was the expression he most regularly employed. It seemed to Canon Moran that the relationship between Harold and Deirdre had a lot to do with Harold's fascination, as though his interest in Deirdre's native land had somehow caused him to become interested in Deirdre herself.

There was something else as well. Fascinated by Ireland, Harold hated his own country. A sneer whispered through his voice when he spoke of England: a degenerate place, he called it, destroyed by class-consciousness and the unjust distribution of wealth. He described in detail the city of Nottingham, to which he appeared to have a particular aversion. He spoke of unnecessary motorways and the stupidity of bureaucracy, the stifling presence of a Royal family. "You could keep an Indian village," he claimed, "on what those corgis eat. You could house five hundred homeless in Buckingham Palace." There was brainwashing by television and the newspaper barons. No ordinary person had a chance because pap was fed to the ordinary person, a deliberate policy going back into Victorian times when education and religion had been geared to the enslavement of minds. The English people had brought it on themselves, having lost their spunk, settling instead for consumer durables. "What better can you expect," Harold demanded, "after the hypocrisy of that empire the bosses ran?"

Deirdre didn't appear to find anything specious in this line of talk, which surprised her father. "Oh, I wonder about that," he said himself from time to time, but he said it mildly, not wishing to cause an argument, and in any case his interjections were not acknowledged. Quite a few of the criticisms Harold levelled at his own country could be levelled at Ireland also and, Canon Moran guessed, at many countries throughout the world. It was strange that the two neighboring

islands had been so picked out, although once Germany was mentioned and the point made that developments beneath the surface
there were a hopeful sign, that a big upset was on the way.

"We're taking a walk," Harold said one afternoon. "She's going to
show me Kinsella's Barn."

Canon Moran nodded, saying to himself that he disliked Harold. It
was the first time he had admitted it, but the feeling was familiar. The
less generous side of his nature had always emerged when his daughters brought to the rectory the men they'd become friendly with or
even proposed to marry. Emma, the eldest girl, had brought several
before settling in the end for Thomas. Linda had brought only John,
already engaged to him. Una had married Carley not long after the
death, and Carley had not yet visited the rectory: Canon Moran had
met him in Dublin, where the wedding had taken place, for in the
circumstances Una had not been married from home. Carley was
an older man, an importer of tea and wine, stout and flushed, certainly not someone Canon Moran would have chosen for his second-
youngest daughter. But, then, he had thought the same about Emma's
Thomas and about Linda's John.

Thomas was a farmer, sharing a sizeable acreage with his father in
County Meath. He always brought to mind the sarcasm of an old
schoolmaster who in Canon Moran's distant schooldays used to refer
to a gang of boys at the back of the classroom as "farmer's sons,"
meaning that not much could be expected of them. It was an inaccu-
rate assumption but even now, whenever Canon Moran found himself
in the company of Thomas, he couldn't help recalling it. Thomas was
mostly silent, with a good-natured smile that came slowly and lingered
too long. According to his father, and there was no reason to doubt the
claim, he was a good judge of beef cattle.

Linda's John was the opposite. Wiry and suave, he was making his
way in the Bank of Ireland, at present stationed in Waterford. He had
a tiny orange-colored moustache and was good at golf. Linda's
ambition for him was that he should become the Bank of Ireland's
manager in Limerick or Galway, where the insurances that went with
the position were particularly lucrative. Unlike Thomas, John talked
all the time, telling jokes and stories about the Bank of Ireland's customers.

"Nothing is perfect," Frances used to say, chiding her husband for an
uncharitableness he did his best to combat. He disliked being so par-

ticular about the men his daughters chose, and he was aware that other people saw them differently: Thomas would do anything for you, John was fun, the middle-aged Carley laid his success at Una's feet. But whoever the husbands of his daughters had been, Canon Moran knew he'd have felt the same. He was jealous of the husbands because ever since his daughters had been born he had loved them unstintingly. When he had prayed after Frances's death he'd felt jealous of God, who had taken her from him.

"There's nothing much to see," he pointed out when Harold announced that Deirdre was going to show him Kinsella's Barn. "Just the ruin of a wall is all that's left."

"Harold's interested, Father."

They set off on their walk, leaving the old clergyman ashamed that he could not like Harold more. It wasn't just his griminess: there was something sinister about Harold, something furtive about the way he looked at you, peering at you cruelly out of his afflicted face, not meeting your eye. Why was he so fascinated about a country that wasn't his own? Why did he refer so often to "Ireland's struggle" as if that struggle particularly concerned him? He hated walking, he had said, yet he'd just set out to walk six miles through woods and fields to examine a ruined wall.

Canon Moran had wondered as suspiciously about Thomas and John and Carley, privately questioning every statement they made, finding hidden motives everywhere. He'd hated the thought of his daughters being embraced or even touched, and had forced himself not to think about that. He'd prayed, ashamed of himself then, too. "It's just a frailty in you," Frances had said, her favorite way of cutting things down to size.

He sat for a while in the afternoon sunshine, letting all of it hang in his mind. It would be nice if they quarrelled on their walk. It would be nice if they didn't speak when they returned, if Harold simply went away. But that wouldn't happen, because they had come to the rectory with a purpose. He didn't know why he thought that, but he knew it was true: they had come for a reason, something that was all tied up with Harold's fascination and with the kind of person Harold was, with his cold eyes and his afflicted face.

In March 1798 an incident had taken place in Kinsella's Barn, which at that time had just been a barn. Twelve men and women, accused of

harboring insurgents, had been tied together with ropes at the command of a Sergeant James. They had been led through the village of
Boharbawn, the Sergeant's soldiers on horseback on either side of the
procession, the Sergeant himself bringing up the rear. Designed as an
act of education, an example to the inhabitants of Boharbawn and the
country people around, the twelve had been herded into a barn owned
by a farmer called Kinsella and there burned to death. Kinsella, who
had played no part either in the harboring of insurgents or in the
execution of the twelve, was afterwards murdered by his own farm
laborers.

"Sergeant James was a Nottingham man," Harold said that evening
at supper. "A soldier of fortune who didn't care what he did. Did you
know he acquired great wealth, Mr. Moran?"

"No, I wasn't at all aware of that," Canon Moran replied.

"Harold found out about him," Deirdre said.

"He used to boast he was responsible for the death of a thousand
Irish people. It was in Boharbawn he reached the thousand. They
rewarded him well for that."

"Not much is known about Sergeant James locally. Just the legend of
Kinsella's Barn."

"No way it's a legend."

Deirdre nodded; Canon Moran did not say anything. They were
eating cooked ham and salad. On the table there was a cake which
Deirdre had bought in McGovern's in Enniscorthy, and a pot of tea.
There were several bunches of grapes from the greenhouse, and a
plate of wafer biscuits. Harold was fond of salad cream, Canon Moran
had noticed; he had a way of hitting the base of the jar with his hand,
causing large dollops to spurt all over his ham. He didn't place his knife
and fork together on the plate when he'd finished, but just left them
anyhow. His fingernails were edged with black.

"You'd feel sick," he was saying now, working the salad cream again.
"You'd stand there looking at that wall and you'd feel a revulsion in
your stomach."

"What I meant," Canon Moran said, "is that it has passed into local
legend. No one doubts it took place; there's no question about that.
But two centuries have almost passed."

"And nothing has changed," Harold interjected. "The Irish people
still share their bondage with the twelve in Kinsella's Barn."

"Round here of course — "

"It's not round here that matters, Mr. Moran. The struggle's world-wide; the sickness is everywhere actually."

Again Deirdre nodded. She was like a zombie, her father thought. She was being used because she was an Irish girl; she was Harold's Irish connection, and in some almost frightening way she believed herself in love with him. Frances had once said they'd made a mistake with her. She had wondered if Deirdre had perhaps found all the love they'd offered her too much to bear. They were quite old when Deirdre was a child, the last expression of their own love. She was special because of that.

"At least Kinsella got his chips," Harold pursued, his voice relentless. "At least that's something."

Canon Moran protested. The owner of the barn had been an innocent man, he pointed out. The barn had simply been a convenient one, large enough for the purpose, with heavy stones near it that could be piled up against the door before the conflagration. Kinsella, that day, had been miles away, ditching a field.

"It's too long ago to say where he was," Harold retorted swiftly. "And if he was keeping a low profile in a ditch it would have been by arrangement with the imperial forces."

When Harold said that, there occurred in Canon Moran's mind a flash of what appeared to be the simple truth. Harold was an Englishman who had espoused a cause because it was one through which the status quo in his own country might be damaged. Similar such Englishmen, read about in newspapers, stirred in the clergyman's mind: men from Ealing and Liverpool and Wolverhampton who had changed their names to Irish names, who had even learned the Irish language, in order to ingratiate themselves with the new Irish revolutionaries. Such men dealt out death and chaos, announcing that their conscience insisted on it.

"Well, we'd better wash the dishes," Deirdre said, and Harold rose obediently to help her.

The walk to Kinsella's Barn had taken place on a Saturday afternoon. The following morning Canon Moran conducted his services in St. Michael's, addressing his small Protestant congregation, twelve at Holy Communion, eighteen at morning service. He had prepared a sermon about repentance, taking as his text St. Luke, 15:32: . . . *for this thy brother was dead, and is alive again; and was lost, and is found.* But at the last moment he changed his mind and spoke instead of the incident in Kinsella's Barn nearly two centuries ago. He tried to make the point that one horror should not fuel another, that passing time contained its own forgiveness. Deirdre and Harold were naturally not in the church, but they'd been present at breakfast, Harold frying eggs on the kitchen stove, Deirdre pouring tea. He had looked at them and tried to think of them as two young people on holiday. He had tried to tell himself they'd come to the rectory for a rest and for his blessing, that he should be grateful instead of fanciful. It was for his blessing that Emma had brought Thomas to the rectory, that Linda had brought John. Una would bring Carley in November. "Now, don't be silly," Frances would have said.

"The man Kinsella was innocent of everything," he heard his voice insisting in his church. "He should never have been murdered also."

Harold would have delighted in the vengeance exacted on an innocent man. Harold wanted to inflict pain, to cause suffering and destruction. The end justified the means for Harold, even if the end was an artificial one, a pettiness grandly dressed up. In his sermon Canon Moran spoke of such matters without mentioning Harold's name. He spoke of how evil drained people of their humor and compassion, how people pretended even to themselves. It was worse than Frances's death, he thought as his voice continued in the church: it was worse that Deirdre should be part of wickedness.

He could tell that his parishioners found his sermon odd, and he didn't blame them. He was confused, and naturally distressed. In the rectory Deirdre and Harold would be waiting for him. They would all sit down to Sunday lunch while plans for atrocities filled Harold's mind, while Deirdre loved him.

"Are you well again, Mrs. Davis?" he inquired at the church door of a woman who suffered from asthma.

"Not too bad, Canon. Not too bad, thank you."

He spoke to all the others, inquiring about health, remarking on the beautiful autumn. They were farmers mostly and displayed a farmer's gratitude for the satisfactory season. He wondered suddenly who'd replace him among them when he retired or died. Father Gowan had had to give up a year ago. The young man, Father White, was always in a hurry.

"Goodbye so, Canon," Mr. Willoughby said, shaking hands as he always did, every Sunday. It was a long time since there'd been the trouble about Eugene Dunlevy's grazing rights; three years ago Mr. Willoughby had been left a widower himself. "You're managing all right, Canon?" he asked, as he also always did.

"Yes, I'm all right, thank you, Mr. Willoughby."

Someone else inquired if Deirdre was still at the rectory, and he said she was. Heads nodded, the unspoken thought being that that was nice for him, his youngest daughter at home again after all these years. There was forgiveness in several faces, forgiveness of Deirdre, who had been thoughtless to go off to an egg-packing factory. There was the feeling, also unexpressed, that the young were a bit like that.

"Goodbye," he said in a general way. Car doors banged, engines started. In the vestry he removed his surplice and his cassock and hung them in a cupboard.

"We'll probably go tomorrow," Deirdre said during lunch.

"Go?"

"We'll probably take the Dublin bus."

"I'd like to see Dublin," Harold said.

"And then you're returning to London?"

"We're easy about that," Harold interjected before Deirdre could reply. "I'm a tradesman, Mr. Moran, an electrician."

"I know you're an electrician, Harold."

"What I mean is, I'm on my own; I'm not answerable to the bosses. There's always a bob or two waiting in London."

For some reason Canon Moran felt that Harold was lying. There was a quickness about the way he'd said they were easy about their plans, and it didn't seem quite to make sense, the logic of not being answerable to bosses and a bob or two always waiting for him. Harold was being evasive about their movements, hiding the fact that they would probably remain in Dublin for longer than he implied, meeting other people like himself.

"It was good of you to have us," Deirdre said that evening, all three of them sitting around the fire in the drawing-room because the evenings had just begun to get chilly. Harold was reading a book about Che Guevara and hadn't spoken for several hours. "We've enjoyed it, Father."

"It's been nice having you, Deirdre."

"I'll write to you from London."

It was safe to say that: he knew she wouldn't because she hadn't before, until she'd wanted something. She wouldn't write to thank him for the rectory's hospitality, and that would be quite in keeping. Harold was the same kind of man as Sergeant James had been: it didn't matter that they were on different sides. Sergeant James had maybe borne an affliction also, a humped back or a withered arm. He had ravaged a country that existed then for its spoils, and his most celebrated crime was neatly at hand so that another Englishman could make matters worse by attempting to make amends. In Harold's view the trouble had always been that these acts of war and murder died beneath the weight of print in history books, and were forgotten. But history could be rewritten, and for that Kinsella's Barn was an inspiration: Harold had journeyed to it as people make journeys to holy places.

"Yes?" Deirdre said, for while these reflections had passed through his mind he had spoken her name, wanting to ask her to tell him the truth about her friend.

He shook his head. "I wish you could have seen your mother again," he said instead. "I wish she were here now."

The faces of his three sons-in-law irrelevantly appeared in his mind: Carley's flushed cheeks, Thomas's slow good-natured smile, John's little moustache. It astonished him that he'd ever felt suspicious of their natures, for they would never let his daughters down. But Deirdre had turned her back on the rectory, and what could be expected when she came back with a man? She had never been like Emma or Linda or Una, none of whom smoked Three Castles cigarettes and wore clothes that didn't seem quite clean. It was impossible to imagine any of them becoming involved with a revolutionary, a man who wanted to commit atrocities.

"He was just a farmer, you know," he heard himself saying. "Kinsella."

Surprise showed in Deirdre's face. "It was Mother we were talking about," she reminded him, and he could see her trying to connect her mother with a farmer who had died two hundred years ago, and not being able to. Elderliness, he could see her thinking. "Only time he wandered," she would probably say to her friend.

"It was good of you to come, Deirdre."

He looked at her, far into her eyes, admitting to himself that she had always been his favorite. When the other girls were busily growing up she had still wanted to sit on his knee. She'd had a way of interrupting him no matter what he was doing, arriving beside him with a book she wanted him to read to her.

"Goodbye, Father," she said the next morning while they waited in Enniscorthy for the Dublin bus. "Thank you for everything."

"Yeah, thanks a ton, Mr. Moran," Harold said.

"Goodbye, Harold. Goodbye, my dear."

He watched them finding their seats when the bus arrived and then he drove the old Vauxhall back to Boharbawn, meeting Slattery in his postman's van and returning his salute. There was shopping he should have done, meat and potatoes, and tins of things to keep him going. But his mind was full of Harold's afflicted face and his black-rimmed fingernails, and Deirdre's hand in his. And then flames burst from the straw that had been packed around living people in Kinsella's Barn. They burned through the wood of the barn itself, revealing the writhing bodies. On his horse the man called Sergeant James laughed.

Canon Moran drove the car into the rectory's ramshackle garage, and walked around the house to the wooden seat on the front lawn. Frances should come now with two cups of coffee, appearing at the front door with the tray and then crossing the gravel and the lawn. He saw her as she had been when first they came to the rectory, when only Emma had been born; but the gray-haired Frances was somehow there as well, shadowing her youth. "Funny little Deirdre," she said, placing the tray on the seat between them.

It seemed to him that everything that had just happened in the rectory had to do with Frances, with meeting her for the first time when she was eighteen, with loving her and marrying her. He knew it was a trick of the autumn sunshine that again she crossed the gravel and the lawn, no more than pretense that she handed him a cup and saucer. "Harold's just a talker," she said. "Not at all like Sergeant James."

He sat for a while longer on the wooden seat, clinging to these words, knowing they were true. Of course it was cowardice that ran through Harold, inspiring the whisper of his sneer when he spoke of the England he hated so. In the presence of a befuddled girl and an old Irish clergyman England was an easy target, and Ireland's troubles a kind of target also.

Frances laughed, and for the first time her death seemed far away, as her life did too. In the rectory the visitors had blurred her fingerprints to nothing, and had made of her a ghost that could come back. The sunshine warmed him as he sat there, the garden was less melancholy than it had been.

John Updike

....

Made in Heaven

BRAD SCHAEFFER was attracted to Jeanette Henderson by her Christianity; at an office Christmas party, in Boston in the thirties, in one of those eddies of silence that occur amid gaiety like a swirl of backwater in a stream, he heard her crystal-clear voice saying, "Why, the salvation of my soul!"

He looked over. She was standing by the window, pinned between a hot radiator and Arthur Gleb, the office Romeo. Outside, behind the black window, it had begun to snow, and the lighted windows of the office building across Milk Street were blurring and fluttering. Jeanette had come to the brokerage house that fall, a tidy secretary in a pimento wool suit, with a prim ruffled blouse. For this evening's event she had dared open-toed shoes and a dress of lavender gabardine, with zigzag pleats marked at their points by flattened bows. The flush the party punch had put in her cheeks and throat helped him see for the first time the something highly polished about her compact figure, an impression of an object finely made, down to the toenails that peeked through the tips of her shoes. Her profile showed pert and firm as she strained to look up into Arthur's overbearing, beetle-browed face. Brad stepped over to them, into the steamy warmth near the radiator. The snow was intensifying; across the street the golden windows were softening like pats of butter.

Jeanette turned her face to her rescuer. She was lightly sweating. The excited blush of her cheeks made the blue of her eyes look icy. "Arthur was saying," she appealed, "that only money matters."

"Then I asked this crazy little gal what mattered to her," Arthur said, giving off heat through his black serge suit. A sprig of mistletoe, pale and withering, was pinned to his lapel.

"And I told him the first thing I could think of," Jeanette said. Her hair, waved and close to her head, was a soft brown that tonight did not look mousy. "Of course a lot of things matter to me," she hurried on, "more than money."

"Are you Catholic?" Brad asked her.

This was a question of another order than Arthur's badinage. Her face composed itself; her voice became secretarial, factual. "Of course not. I'm a Methodist."

Brad felt relief. He was free to love her. In Boston one did not love Catholics, even if one came from Ohio with the name of Schaeffer.

"Did I sound so silly?" she asked, when Arthur had gone off in search of another cup of punch and another little gal.

"Startling, but not silly." In his heart Brad did not expect capitalism to last another decade, and it would take with it what churches were left. He assumed that religion was already as dead as Marx and Mencken had claimed. There was a gloom in the December streets, and in the statistics that came to the office, that made the cheer of Christmas carols sound obscene. From the deep doorways of Boston's business buildings, ornamented like little Gothic chapels with carvings and ironwork, people actually starving peered out, too bitter and numb to beg. Each morning the Common was combed for bodies.

"I *do* believe," Jeanette said, as if in apology. The contrast between her blue eyes and rosy, glazed skin had become almost garish. "Ever since I can remember, even before anything was explained to me. It seems so natural, so necessary. Do you think that's strange?"

"I think that's lovely," he told her.

By Lententime they were going together to church. It was his idea, to accompany her; he loved seeing her in new settings, in the new light each placed her in. At work she was drab and brisk, a bit aloof from the other "girls," with a dry way of pursing her lips into crinkles that made her look older than she was. At her ancestral home in Framingham, with her parents and brothers, she became girlish and slightly drunk on family atmosphere, as she had been on punch; he greedily inhaled the air of this spicy old house, with its worn orientals and sofas of leather and horsehair, knowing that this was the aroma of her childhood. On the streets and in restaurants Jeanette was perfectly the lady, like a figure etched on a city scene, making him, in their scenic anonymity, a gentleman, an escort, a gallant. Her smiling face, and the satin lapels of her blue wool coat, and the pointed tips of her shiny black boots, all gleamed. Involuntarily his arm encircled her waist at street corners, and he could not let go even when they had safely crossed the street. Her bearing was so nicely honed in every move — the pulling off, for instance, finger by finger, of her gloves in Locke-Ober's — that Brad would sometimes clown or feign clumsiness just to crack her composure with a blush or a grimace. He was afraid that otherwise he might slip from her mind. It did not occur to him, when, during a rapt *pianissimo* moment in Symphony Hall, he nudged her and whispered a joke, that he was rending something precious to her, invading a fragile feminine space. In church he loved standing tall at her side and hearing her frail, crystalline voice lift up the words of the hymns. He basked in her gravity, which had something shy about it, and even uncertain, as if she feared that an excess of feeling might leap from the musty old forms and overwhelm her. He knew the forms: he had been raised as a Presbyterian, though only his mother attended services, and then only on those Sundays when she wasn't needed in the fields or at the barn. Jeanette had at first resisted his accompanying her. It would be, she murmured, distracting. And it was true: her shy, uncertain reverence made him, perversely, want to turn and hug her and lift her up with a shout of pride and animal gladness.

He was twenty-eight, and she was twenty-five — old enough that marriage might have slipped her by. Her composure, the finished neatness of her figure, already seemed a touch old-maidenly. She shared rooms with another young woman on Marlborough Street; he lived on Joy, on the dark, Cambridge Street side of Beacon Hill. She had been going to church at the brick Copley Methodist over on Newbury Street, with its tall, domed bell tower and Byzantine gold-leaf ceiling. Brad found within an easy walk of his own apartment a precious oddity, a Greek Revival clapboard church tucked among the brick tenements of the West End. Built by the Unitarians in the 1830s and taken over by the Wesleyans during their post–Civil War resurgence, the little building had box pews, small leaded panes of gray glass, and an oak pulpit shaped somewhat like a bass viol. Brad was to remember with special fondness coming here with Jeanette for the Wednesday-night Lenten services. On these raw spring nights the east wind brought the smell of brine in from the harbor. The couple walked through dim-lit streets crowded with the babble and cooking odors of Jewish and Italian families, and then came to this closet of Protestantism, this hushed vacant space — scarcely a dozen heads in the pews, and the church so chilly that overcoats were left on. There was no choir, and each shift of weight on a pew seat rang out like a cough. Perhaps Brad was still an unbeliever at that point, for he relished — as if he were whispering a joke to Jeanette — the emptiness, the chill, the pathos of the aged minister's trite and halting sermon as once again the old clergyman, set down to die in this dying parish, led his listeners along the worn path to the Crucifixion and the bafflement beyond. During these pathetic sermons Brad's mind would range wonderfully far, a falcon scouting his future, while Jeanette sat at his side, compact and still and exquisite. She would lift him up, he felt. In the virtual vacancy of this old meetinghouse she seemed most intimately his.

Roosevelt was newly President then, and Curley was still mayor; their boasts came true, the country survived. The precious little hollow church, with its wooden Ionic columns and viol-shaped pulpit, was swept away in the fifties along with the tenements of the West End. By this time Brad and Jeanette had moved with their children to Newton and become Episcopalians.

On their wedding night, hoping to please her, he held her body in his arms and prayed aloud. He thanked God for bringing them together, and asked that they be allowed to live fruitful and useful lives together. The prayer was, in time, answered, though on this occasion it did little to relax Jeanette. Always his love of her, when distinctly professed, made her a little reserved and tense, as if a certain threat was being masked and a trap might be sprung.

Their four children were all born healthy, and Brad's four years as a naval officer passed with no more harm to him than the devastating impression that the black firmament of spattered stars made when seen from the flight deck of an aircraft carrier, in the middle of the Pacific. How little, little to the point of nothingness, he was under those stars! Even the great ship, the *Enterprise,* that held him a tall building's height above the monotonous swells was reduced to the size of a pinpoint in such perspective. And yet, it was he who was witnessing the stars. They knew nothing of themselves, so in this dimension he was greater than they. As far as he could reason, religion begins with this strangeness, this standstill; faith tips the balance in favor of the pinpoint. So, though he had never had Jeanette's intuitions or sensations of certainty, he became in his mind a believer.

Ten years later he suggested they become Episcopalians, because the

church was handier to the Newton house — a shingled, many-dor-
mered affair with corridors for vanished servants and even a cupola.
Narrow stairs wound up to a small round room that became Jeanette's
"retreat." She installed rugs and pillowed furniture, did needlepoint
and watercolors. From its windows one could see to the east the red
warning light topping the spire of the John Hancock Building. Brad did
not need to say that his associates and clients tended to be Episcopalian
and that this church held more of the sort of people they would like to
get to know. Although he never quite grew accustomed to the droning
wordiness of the service and the awkward and repetitive kneeling, he
did love the look of the congregation — the ruddy men with their blue
blazers and ever-fresh haircuts, the sleek Episcopalian women with
their furs in winter and in summer their wide pastel garden hats that
showed the backs of their necks when they bowed their heads. He
loved Jeanette among them, in her black silk dress and the strand of
real pearls, each costing as much as a refrigerator, with which he had
paid tribute to their fifteenth anniversary. Money gently glimmered on
her fingers and ears. All capitalism had needed, it had turned out, was
an infusion of war. The postwar stock market climbed; even plumb-
ers and grocers needed a stockbroker now. Shares Brad had picked up
for peanuts in the Depression doubled in value, and doubled again, and
more.

Jeanette never took quite as active a role in the life of the church as
he had expected. He himself taught Sunday school, passed the plate,
sat on the vestry, read the lesson. It was like a playful extension of his
business life; he felt at home in the committee room, in the linoleum-
floored offices and robing rooms that mere worshippers never saw. He
always found some practical reason to be at the church Sunday mornings, whereas in growing season Jeanette often stayed home to garden,
much as Brad's mother had worked in the fields. Jeanette's body had
added a sturdy plumpness to that polished, glossy quality that had first
enchanted him. Her Christianity, as he imagined it, was, like water
sealed in an underground cistern, unchangingly pure. Standing beside
her in church, hearing her small, true voice lifted in song, he still felt
empowered by her fineness, so that in the jostle after the service his
hands involuntarily crept around her waist, and he would let go only to
shake the minister's overworked hand.

"I wish you wouldn't paw me in church," she said one Sunday as
they drove home. "We're too middle-aged."

"I wasn't so much pawing you as steering you through the mob," he said, embarrassed.

"I don't *need* to be steered," Jeanette said. She tried to stamp her foot, but the gesture was ineffectual on the carpeted car floor.

Here we are, Brad thought, in our beige Mercedes, coming home from church, having a quarrel; and he had no idea why. He saw them from afar, with the eyes of aspiration, like a handsome, mature couple in a four-color ad, and there was no imperfection in the picture. "If I can't help touching you," he said, "it's because I still love you. Isn't that nice?"

"It is," she said sulkily, then added, "Are you sure it's me you love, or some idea you have of me?"

This seemed to Brad a finicking distinction. She was positing a "real" her, a person apart from the one he was married to. But who would this be, unless it was the woman who took a cup of tea and went up the winding stairs to her cupola at odd hours? This woman disappeared. And no sooner did she disappear, when he was home, than two children began fighting, or the dry cleaner's delivery truck pulled into the driveway, and she had to be called down.

"Did it ever occur to you," she asked now, "that you love me because it suits you? That for you it's an exercise in male power?"

"My God," he said indignantly, "who have you been reading? Would you rather I loved you because it *didn't* suit me?"

"That *would* be more romantic," she admitted, in her smallest, tidiest voice, and he knew this was a conciliatory joke, and their mysterious lapse of harmony would be smoothed away.

He became head of the vestry and spent hours at the church, politicking, soothing ruffled feathers. After the last of their children had been confirmed and was excused from faithful attendance, Jeanette began to go to the eight o'clock service, before Brad was fully awake. She would return, shiny-faced, just as he was settling, a bit foggy and hung over, into a second cup of coffee and the sheaves of the Sunday *Globe*. She loved the lack of a sermon, she said, and the absence of that oppressive choir with those Fred Waring–like arrangements. She did not say that she enjoyed being by herself in church, as she had been in Boston twenty-five years earlier. At the ten o'clock service he missed her, the thin, sweet piping of her singing beside him. He felt naked, as when alone on the deck of the imperiled *Enterprise*. He explained to Jeanette that he would happily push himself out of bed and go with her to the eight o'clock, but the committee people he had to talk to expected him to be at the ten o'clock. She relented and resumed her place at his side. But she complained at the length of the sermon and winced when the choir came on too strong. Brad wondered if their sons, who had become more or less anti-establishment, and incidentally anti-church, had infected her with their rebellion.

Ike was President, and then JFK. Joseph Kennedy, when Brad was young, had been a man to gossip about in Boston financial circles — a cocky mick with the bad taste not only to make a pot of money but also then to leave Boston and head up the SEC under Roosevelt and his raving liberals. The nuances of the regional Irish–Yankee feud escaped and amused Brad, since to his midwestern eyes the two hostile camps were very similar — thin-skinned, clubby men from damp green islands, fond of a nip and long, malicious stories. Though Brad had lived all of his adult life in and around Boston, he never could catch the accent, never could bring himself to force his *as* and to say "Cuber" and "idear," the way the young President did so ringingly on television.

With their own young the Schaeffers were lucky — the boys were a little too old to fall into the heart of the drug craze, and the girls were safely married before just living together became fashionable. One boy didn't finish college and became a carpenter in Vermont; the other did finish, at Amherst, but then moved to the West Coast to live. The two girls, however, stayed in the area and provided new grandchildren at regular intervals. So Brad's wedding-night prayer was, to all appearances, still being answered.

As the sixties wore into the seventies, some misfortunes befell the Schaeffers as well as the country. Both daughters went through messy divorces, involving countersuing husbands, scandalous depositions, and odd fits of nocturnal violence on the weedless lawns and in the neo-colonial bedrooms of Wellesley and Dover. Freddy, the son on the West Coast, never could seem to get what would be called a job; he was always "in" things — in real estate, in public relations, in investments — without ever drawing a salary or making, as far as Brad could figure, a profit. Like Brad, Freddy had turned gray early, and suddenly there he was, well over thirty, a gray-haired boy, sweet-natured and with gracious, expensive tastes, who had never found his way into the economy. It worried Jeanette that to keep him going out there they were robbing the other children, especially the carpenter son, who by now had become a condo contractor and part-owner of a ski resort. They were grieved but at some level not surprised when poor Freddy was found dead in Glendale, of what was called an accidental drug overdose. A cocaine habit had backed him, financially, to the wall. He was found neatly dressed in a blue blazer and linen slacks — to the end a gentleman, something Brad, in his own mind, had never become.

The Newton house huge and empty around them, the couple talked of moving to an apartment, but it seemed easier to turn off the radiators in a few rooms and stay where they were. Throughout the rooms of familiar furniture were propped and hung photographs of the children at happy turning points — graduations, marriages, trips abroad. This grinning, tinted population extended now into the third generation and was realer than the intermittent notes and phone calls from the children themselves. Brad knew in the abstract that he had changed diapers, driven boys to hockey and girls to ballet, supervised bedtime prayers, paternally stood by while tears were being shed and games played and the traumas of maturation endured; yet he could not muster much actual sensation of parenthood — those years were like a television sitcom in which he sat watching himself play the father. More vivid, returning in such unexpected detail that his eyes stung and the utter lostness of it all made him gasp, were moments of his and Jeanette's Boston days in the L-shaped apartment on St. Botolph Street and then in the fifth-floor Commonwealth Avenue place with its skylight and bird-cage elevator, and of old times at the firm, before it moved from the walnut-paneled offices on Milk Street to a flimsy, flashy new skyscraper on State. Certain business epiphanies — workday afternoons when an educated guess paid off a thousandfold, or a carefully cultivated friendship produced a big commission — could still put the taste of triumph in his mouth. Fun like that had fled the business when the sixties bull market had collapsed. The people he had looked up to, the crusty Yankee money managers, had all retired. Brad himself retired at the age of sixty-eight, the same summer that Nixon resigned. In his loneliness those first months, his guilty unease at not being in a suit, he would visit Jeanette in her cupola.

She did not say she minded, but everything seemed to halt when he climbed the last pie-slice-shaped steps, so the room had the burnished silence of a clock that has just stopped ticking. She sat surrounded by windows, lit from all sides, her soft brown hair scarcely touched by gray. The rug she had been hooking was set in its frame at the side of her armchair, and a magazine lay in her lap, but she did not appear to be doing anything — so deeply engaged in gazing out a window through the tops of the beeches that she did not even move her head at his entrance. Her motionlessness slightly frightened him. He stood a second, getting his breath. Where just the tip of the old Hancock Building had once shown above the treetops, now a silvery cluster of tall glass boxes reflected the sun. He had always been nervous in high places, and as his eyes plunged down, parallel with her gaze, through the bare winter branches toward the dead lawn, three stories below, his thighs tightened and he shuffled self-protectively toward the center of the room.

Since she said nothing, he asked, "Do you feel all right?"

"Of course," Jeanette answered, firmly. "Why wouldn't I?"

"I don't know, my dear. You seem so quiet."

"I like being quiet. I always have. You know that."

"Oh, yes." He felt challenged and slightly dazed. "I know that."

"So let's think of something for you to do," she said, at last turning, with one of her usual neat motions, to give him her attention. And she would send him back down, down to the basement, to reglaze, say, a storm window that a neighbor child had broken with a golf ball. It was strange, Brad reflected, that in this room of her own Jeanette had hung no pictures of the children or of him. But then, there was little wall space between the many windows, and the cushioned window seats, two thirds of the way around the room, were littered with old paintings, needlepoint cushions, and books whose cloth covers the circling sun had bleached. He thought of it as her meditation room, though he had no clear idea of what meditation was; his own brain skidded off, in even the silent seconds inserted between rote petitions at church, into that exultant plotting that divine service stimulated in him.

Her illness came on imperceptibly at first, and then with devastating speed. They were watching television one night — the hostages had been taken in Iran, and every day, it seemed, something *had* to happen. Suddenly Jeanette put her hand on his wrist. They were sitting side by side on the red upholstered Hepplewhite-style settee, or love seat, that they had impulsively bought at Paine's in the late forties, during a blizzard, before the move to Newton. Because of the storm, the vast store had been nearly empty, and they had felt they must do something to justify their presence, to celebrate the weather. His love for her always returned full force when it snowed. "What?" he asked now, startled by her unaccustomed gesture.

"Nothing." She smiled. "A tiny pain."

"Where?" he asked, monosyllabic as if just awakened. On the news at that moment a reporter was interviewing a young Iranian revolutionary who spoke fluent, midwestern-accented English, and Jeanette's exact answer escaped Brad. If in the course of their marriage there was one act for which he blamed himself, could identify as a sin for which he deserved to be punished, it was this moment of inattention, when Jeanette first, after weeks of hugging her discomforts to herself, began to confide, in her delicate voice, what she would rather have kept hidden.

The days that followed, full of doctors and their equipment, lifted all secrecy from the disease and its course. It was cancer, metastasizing from the liver, though she had never been a drinker. For Brad, these days were busy ones. After five years of retirement, of not knowing quite what to do with himself, he was suddenly housekeeper, cook, chauffeur, switchboard operator, nurse. Isolated in their big house, while their three children anxiously visited and then hurried back to their own problems, and their friends and neighbors tried to tread the thin line between kindness and interference, the couple that winter had a kind of honeymoon. An air of adventure, of the exotic, tinged their excursions to clinics and specialists tucked into sections of Boston they had never visited before. They spent all their hours together and became, more than ever, one. His own scalp itched as her soft hair fell away under the barrage of chemotherapy; his own stomach ached when she would not eat. She would greet with a bright smile the warmth and aroma of the food he would bring to the table or her bed, and she would take one forkful, so that she could tell him how good it was; then, with a magical slowness meant to make the gesture invisible, Jeanette would let the fork slowly sink back to the plate, keeping her fingers on its silver handle as if at any moment she might decide to use it again. In this position she sometimes even dozed off, under the sway of medication. He learned to treat her refusal to eat as a social lapse he must overlook. If he urged the food upon her, sternly or playfully, real irritation broke through her stoical, drugged calm.

The other irritant, strangely, seemed to be the visits of the young Episcopalian clergyman. He had come to their church this year, after the long reign of a hearty, facetious man no one had had to take seriously. The new man had a self-conscious, honey-smooth voice and curly blond hair already receding, young as he was, from his temples. Brad, who of course knew of the infighting among the search-committee members that had preceded the rector's selection, admired his melodious sermons and his conservative demeanor; ten years ago a clergyman his age would have been trying to radicalize everybody. But Jeanette complained that his visits to the house tired her, though they rarely lasted more than fifteen minutes. When she became too frail, too emaciated and constantly drowsy, to leave her bedroom and the young man offered to bring Communion to her, she asked Brad to tell him, "Another time."

The room at Mass. General Hospital to which she was eventually moved overlooked, across a great air well, a brick wall of windows identical with hers. The wing was modern, built on the rubble of the old West End. It was late March, the first spring of a new decade. Though on sunny days a few giggling nurses and hardy patients took their lunches on cardboard trays out to the patio at the base of the air well, the sky was usually an agitated gray and the hospital heat was still on full blast. During his visits Brad often removed his suit coat, it was so hot in Jeanette's room.

Dressed in a white hospital johnny and a pink quilted bed jacket with ribbons, she looked pretty against her pillows. Her cheeks still had some plumpness, and her fine, straight nose and clear eyes and narrow, arched brows — old-fashioned eyebrows, that looked plucked though they weren't — still made the compact, highly finished impression that had always kindled pride within him. Her hair was growing back, a cap of soft brown bristle, now that chemotherapy had been abandoned. Only her hands, inert and fleshless on the blanket, betrayed that something terrible was happening to her.

One day she told him, with a touch of mischief, "Our young parson was in from Newton this morning, and I told him not to bother anymore."

"You sent the priest away?" Brad's aged voice seemed to rumble and crackle in his ears, in contrast to Jeanette's, crystalline and distant as wind chimes.

"Priest, for heaven's sake," she said. "Why can't you just call him a minister?" It had been a joke of sorts between them, how High Church he had become. When on occasion they had visited the Church of the Advent, on Brimmer Street, she had scorned the incense, the robed teams of acolytes. "He makes me tired," she said.

"But don't you want to keep up with Communion?" It was his

favorite sacrament; he harbored an inner image, a kind of religious fantasy, of the wafer and wine turning, with a muffled explosion, to pure light in the digestive system.

"Like keeping up an insurance policy," she sighed, and did sound tired, tired to death. "It seems so pointless."

"But you *must*," Brad said, panicked.

"I must? Why must I? Who says I must?" The blue of her challenging eyes and the fevered flush of her cheeks made a garish contrast.

"Why, because . . . you know why. Because of the salvation of your soul. That's what you used to talk about when I first met you."

She looked toward the window with a faint smile. "When I used to go alone to Copley Methodist. I loved that church; it was so bizarre, with its minaret. Dear old Doctor Stidger, on and on. Now it's just a parking lot. Salvation of the soul." Her gaunt chest twitched — a laugh that didn't reach her lips.

He lowered his eyes, feeling mocked. His own hands, an old man's gnarled, spotted claws, were folded together between his knees. "You mean you don't believe?" In his inner ear he felt all the height of space concealed beneath the floor.

"Oh, darling," she said. "Doesn't it just seem an awful lot of bother?"

"Not a bit?" he persisted.

Jeanette sighed again and didn't answer.

"Since when?"

"I don't know. No," she said, "that's not being honest. We should start being honest. I do know. Since you took it from me. You moved right in. It didn't seem necessary for the two of us to keep it up."

"But — " He couldn't say, so late, how fondly he had intended it, enlisting at her side.

She offered, to console him, "It doesn't matter, does it?" When he remained silent, feeling blackness all about him, to every point on the horizon, as on those nights in the Pacific, she shifted to a teasing note: "Honey, why does it matter?"

She knew. Because his death was also close. He lifted his eyes and saw her as enviably serene, having wrought this vengeance. A nurse rustled at the door, her syringe tingling in its aluminum tray, and across the air well, in the blue spring twilight, the lights had come on, rectangles of gold. Snow, a few dry flakes, had begun to fall.

Though she had asked that there be absolutely no religious service,

Brad and the young minister arranged one, following the oldest-fash-ioned, impersonal rite. Jeanette would have been seventy-one in May, and he was three years older. He continued to go to the ten o'clock service, his erect figure carrying his white hair like a flag. But it was sheer inert motion; there were no falcon flights of his mind anymore, no small, true voice at his side. There was nothing. He wished he could think otherwise, but he had believed in her all those years and could not stop now.

Eudora Welty

....

A Still Moment

L ORENZO DOW RODE the Old Natchez Trace at top speed
upon a race horse, and the cry of the itinerant Man of God, "I
must have souls! And souls I must have!" rang in his own windy
ears. He rode as if never to stop, toward his night's appointment.

It was the hour of sunset. All the souls that he had saved and all
those he had not took dusky shapes in the mist that hung between the
high banks, and seemed by their great number and density to block his
way, and showed no signs of melting or changing back into mist, so
that he feared his passage was to be difficult forever. The poor souls
that were not saved were darker and more pitiful than those that were,
and still there was not any of the radiance he would have hoped to see
in such a congregation.

"Light up, in God's name!" he called, in the pain of his disappointment.

Then a whole swarm of fireflies instantly flickered all around him,
up and down, back and forth, first one golden light and then another,
flashing without any of the weariness that had held back the souls.
These were the signs sent from God that he had not seen the accumu-
lated radiance of saved souls because he was not able, and that his eyes
were more able to see the fireflies of the Lord than His blessed souls.

"Lord, give me the strength to see the angels when I am in Paradise," he said. "Do not let my eyes remain in this failing proportion to
my loving heart always."

He gasped and held on. It was that day's complexity of horse-trading
that had left him in the end with a Spanish race horse for which he was
bound to send money in November from Georgia. Riding faster on the

beast and still faster until he felt as if he were flying he sent thoughts of love with matching speed to his wife Peggy in Massachusetts. He found it effortless to love at a distance. He could look at the flowering trees and love Peggy in fullness, just as he could see his visions and love God. And Peggy, to whom he had not spoken until he could speak fateful words ("Would she accept of such an object as him?"), Peggy, the bride, with whom he had spent a few hours of time, showing of herself a small round handwriting, declared all in one letter, her first, that she felt the same as he, and that the fear was never of separation, but only of death.

Lorenzo well knew that it was Death that opened underfoot, that rippled by at night, that was the silence the birds did their singing in. He was close to death, closer than any animal or bird. On the back of one horse after another, winding them all, he was always riding toward it or away from it, and the Lord sent him directions with protection in His mind.

Just then he rode into a thicket of Indians taking aim with their new guns. One stepped out and took the horse by the bridle, it stopped at a touch, and the rest made a closing circle. The guns pointed.

"Incline!" The inner voice spoke sternly and with its customary lightning-quickness.

Lorenzo inclined all the way forward and put his head to the horse's silky mane, his body to its body, until a bullet meant for him would endanger the horse and make his death of no value. Prone he rode out through the circle of Indians, his obedience to the voice leaving him almost fearless, almost careless with joy.

But as he straightened and pressed ahead, care caught up with him again. Turning half-beast and half-divine, dividing himself like a heathen Centaur, he had escaped his death once more. But was it to be always by some metamorphosis of himself that he escaped, some humiliation of his faith, some admission to strength and argumentation and not frailty? Each time when he acted so it was at the command of an instinct that he took at once as the word of an angel, until too late, when he knew it was the word of the devil. He had roared like a tiger at Indians, he had submerged himself in water blowing the savage bubbles of the alligator, and they skirted him by. He had prostrated himself to appear dead, and deceived bears. But all the time God would have protected him in His own way, less hurried, more divine.

Even now he saw a serpent crossing the Trace, giving out knowing glances.

He cried, "I know you now!", and the serpent gave him one look out of which all the fire had been taken, and went away in two darts into the tangle.

He rode on, all expectation, and the voices in the throats of the wild beasts went, almost without his noticing when, into words. "Praise God," they said. "Deliver us from one another." Birds especially sang of divine love which was the one ceaseless protection. "Peace, in peace," were their words so many times when they spoke from the briars, in a courteous sort of inflection, and he turned his countenance toward all perched creatures with a benevolence striving to match their own.

He rode on past the little intersecting trails, letting himself be guided by voices and by lights. It was battle-sounds he heard most, sending him on, but sometimes ocean sounds, that long beat of waves that would make his heart pound and retreat as heavily as they, and he despaired again in his failure in Ireland when he took a voyage and persuaded with the Catholics with his back against the door, and then ran away to their cries of "Mind the white hat!" But when he heard singing it was not the militant and sharp sound of Wesley's hymns, but a soft, tireless and tender air that had no beginning and no end, and the softness of distance, and he had pleaded with the Lord to find out if all this meant that it was wicked, but no answer had come.

Soon night would descend, and a camp-meeting ground ahead would fill with its sinners like the sky with its stars. How he hungered for them! He looked in prescience with a longing of love over the throng that waited while the flames of the torches threw change, change, change over their faces. How could he bring them enough, if it were not divine love and sufficient warning of all that could threaten them? He rode on faster. He was a filler of appointments, and he filled more and more, until his journeys up and down creation were nothing but a shuttle, driving back and forth upon the rich expanse of his vision. He was homeless by his own choice, he must be everywhere at some time, and somewhere soon. There hastening in the wilderness on his flying horse he gave the night's torch-lit crowd a premature benediction, he could not wait. He spread his arms out, one at a time for safety, and he wished, when they would all be gathered in by his tin horn blasts and the inspired words would go out over their heads, to

brood above the entire and passionate life of the wide world, to become its rightful part.

He peered ahead. "Inhabitants of Time! The wilderness is your
souls on earth!" he shouted ahead into the treetops. "Look about you,
if you would view the conditions of your spirit, put here by the good
Lord to show you and afright you. These wild places and these trails of
awesome loneliness lie nowhere, nowhere, but in your heart."

A dark man, who was James Murrell the outlaw, rode his horse out of
a cane brake and began going along beside Lorenzo without looking at
him. He had the alternately proud and aggrieved look of a man believing himself to be an instrument in the hands of a power, and when he
was young he said at once to strangers that he was being used by Evil,
or sometimes he stopped a traveler by shouting, "Stop! I'm the Devil!"
He rode along now talking and drawing out his talk, by some deep
control of the voice gradually slowing the speed of Lorenzo's horse
down until both the horses were softly trotting. He would have wondered that nothing he said was heard, not knowing that Lorenzo listened only to voices of whose heavenly origin he was more certain.

Murrell riding along with his victim-to-be, Murrell riding, was Murrell talking. He told away at his long tales, with always a distance and a
long length of time flowing through them, and all centered about a
silent man. In each the silent man would have done a piece of evil, a
robbery or a murder, in a place of long ago, and it was all made for the
revelation in the end that the silent man was Murrell himself, and the
long story had happened yesterday, and the place *here* — the Natchez
Trace. It would only take one dawning look for the victim to see that
all of this was another story and he himself had listened his way into it, and that he too was about to recede in time (to where the dread
was forgotten) for some listener and to live for a listener in the long
ago. Destroy the present! — that must have been the first thing that
was whispered in Murrell's heart — the living moment and the man
that lives in it must die before you can go on. It was his habit to bring
the journey — which might even take days — to a close with a kind of
ceremony. Turning his face at last into the face of the victim, for he
had never seen him before now, he would tower up with the sudden
height of a man no longer the tale teller but the speechless protagon-
ist, silent at last, one degree nearer the hero. Then he would murder
the man.

But it would always start over. This man going forward was going backward with talk. He saw nothing, observed no world at all. The two ends of his journey pulled at him always and held him in a nowhere, half asleep, smiling and witty, dangling his predicament. He was a murderer whose final stroke was over-long postponed, who had to bring himself through the greatest tedium to act, as if the whole wilderness, where he was born, were his impediment. But behind him and before him he kept in sight a victim, he saw a man fixed and stayed at the point of death — no matter how the man's eyes denied it, a victim, hands spreading to reach as if for the first time for life. Contempt! That is what Murrell gave that man.

Lorenzo might have understood, if he had not been in haste, that Murrell in laying hold of a man meant to solve his mystery of being. It was as if other men, all but himself, would lighten their hold on the secret, upon assault, and let it fly free at death. In his violence he was only treating of enigma. The violence shook his own body first, like a force gathering, and now he turned in the saddle.

Lorenzo's despair had to be kindled as well as his ecstasy, and could not come without that kindling. Before the awe-filled moment when the faces were turned up under the flares, as though an angel hand tipped their chins, he had no way of telling whether he would enter the sermon by sorrow or by joy. But at this moment the face of Murrell was turned toward him, turning at last, all solitary, in its full, and Lorenzo would have seized the man at once by his black coat and shaken him like prey for a lost soul, so instantly was he certain that the false fire was in his heart instead of the true fire. But Murrell, quick when he was quick, had put his own hand out, a restraining hand, and laid it on the wavelike flesh of the Spanish race horse, which quivered and shuddered at the touch.

They had come to a great live-oak tree at the edge of a low marshland. The burning sun hung low, like a head lowered on folded arms, and over the long reaches of violet trees the evening seemed still with thought. Lorenzo knew the place from having seen it among many in dreams, and he stopped readily and willingly. He drew rein, and Murrell drew rein, he dismounted and Murrell dismounted, he took a step, and Murrell was there too; and Lorenzo was not surprised at the closeness, how Murrell in his long dark coat and over it his dark face darkening still, stood beside him like a brother seeking light.

But in that moment instead of two men coming to stop by the great forked tree, there were three.

★　　★　　★

From far away, a student, Audubon, had been approaching lightly on the wilderness floor, disturbing nothing in his lightness. The long day of beauty had led him this certain distance. A flock of purple finches that he tried for the first moment to count went over his head. He made a spelling of the soft *pet* of the ivory-billed woodpecker. He told himself always: remember.

Coming upon the Trace, he looked at the high cedars, azure and still as distant smoke overhead, with their silver roots trailing down on either side like the veins of deepness in this place, and he noted some fact to his memory — this earth that wears but will not crumble or slide or turn to dust, they say it exists in one other spot in the world, Egypt — and then forgot it. He walked quietly. All life used this Trace, and he liked to see the animals move along it in direct, oblivious journeys, for they had begun it and made it, the buffalo and deer and the small running creatures before man ever knew where he wanted to go, and birds flew a great mirrored course above. Walking beneath them Audubon remembered how in the cities he had seen these very birds in his imagination, calling them up whenever he wished, even in the hard and glittering outer parlors where if an artist were humble enough to wait, some idle hand held up promised money. He walked lightly and he went as carefully as he had started at two that morning, crayon and paper, a gun, and a small bottle of spirits disposed about his body. (*Note: "The mocking birds so gentle that they would scarcely move out of the way."*) He looked with care; great abundance had ceased to startle him, and he could see things one by one. In Natchez they had told him of many strange and marvelous birds that were to be found here. Their descriptions had been exact, complete, and wildly varying, and he took them for inventions and believed that like all the worldly things that came out of Natchez, they would be disposed of and shamed by any man's excursion into the reality of Nature.

In the valley he appeared under the tree, a sure man, very sure and tender, as if the touch of all the earth rubbed upon him and the stains of the flowery swamp had made him so.

Lorenzo welcomed him and turned fond eyes upon him. To transmute a man into an angel was the hope that drove him all over the world and never let him flinch from a meeting or withhold good-byes for long. This hope insistently divided his life into only two parts, journey and rest. There could be no night and day and love and despair and longing and satisfaction to make partitions in the single ecstasy of this alternation. All things were speech.

"God created the world," said Lorenzo, "and it exists to give testimony. Life is the tongue: speak."

But instead of speech there happened a moment of deepest silence.

Audubon said nothing because he had gone without speaking a word for days. He did not regard his thoughts for the birds and animals as susceptible, in their first change, to words. His long playing on the flute was not in its origin a talking to himself. Rather than speak to order or describe, he would always draw a deer with a stroke across it to communicate his need of venison to an Indian. He had only found words when he discovered that there is much otherwise lost that can be noted down each item in its own day, and he wrote often now in a journal, not wanting anything to be lost the way it had been, all the past, and he would write about a day, "Only sorry that the Sun Sets."

Murrell, his cheated hand hiding the gun, could only continue to smile at Lorenzo, but he remembered in malice that he had disguised himself once as an Evangelist, and his final words to this victim would have been, "One of my disguises was what you are."

Then in Murrell Audubon saw what he thought of as "acquired sorrow" — that cumbrousness and darkness from which the naked Indian, coming just as he was made from God's hand, was so lightly free. He noted the eyes — the dark kind that loved to look through chinks, and saw neither closeness nor distance, light nor shade, wonder nor familiarity. They were narrowed to contract the heart, narrowed to make an averting plan. Audubon knew the finest-drawn tendons of the body and the working of their power, for he had touched them, and he supposed then that in man the enlargement of the eye to see started a motion in the hands to make or do, and that the narrowing of the eye stopped the hand and contracted the heart. Now Murrell's eyes followed an ant on a blade of grass, up the blade and down, many times in the single moment. Audubon had examined the Cave-In Rock where one robber had lived his hiding life, and the air in the cave was the cavelike air that enclosed this man, the same odor, flinty and dark. O secret life, he thought — is it true that the secret is withdrawn from the true disclosure, that man is a cave man, and that the openness I see, the ways through forests, the rivers brimming light, the wide arches where the birds fly, are dreams of freedom? If my origin is withheld from me, is my end to be unknown too? Is the radiance I see closed into an interval between two darks, or can it not illuminate them both and discover at last, though it cannot be spoken, what was thought hidden and lost?

In that quiet moment a solitary snowy heron flew down not far away and began to feed beside the marsh water.

At the single streak of flight, the ears of the race horse lifted, and the eyes of both horses filled with the soft lights of sunset, which in the next instant were reflected in the eyes of the men too as they all looked into the west toward the heron, and all eyes seemed infused with a sort of wildness.

Lorenzo gave the bird a triumphant look, such as a man may bestow upon his own vision, and thought, Nearness is near, lighted in a marsh-land, feeding at sunset. Praise God, His love has come visible.

Murrell, in suspicion pursuing all glances, blinking into a haze, saw only whiteness ensconced in darkness, as if it were a little luminous shell that drew in and held the eyesight. When he shaded his eyes, the brand "H.T." on his thumb thrust itself into his own vision, and he looked at the bird with the whole plan of the Mystic Rebellion darting from him as if in rays of the bright reflected light, and he stood looking proudly, leader as he was bound to become of the slaves, the brigands and outcasts of the entire Natchez country, with plans, dates, maps burning like a brand into his brain, and he saw himself proudly in a moment of prophecy going down rank after rank of successively bow-ing slaves to unroll and flaunt an awesome great picture of the Devil colored on a banner.

Audubon's eyes embraced the object in the distance and he could see it as carefully as if he held it in his hand. It was a snowy heron alone out of its flock. He watched it steadily, in his care noting the exact inevitable things. When it feeds it muddies the water with its foot. . . . It was as if each detail about the heron happened slowly in time, and only once. He felt again the old stab of wonder — what structure of life bridged the reptile's scale and the heron's feather? That knowledge too had been lost. He watched without moving. The bird was defense-less in the world except for the intensity of its life, and he wondered, how can heat of blood and speed of heart defend it? Then he thought, as always as if it were new and unbelievable, it has nothing in space or time to prevent its flight. And he waited, knowing that some birds will wait for a sense of their presence to travel to men before they will fly away from them.

Fixed in its pure white profile it stood in the precipitous moment, a plumicorn on its head, its breeding dress extended in rays, eating steadily the little water creatures. There was a little space between each man and the others, where they stood overwhelmed. No one could say the three had ever met, or that this moment of intersection had ever come in their lives, or its promise fulfilled. But before them the white heron rested in the grasses with the evening all around it, lighter and more serene than the evening, flight closed in its body, the circuit of its beauty closed, a bird seen and a bird still, its motion calm as if it were offered: Take my flight . . .

What each of them had wanted was simply *all*. To save all souls, to destroy all men, to see and to record all life that filled this world — all, all — but now a single frail yearning seemed to go out of the three of them for a moment and to stretch toward this one snowy, shy bird in the marshes. It was as if three whirlwinds had drawn together at some center, to find there feeding in peace a snowy heron. Its own slow spiral of flight could take it away in its own time, but for a little it held them still, it laid quiet over them, and they stood for a moment unburdened. . . .

Murrell wore no mask, for his face was that, a face that was aware while he was somnolent, a face that watched for him, and listened for him, alert and nearly brutal, the guard of a planner. He was quick without that he might be slow within, he staved off time, he wandered and plotted, and yet his whole desire mounted in him toward the end (was this the end — the sight of a bird feeding at dusk?), toward the instant of confession. His incessant deeds were thick in his heart now, and flinging himself to the ground he thought wearily, when all these trees are cut down, and the Trace lost, then my Conspiracy that is yet to spread itself will be disclosed, and all the stone-loaded bodies of murdered men will be pulled up, and all everywhere will know poor Murrell. His look pressed upon Lorenzo, who stared upward, and Audubon, who was taking out his gun, and his eyes squinted up to them in pleading, as if to say, "How soon may I speak, and how soon will you pity me?" Then he looked back to the bird, and he thought if it would look at him a dread penetration would fill and gratify his heart.

Audubon in each act of life was aware of the mysterious origin he half concealed and half sought for. People along the way asked him in their kindness or their rudeness if it were true, that he was born a prince, and was the Lost Dauphin, and some said it was his secret, and some said that that was what he wished to find out before he died. But if it was his identity that he wished to discover, or if it was what a man had to seize beyond that, the way for him was by endless examination, by the care for every bird that flew in his path and every serpent that shone underfoot. Not one was enough; he looked deeper and deeper, on and on, as if for a particular beast or some legendary bird. Some men's eyes persisted in looking outward when they opened to look inward, and to their delight, there outflung was the astonishing world under the sky. When a man at last brought himself to face some mirror-surface he still saw the world looking back at him, and if he continued to look, to look closer and closer, what then? The gaze that looks outward must be trained without rest, to be indomitable. It must see as slowly as Murrell's ant in the grass, as exhaustively as Lorenzo's angel of God, and then, Audubon dreamed, with his mind going to his pointed brush, it must see like this, and he tightened his hand on the trigger of the gun and pulled it, and his eyes went closed. In memory the heron was all its solitude, its total beauty. All its whiteness could be seen from all sides at once, its pure feathers were as if counted and known and their array one upon the other would never be lost. But it was not from that memory that he could paint.

His opening eyes met Lorenzo's, close and flashing, and it was on seeing horror deep in them, like fires in abysses, that he recognized it for the first time. He had never seen horror in its purity and clarity until now, in bright blue eyes. He went and picked up the bird. He had thought it to be a female, just as one sees the moon as female; and so it was. He put it in his bag, and started away. But Lorenzo had already gone on, leaning a-tilt on the horse which went slowly.

Murrell was left behind, but he was proud of the dispersal, as if he had done it, as if he had always known that three men in simply being together and doing a thing can, by their obstinacy, take the pride out of one another. Each must go away alone, each send the others away alone. He himself had purposely kept to the wildest country in the world, and would have sought it out, the loneliest road. He looked about with satisfaction, and hid. Travelers were forever innocent, he believed: that was his faith. He lay in wait; his faith was in innocence and his knowledge was of ruin; and had these things been shaken? Now, what could possibly be outside his grasp? Churning all about him like a cloud about the sun was the great folding descent of his thought. Plans of deeds made his thoughts, and they rolled and mingled about his ears as if he heard a dark voice that rose up to overcome the wilderness voice, or was one with it. The night would soon come; and he had gone through the day.

Audubon, splattered and wet, turned back into the wilderness with the heron warm under his hand, his head still light in a kind of trance. It was undeniable, on some Sunday mornings, when he turned over and over his drawings they seemed beautiful to him, through what was dramatic in the conflict of life, or what was exact. What he would draw, and what he had seen, became for a moment one to him then. Yet soon enough, and it seemed to come in that same moment, like Lorenzo's horror and the gun's firing, he knew that even the sight of the heron which surely he alone had appreciated, had not been all his belonging, and that never could any vision, even any simple sight, belong to him or to any man. He knew that the best he could make would be, after it was apart from his hand, a dead thing and not a live thing, never the essence, only a sum of parts; and that it would always meet with a stranger's sight, and never be one with the beauty in any other man's head in the world. As he had seen the bird most purely at its moment of death, in some fatal way, in his care for looking outward, he saw his long labor most revealingly at the point where it met its limit. Still carefully, for he was trained to see well in the dark, he walked on into the deeper woods, noting all sights, all sounds, and was gentler than they as he went.

In the woods that echoed yet in his ears, Lorenzo riding slowly looked back. The hair rose on his head and his hands began to shake with cold, and suddenly it seemed to him that God Himself, just now, thought of the Idea of Separateness. For surely He had never thought of it before, when the little white heron was flying down to feed. He could understand God's giving Separateness first and then giving Love to follow and heal in its wonder; but God had reversed this, and given Love first and then Separateness, as though it did not matter to Him which came first. Perhaps it was that God never counted the moments of Time; Lorenzo did that, among his tasks of love. Time did not occur to God. Therefore — did He even know of it? How to explain Time and Separateness back to God, Who had never thought of them, Who could let the whole world come to grief in a scattering moment?

Lorenzo brought his cold hands together in a clasp and stared through the distance at the place where the bird had been as if he saw it still; as if nothing could really take away what had happened to him, the beautiful little vision of the feeding bird. Its beauty had been greater than he could account for. The sweat of rapture poured down from his forehead, and then he shouted into the marshes.

"Tempter!"

He whirled forward in the saddle and began to hurry the horse to its high speed. His camp ground was far away still, though even now they must be lighting the torches and gathering in the multitudes, so that at the appointed time he would duly appear in their midst, to deliver his address on the subject of "In that day when all hearts shall be disclosed."

Then the sun dropped below the trees, and the new moon, slender and white, hung shyly in the west.

Tobias Wolff

....

The Missing Person

F ATHER LEO had started out with the idea of becoming a missionary. He had read a priest's account of his years among the Aleuts and decided that this was the life for him — trekking from trapper's hut to Indian village, a dog for company, sacramental wine in his knapsack, across snowfields that gleamed like sugar. He knew it would be hard. He would suffer things he could not imagine in that polar solitude. But that was the life he wanted, a life full of risk among people who needed him and were hungry for what he had to give.

Shortly before his ordination he asked to be sent to Alaska. The diocese turned down his request. The local parishes were short of young priests, and their needs came first. Father Leo was assigned to a parish in West Seattle, where the pastor took an immediate dislike to him and put him on what he called "crone duty" — managing rummage sales, bingo, and the Legion of Mary, and visiting old parishioners in the hospital. Father Leo worked hard at everything he put his hand to. He hoped that the old priest would notice and begin to soften toward him, but that never happened.

He stayed on in the parish. The old priest kept going, though his mind had begun to wander and he could not walk without a stick. He repeated his sermons again and again. There was one story he told at least once a month, about an Irishman who received a visitation from his mother the night after her death, a visit that caused him to change his whole life. He told the story with a brogue, and it went on forever.

The parishioners didn't seem to mind. More of them came every year, and they kept the old priest busy from morning to night. He liked to say that he didn't have time to die. One night he said it at dinner and Father Leo thought, *Make time.* Then he felt so ashamed that he couldn't eat the rest of his meal. But the thought kept coming back.

Finally the old priest did die. Father Leo collected his papers for the diocese and found copies of several reports the old priest had made on him. They were all disparaging, and some of them contained charges that were untrue. He sat on the floor and read them through carefully. Then he put them down and rubbed his eyes. It was the first warm night of the year. The window was open. A moth fluttered against the screen.

Father Leo was surprised at what he'd found. He couldn't understand why the old priest had hated him. But the more he thought about it the less strange it seemed. Father Leo had been in love once, before entering the seminary, and remembered the helplessness of it. There had been no reason for him to be in love with the girl: she was no better than other girls he knew, and apart from loving her he didn't like her very much.

Still, he probably would have married her if he had not felt even greater helplessness before his conviction that he should become a priest. He thought that as a priest he would be necessary to people. She didn't seem to need him all that much. Nevertheless, she was desolate when he told her what he was planning to do, to the point that he nearly changed his mind. Then she lost interest. A few months later, she married another man.

Vocation was a mystery, love was a mystery, and Father Leo supposed that hatred was a mystery. The old priest had been pulled under by it. That was a shame, but Father Leo knew better than to ponder its meaning for him.

A monsignor from the chancery was named to succeed the old priest. Father Leo brooded. He began to fear that he would never get his own parish. One night, driving back to the rectory from a visit to the home of a sick woman, he suddenly began to shake. He was shaking so badly that he had to pull off the road until it passed. For the first time, Father Leo considered leaving the priesthood, as many of his friends had done. But he could not get it out of his head that he was meant to be a priest. *Patience,* he told himself.

The monsignor asked Father Leo to stay on and teach religion in the parish elementary school. Father Leo agreed. At the end of their interview, the monsignor asked if there were any hard feelings.

"Not at all," Father Leo said, and made himself smile.

When school began in September his feelings of resentment left him. The students liked Father Leo. They were troubled and cruel to each other but they were still curious about things that mattered: what they should believe in, how they should live. They paid attention to what Father Leo said, and he felt happy enough to be where he was.

Every couple of years or so the diocese sent out new books to religion teachers. Father Leo found the changes confusing and stopped trying to keep up. When the books came in he put them on a shelf and forgot about them. That was how he got fired. His classes were inspected by a priest from the education office that sent the books, and soon afterward Father Leo received a summons. He went before a committee. After they questioned him, the chairman sent a letter to the monsignor saying that Father Leo's ideas were obsolete, and peculiar. The committee suggested that he be replaced.

The monsignor took Father Leo out to dinner at a seafood house and explained the situation to him. The suggestion of the committee was actually a directive, he said. The monsignor had no choice in the matter. But he had been calling around and had found an open position, if Father Leo was interested. Mother Vincent at Star of the Sea needed a new chaplain. Their last chaplain had married one of the nuns. It so happened, the monsignor said, looking into his wine, swirling it gently, that he had done several favors for Mother Vincent in his days at the chancery. In short, if Father Leo wanted the position he could have it. The monsignor lit a cigarette and looked out the window, over the water. Gulls were diving for scraps.

He seemed embarrassed, and Father Leo knew why. It was a job for an old priest, or one recovering from something: sickness, alcohol, a breakdown. Father Leo looked at his hands folded on the tablecloth. He thought of Bishop Thangbrand, who had come among the savage Vikings of Iceland and converted the entire population in three weeks by beating to death with a heavy crucifix anyone who dared to argue with him.

"Where will I live?" he asked.

"At the convent," the monsignor said.

Something had gone wrong at Star of the Sea. It was an unhappy place. Some of the sisters were boisterous, and their noise made the silence of the others seem that much deeper. Coming upon these sad, silent nuns in the corridor or on the grounds, Father Leo felt a chill. It was like swimming into a cold pocket in a lake.

Several nuns had left the order. Others were thinking of it. They came to Father Leo and complained about the noise and confusion. They couldn't understand what was happening. Father Leo told them what he told himself — Be patient. But the truth was that his own patience had begun to give out.

He was supposed to be spiritual adviser to the convent. Many of the nuns disregarded him, though. They went their own way. The director of novices described herself as a "Post-Christian" and at Easter sent out cards showing an Indian god ascending to the clouds with arms waving out of his sides like a centipede's. Some held jobs in town. The original idea had been for the nuns to serve the community in some way, but now they did what they wanted to do. One was a disc jockey.

The rowdy nuns ran around together and played pranks. Their jokes were good-natured but often in bad taste, and they didn't know when to stop. A couple of them had stereos and played weird music at night. The hallways echoed with their voices.

They called Father Leo "Padre," or just "Pod." When he walked past them they usually made some crack or asked a cute question. They made racy jokes about Jerry, the fellow Mother Vincent had hired to raise funds. They were always laughing about something.

One evening he went to Mother Vincent's office and told her, again, that the convent was in trouble. This was his third visit that month, and she made it plain that she was not glad to see him. She neither rose to meet him nor invited him to sit down. While he talked she gazed out the open window and rubbed the knuckles of her huge red hands. Father Leo could see that she was listening to the crickets, not to him, and he lost heart.

Mother Vincent was strong, but old and drifting. She had no idea what was going on downstairs. Her office and rooms were on the top floor of the building, separate from the others, and her life took place even further away than that. She lived in her dream of what the convent was. She believed that it was a perfect song, all voices tuned, sweet and cool and pure, rising and falling in measure. Her strength had hardened around that dream. It was more than Father Leo could contend with.

He broke off, though he hadn't finished what he had come to say. She went on staring out the window at the darkness. Her hands grew still in her lap.

"Father," she said, "I wonder if you are happy with us."

He waited.

"Because if you are not happy at Star of the Sea," she went on, "the last thing I would want to do is keep you here." She looked at him. She said, "Is there anywhere else you want to be?"

Father Leo took her meaning, or thought he did. She meant, Is there anywhere else that would have you? He shook his head.

"Of course you hear complaints," she said. "You will always hear complaints. Every convent has its sob-sister element. Myself, I would trade ten wilting pansies for one Sister Gervaise any day. High spirits. A sense of humor. You need a sense of humor in this life, Father."

Mother Vincent drew her chair up to the desk. "If you don't mind my saying so, Father," she said, "you are inclined to take yourself too seriously. You think too much about your own problems. That's because you don't have enough to keep you busy here." She put her hands on the desk top and folded them together. She said that she had a suggestion to make. Jerry, her fund-raiser, needed some help. The convent could not afford to hire another man, but she saw no reason why Father Leo couldn't pitch in. It would be good for him. It would be good for everyone.

"I've never done any fund-raising before," Father Leo said. But later that night, back in his room, he began to like the idea. It meant that he would meet new people. He would be doing something different. Most of all, it meant that he would be getting out every day, away from this unhappy place.

Father Leo had coffee with Jerry a few mornings later. Though the weather was warm, Jerry had on a three-piece suit, which he kept adjusting. He was nearly as tall as Father Leo but much thicker. There were lines across the front of his vest where the buttons strained. Rings sparkled on his thick, blunt fingers as he moved his hands over the sheets of paper he had spread on the table. The papers were filled with figures showing what the convent's debts were, and how fast they were growing.

Father Leo hadn't known any of this. It came as a surprise to him to learn that they could owe so much — that it was allowed. He studied the papers. He felt good bending over the table with Jerry, the smell of coffee rising up from the mug in his hand.

"That's not all of it," Jerry said. "Not by a long shot. Let me show you what we're actually looking at here." He took Father Leo on a tour. He pointed out the old pipes, the warped window frames, the cracked foundations. He dug at the crumbling mortar in the walls and even pulled out a brick. He turned a flashlight on pools of scummy water in the vast basement. At the end of the tour, Jerry added everything up — debts, operating expenses, and the cost of putting the physical plant back in shape.

Father Leo looked at the figures. He whistled.

"I've seen worse," Jerry said. "Our Lady of Perpetual Help was twice as bad as this, and I had them in the black in two years. It's easy. You go where the money is and you bring the money back."

They were standing beside an empty greenhouse with most of the windows broken out. Shards of glass glittered at their feet. It had rained earlier, and now everything seemed unnaturally bright: the snowcap on Mount Rainier, the grass, the white sails of the boats on Puget Sound. The sun was at Father Leo's back, shining into Jerry's face. Jerry squinted as he talked. Father Leo saw little scars under his eyes. His nose was puffy.

"I should tell you," Father Leo said. "I've never raised funds before."

"Nothing to it," Jerry said. "But first you have to make up your mind whether you really want the money. You ask yourself, is it worth going after or isn't it? Then, if the answer is yes, you go after it." He looked at Father Leo. "So, what is it? Yes or no?"

"Yes," Father Leo said.

"All right! That's the big step. The rest is easy. You don't mess around. You don't get hung up on details. You do whatever you have to do and keep going. It's the only way. The question is, can you work like that?" Jerry brushed some brick dust off his jacket. He straightened his vest. He looked down at his shoes, then at Father Leo.

"I think so," Father Leo said.

"You have to be a gunslinger," Jerry said. "No doubts. No pity."

"I understand," Father Leo said.

"All right," Jerry said. "Just so you know how I work. My philosophy." He pulled a flask from his jacket pocket, drank from it, and held it out to Father Leo. "Go on," he said. Father Leo took it. The flask was silver, half-covered with leather, and engraved with initials below the neck. They weren't Jerry's initials. The liquor burned. Father Leo became aware of the sun on the back of his neck, the sighing of the trees. They each had another drink, then Jerry put the flask away. "Cognac," he said. "Napoleon's brand. So, what do you think? Partners?"

"Partners," Father Leo said.

"Bueno," Jerry said. He slapped his leg and brought his hand up like a pistol. "Okay," he said, "let's ride."

The plan was for Father Leo to go with Jerry and watch how he approached potential donors. Then, once he got the hang of it, he could go out on his own. Jerry coached him on the way to their first interview. He said that the big thing was to make it personal. Nobody wanted to hear about old furnaces. You had to do your homework, you had to know your man — in this case, your woman. Here they had a lady who went to Lourdes every year. She'd been to Lourdes more than twenty times. That meant she had a special interest in crippled people. She had a big heart and she had money. Going to France wasn't like going to Mexico.

The woman was standing at the door when they arrived. Father Leo followed Jerry up the walk, moving slowly, because Jerry had assumed what appeared to be a painful limp. He had endless trouble with the steps but refused the woman's help. "I can manage," he said. "There's plenty worse off than me. I just think of them and it's easy."

Jerry did all the talking when they got inside. Now and then the woman looked over at Father Leo, but he would not meet her eyes. Jerry was describing a number of projects that Star of the Sea had developed for the handicapped, all of them imaginary. He implied that most of the nuns were devoted to this particular work and that he himself had been rescued by their efforts. Jerry's voice cracked. He looked away for a moment, then went on. When he finished, the woman served tea and wrote out a check.

Not everyone they visited gave them money. One old man laughed in their faces when Jerry told him that the convent had been built on orders from the Blessed Mother, and that she was taking a personal interest in the fund drive. When the old man stopped laughing he threw them out. "You must take me for an idiot," he said.

Not everyone gave, but most people did. Jerry would say anything. He said that the convent helped orphans, lepers, Navahos, earthquake victims, even pandas and seals. There was no end to what he would do.

Jerry had a saying: "If you want the apples, you have to shake the tree."

Father Leo knew that he should disapprove of Jerry's methods, but he didn't. That is, he felt no disapproval. The people they visited lived in Broadmoor and Windermere. They had plenty of money, too much money. It was good for them to share it. Anyway, Jerry was a performer, not a liar. Lying was selfish, furtive, low. What Jerry did was reckless and grand, for a good cause.

Father Leo did not want to go out on his own. He would never be able to carry on the way Jerry did in front of complete strangers. He did not have the courage. He would fail.

Besides, he was having the time of his life. Jerry called him "Slim," and he liked that. He liked getting into Jerry's big car and driving through the convent gate with no idea what would happen that day. He looked forward to the lunches they ate downtown — club sandwiches, fruit platters, big salads covered with diced cheese and ham. Then the coffee afterward, and one of Jerry's stories about his days in the Navy. Father Leo came to need these pleasures, most of all the pleasure of watching Jerry have it his way with people who were used to having it their way.

As it happened, they did not split up after all. Jerry tallied their take for the month and decided that they should stick together. The receipts were almost double the average. He said that as a team they were unbeatable. He had the blarney and Father Leo had the collar, which Jerry called "The Persuader."

They would go on as before. Father Leo's job was just to sit there. He didn't have to say anything. If someone should look at him in a questioning way, all he had to do was close his eyes. No nodding. No murmuring.

"We'll rake it in," Jerry said, and they did.

When they finished their rounds, Jerry and Father Leo usually had a drink at a fern bar on the wharf. They sat in a booth and Jerry told stories about his life. He'd sold cars and worked as a private detective. For two years, he had been a professional fighter. He had been everywhere and seen everything. In Singapore he had witnessed a murder, one man shooting another man right in the face. "Just like you'd shoot a can," Jerry said. Later he'd heard the men were brothers. He had seen men make love to each other on board ship. In Dakar he'd watched a woman with knobs where her arms should have been paint pictures of sailors, take their money, and give them change, all with her toes. He had seen children chained to a wall, for sale.

So he said. Father Leo did not believe all the stories Jerry told him. He couldn't. Roughly speaking, he believed about half of what he heard. That was fine with him. He didn't mind having his leg pulled. He thought it was the sort of thing men did in lumber camps and on ships — sitting around, swapping lies.

Just before Thanksgiving they had a meeting with a vice president of an airplane corporation. The man wore sunglasses during the interview. It was hard to tell what he was thinking. Father Leo guessed that he was trying to keep his temper, because in his opinion Jerry had chosen the wrong line to follow. Jerry was going on about missiles and bombers and instruments of destruction. He suggested that the man had a lot to make amends for. Father Leo wanted to get out. When Jerry was through, the vice president sat there behind his desk and stared at them. He said nothing. Father Leo became uncomfortable, then angry. This was obviously some technique the vice president used to bully his subordinates. "You ought to be ashamed of yourself," Father Leo said.

The vice president suddenly bent over. He buried his face in the crook of his arm. "You don't know the half of it," he said. His shoulders began to jerk.

Jerry looked at Father Leo and gave the thumbs-up. He went around the desk and stood behind the man. "There, there," he said.

Finally the vice president stopped crying. He took off his sunglasses and wiped his eyes. "I needed that," he said. "By God, I needed that." He went into the adjoining room and came back with a plastic garbage bag. It was full of money, but he would not let Jerry count it in the office or give him a receipt. He insisted that the gift remain anonymous. As he showed them out of the office he took Father Leo by the sleeve. "Pray for me," he said.

They counted the money in the car. It came to almost seven thousand dollars, all in twenties. Jerry locked it in the trunk and they went to the fern bar to celebrate. Jerry's cheeks were red and they grew redder as he drank cognac after cognac. Father Leo did not try to keep up with him, but he drank more than usual and became a little giddy. Now and then the young people at the bar turned and smiled at him. He could see that they were thinking, What a jolly priest! That was all right. He wanted to look like someone with good news, not like someone with bad news.

Jerry held up his glass. "The team," he said, and Father Leo said, "The team." They toasted each other. "I'll tell you what," Jerry said. "We have a bonus coming, and I'm going to see that we get it if I have to break Vincent's arm." When Father Leo asked what kind of a bonus Jerry had in mind, Jerry said, "How about Thanksgiving in Vegas?"

"Las Vegas?"

"You bet. We're riding a streak. We've made plenty for Vincent, why shouldn't we make a little for ourselves?"

Father Leo knew that Mother Vincent would never agree, so he said, "Sure. Why not?" and they touched glasses again.

"Slim, you're something," Jerry said. "You're really something." He shook his head. "You're as bad as I am."

Father Leo smiled.

Jerry said, "I'm going to tell you something I've never told anyone before. Maybe I shouldn't even tell you." He lit a cigar and blew smoke at the ceiling. "Hell with it," he said. He leaned forward. In a low voice he told Father Leo that Jerry was not his real name. Royce, his last name, was also made up. He'd taken it from Rolls-Royce, his favorite car.

It happened like this. He had been selling insurance in San Diego a few years back, and some of his clients complained because they didn't get the benefits he had promised them. It was his own fault. He had overdone it, laid it on too thick. He would be the first to admit that. Anyway, he'd had to change names. There was no choice, not if he wanted to keep working and stay out of jail. The worst of it was that his wife left town with their son. He hadn't seen them since, had no idea where they were. In some ways, looking back on it, he thought that it was for the best. They didn't get along and she was holding him back. Always criticizing. If she'd had her way he'd still be in the Navy, pulling down a hundred and forty dollars a month. "She loved it," he said. "So did I, at least for a while. We were just kids. We didn't know from Adam."

Jerry looked at the people in the next booth, then at Father Leo. He said, "Do you want to know what my real name is?"

Father Leo nodded. But just when Jerry was about to speak he interrupted. "Maybe you'd better not tell me," he said. "It's probably not such a good idea."

Jerry looked disappointed. Father Leo felt bad, but he didn't want that kind of power, the power to send a man to jail. He was also afraid that Jerry would start wondering about him all the time, whether he could be trusted, whether he would tell. It would spoil everything. They sat for a while without talking. Father Leo knew that it was his turn. He should open up and talk about himself for a change. But there was nothing to tell. He had no stories. Not one.

Outside it was raining. Cars went past with a hissing sound. Father Leo said, "Jerry?" His throat felt scratchy. He did not know what he would say next.

Jerry moved in his seat and looked at him.

"You've got to keep this to yourself," Father Leo said.

Jerry pulled his thumb and forefinger across his lips as if he were closing a zipper. "It stops here," he said.

"All right," Father Leo said. He took a sip from his drink. Then he started talking. He said that when he was a senior in high school he had been waiting for a bus when he heard someone scream across the road. He ran over and saw a woman on her knees, hanging on to the belt of a man with a purse in his hand. The man turned and kicked the woman in the face. "I guess I went berserk," Father Leo said. The next thing he knew, the police were dragging him off the man's body. The man was dead. Father Leo said that they'd had to pry his fingers off the man's throat one by one.

"Jesus," Jerry said.

Father Leo looked out the window. "That's why I became a priest," he said. "To atone for the blood on my hands."

"Jesus," Jerry said again. His face dissolved and came together in a way that was new to Father Leo. He looked young and amazed, fresh as he must have been when he stepped for the first time onto a strange land, before his name was Jerry. There were tears in his eyes. He looked at Father Leo and tried to smile but his mouth wouldn't hold the shape. Finally he reached out and squeezed Father Leo's shoulder. He squeezed it again, then got up and went to the bar.

Oh, no, Father Leo thought. What have I done?

Jerry came back with fresh drinks. He sat down and slid one over to Father Leo. His eyes were still misty. "Vegas," he said, and raised his glass.

"Vegas," Father Leo said.

Mother Vincent gave them the bonus. Thanksgiving weekend in Las Vegas, all expenses paid — air fare, hotel, meals, and a hundred dollars apiece in gambling coupons. The trip was arranged at discount by a nun who worked as a travel agent.

When Jerry picked Father Leo up for the ride to the airport he shook his head. "I knew it," he said.

"Knew what?"

"The outfit," Jerry said. "There's nothing in the rules that says you have to wear your outfit on vacation, is there?" He stopped at a clothing store and bought Father Leo two Western shirts with mother-of-pearl buttons and a pair of Western pants. The store did not carry boots. Father Leo was glad, though he could see that Jerry didn't think much of the square black shoes showing beneath his cuffs.

"Something is going to happen," Jerry said later, on the plane. "I feel it. Something big. We're going to come home with gold in our saddlebags."

"I don't know," Father Leo said.

"Listen," Jerry said. "We are two serious hombres and we are about to bust this town wide open. We'll never work again. It is written." He leaned past Father Leo and looked down at the cluster of lights that pulsed in the darkness below. "Vegas," he whispered.

They found a commotion in the hotel lobby when they arrived. A woman was yelling that her room had been broken into. Two men in fringed leather jackets tried to calm her down, and finally managed to lead her to an office behind the registration desk. As he stood in line Father Leo could hear her voice, high and breaking. He picked up the room keys and meal coupons and gambling chips, and turned around just in time to see Jerry win twelve dollars at one of the quarter slots by the Hertz counter. The coins slid out of the machine onto the tile floor with a steady ringing sound and rolled in every direction. Jerry got down on his hands and knees and crawled after them. Nobody paid any attention except a red-haired man in silver pants who went over to Jerry and touched his shoulder, then hurried away.

They ate dinner in the hotel, the only place where their coupons were good. Jerry spent his winnings on a bottle of wine, to celebrate. He couldn't get over it — a jackpot the first time around. "Figure the odds on that," he said. "It's an omen. It means we can't lose."

"I'm not much of a gambler," Father Leo said. It was true. He had never won a bet in his life. The chips they'd been given were negotiable and he intended to cash them in just before he left and buy his sister something nice for Christmas, something he would not usually be able to afford. For now they were squirreled away in the bottom of his suitcase.

"Who's talking about gambling?" Jerry said. "I'm talking about fate. You know what I mean."

"I guess I don't," Father Leo said. "Not really."

"Sure you do. What about the guy you killed? It was fate that put you there. It was fate that you became a priest."

Father Leo saw how the lie had grown. It had taken on a meaning and the meaning was false. He felt tired of himself. He said, "Jerry, it isn't true."

"What isn't true?"

"I never killed anyone."

Jerry smiled at him. "Come off it."

"I've never even been in a fight," Father Leo said.

Jerry looked at him. "Then why are you a priest?"

Father Leo wanted to explain, but the words wouldn't come. The moment passed.

Jerry leaned forward. "Look," he said, "you shouldn't feel guilty about it. It was that kind of a situation. I would have done the same thing in your shoes. That's what I told Sister Gervaise."

"No," Father Leo said. "You didn't."

"Don't worry," Jerry said. "She promised not to tell anyone. The thing is, she made a crack about you and I wanted to set her straight. It worked, too. She went white as a ghost. She looked about ready to hemorrhage. You should have seen her."

"She's a gossip," Father Leo said. "She'll tell everyone. She'll tell Mother Vincent."

"I made her promise," Jerry said. "She gave her word."

"So did you."

Jerry tore out a coupon and put it on the table. He ground out his cigar. "This conversation isn't going anywhere," he said. "What's done is done. We're in Get Rich City now, and it's time to start raking it in."

There was a small casino on the other side of the lobby. Jerry suggested that they start there. He sat down at the blackjack table. Father Leo moved up and watched the play. He was pretending to study Jerry's tactics, but none of it made any sense to him. He could think only of Sister Gervaise turning white. He felt as if he must be turning white himself. "I'm going upstairs," he told Jerry. "I'll be back in a little while."

*   *   *

Father Leo sat on the balcony outside his room. In the courtyard below he saw a pool, turquoise, heart-shaped, lit by underwater lights. He gripped the armrests of his chair. His body felt strange to him and far away. He could not stop thinking of Sister Gervaise, stricken and pale. What was he supposed to do? He couldn't have Mother Vincent and the others believing that he had killed a man. It would terrify them. On the other hand, he didn't want them to think that he went around telling crazy lies about himself. In its own way, that was just as bad. He put his head in his hands. He couldn't think. Finally he gave up and went back downstairs.

Another man had taken Jerry's place at the blackjack table. Father Leo couldn't find Jerry at any of the other tables and he wasn't at the bar or in the lobby. On the chance that he'd gone to his room, Father Leo called upstairs on the house phone. No one answered. Finally he went outside and stood under the awning beside the doorman. A greyhound wearing a sweater and pulling an old woman behind him stopped and lifted his leg over a small border of flowers in front of the hotel. While the dog relieved itself, the woman glared at the doorman. He looked back at her but didn't say anything.

People spilled over into the street, all moving in different directions. Everyone was shouting and the cars were blowing their horns. All along the street colored lights flashed names and pictures. Farther down was a sign that must have been twenty feet high, showing a line of girls in cowboy boots and bikinis. Every so often they kicked up their legs this way and that. They were smiling, and every tooth was a little light.

There was no point in looking for anyone out there. Father Leo went back inside and took a seat at the bar. From the bar he could keep an eye on both the lobby and the casino. He sipped at his drink and glanced around. A young couple in identical Hawaiian shirts sat silently side by side. A heavy-set Indian was poking out numbers on a punchboard. At the end of the bar a pretty woman was ransacking a handbag and muttering to herself. Finally she found what she was after — cigarettes. She lit one, pursed her lips, and blew out a long stream of smoke. She had on bright red lipstick. Her hair was blonde, almost white against her sun-darkened skin. She noticed that Father Leo was looking at her, and she looked back. She smiled. He gave a little nod. His drink was almost full, but he finished it off and left the bar.

Father Leo sat in the lobby for an hour, reading newspapers. Every time someone came in he looked up. When he felt himself beginning to doze off he went to the desk and talked to the clerk. Jerry had left his key, but no message. "That's strange," Father Leo said. He walked across the lobby to the elevator. The woman from the bar was standing inside, holding the door for him. "What floor?" she said.

"Five. Thank you."

"Coincidence," she said. "That's my floor, too." She smiled. Father Leo stared at himself in the mirrored wall. Next to him the woman kept smiling at his reflection. She was about his age, older than he'd thought. He saw that she was badly sunburned except for a white circle around each eye. He could almost feel the heat coming off her pink skin. She was tapping one foot.

"Been here long?" she asked.

He shook his head. The elevator stopped and they got out. She walked beside him down the corridor. "I flew in two days ago," she said. "I don't mind telling you I've been having a ball." When Father Leo put his key into the lock she read the number of his door. "Five-fifteen. That's easy to remember. I always leave work at five-fifteen. I could leave at five but I like it when everyone's gone. I like to just sit and look out the window. It's so peaceful."

"Good night," Father Leo said. She was still talking when he closed the door. He sat for a time on his balcony. High palms surrounded the pool, and overhead shone a silver crescent moon. Father Leo thought of a band of marauders camped by a well in the desert, roasting a lamb over a spitting fire, the silver moon reflected in the chasing of their long inlaid rifles: veiled women moving here and there in silence, doing as they were told.

Before he went to bed Father Leo called the desk. Jerry's key was still on its hook.

"It's only twelve-thirty," the clerk said. "You could try later."

Father Leo turned out the lights. The ceiling sparkled. He was staring at it when he thought he heard a sound at the door. He sat up. "Who's there?" he called. When no one answered he said, "Jerry?" The sound did not come again, and Father Leo lay back on the bed. After a while he slept.

On his way to breakfast the next morning Father Leo stopped by the front desk. Jerry still hadn't come in. Father Leo left a message — "I'm in the coffee shop" — and when he finished eating he changed it to "Went out. Be back soon."

Though it was just after eleven, the street was already jammed with people. A dry breeze blew, bearing a faint smell that was strange to Father Leo but made him think of the word "sage." The light shimmered. Off in the distance, purple mountains floated on a lake of blue that appeared and vanished to the beat of Father Leo's pulse, which he felt in his temples and wrists. The sidewalk glowed.

For the rest of the morning Father Leo searched the casinos across the street. He thought that Jerry might have wandered over and got caught up in one of those games that went on forever. But he didn't see him, or if he saw him he didn't recognize him. That was possible. There were so many people. Bent over their machines, faces fixed and drained by the hot lights, they all began to look the same to Father Leo. He couldn't make out who he was looking at, and it wore him out to try. At two o'clock he went back to the hotel, intending to search the casinos on the other side of the street after he'd eaten lunch.

He sat at the counter and watched the crowd move past outside. It was noisy in the coffee shop, which was full of Japanese men in business suits. They all wore cowboy hats and string ties with roadrunner clasps. At the back of the room a bunch of them were playing slot machines. There weren't enough machines to go around so they took turns, standing behind each other in little lines. Finally one of them hit a jackpot and all the others, including those at the tables, stopped talking and applauded.

"If it isn't five-fifteen." The woman from the night before sat down at the next stool and offered Father Leo a package of Salems with one cigarette sticking halfway out. He shook his head. She slipped the cigarette from the pack, tapped it once on the countertop, and put it in the ashtray. "For later," she said. "I can't smoke on an empty stomach." The color of her face had gone from pink to red. It was painful for Father Leo to look at her and to think of how hot and tight her skin must feel, and how it must hurt her to keep smiling the way she did.

"By the way," she said, "I'm Sandra."

Father Leo did not want to know this woman's name and he did not want her to know his name. But she kept waiting. "Slim," he said.

"Then you must be a westerner."

He nodded. "Seattle and thereabouts."

She said, "I met a fellow in the casino named Will. In Chicago you just don't hear names like that. Will and Slim. I love it. It's so different."

The waitress took Sandra's order and slipped Father Leo's check under his plate. He picked it up and looked at it.

"Let me treat you to a refill," Sandra said, pointing at his coffee cup.

He stood. "No thanks," he said. "I've got to be going. Much obliged."

Jerry hadn't called in yet or used his key. Father Leo left another message for him and went upstairs to his room. He thought he would lie down for a while before making another tour of the casinos. When he stepped inside he saw that his suitcase was open, though he could remember closing it. On the table next to the suitcase a cigarette was coming apart in a glass of water.

He knelt and went through the suitcase. He sat back for a moment, caught his breath, and searched the suitcase again. The chips were gone.

Father Leo flushed the cigarette down the toilet and dropped the glass in the wastebasket. His heart was jumping; every time it struck it surprised him and shook him as if he were hollow. He sat on the bed and felt the hollowness spreading up from his chest into his neck and head, down into his legs. When he stood he rose up and up. He saw his shoes side by side on the rug, a long way below. He walked over to the balcony door and back. Then he began to talk to himself, just to hear the sound.

The things he said didn't make any sense. They were only noises. He kept pacing the room. He struck himself over the heart. He gripped his shirt in both hands and tore it open to his waist. He struck himself again. Back and forth he walked.

The sounds he made grew soft and distant, then stopped. Father Leo stood there. He looked down at the front of his shirt. One button was missing. Another hung by a thread. The room was hot and still smelled faintly of the thief's cigarette. Father Leo slid open the glass door and went out onto the balcony. The desert was hidden by casinos but he could feel it all around him and taste its dryness in the breeze. The breeze ruffled the surface of the pool below, breaking the sun's reflection. The broken light glittered on the water.

Two young girls came into the courtyard. One of them had a radio as big as a briefcase. She turned it up full blast and they started doing cannonballs off the diving board.

When the desk clerk saw Father Leo coming he shook his head. Father Leo walked up to him anyway. "No message?"

"Not a thing," the desk clerk said. He went back to his magazine.

Father Leo had meant to report the theft, but now he didn't see the point. The police would come and make him fill out a lot of forms. They would ask him questions, and he felt uneasy about that, about explaining his presence in Las Vegas.

For the rest of the afternoon he went up and down the street, looking for Jerry. Once he thought he saw him going into a casino but it turned out to be somebody else, a much older man with a pink, shiny face. Father Leo returned to the hotel. He didn't feel like going back to his room, so he sat in the lobby for a while. Then he bought a copy of *Omni* and went out to the pool.

The two girls were still at the pool. The radio sat there screaming. Father Leo tried to read an article about the creation of the universe but he couldn't keep his attention fixed. After a time he gave up and watched the girls, who sensed his attention. They began to show off. First they did swan dives. Then one of them tried a flip. She hit the water with a loud crack, flat on her stomach. Father Leo started out of his chair, but she seemed to be all right. She pulled herself up the ladder, grabbed the radio, and left the courtyard crying. Her friend walked carefully out to the end of the board, turned around, bounced twice, and executed a perfect backward flip. Then she walked away from the pool, feet slapping on the wet cement.

"Coincidence," Sandra said. "Looks like we've got the pool to ourselves." She was standing beside the next chair, looking down at him. She stepped out of her high-heeled clogs and took off her robe. Then she raised her arms above her head and stood on her toes. Her head blocked out the sun. She dropped her arms and touched her feet several times.

"You shouldn't be out here," Father Leo said. "Not with that burn of yours."

"This is my last day," she said. "I wanted to catch the sunset."

Father Leo glanced up. The sun was just touching the roof of the hotel across from them. It looked like another sign.

Sandra sat down and took a bottle of baby oil out of her tote bag. She rubbed the oil along her arms and across her chest, under the halter of her bathing suit. Then she raised her legs one at a time and slowly oiled them until they glistened. They were deep red. "So," she said, "where's the wife?"

"I'm not married."

"Me either," she said.

Father Leo closed his magazine and sat up.

"What shows have you been to?" she said.

"None."

"You should go," she said. "The dancers are so beautiful. I don't think I've ever seen such beautiful men and women in my whole life. Do you like to dance?"

Father Leo shook his head.

Sandra drew her legs up. She rested her chin between her knees. "What do you like?"

Father Leo was about to say, "I like peace and quiet." He stopped himself, though. She was lonely. There was no reason to hurt her feelings. "I like to read," he said. "Music. Good music, not weird music. Eating in restaurants. Talking to friends."

"Me too," Sandra said. "Those are the same things I like." She lowered the back of the deck chair and rolled onto her stomach. She rubbed baby oil over her shoulders, then held the bottle out toward Father Leo. "Could you give a lady a hand?" she said.

He saw that she wanted him to oil her back, which looked swollen and painful, glowing in the little sun that was left. "I'm afraid I can't do that," he said.

"Oh," she said. She put the bottle down. "Sorry I asked."

"I'm a priest," he said.

"That's a new one," she said, not looking at him. "A priest named Slim."

"Slim is my nickname," he said.

"Sure," she said. "Your nickname. What kind of a priest are you, anyway?"

Father Leo began to explain but she cut him off. "You're no priest," she said. She sat up and began stuffing things into her tote bag — lighter, cigarettes, baby oil, sunglasses. She put her robe on and stepped into her clogs. "If you were a priest you wouldn't have let me go on like I did. You wouldn't have let me make a fool of myself." She stood there, looking down at him. "What are you, anyway?"

"I came here with a friend," Father Leo said. "He's been gone ever since last night. I don't have any idea where he is. Then, this afternoon . . ." He shook his head. "I think I'm a little confused."

"I don't know what you are," she said, "but if you come near me again I'll scream."

She left. The sun went down. Father Leo sat by the pool and stared up at the window of Jerry's room, which was next to his own. The breeze picked up, rustling the palm fronds overhead. The water slapped softly against the sides of the pool. A boy and a girl came into the courtyard, holding hands, and sat on the diving board. They stared down at the water. After a while they started to kiss.

Father Leo didn't know what to do. He was afraid to call the police, because if they did find Jerry they might discover his real name and put him in prison. He borrowed a telephone book from the desk clerk and wrote down the numbers of all the hospitals in town. There were seven, including one convalescent home and one women's hospital. He tried them all. There was no Jerry Royce registered at any of the hospitals, but at Desert Springs the nurse who took the call said that on the previous night they had admitted a John Doe with what she called "a sucking chest wound." Father Leo asked for a description of the man, but she did not have his file and the line to Intensive Care was busy. "It's always busy," the nurse said. "If you're in town, the easiest thing to do is just come over."

Father Leo rode up to Intensive Care in a padded elevator. When he stepped out, a gurney almost ran into him. He moved aside and watched it pass. One nurse was pushing it at a brisk pace while another adjusted a strap across the knees of the man lying on the gurney, who smiled at Father Leo.

The John Doe was dead. He had died that afternoon and they had sent his body to the morgue. Father Leo put his hands on the desk. "The morgue?" he said.

The nurse nodded. "We have a picture," she said. "Would you like to see it?"

"I guess I'd better," Father Leo said. He was afraid to look at the picture, but he didn't feel ready for a trip to the morgue. The nurse opened a folder and took out a large glossy photograph and handed it to him. He looked at it. The face was that of a boy with narrow features. His eyes were open, staring without defiance or shyness into the blaze of the flash. Father Leo knew that the boy had died before the picture was taken. He gave the picture back.

The nurse looked at it. "Not your friend?" she asked.

He shook his head. "What happened?"

"He was stabbed." She put the folder away.

"Did they catch the person who did it?"

"Probably not," she said. "We get over one hundred murders a year in town."

On his way back to the hotel Father Leo watched the crowd through the window of the cab. A group of sailors ran across the street. The one in front was throwing coins over his shoulder and the rest were jumping for them. Signs flashed. People's faces pulsed with reflected light.

Father Leo bent forward. "I just heard that you get over one hundred murders a year in town. Is that true?"

"I don't know," the cabby said. "I suppose it's possible." He shook his head. "This place has its drawbacks, all right. But I'm glad to be here. They've got a foot of snow in Albany right now and there's more on the way." He grinned at Father Leo in the mirror.

There were no messages. Father Leo sat in the lobby for a while, then went up to bed.

At a little past two in the morning Jerry called. He said that he was sorry about the mix-up, but he could explain everything. It turned out that while Father Leo was upstairs that first night Jerry had met a fellow on his way to a poker game outside town. It was a private game. The players were rich and there was no limit. They'd had to leave right away, so Jerry wasn't able to tell Father Leo. And after he got there he'd had no chance to call. The game was that intense. Incredible amounts of money had changed hands. It was still going on, he'd just broken off to catch a few winks and let Father Leo know that he would not be going back to Seattle the next morning. He couldn't, not now. Jerry had lost every penny of his own savings, the seven thousand dollars from the airplane executive, and some other cash he had held back. "I'm really sorry," he said. "I know this is going to put you in an awkward position."

"I think you ought to come home," Father Leo said. "We can make it up. We can work something out."

"No," Jerry said. "I don't think so. I still have four hundred left. I've been down further than that and bounced back. I'm just getting warmed up."

"Jerry, listen."

"Look," Jerry said, "haven't you ever had the feeling that you're bound to win? Like you've been picked out and you'll get taken care of no matter what?"

"Sure," Father Leo said. "I've had that feeling. It doesn't mean a damn thing."

"That's what you say. I happen to feel differently about it."

"For God's sake. Jerry, use your head. Come home."

But it was no good. Jerry said good-bye and hung up. Father Leo sat on the edge of the bed. The telephone rang again. He picked it up and said, "Jerry?"

It wasn't Jerry, though. It was Sandra. "I'm sorry if I woke you up," she said.

"Sandra," he said. "What on earth do you want?"

"Are you really a priest?" she asked.

"What kind of a question is that? What do you mean by calling me at this hour?" Father Leo knew that he had every right to be angry but he wasn't, not really. The sound of his own voice, fussy and peevish, embarrassed him. "Yes," he said.

"Oh, thank God. I'm so frightened."

He waited.

"Someone's been trying to get into my room," she said. "At least I think they have. I could have been dreaming," she added.

"You should call the police."

"I already thought of that," she said. "What would they do? They'd come in and stand around and then they'd go away. And there I'd be."

"I don't know how I could help," Father Leo said.

"You could stay."

"My friend still isn't back," Father Leo said. "We have to leave to-morrow morning and I should be here in case he calls. What if you were dreaming?"

"Please," she said.

Father Leo slammed his fist into the pillow. "Of course," he said. "Of course. I'll be right down."

After Sandra unlocked the door she told Father Leo to wait a second. Then she called, "Okay. Come on in." She was wearing a blue nightgown. She slid into bed and pulled the covers up to her waist. "Please don't look at me," she said. "And in case you wondered, I'm not making this up. I'm not so desperate for company. Almost but not quite."

There were two beds in the room with a night table in between. Father Leo sat at the foot of the other bed. He looked at her. Her face was red and puffy. She had white stuff on her nose.

"I'm a sight," she said.

"You should have that burn looked at when you get home."

She shrugged. "It's going to peel no matter what. In a couple of weeks I'll be back to normal." She tried to smile and gave it up. "I thought I'd at least come home with a tan. This has been the worst vacation. It's been one thing after another." She picked at the covers. "My second night here I lost over three hundred dollars. Do you know how long it takes me to save three hundred dollars?"

"This is an awful place," Father Leo said. "I don't know why anybody comes here."

"That's no mystery," Sandra said. "At a certain point it's the logical place to come."

"The whole thing is fixed," Father Leo said.

Sandra shrugged. "At a certain point that doesn't matter."

Father Leo went over to the sliding glass door. He opened it and stepped out onto the balcony. The night was cold. A mist hung over the glowing blue surface of the pool.

"You'll catch your death out there," Sandra called.

Father Leo went back inside and closed the door. He was restless. The room smelled of coconut oil.

"I have a confession to make," Sandra said. "It wasn't a coincidence when I came out to the pool today. I saw you down there."

Father Leo sat in the chair next to the TV. He rubbed his eyes. "Did somebody really try to break into the room?"

"I'm scared," Sandra said. "Can't you tell I'm scared?"

"Yes," he said.

"Then what difference does it make?"

"None," Father Leo said.

"This has been the worst vacation," Sandra said. "I won't tell you all the things that happened to me. Let's just say the only good thing that's happened to me is meeting you."

"This is a terrible place," Father Leo said. "It's dangerous, and everything is set up so you can't win."

"Some people win," she said.

"That's the theory. I haven't seen any winners. Do you mind if I use your phone?"

Sandra smoked and watched Father Leo while he talked to the desk clerk. Jerry had not called back. Father Leo left Sandra's room number and hung up.

"You told him you were here?" she said. She was smiling. "I wonder what he'll think."

"He can think whatever he wants to think," Father Leo said.

"He probably isn't thinking anything," Sandra said. "I'll bet he's seen it all."

Father Leo nodded. "I wouldn't be surprised."

"It's strange," she said. "Usually, when I'm about to go home from a vacation, I get excited — even if I've had a great time. This year I just feel sad. How about you? Are you looking forward to going home?"

"Not much," Father Leo said.

"Why not? What's it like where you live?"

Father Leo thought of the noise in the refectory. Sister Gervaise shrieking at one of her own wisecracks. Then he saw her face go bone-white as she listened to the lie he'd told Jerry. It would be all over the convent by now. By now Mother Vincent would have heard. There was no way to undo it. When you heard a story like that it became the truth about the person spoken of. Denials would only make it seem more true.

He would have to live with it. And that meant that everything was going to change. He saw how it would be. The hallways empty at night and quiet. The sisters falling silent as he walked past them, their eyes downcast.

"What are you smiling at?" Sandra asked.

He shook his head. "Nothing. Just a thought."

Sandra stubbed her cigarette out. "To get back to what we were talking about before," she said. "Some people do win. You just have to be in the right place at the right time, that's all. A friend of mine met her husband at the dentist's. They were both in the waiting room and got to talking about one thing and another. If either he or my friend hadn't made an appointment for that particular morning, they wouldn't have met. If the dentist hadn't taken so long with the patient he was working on, they wouldn't have discovered all the things they have in common, music and so on. It happens all the time. Take you and me. Say you weren't a priest. I know you are, but say you weren't. If we were to meet and you were to fall in love with me, think how lucky I would be. I would have the man I always dreamed of."

"You don't know me, Sandra."

"Not in the usual way, maybe. But I recognize you. I have these dreams, and the person I dream about is like you. Intelligent. Kind. Gallant. He even looks like you."

"Gallant," Father Leo said.

Sandra nodded. "You're here, aren't you?"

A group of people went past the door, talking loudly. When it was quiet again Father Leo said, "Too many ifs. We would have to be different people. Everything would have to be different."

She said, "Don't you think you could love me?"

"That's not the point," Father Leo said. "That's not what I'm talking about."

"But could you?"

"Yes," he said.

"What for? What is it about me that you would love if you loved me?" She leaned forward and clasped her arms around her knees. She watched him. Her blue eyes glittered.

"It's hard to put into words," Father Leo said.

Sandra said, "You don't have to." She shook another cigarette out of the pack, stared at it, and put it down on the night table.

"I like the way you talk," Father Leo said. "Straight out — just what's on your mind."

She nodded. "I do that all right. Let the chips fall where they may."

"Your spirit," Father Leo said. "Coming here all alone the way you did."

"Last year I went to Nassau."

"How friendly you are," Father Leo said. "The way you listen."

She leaned back against the pillow.

"Your eyes," he said.

"My eyes? Really?"

"You have beautiful eyes."

Father Leo went on. He did not think, he just listened to himself. His voice made a cool sound in the stuffy room. After a time Sandra whispered, "You won't leave, will you?"

"I'll be right here," he said.

She slept. Father Leo turned off the lights and moved his chair in front of the door. If anyone tried to break in he would be in the way. They would have to get past him.

He sat and listened. Every so often, faintly, he heard the elevator open at the end of the hall. Then he tried to hear the voices of people who got out, to see if they were men or women. Whenever he heard a man's voice, or no voice at all, he tensed. He listened for sounds in the corridor. Several people went by Sandra's door. Nobody stopped.

The only sounds in the room were his own and Sandra's breathing: his deep, almost silent, hers quick and shallow.

After a few hours of this he began to drift. Finally he caught himself dozing off, and went outside onto the balcony. A few stars still glimmered. The breeze stirred the fronds of the palm trees. The palms were black against the purple sky. The moon was white.

Father Leo stood against the railing, chilled awake by the breeze. A car horn honked, a small sound in the silence. He listened for it to come again but it didn't, and the silence seemed to grow. Again he felt the desert all around him. He thought of a coyote loping home with a rabbit dangling from its mouth, yellow eyes aglow.

Father Leo rubbed his arms. The cold began to get to him and he went back inside.

The walls turned from blue to gray. A telephone started ringing in the room above. He heard heavy steps.

Sandra turned. She said something in her sleep. Then she turned again.

"It's all right," Father Leo said. "I'm here."

Biographical Notes

James Baldwin (1924–1987), the son of a Harlem minister, had a brief preaching career as a teenager in a Harlem Pentecostal church. After experiencing a religious crisis, he left the church and began writing articles and working at various menial jobs. He made his literary debut with *Go Tell It on the Mountain* (1953), a novel that reflected his coming to terms with his religious and social convictions. His other novels include *Giovanni's Room* (1956), *Tell Me How Long the Train's Been Gone* (1968), and *Just Above My Head* (1979). Baldwin died of stomach cancer in France at the age of sixty-three.

Richard Bausch (1945–) is the author of six novels and several volumes of short stories. His stories have appeared in *The Atlantic Monthly, Harper's, The New Yorker, Esquire, Prize Stories: The O. Henry Awards,* and *Best American Short Stories.* He lives in rural Virginia with his wife and five children.

Mary Ward Brown (1917–) lives on a 300-acre plantation in Alabama, where she has resided for most of her life. She studied creative writing at the University of Alabama and the University of North Carolina in the 1950s, and her short-story collection *Tongues of Flame* won the Ernest Hemingway Award for best first work of fiction in 1987. "A New Life" first appeared in *The Atlantic Monthly.*

Andre Dubus (1936–) was born in Louisiana and served as a captain in the Marine Corps before pursuing an M.F.A. at the University of Iowa. He is the author of eleven books, including a novel, two novellas, a collection of essays, and several collections of short stories, and has been the recipient of fellowships from the Guggenheim and MacArthur foundations. The father of six children, he currently resides in Massachusetts.

Louise Erdrich (1954–) was born in Minnesota and grew up in North Dakota, a member of the Turtle Mountain band of Chippewa. She received her B.A. from Dartmouth College in 1976 and an M.A. in creative writing from Johns Hopkins University. Erdrich's first novel, *Love Medicine* (1984), won the National Book Critics Circle Award and the best first fiction award from the American Academy and Institute of Arts and Letters. Her work has been published in *The Atlantic Monthly* (where "Satan: Hijacker of a Planet" first appeared), *The New Yorker, Best American Short Stories,* and *Prize Stories: The O. Henry Prize Awards.* Her latest novel, *The Antelope Wife,* was published in 1998.

John Gardner (1933–1982) was a novelist, poet, critic, educator, and translator, who taught at Oberlin College, Southern Illinois University, and the State University of New York at Binghamton. He was born in upstate New York and grew up in a household where the Bible, Shakespeare, and poetry were strong influences. He received his B.A. from Washington University, St. Louis, and his M.A. and Ph.D. from the University of Iowa. His 1976 novel, *October Light,* won the National Book Critics Circle Award for fiction. "Redemption" first appeared in *The Atlantic Monthly.*

Brendan Gill (1914–1997) was born in Hartford, Connecticut, and attended Yale University. He became a regular contributor to *The New Yorker* in 1936 and wrote the best-selling *Here at the New Yorker* (1973) about his time there. Gill is the author of thirteen other books, including novels, a book of poetry, and several books on architecture; he also wrote short stories, essays, and film and drama reviews.

John Hersey (1914–1993) began his writing career as an editor, writer, and correspondent at *Time* magazine and later spent eighteen years as a professor of writing at Yale University and the Massachusetts Institute of Technology. In 1945 he won a Pulitzer Prize for *A Bell for Adano,* a work of nonfiction about World War II. "God's Typhoon" was first printed in *The Atlantic Monthly.* Hersey was born in Tientsin, China, and died in Key West, Florida.

William Hoffman (1925–) was born in West Virginia and is the author of eleven novels, including *Godfires* (1985) and *Tidewater Blood* (1998), as well as three collections of short stories. His stories have appeared in *Best American Short Stories,* the O. Henry Prize collection, and *The Atlantic Monthly,* where "The Question of Rain" first appeared. He has lived in Virginia for forty years and currently serves as a professor and writer-in-residence at Hampden-Sydney College.

James Joyce (1882–1941) was born in Dublin, Ireland, and graduated from University College in Dublin. In 1905 he settled in Trieste with his wife, Nora Barnacle. They had two children. He published his first book in 1907, a collection of poems called *Chamber Music. Dubliners* was published in 1914, followed by *A Portrait of the Artist as a Young Man* (1916); *Exiles,* a play, in 1918; *Ulysses* (1922); and *Finnegans Wake* (1939). He lived for a time in Paris and died in Zurich.

Bernard Malamud (1914–1986) was born and raised in New York City, receiving his M.A. from Columbia University in 1942. He wrote his first novel, *The Natural* (1952), while a teacher at Oregon State University. From 1961 until his death he taught at Bennington College in Vermont. His books, which often reflect his keen interest in Jewish-American life, include *The Assistant* (1957), *God's Grace* (1982), and *The Fixer* (1966), which won both the National Book Award and the Pulitzer Prize. His first collection of short stories, *The Magic Barrel* (1958), also won a National Book Award. His stories appeared in *The Atlantic Monthly* and other magazines.

Bobbie Ann Mason (1940–) is the author of six books of fiction. She earned a degree in journalism from the University of Kentucky and a Ph.D. from the University of Connecticut. In 1983 her collection *Shiloh and Other Stories* won the Ernest Hemingway Foundation/PEN Award for best first fiction and was also a finalist for a National Book Critics Circle Award, American Book Award, and PEN/Faulkner Fiction Award. Her work has appeared in *Best American Short Stories, Prize Stories: The O. Henry Prize Awards, The Atlantic Monthly* (where "The Retreat" was first published), *The New Yorker,* and *Harper's.* She lives in Kentucky.

Alice Munro (1931–) was born in Ontario, Canada, the setting for most of her short stories. She has been awarded the Governor General's Literary Award (Canada's highest award) three times, for her first collection of short stories, *Dance of the Happy Shades* (1968), for *Who Do You Think You Are?* (1978), and for *The Progress of Love* (1986). Munro's stories have appeared in *The Atlantic Monthly* (where "Pictures of the Ice" was first published), *The New Yorker, The Paris Review,* and elsewhere.

Flannery O'Connor (1925–1964), a novelist and short-story writer, was raised as a Roman Catholic in the deep South's Bible Belt. She received a B.A. from Women's College of Georgia in 1945 and an M.F.A. from the Iowa Writers Workshop in 1947. She wrote two novels, *Wise Blood* (1952) and *The Violent Bear It Away* (1960), and three collections of short stories, *A Good Man Is Hard to Find* (1955), *Everything That Rises Must Converge* (1965), and *Collected Stories.*

O'Connor, who died of lupus at age thirty-nine, spent the last ten years of her life as an invalid, writing and raising peacocks on her mother's farm near Milledgeville, Georgia.

Cynthia Ozick (1928–), the author of novels, short stories, essays, literary criticism, translations, and a play, was born in New York City and studied at New York and Ohio State Universities. She has been awarded four first prizes in the *O. Henry Prize Stories* anthology and is a member of the American Academy of Arts and Letters. Ozick's work has appeared in publications such as *The Atlantic Monthly* and in *Best American Short Stories*. Her most recent books include *Fame and Folly: Essays* and *The Puttermesser Papers*, a novel.

Peggy Payne (1949–), a freelance writer since 1972, has published in most major U.S. newspapers and in magazines such as *Travel & Leisure, MS, Cosmopolitan,* and *Family Circle*. Her work has also been cited in *Best American Short Stories*. Her novel *Revelation* is an expansion of "The Pure in Heart." She lives with her husband near Chapel Hill, North Carolina.

Eileen Pollack (1956–) is the author of a collection of short fiction, *The Rabbi in the Attic and Other Stories* (1991); a novel, *Paradise, New York* (1998); and a children's book about AIDS, *Whisper Whisper Jesse* (1992). She has published stories in a number of literary journals. Pollack directs the undergraduate creative writing program at the University of Michigan in Ann Arbor, where she lives.

Joe Ashby Porter (1942–) was born and grew up in Madisonville, Kentucky, and studied at Harvard, Oxford, and Berkeley. He is the author of *Eelgrass* (1977), a novel, and the collections *Lithuania: Short Stories* (1997) and *The Kentucky Stories* (1983), for which he was a Pulitzer Prize nominee. Porter is a professor of English at Duke University in Durham, North Carolina, where he teaches creative writing.

J. F. Powers (1917–) was born in Jacksonville, Illinois, and attended Northwestern University. His first two books were collections of short stories, *Prince of Darkness and Other Stories* (1947) and *The Presence of Grace* (1956). His first novel, *Morte D'Urban* (1962), won a National Book Award. *Look How the Fish Live* (1975), a third collection of stories, and *Wheat That Springeth Green* (1988), a novel, followed. Powers has taught writing at four universities and colleges.

Philip Roth (1933–) was born in Newark, New Jersey, and taught comparative literature for many years, mainly at the University of Pennsylvania, before his retirement from Hunter College in 1992. He is the author of more than twenty books, including *Goodbye, Columbus* (1960), *Sabbath's Theater* (1995) (both National Book Award winners), and *American Pastoral* (1997), which won the Pulitzer Prize for fiction. Roth now lives in Connecticut.

Elizabeth Spencer (1921–) was born in Carrollton, Mississippi. She received her B.A. from Belhaven College in 1942 and her M.A. from Vanderbilt in 1943. She has taught writing at Concordia University in Montreal, Canada, and at the University of North Carolina. She is the author of thirteen books, including *The Light in the Piazza* (1960), *The Salt Line* (1984), and *Landscapes of the Heart: A Memoir* (1997). "A Christian Education" first appeared in *The Atlantic Monthly*. She now lives in Chapel Hill, North Carolina.

William Trevor (1928–), born in Mitchelstown, County Cork, Ireland, spent his childhood in provincial Ireland and attended Trinity College in Dublin. A number of his stories have appeared in *The Atlantic Monthly*, *The New Yorker*, and other magazines. Among Trevor's books, *The Children of Dynmouth* and *Fools of Fortune* were both awarded the Whitbread Award; *The Silence in the Garden* was the winner of the Yorkshire Post Book of the Year Award; *Reading Turgenev* was short-listed for the Booker Prize; and *My House in Umbria* was short-listed for the Sunday Express Prize.

John Updike (1932–) was born in Shillington, Pennsylvania, graduated from Harvard in 1954, and spent a year at the Ruskin School of Drawing and Fine Art, in Oxford, England. From 1955 to 1957 he was a staff member of *The New Yorker*, to which he has contributed poems, short stories, essays, and book reviews. In 1957 he moved to Massachusetts and has since produced more than forty books, among which are *Rabbit Is Rich* (1981), which received a National Book Award and the Pulitzer Prize, and *Rabbit at Rest* (1991), which also won a Pulitzer. "Made in Heaven" first appeared in *The Atlantic Monthly*. The father of four children, he lives north of Boston.

Eudora Welty (1909–) was born in Jackson, Mississippi, where she has lived for most of her life. She studied at the University of Wisconsin and Columbia University and was for a time a staff member at *The New York Times Book Review*. She has published several collections of short stories and novels, mostly drawn from Mississippi life, including *The Robber Bridegroom* (1942), *The Ponder Heart* (1954), and *The Optimist's Daughter* (1972), for which she was awarded the Pulitzer Prize. Her stories have appeared in *The Atlantic Monthly*, among other publications.

Tobias Wolff (1945–) was born in Alabama and joined the U.S. Army in 1964. He is the author of seven books, including a short novel, *The Barracks Thief*

(1984), which won a PEN/Faulkner Award; *In Pharaoh's Army: Memories of the Lost War* (1994), a National Book Award finalist; and *This Boy's Life* (1989), a memoir. He received an M.A. from Stanford University, where he was a Wallace Stegner Fellow. "The Missing Person" first appeared in *The Atlantic Monthly*. Wolff lives with his wife and three children in Palo Alto, where he directs the graduate writing program at Stanford.